Their eyes were suc̲ ̲ ̲ ̲ ̲ ̲ ̲ ̲ ̲ ̲ ̲ ̲ ̲ ̲ ̲ e neither could control. Their hands reached out to each other, entwining in an impassioned embrace. Erika wanted so desperately to speak, but her words would have no voice behind them, so she continued to lose herself in the depths of his hazel reflectors.

Michael lost himself, too—not caring whether he'd be found, unless he could be found with her, totally locked in this magical world that evil could never penetrate, the magical world they now shared together.

The almost tangible silence between them grew in intensity—and went on and on. Erotic tension mounted; primitive needs screamed to be fulfilled, desire flooded their souls. Slowly, deeply, he possessed her mouth, as though this was the first and final drink of sweet wine he'd ever taste from her intoxicating lips. Sensuously drugged out of their minds, Erika and Michael let their tongues rove, sweetly plundering; trembling hands groped tenderly; fresh breaths of life mingled. Sheer bliss.

In a dimly lit hospital cafeteria, which they no longer solely occupied, the seed of love was planted in their hearts—a seed they'd hopefully nurture, until it could mature into a full, exquisite blossom. Separated by a mere inch, they trembled from the coldness lodged in the minute space between them.

BOOK YOUR PLACE ON OUR WEBSITE AND MAKE THE ARABESQUE ROMANCE CONNECTION!

We've created a customized website just for our very special Arabesque readers, where you can get the inside scoop on everything that's going on with Arabesque romance novels.

When you come online, you'll have the exciting opportunity to:

- View covers of upcoming books

- Learn about our future publishing schedule (listed by publication month and author)

- Find out when your favorite authors will be visiting a city near you

- Search for and order backlist books

- Check out author bios and background information

- Send e-mail to your favorite authors

- Join us in weekly chats with authors, readers and other guests

- Get writing guidelines

- AND MUCH MORE!

Visit our website at
http://www.arabesquebooks.com

DESPERATE DECEPTIONS

Linda Hudson-Smith

BET Publications, LLC
www.bet.com
www.arabesquebooks.com

> *This book is dedicated to the loving memory of my dear mother, Bernice Alice Hudson.*
> *Sunrise: August 10, 1919   Sunset: May 9, 1996*

ARABESQUE BOOKS are published by

BET Publications, LLC
c/o BET BOOKS
One BET Plaza
1900 W Place NE
Washington, D.C. 20018-1211

Copyright © 2001 by Linda Hudson-Smith

All rights reserved. No part of this book may be reproduced, stored in a retrieval system, or transmitted in any form or by any means without the prior written consent of the Publisher.

If you purchased this book without a cover, you should be aware that this book is stolen property. It was reported as "unsold and destroyed" to the Publisher and neither the Author nor the Publisher has received any payment for this "stripped book."

All Kensington Titles, Imprints, and Distributed Lines are available at special quantity discounts for bulk purchases for sales promotion, premiums, fund-raising, and educational or institutional use. Special book excerpts or customized printings can also be created to fit specific needs. For details, write or phone the office of the Kensington special sales manager: Kensington Publishing Corp., 850 Third Avenue, New York, NY 10022, attn: Special Sales Department, Phone: 1-800-221-2647.

BET Books is a trademark of Black Entertainment Television, Inc. ARABESQUE, the ARABESQUE logo and the BET BOOKS logo are trademarks and registered trademarks.

First Printing: March 2001

10 9 8 7 6 5 4 3 2 1
Printed in the United States of America

ACKNOWLEDGMENTS

My Father in heaven: Thank you for the continued blessings as I continue to count on you to take charge of my life, day in and day out, and for being a constant force of love and light in my life.

My husband, my other wing: Thanks, Rudy, for being the best navigator, willing to fly on short notice.

Linda Gill-Cater: Thank you for your willingness to listen to my ideas and for the tireless contribution you made in bringing about the success of the Arabesque Armed Forces Tour 2000.

Kicheko Driggins: Thanks for all that you do at Arabesque Books and for helping our book signings to run smoothly. Your great personality and positive attitude are greatly appreciated.

Tanya Rutledge, M.D.: Thank you so much for writing the enlightening medical awareness article on pernicious anemia and for sharing your expertise with Arabesque readers and myself. May God bless you always.

All the authors and readers that nominated and voted for me in the category of best new author for the Gold Pen Award 2000: Thank you so much. Receiving the award has been one of the greatest highlights of my writing career. A very special thanks to two extraordinary women, Tia Shabazz of African-American Online Writers Guild and Nicki Hand of Romantic Tales Organization.

My Pennsylvania family: Thanks to all of you for making my July 2000 homecoming such a spectacular event! A special thanks to my cousins, Jim McDonald, Louise Brown, Arlene & Eugene Stevens, and to my aunt, Josephine Jenkins. I also want to thank my surrogate parents, Ena & Walter Poole, and my dearest sister-friend, Denise Poole-Mull. The time I spent with each of you created new magnificent memories.

Prologue

A heavy snowstorm, bitter-cold and violent, had all but crippled the Pittsburgh area, nearly devastating the northeastern community of Lebanon. Shimmering white snowflakes still descended from the heavens, but weren't falling nearly as heavily as on the previous night.

The tiny community of Lebanon could easily be a calendar scene of a white Christmas. Barely detectable, sidewalks and driveways lay buried beneath the still whiteness. The shimmering white powder heavily blanketed rooftops, icicles hung from rainspouts, and windows and doors appeared to be covered with thin sheets of transparent ice. Fluffy white nests of snow filled the tall pine trees.

Erika Edmonds stood rooted to a spot in front of the picture window in the formal living room that she shared off and on with her ailing mother, Vernice. Erika's large eyes, the color of dark chocolate, strained against the blinding whiteness bouncing off the glistening snowbanks. As she surveyed the damage the storm had heaped on the area surrounding her mother's single-story, gray-brick home, her liquid-chocolate eyes registered shock and disbelief.

A fire roared in the fireplace, yet Erika felt chilled to the bone. Vigorously, she rubbed her hands up and down her arms, trying to relieve the tingling numbness settling in her limbs. During the past year Erika had lost more than forty pounds and was no longer the chubby, cherub-faced, first-year medical resident who lived on the third floor of Honor Hall dormitory, the one who could stand to lose more than just a few pounds. The only remaining dimples on her body were those deeply embedded in her velvety, café au lait skin, at the corners of her full, wine-colored lips.

At five-foot-two, one hundred and ten pounds, down from one hundred fifty-five, Erika was now described as the Junoesque bombshell resident with the honey-brown hair. Because of the deep indentations in her cheeks, she was often referred to as the doctor with craters for dimples.

Erika wiped off the picture window with a wet paper towel, only to have it frost up in a matter of seconds. "Well, he's probably not coming today, anyway," she said, moving away from the window.

Hearing a crashing noise coming from the back of the house, she dashed down the beige carpeted hallway to check on her mother, who was still in bed asleep.

Her eyes flashing horror, Erika stopped dead in her tracks, taking special note of the open window and Vernice's absence from her bed. Apparently the strong winds had gushed in and knocked over the bedside table, but that was the least of Erika's concerns.

Vernice's health was very fragile. She suffered from pernicious anemia, a condition, often hereditary, caused by a deficiency of vitamin B-12, which was needed for normal production of red blood cells. The symptoms included mental changes, memory loss, depression, and even dementia. The walking gait and balance sometimes became disturbed, and numbness in the hands and feet sometimes occurred.

Pernicious anemia was considered a disease most common among people of northern European descent. Because of the mingling of bloodlines down through the generations, Erika thought it was naive of modern scientists to assume that African-Americans were not at risk.

As Erika frantically searched through the other rooms in the house, a sickening feeling gnawed at her insides. "Oh, no!"

she screamed in anguish, realizing she wasn't going to find Vernice anywhere in the house.

Vernice had simply wandered off again. Even though she'd done that often, Erika could never get used to the shock waves that always rumbled through her brain during the stressful times. Rubbing her left temple in a circular motion, she tried to ease the tension, but she knew her headache wouldn't go away until she found her mother.

Like a windup toy robot, Erika picked up the phone and dialed the emergency number. Due to the storm, it took longer than usual for the operator to respond.

"How may I help you?" came the bland response.

Swiping at her tears, Erika drew in a deep breath. "This is Erika Edmonds. My mother, Vernice Edmonds, has wandered away from our home. She has a serious medical disorder, which has impaired her memory. Her mental coordination has been affected terribly."

Erika listened as the operator echoed their street address. She then asked for a physical description of Vernice, along with a description of the type and color of clothing that she was last seen wearing.

Stretching the phone cord over to the closet, Erika checked to see if anything was disturbed. Everything was still neatly arranged. "I'm afraid she's only wearing a blue-and-white striped flannel nightgown. All of her other clothes are accounted for." Erika grimaced when she noticed the fluffy blue slippers under the bed, which meant her mother was probably barefoot.

"My mother is a black woman, in her late fifties, with an olive-brown complexion. She's approximately five-foot-five and weighs one hundred twenty-five pounds. She has mixed gray hair that's braided across the top of her head."

The second Erika hung up she grabbed a heavy, gray wool coat. As she made her way to the door, she wiggled her hands into a pair of gray leather gloves. At the door, she pulled on a pair of black leather boots and then started outdoors. The raging wind nearly knocked her over as it swirled around her menacingly, biting and stinging her velvety skin. The outdoor temperature registered well below zero.

For all the good the coat was doing, she may as well not have it on, she thought, as she struggled to close the door behind her. Managing to jerk it shut in a forceful swoop, she left the porch and plodded on through the knee-high snow. Making a mental note to call on her neighbor's teenage son to clear the walkway, she battled with the snow impeding her progress.

A heavy snowplow was clearing the streets. She wished the plow's operator could take a one-time pass over the driveway and sidewalk in front of her house, but she already knew the city would never allow it. She'd asked before.

As she headed west, she prayed that the commuter trains had been rendered inoperable, fearing that her mother would wander into their deadly path. Vernice had crossed the tracks when she wandered off before, but Erika knew the angels had been at her mother's side. Erika prayed they'd continue to watch over her now.

As she plodded on, her thoughts turned to David Wells, the administrator of the Golden Age Retirement Center. Months prior to Vernice crossing the tracks David had tried to convince her that her mother needed residential placement, in a center that specialized in caring for patients with memory loss. Whether she chose Golden Age or not, David was convinced Vernice needed the specialized attention that only a professional staff could provide. But Erika had balked at the idea, unable to stand the thought of putting her mother in a home.

"Even if it's for her own safety?" David had asked.

Now, those same words tormented her even though she'd already called David. He was supposed to pick up Vernice this very morning, but the weather had obviously sidelined him, she decided.

In her first year as an OB-GYN resident, with several more years still ahead of her, Erika barely had time to take a shower, let alone give her mother all the attention she so desperately needed and deserved. Though Erika lived on Lebanon's Great Western University Hospital campus, she had several people who looked after Vernice.

Erika's main support came from Vernice's sister, Arlene Wasler, who was a couple of years older than Vernice. Like Vernice, Arlene was retired and widowed. Before Vernice's illness destroyed her chances of having a normal life, she and Arlene had spent their time doing all the exciting things that seniors liked to do in their retirement years.

Twenty-six-year-old Erika had struggled financially in her last year of college. Now in the first year of residency, she still struggled with finances. Money was practically nonexistent. Through the grace of God, scholarships, and school grants, Erika had gotten by over the past several years. But she barely knew where her next meal was going to come from, let alone how she could pay for Vernice's residential care.

When her stepfather, Anthony Edmonds, who had adopted her, passed away in her last year of undergraduate school, things had gotten really tough. Although he'd left Vernice in pretty good financial shape, there wasn't enough money for her to continue to help pay the rising costs of Erika's school expenses.

With no sign of her mother anywhere, Erika retraced her steps. While her legs and hands had no feeling in them, her cheeks had turned a flame-red and her eyes had the appearance of frosted glass. As she approached her front door, she heard the phone ringing. After forcing the nearly frozen door open, she ran into the house and snatched up the receiver. Breathlessly, she spoke into the mouthpiece.

"Miss Edmonds, this is the Lebanon County Sheriffs Department. We just received a call from a lady who thinks she might have your mother at her house. She called to report having found a lady wandering around near the commuter tracks." Erika gasped and her hands began to shake. "From the description she gave, we're pretty sure it's your mother.

However, this woman isn't wearing nightclothes. She's fully dressed but has no hat or coat."

Erika's entire body trembled as she unleashed a sigh of relief. "Did the lady leave a phone number or an address?" Erika inquired anxiously.

"Yes, she did, Miss Edmonds. She lives very close to you. Two officers have been dispatched to that location. They're going to pick the woman up and bring her to you for identification. They should arrive momentarily. We hope it's your mom. If not, the officers will instruct you what to do next. Good luck, Miss Edmonds." Erika thanked the operator and ran to the window.

A small van was pulling up to the curb, but she saw that there was only one man in it. When he got out, she immediately recognized David Wells. Nearly falling over the leather hassock as she scrambled to the door, she righted herself and flung the door open.

David looked up at her, giving her a flash of even pearly whites as he dug his boots into the snow and cleared the path with a small, square-edged shovel. Looking ahead at Erika, David brushed the snow from his coat as he stepped onto the porch. Taking off his hat, revealing a thick mass of soft, brown waves, he hit the cap across his thigh to knock the loose snow to the floor. "Hello, Dr. Edmonds. Looks like you've got some heavy work ahead of you," he said, stepping inside the warm interior.

Though her face felt as if it had cracked, she managed a weak smile. "It's a mess, isn't it? But we have a neighbor kid who will make light work of it. Come on in, Mr. Wells. Have a seat by the fireplace."

David entered the living room, his tobacco-brown eyes surveying the plastic-covered, creamy beige French provincial sofa and loveseat facing the fireplace. Handsome with finely chiseled features, David had a rugged complexion the color of cinnamon. Placing his briefcase on the cherry-wood coffee table, he walked over to the fireplace and stood with his back to the warm flames.

As he rubbed his hands together, his eyes made direct contact with Erika's. "How's your mom, Dr. Edmonds?"

Exhausted, Erika dropped down onto the sofa. "I really don't know, Mr. Wells. She's wandered off again. This is the second time since I made the decision to contact you. I'm waiting for the police now," she informed him, biting back the wrenching sob in her throat. "They think they've found her." David didn't say anything, but she knew what he was thinking. His I-warned-you gaze was confirmation enough.

Moving toward the ivory leather reclining chair, David knelt beside it. "These kinds of things are going to keep happening, Dr. Edmonds. That's why it's necessary for your mother to have the kind of protection our facility offers. This is no one's fault. It's all a part of her illness. No one person can handle all the situations that are direct results of these types of serious ailments."

Tears glistened in Erika's eyes. "I keep telling myself that, but I'm still having a hard time listening to my own voice of reason." Picking up a multicolored crocheted blanket, she draped it over her knees, poking her pinkie finger in and out of the small spaces. "It's so hard to come to terms with what's happening to my mother."

His rapt attention on Erika, David deposited his tall, lanky frame onto the reclining chair. "Are you still prepared to let your mother go with me today?"

Erika looked down at the floor and back at David. "I don't think I have a choice. This has been going on for close to four years now and it's only getting worse." Erika felt as though a good scream would relieve the tension in her head.

His smile was sympathetic. "Unfortunately, it can only get worse, unless it's treated early on. Did you talk with other medical professionals as I suggested, Dr. Edmonds?" He swiped at his fine leather boots with a white handkerchief.

Erika stood and wandered over to the window, feeling as

though bricks of lead had somehow gotten into her shoes. Each step she took was burdensome. "I've talked to several doctors, but it's always the same destructive diagnosis. We all should rely on the Master Physician. He's never lost a case."

David understood her frustration, but he wished she would talk to him face-to-face, instead of staring blankly out the window. However, he knew that this was probably the hardest decision she'd ever have to make in her life. The decision to place a loved one was never easy. But he couldn't talk to her about it, or help her with it, if she kept herself so far removed from the reality of it all. As he was about to coax her into discussing her feelings, she ran out the front door, and he moved over to the spot where she'd been standing.

Erika slipped and skated her way to the police car. She'd already recognized her mother in the backseat. "Mom!" she shouted gleefully, gathering the fragile Vernice in her arms. "I've been worried sick about you," she admonished gently.

What amazed Erika most was her mother's attire. Even though she had no coat and hat, she had dressed herself in warm clothing. Vernice looked as though she'd just stepped out for a shopping spree. Her brown wool slacks were shoved into brown leather boots. Along with her brown sweater, they looked impeccably neat on her slender frame. Erika hadn't missed this particular outfit because she'd never seen it before.

"Ma'am," the officer said, "I don't need to ask if this is your mother. You two look well-acquainted. If you'll take her inside, I'd like to have a word with you in private, if I may?"

"Certainly. Thank you both." Erika looked at the officer who sat behind the wheel, inside the patrol car.

Keeping her arms around Vernice, Erika guided her into the house, worried because her mother hadn't yet spoken. After making Vernice comfortable, Erika left her in the care of David and dashed back to the waiting officers.

"I'm all ears," she said, nearly slipping on a patch of ice. The officer broke her fall. Embarrassed, Erika thanked him.

Officer Easton leaned against the door of the patrol car.

"Ma'am, uh, how long has your mother been wandering off like this?"

"It just started a few months ago, but there's been a problem with her memory for several years. I'm really sorry for putting you through all this. I know it's a big problem for you."

He smiled warmly. "It's not a problem. It's our job. I'm glad we could be of service. Protect and serve is our motto. And you can use me in any way you see fit." Laughing, he tipped the bill of his hat. His expression suddenly grew somber. "Are you aware that if anything happens to your mother when she's in your care, you can be held liable?"

Erika looked stunned. "Liable for what? I'd never do anything to harm my mother," she objected loudly.

He cleared his throat. "I think you've misunderstood what I was trying to say here. But it's my duty to inform you of the laws that protect those who are incapable of caring for themselves. The courts might take the position that you've been negligent in caring for her. They could bring charges against you."

Hoping to soften the staggering blow he'd just delivered, the officer touched her arm briefly. "I strongly advise you to seek professional help in this matter. No malice intended."

Her rigid stance screamed out her obvious indignation as she eyed him coolly. "Consider me informed. Thanks for all that you've done." With no need for further communication, she returned to the house, feeling the icy coldness from the officer's eyes squaring off with her retreating form. Without looking back, she entered the house and went straight to the kitchen.

Erika prepared a pot of hot tea and pulled out a care package of chocolate chip cookies, compliments of her Aunt Arlene. After placing cups and saucers on a heavy metal tray, she carried the refreshments into the living room, where Vernice and David chatted like old friends.

"Your mother's a live wire," David began. Erika carried her cup of tea over to the sofa and sat down. "She's got a darn good sense of humor. She's been telling me a lot of spicy jokes. My sides are splitting."

Erika smiled at her mother. "Yes, she does. She has quite an ornery side, as well. Mother, where were you off to this morning?" Erika asked, trying to get a feel for what had happened without making Vernice feel as if she was being brought to task.

Vernice carefully set her cup of tea on the tray. Staring blankly at her daughter, she struggled to recall the earlier events. Erika could see the frustration in her mother's sable-brown eyes, and it broke her heart.

Vernice suddenly smiled. "Oh, I was going to the bank, but the strangest thing happened before I made it. I simply got turned around and I couldn't remember how to get to the bank or back here," she explained nervously. A puzzled look gleamed in her eyes. "David tells me he has an apartment he'd like me to take a look at. What do you think about that, Erika?"

Erika quickly diverted her eyes, fighting the urge to cry. She couldn't meet her mother's trusting gaze, knowing she didn't deserve her trust. Turning her head back around, she focused on the flames. "Well, you've been talking about getting a smaller place, so I guess it wouldn't hurt to take a look at it."

Traitor, Erika screamed inwardly, feeling like the world's largest, slimiest rat. A few tears rushed from her eyes and she hurriedly swiped them away.

Sensing the mounting tension, David stood up and glanced at his watch. "Mrs. Edmonds, we'd better get going. It's getting late. I don't want you to miss out on having lunch with the other residents. You're our special guest today."

Vernice smiled brightly. "Now that sounds like my kind of fun, young man. But let me go to the bathroom first." As Vernice ambled to the back of the house, Erika put her face in her trembling hands.

David touched Erika's shoulder. "We have to move fast," he said when she looked up at him. "Are her bags packed?"

Erika glanced at the hall closet, where she'd stored some of her mother's personal belongings. "They're in there."

"Good. I'm going to hurry out and put them in the van. You two take a few minutes alone. I'll call you once she's settled in." He moved rapidly toward the closet. "Don't worry," he tossed back over his shoulder.

Erika got up and started toward the back of the house, hoping she could hold up emotionally for the next few minutes. When she reached Vernice's bedroom, she leaned against the doorjamb, watching her mother fuss with her braided hair.

Sensing Erika's presence, Vernice turned to look at her daughter. "This hairdo has got to go. This gray has to go, too. I look like a little old lady, and I'm not yet sixty. I think I'll have Bertha rinse my hair tomorrow."

The resounding weight of her mother's words was almost too much for Erika to bear. The entire situation was just one cross too many to have to carry. Doing it all alone made it even more frightening. Moving over to stand next to her mother, Erika draped her arm around Vernice's shoulders. "Mother, you look just fine. This style is so much easier to care for. Give me a hug," she commanded gently, trying to hold her emotions in check.

Vernice was not known for being overly affectionate, but she easily went into her daughter's loving arms, knowing she'd find all the warmth of early summer there. Erika squeezed her mother so tightly that Vernice moaned in protest.

Reluctantly, Vernice moved away from her daughter's warmth. "From the way you were holding on to me, you'd think I was never coming back home, child," Vernice chided lovingly. "You can't get rid of me that easy. I'm going to hang around here so that I can see how you deal with your own kids. I just hope they're not as stubborn and fiery tempered as you are, my dear child."

Vernice started for the front of the house. "I don't want to keep the young man waiting any longer. If he were a couple of years older, I'd make a play for him," she teased, laughing.

Erika couldn't respond, knowing that if she opened her mouth she'd start begging for forgiveness. Unwittingly, Vernice had driven the final nail into Erika's coffin, and she felt as if her life were slowly ebbing away.

As they walked toward the front door, Erika felt a tear slide down her cheek and she rapidly wiped it away. When the door opened, David came back up the walk and helped Vernice to the van. No other words were exchanged between mother and daughter, but enough words floated around in Erika's head to fill a book.

Like a zombie, Erika moved back inside, where she rushed to the window. Morosely, she watched the van that would take her mother away to strangers and an unfamiliar place, away from all the people and all the things she loved, away from the comfort of her own home, permanently away from her lifelong neighborhood.

Guilt washed through Erika, and in that moment she would've done anything to keep her mother at home. At the same time that the van pulled away from the curb, gut-wrenching sobs pulled her resolve apart.

Falling to her knees, she cried and screamed herself hoarse, knowing this was hardly the end of her anguish. She suddenly felt as if the end of the world had come, fearing that this move might prove to be the beginning of the worst chapter of Vernice's life story. . . .

One

Erika walked around the house in a trance touching all the things her mother had cherished. Though barely able to see them through the blur of her tears, she felt them. The mantelpiece was loaded with family photographs, invoking memories.

Although Erika was an only child, Vernice had siblings and plenty of nieces, nephews and cousins. Almost all of her relatives had come for Vernice's funeral. When Erika had brought her home to spend the weekend, she had been in residential placement less than a month. During her second night at home Vernice had died in her sleep from heart failure.

Erika picked up one of the lace doilies crocheted by her mother's hands, hands that had forgotten how to work the needles. On built-in wall shelves rested a variety of dolls dressed in hand-sewn lace and satin clothes. Vernice had made them, too, along with the decorative matchboxes gracing the antique end tables. She'd been so creative. Once she'd taken ill, she no longer had the patience to work at arts and crafts. It was possible that she just couldn't remember how to do any of it anymore, Erika sadly considered. The pernicious anemia had gone undiagnosed for too long, and the outcome could've been avoided had it been caught sooner.

Consumed by grief, Erika vowed to make it her life's work to educate her people about pernicious anemia. Because it mimicked Alzheimer's disease it often went undiagnosed. Knowing she couldn't do what she'd come there to do, which was to decide which things she wanted to keep, Erika decided to leave. The house was already on the market, but the contents had to be removed. Erika hated the thought of selling the house, but she couldn't afford to keep it. Her bank account was practically empty.

Scheduled for afternoon rounds, Erika gathered her belongings and started for the front door. She then remembered that her car was blocked in from yet another storm. The neighbor kid was probably in school, she figured, so she'd have to dig the car out herself. Dropping everything on the dining room table, she went to the door that led to the garage.

Thirty minutes later, she backed the car out onto the salt-sprinkled streets.

Rushing onto the university grounds, with only ten minutes left to arrive at her destination, Erika hustled toward the dormitory apartments. As she rounded the corner of the building, she collided with what she thought was a brick wall. But when strong, Indian-brown hands tenderly caught her by the waist, she could feel and smell the fiery heat of a hot-blooded male—a tall, muscular male, possessing the kind of looks that were to die for.

Smiling broadly, he steadied her. Sure that he had rare white diamonds for teeth, Erika watched in awe as they flashed and sparkled with brightness. "Where's the fire, gorgeous?" Stooping over, he picked up her belongings, which were scattered all over the cleared walkway.

In your touch, she sang out inwardly, marveling at the wavy, maple-brown hair that fell just short of his stiff white collar. When he straightened, she felt like a midget standing toe-to-toe with Kareem Abdul Jabbar. In reality he looked approximately six-foot-two, give or take an inch. For sure, he looked good enough to order for dessert.

He handed over her belongings, making sure that she had a firm grip on them before relaxing his hold. "I hope the fire is out by the time you get there, gorgeous. I'd hate for you to get caught in a firestorm. You're bewitching and too beautiful to be burned at the stake."

She'd ignored his term of endearment once, but he was beginning to push her tolerance button. That could put him up to his neck in boiling-hot water, especially if he pressed too hard.

Erika squashed her childish desire to make a farcical face at him. "Maybe if you'd watched where you were going I could've put the fire out myself. Thank you," she retorted.

He laughed. "Ah, yes! I'm sure that you're quite capable of getting a blazing fire under control, but I didn't realize that I was the one in such a rush." The intense heat in his hazel gaze told her that he knew exactly how to get an alarming fire started, and that he'd love to have her put it out for him.

"Thanks for retrieving my things," she said through tightly clenched teeth. Turning away from his piercing eyes, she walked off, an infusion of color surfacing in her cheeks.

As she turned around to steal a glance at his back, she found him standing there, checking her out. When he grinned and waved, she turned around and ran like the wind. He looked good enough to drool over, but now wasn't the time, and on the hospital grounds wasn't the place.

Dr. Jules Baker, the chief of obstetrics and gynecology, was already going to have her hide for his coffee break, she thought nervously. Erika was going to be late for the second time this week. Dr. Baker detested tardiness, regardless of how legitimate the reason.

Inside her tiny, brightly decorated apartment Erika snatched a freshly starched white lab coat instead of changing clothes as she'd originally planned. Snatching her backpack from the small desk, she lodged it snugly against her back. Grabbing her stethoscope and daily schedule, she rushed out the door.

* * *

Dr. Baker and his team of residents were already making rounds, she learned, reaching the third-floor reception desk ten minutes later. Maggie England, the ward clerk, informed her that the team was in room 204.

Skidding into the room, Erika did her best to blend in with her colleagues. She hoped Dr. Baker wouldn't notice the time, since he was busy writing in a medical chart.

"Dr. Edmonds, so glad you could join us," Dr. Baker said without looking up. "What's your excuse this time, young lady?" he demanded impatiently.

Dr. Baker had four eyes with his glasses, but six—having two more in the back of his head—was utterly ridiculous, she thought, suddenly feeling a swarm of butterflies stirring in her stomach. "Sir, would you mind if I gave it to you after rounds? It's very personal."

"Dr. Edmonds," he thundered, "dedicated residents don't have personal lives, period. I'm waiting to hear your excuse."

How insensitive, she charged silently, wondering what he would've done in her situation. "Sir, I can appreciate what you've said, but I don't feel the necessity to air my personal problems in front of everyone. I'd be eternally grateful if I could discuss this with you in private," she challenged boldly, her voice carrying a spark of anger and noticeable quiver.

He looked up from the medical chart. Peering at her over the metal-rimmed glasses lodged on the once-broken bridge of his nose, agitated, he ran fingers through the premature silver hair at his temples. His air of authority waving like a red flag, Dr. Baker removed his glasses, causing Erika to shudder. "I sense an urgency here, so I'll grant your wish. But if you're late one more time, you're going on probation," he ground out furiously.

Sixteen insensitive expressions were now turned her way. Bursting into tears, Erika threw her belongings to the floor and sped from the room. Out in the hallway, she pressed her face against the cool, stark white wall. Breaking down, she cried bitterly. Ever since her mother's untimely death she'd been overly sensitive. Knowing that she now had to sell her childhood home had made her even more vulnerable.

Soothing hands firmly gripped her shoulders. "What's happened? Lose everything you own in the fire?" a sexy and slightly familiar voice queried.

Trembling from his soothing touch, tearful, she sucked in a deep breath. "Go away. Maybe you should try your hand at the local comedy club. But I think that I should warn you . . . your routine sucks."

He moaned softly. "Hmm. I seem to have hit an exposed nerve. Can I make it up to you by offering you a very sensitive shoulder to cry on?"

Lifting her head, she looked right into his eyes. Her drop-dead glare gave him an idea of just how spunky she might be. The devastation that he also saw in her eyes caused him a bit of concern. "First, you nearly caused me to break my neck. Now you're goading me into losing my temper. Mr. whoever you are, don't you have a job somewhere? Or do you make a living harassing people?"

The tantalizing sound of his laughter trickled through her like liquid fire. "As a matter of fact, I do have a job. A very important one, I might add."

She glanced at her wristwatch. "If you leave right away, you can probably get to your job on time. Wouldn't want you to be late on my account." Erika knew she would usually never be this rude to anyone, but this wasn't just a normal day. It was an emotionally horrendous one.

"Edmonds, physicians' library. Right now," Dr. Baker shouted from the doorway of room 204, embarrassing her to no end. Color crept in again, staining her cheeks crimson.

"Edmonds, huh?" her new personal nemesis breathed. "Does Ms. Edmonds have a first name?"

A new flood of tears stung her eyes. "Mud," she snapped, storming off toward the doctors' library.

Watching her intently, he chuckled as she raced down the hall. *Under that honey-glazed hair lies a fiery redhead. I'd be willing to stake my reputation on it,* he ruminated mischievously. Put to the test, his reputation would've been worthless—the shoulder length honey-brown hair was as natural as the golden flecks of sunlight streaking through it.

After giving further instructions to his team, Dr. Baker hurried to the physicians' library. When he walked into the room, Erika's head was down on the conference table, and he could see the slight trembling of her shoulders. Quietly, he observed her for a few seconds, then strolled across to where she sat. Clearing his throat, he pulled out a chair and sat down on the opposite side of the table. Erika quickly jerked her head up.

He eyed her intently for several more seconds. "You have the floor, Dr. Edmonds. This interruption in my schedule had better be damn good."

Her eyes puffy from crying, Erika shifted uncomfortably in her seat. "Dr. Baker," she began, attempting a smile, "I was late this afternoon . . . because I had to go to my mother's house to try to decide which of her things I want to keep. I'm going to have to sell the house, but I need to clear out everything before the realtor can show it."

She breathed in deeply, gaining temporary control of her emotional agony. "I have to sell the home I grew up in. The same home both my mother and father died in." Hysteria forced its way to the top of her throat, but she gulped it back down.

Dr. Baker hadn't prepared himself for such an emotional response from Erika, yet understanding flashed in his eyes. Swallowing hard, he rose from his seat. Quickly, he moved around the table and dropped down in the chair next to hers. For several moments his voice was stuck in his throat, but his burgundy-brown eyes easily conveyed the empathy he felt for his young resident. "I now understand your request for privacy. It was insensitive of me to call you on the carpet in front of your colleagues."

Sorry for what she was faced with, he momentarily lowered his eyes. "I'm sorry, Dr. Edmonds, and I know just how you feel. After both of my parents passed away, I was faced with the same dilemma. I held on to that house and its contents until it became an albatross around my neck. I wouldn't even consider allowing someone else to move in there," he said shakily.

Digging her fingernails deeply into her thighs, she was as stunned by his response as he had been by hers. "I'm sorry. I had no idea, Dr. Baker. How did you cope with it at first?" Because of her emotional agony, she just barely felt her nails ripping into her flesh.

Pushing a salt-and-pepper curl back from his forehead, he sighed. "I'm afraid I didn't. That house meant everything to me. There were so many wonderful memories crammed into that old place, and I didn't want to let go of them. Letting go was tough on the entire family." He gripped her shoulder. "Give yourself some time to settle down. Your grief is still very fresh. Is selling the house a decision you have to make right now?"

As she gripped his hand tightly, more tears sprang to her eyes. How could she tell him that she had to either sell the house or drop out of the residency program? Vernice had cashed in her own insurance policy a long time ago, and Erika had taken the last of the money out of savings to give her mother a decent burial. Crying softly and moaning in despair, Erika again lowered her head to the table.

"It's all right, Erika," Dr. Baker comforted.

"No it's not," she sobbed. "I keep thinking that if I hadn't put my mother away she might still be alive. Now I'm left alone to face these very cold, stark realities."

A tidal wave of sympathy darkened his eyes. "You have to stop referring to your very wise decision to have your mother placed in a controlled setting as 'putting her away.' You did the right thing. You saw her every day. Even with the sort of hectic schedule you carry, you found the time to be directly involved in your mother's care. You did the right thing for her, young lady. Her safety was at grave risk. There weren't any alternatives."

"Oh, God, I hope so. I pray that both she and God knew where my heart was when I made the most difficult decision of my life. I don't like feeling this way. It scares me."

Dr. Baker let his hands rest innocently on her shoulders. "Listen, I want you to go down to the cafeteria and have a hot drink or something. We can handle the afternoon rounds without you today. Come see me in my office later this afternoon. Okay?"

Erika managed a smile. "Okay. Thanks, Dr. B. You've been very understanding. I'll try to be on time from now on."

He laughed lightly. "Dr. Edmonds, you had a very legitimate excuse. Despite the fact that I rarely tolerate any excuse, I accept yours. And I rarely apologize for anything, but I'm sincerely sorry about lashing out at you at a time like this. It wasn't as if I didn't know you'd recently lost your mother. Forgiven?"

"Without question," she responded, taking flight toward the door. Stopping briefly, she encompassed him with a smile.

He saw Dr. Erika Edmonds as a genuinely warm individual who possessed unadulterated sweetness and sincerity. Seeing so much more of her than what was so obviously on the surface, he smiled. "Wherever your mom is, I'm sure she's proud of you. She has a delightfully challenging minx for a daughter, not to mention a highly intelligent one. Her daughter is going to be one of the best African-American female doctors that Great Western University will ever send out into the medical world. You are definitely an invaluable asset to your rich ancestry. Now all you have to do is learn to be on time."

Erika's laughter rang out as she left the library.

The cafeteria was crowded. Erika's first thought was that this was the last place she needed to be. She then decided that it might be exactly where she should be. It just might do her a wealth of good. Being alone certainly wasn't going to cure what ailed her. Loneliness was another of those incurable diseases. One should avoid it like the plague, she mused.

Erika knew that she was going to have to learn a lot of clever maneuvers just to cope with life itself, let alone all the other ever-rising problems. If she couldn't manage to get hold of some financial assistance, she was going to be more than just lonely.

After paying for a cup of orange spice tea, Erika carried it to a far corner table, ready to watch the cast of colorful characters who trooped in and out of the drafty cafeteria at regular intervals. Before sitting down, she waved back at Marlon Hale, hoping he'd stay with his group of loudmouth friends. She was lonely, but not desperate enough to want to share her space with him. He should've been an X-rated comedian instead of a doctor. When Marlon turned his attention back to his friends, she exhaled a sigh of gratifying relief.

Just as she took a sip of her hot tea, she felt warm hands on her neck. Erika quickly looked to see if Marlon had in fact moved, but he was still in his original seat. Then she heard the voice that made her insides sizzle like pancakes on a hot grill. It felt as if melted butter flowed rapidly through her.

"Trying to recoup your losses?" He smiled at her as if she was the right answer to all the wrong in his life, as well as the missing piece of a puzzle. Without asking, he sat down across from her, tenderly stroking her face with the heat from his eyes.

As she tapped her squared fingernail tips on the Formica tabletop, his awesome smile made her feel insane with longing. "You seem so obsessed with my losses. Are you always this annoying?" There was no nearby escape route available to her, but she realized she wasn't looking for one. She felt mesmerized by his winsome gaze.

Looking directly at her, he rested his elbows on the table. He grinned. "Annoying, sometimes. Charming, always," he said with confidence, shrugging his broad shoulders. She was amazed that there didn't seem to be any arrogance in his softly voiced statement. "Maybe I am a little obsessed with you, but are you always this hard to get to know?"

"Oh, is that what we're doing here?" she inquired sarcastically. Despite her growing irritation, she smiled.

Her craterlike dimples caught him off guard. Sucking in a deep breath, he extended a marvelous hand with beautiful, long, lean fingers. "Michael Mathis, Miss Edmonds," he enchanted sweetly. "I'd love to make your acquaintance."

Lightly gripping the long, sensuous fingers, she felt his warmth shoot straight through her. "Dr. Erika Edmonds," she responded casually, wondering why his name rang a bell.

A slight smile played at the corners of his generous mouth. "So, you do have another name besides Mud. I like Erika better. It's such a lovely name." He hadn't responded to the prestigious title in front of her name, she noted, but neither did he seem threatened by it.

Folding her hands, she placed her elbows on the table. "Thank you, I guess," she commented coolly. "Tell me, Michael, why is it that you seem to have nothing to do but harass me? This is our third encounter and the day has just gotten under way."

Michael took a quick swig of coffee from a Styrofoam cup. "I have plenty to do, but none of it seemed as important as finding out who you were. Now that I've met you, I'm dying to learn more about who you are and what you aspire to be."

She flashed him a mischievous smile. "If you're dying, you're in the right place. Shall I escort you to the emergency room, Michael?"

He laughed from deep within his chest. "The emergency room won't be necessary, but I'd be honored if you'd escort me to dinner this evening. I'm really a tame guy, Dr. Edmonds," he said, giving her the recognition she had earned and deserved.

She smiled at the respect he'd shown her, yet she still sensed the need to be on guard. "Wild animals are tame. That is, when they're caged." She suddenly felt very foolish for being so arrogant. He hadn't offended her one single time, unless she considered being called "gorgeous" offensive; she didn't. "I'm sorry for being so rude, but I've had a horrendous day so far."

"I know," he commiserated tenderly. Even his eyes grew sympathetic.

She got the strangest feeling that he really did know, that he somehow felt her pain, soulfully. It was as though she felt him, too—way down, deep inside of her.

He raised his eyebrows in a knowing manner. "That's why you should accept my dinner invitation. It might help change the course of your day."

Was the charming Michael Mathis dealing from the top of the deck, she wondered, or straight from the bottom? She sighed again. "I'm not up to going out to dinner. I'm afraid I'm not feeling very sociable. Nothing personal."

His smile was gentle. "The loan of my shoulder is still available. Do you live here on campus?" he asked with keen interest.

"Honor Hall," she answered, wishing she could muster up enough enthusiasm to accept his invitation.

"Why don't you let me grab some take-out food later on this evening? We can eat here in the cafeteria. We can even eat in silence if you prefer it that way."

Looking directly at him, she tried to figure out why he was so persistent about spending time with her, inwardly admitting that she liked his persistence. She also liked the way he presented himself, very much a gentleman.

She formed a steeple with her hands. "Will seven-thirty fit into your schedule, Michael Mathis?"

"Perfectly, Erika Edmonds. Now that we have that settled, why don't you tell me why you were crying earlier?"

No traces of sarcasm laced her laughter. "I agreed to eat with you, not share my life story. Let's save it for another time.

The pain is so close to the surface I couldn't possibly discuss it calmly. Rain check, Michael?"

He smiled broadly. "Count on it, Erika." He stood and threw his cup in the trash bin. "Since I'm not going to be able to coerce any more interesting facts from you, I'm going to go and take care of my duties. I'll meet you right here at six-thirty."

"Seven-thirty," she corrected, wishing he didn't have to leave at all. She had enjoyed his company thoroughly, though she thought she probably shouldn't have.

Laughing, he wagged his finger at her playfully. "Just checking to see if you're on your toes." Bending over, he planted a petal-soft kiss on her right cheek. "Good-bye, Erika."

Moist heat stole into her face at the way he'd seductively breathed her name. Erika whistled softly as she studied the sexy swagger of his powerful legs and lean, mean hips. When the paging system boomed overhead, startling her, she realized that she hadn't even heard it during the course of their meeting. She'd been completely captivated by his presence. Normally the paging system drove her nuts, especially when she tried to talk to someone over it.

Erika tossed her cup into the trash bin and strolled from the cafeteria on some type of cloud. She couldn't put a name or number to it, but she knew it wasn't a rain cloud. Groping in her backpack for some change, Erika darted to the nearest pay phone. After depositing the coins into the slot, she dialed her aunt's phone number. Fumbling with her hair, she awaited a response.

"Aunt Arlene," she called out when her aunt answered, "it's Erika. I'm calling to see how you're doing." The transitory silence seemed almost eerie as she dug her sharp nails into her palm. This time, she grimaced at the pain.

"Erika, child," Arlene greeted, her voice full of cheer. "I'm fine, but I stayed up half the night watching television. Some of the shows on those cable channels are spicy-hot, but I can't say that I complained too loudly." Arlene chuckled. "For sure,

I didn't bother to change the channel. Had your mother been here we probably would've stayed up all night."

At the mention of her mother, Erika swallowed the uncomfortable lump in her throat. "You are so naughty," she teased. "Mother would've had a fit if she'd ever caught me watching some of those spicy programs. I guess there's no need for me to worry about you, is there? You sound wonderful."

Aunt Arlene sucked her teeth. "I can't begin to imagine what you'd have to worry about, child. For sure, not about me. Other than missing your mother, I'm doing just fine. Everything else is going to be just fine, too. Vernice is resting in peace now. She'd suffered enough. Do you want me to come out there and see about you?"

"No, no," Erika said quickly, wondering when things were going to be just fine for her. "I'm pulling it together, but I'm afraid it's going to take a lot more time for me." Erika hadn't yet come to terms with her mother's death the way her aunt had, but she knew she had to get used to the change. Change was always hard to accept, but there really was no other option left to her. "If you were up most of the night, you need to rest. I'll call back later on. Love you, Auntie."

"Erika, child, I can hear the distress in your voice, but I want you to take time out to think about what your mother would've wanted you to do. I can tell you one thing for sure. She'd want you to get on with your career and your life. Until her illness, your mother had a pretty good life. With school and all, you already have too much to worry about. I love you, niece," she remarked warmly, disconnecting the line without further comment.

Erika hung up the phone, but she couldn't hang up on the echoes violently attacking her ears. "Deserter, deserter, deserter," they seemed to scream boisterously.

Clamping her hands over her ears, Erika ran through the halls like a woman stalked by the devil. So intent on escaping the loud echoes, she didn't even notice the worried glances from those passing by. Nothing would get in the way of her getting to her apartment so she could sort things out. Erika knew she wasn't a weak person, but feelings of hopelessness and guilt had begun to usurp every ounce of her strength.

Upon entering her apartment, the first thing she saw was the color portrait of Vernice hanging on the wall behind the sand-colored, saddle back sofa. Vernice had been a beautiful woman who possessed much poise and grace. The portrait was several years old, but Vernice had hardly changed. Not a single wrinkle had creased her lovely, olive-brown face, and her figure had been one to be envied, especially by women of her age group.

Like Erika, Vernice had once been obese. She had also made the conscious decision to take off the unwanted pounds and keep them off. She'd loved to dress up. Even during her illness, her fashion sense was no less than extraordinary. Not a day went by when Vernice didn't look as though she was off to church. That had been a real treat for her husband, Erika remembered with fondness. During her brief stay at Golden Age Retirement Center, Erika made sure her mother's style of dress wasn't compromised.

Erika tossed her gear onto the round, oak dining table, which was large enough to accommodate only two people. A ceramic vase of colorful silk flowers was in the center of the table, and a clear plastic place mat was laid out at each place setting.

Dropping down on the sofa, Erika closed her eyes, willing her mind to nothingness. When it refused to obey, she began to wallow in self-pity. Devastated beyond solace, Erika began to think about all the reasons why she'd gone into the medical profession. For one, she simply hated to see people suffer from any sort of pain. As a child, she had suffered terribly with asthma. When she was ten, one severe attack had nearly claimed her life. By the time she'd reached puberty, she'd been fortunate enough to grow out of the horrendous disease. The memory of that cold night in January, when she'd suffered the nearly fatal attack, would forever live on in her mind.

The death of her little friend, Sally Thomas, seemed to be

the worst thing she'd had to deal with as a child. They had both been only seven years old when Sally's diseased kidneys had ceased to function, robbing Sally of her precious life.

It was then that Erika had first voiced her desire to become a physician. She couldn't help Sally then, but there were millions of others with debilitating diseases who desperately needed her help now. Closing her eyes, she prayed for strength and courage. Finished with her reverent prayer, she made another commitment to herself. She vowed to crusade for those in need of proper medical care who couldn't afford it, along with educating people about pernicious anemia. She didn't have any money to offer, but she had a God-given talent, and she was going to use it to make a difference. Feeling somewhat at peace, Erika left the tiny apartment, hoping Dr. Baker was still in his office.

Five minutes later, when she knocked on Dr. Baker's door, he was there.

After chatting impersonally for a few minutes, they entered into a lengthy discussion about pernicious anemia. Dr. Baker was very supportive of her desire to educate others about the disease, which made her feel much better. Afterward, Dr. Baker even asked her to have dinner with him and his wife, Jada, but Erika had to decline, due to the prior commitment she'd made to Michael Mathis.

It was close to six o'clock when Erika reentered her apartment. *Just enough time for a hot bath,* she thought, tired. Perhaps Michael Mathis would chase away a few hours of the loneliness that had become her constant companion.

Erika rummaged through her scant wardrobe and came up with a classy pair of heather-gray slacks and a gray-and-white tunic sweater. These would do nicely for an informal meal in a hospital cafeteria, she decided, an amused expression softening the heavy scowl threatening to harden her pretty, heart-shaped face.

Minutes later, her body was submerged in a swirling tub of hot water and deliciously scented bubbles. At that very moment, she had no desire to leave the relaxing atmosphere of her small, serenely decorated bathroom.

As the flame from a single candle cast dancing shadows on the walls, Erika slipped into a state of sweet exultation. Somewhere in the distance, a slow song could be heard. Its melody, fraught with sadness and loneliness, caused a restlessness to stir in her soul. Having been preoccupied with her grief over the absence of her mother, she was now preoccupied with the strength and warmth of the Indian-brown hands that had made only brief contact with her creamy skin, along with the quiet spirit in him that reminded her of her step-father.

Michael Mathis intrigued her in more ways than one. She strongly suspected there was so much more to the man than the naked eye could see. Michael Mathis had something very special going on. Something very special, indeed. It suddenly dawned on her that the absence of a man in her life could be one of the causes of the "poor me" saga she'd been so selfishly creating.

As the memory of Michael's gaze pierced her like an arrow, she began to realize that the arrow belonged to Cupid. Its very pointed end had hit the dead center of her heart. But how could that be? She'd only seen the man three times and all the encounters had come in the same day. Whatever she felt was ridiculous, yet so wonderfully sensuous.

How could a few mere touches reach her so deeply? But then again, the first encounter had almost knocked her senseless. Had the impact of that caused her to think irrationally? Whatever it was, the direct hit had had a profound impact on her lonely heart.

Two

Although it was dark outside, Erika sat at a window table in the cafeteria. The lights on the building's exterior shone down on the snowy landscape, turning the snowbanks into glistening jewels. *Perfect,* Erika thought, pulling a sketchpad from a large, hand-knitted satchel.

Michael wasn't due for another half an hour, and she could use the time to sketch and relax. She would've loved for him to have been sitting there waiting for her to make an appearance, but she hadn't been able to deal with herself for another second, not in that lonely, tiny space she called home away from home.

Erika selected a few colored pencils and began to sketch the landscape, adding other fine details she relied on her imagination to create. Her fingers moved fast and furiously, slowing to a lazy pace as she used a shading pencil to fill in the rest of the blank spaces. The etchings came to life before her eyes, which always amazed her.

"That's beautiful," Michael said. Leaning over her shoulder, he inhaled the sweet, engaging scent of her, which made him want to bury his nose in the softness of her elegant neck.

She looked up at him and gave him a full, dimpled smile, melting his insides like a chocolate bar left too long in the heat. "Hello," she said, barely above a whisper.

The desire to kiss her wine-colored lips had never been stronger than it was at that very moment, but he didn't want to make her think that his interest in her was only physical. Coming on too strong, too soon, could end their relationship before it got a chance to breathe life on its own. Had he known that her desire to be kissed equaled his own, he wouldn't have hesitated. Smiling sweetly, he placed a box of steaming pizza and two soft drinks on the table.

He took the seat next to her. "Hello, Erika. Am I late? Or are you early?"

Smiling gently, she entombed him with her eyes. "Let's just say we're both right on time, Michael Mathis."

"Long overdue, if you ask me. But you didn't ask, so I'll just let it go at that. Hungry?"

Smiling at his comment, Erika nodded, putting her drawing away.

Gently, he stilled her hand. "I'd like to take a closer look at it, if I could?" She slid the drawing in front of him. Picking it up, he studied it closely. "It's magnificent, Erika."

"Thank you. I knew that if I couldn't make it as a doctor, I could always try to keep from starving by working as an artist," she commented thoughtfully, not sure that she was going to keep from starving as a doctor.

Money was so difficult to come by these days. The residency stipend was just enough to keep her head above water, and her school expenses, along with a few other necessary encumbrances, were eating her alive.

He chuckled. "I think you're talented enough to do both." He pointed at the two intimately entwined figures in the drawing. "Are these two in love?"

She couldn't stop herself from smiling at his keen perception. "They are love," she remarked timidly. "I created them with the love God transplanted into my heart for all mankind. Therefore, anything created from love is love."

As he stared at her in utter bewilderment, she thought she actually saw tears in his eyes. But the lighting was so dim she couldn't be sure. Whatever she'd seen had nearly taken her breath away. In the next instant he claimed what little breath she had left. His lips touched hers so lightly she wasn't sure that it had happened, either, until another light kiss confirmed the first. A deeper, probing kiss brought the prior events sharply into focus.

He lifted his head and looked into her eyes. "In two words, how would you describe what just happened here?" His voice sounded thick with emotion.

"Breathless wonder!"

"Dr. Michael Mathis, please call the operator," the paging system blared, intruding upon the most electrifying moment either of them had ever encountered. An immediate apology for the untimely intrusion swirled in his eyes.

Michael groaned. "This could only happen to me. Erika, go ahead and eat, and pray that this call isn't going to tear us away from each other." He then rushed off to grab a nearby phone.

Erika hadn't heard a word he'd said. She was in a state of shock. The name of the doctor on the paging system kept pealing in her brain, making her dizzy with disbelief. *It can't be,* she thought reverently. *Dr. Michael Mathis, the brilliant surgeon?* He had saved a baby's life by using a microsurgery technique that hadn't been certified for use at the time the surgery was performed. The technique was now certified because of the irrefutable evidence of its credibility and the overwhelming success of the surgery that the incredible, young Dr. Mathis had so skillfully performed. "No, no way," she said firmly, shaking her head from side to side.

He'd never even mentioned that he was a doctor. And he wasn't at all arrogant, which she believed was an absolute prerequisite for all males entering medical school. She was still lost somewhere in a dense fog when Michael returned to the table.

Quietly, he observed the perplexed expression shrouding her delicate features. He couldn't help wondering what she could possibly be thinking about. Whatever her thoughts, they had suddenly transformed her into a bewitching enigma.

As he sat down, he pulled her into his arms. "Where are you, Erika Edmonds? Are you too far out there for me to reach?"

Blinking hard, she tried to return to his lofty presence, but something unexplainable kept her quietly aloof. Their eyes were suddenly locked together by an alien force neither of them could control. Their hands reached out to each other, entwining in an impassioned embrace. Erika wanted so desperately to speak, but her words would have no voice behind them, so she continued to further lose herself in the depths of his hazel reflectors.

Michael lost himself, too—not caring whether he'd be found, unless he could be found with her, totally locked in this magical world that evil could never penetrate. The magical world they now shared together.

The tangible silence between them grew in intensity—and went on and on. Erotic tension mounted; primitive needs screamed to be fulfilled, desire flooded their souls. Slowly, deeply, he possessed her mouth, as though this was the first and final drink of sweet wine he'd ever taste from her intoxicating lips. Sheer bliss.

In a dimly lit hospital cafeteria, which they no longer solely occupied, the seed of love was planted in their hearts—a seed they'd hopefully nurture, until it could mature into a full, exquisite blossom. Separated by a mere inch, they trembled from the coldness lodged in the minute space between them.

Sure that the pizza was cold by now, Michael opened the box, anyway, offering a slice to Erika. Taking it from his hand, she held it to his mouth and watched as his strong, white teeth bit into the soft dough. He then did the same for her. After three slices had been consumed between them, Michael closed the lid and shoved the box aside.

Erika gently touched his hand. "The phone call. Anything important?"

He shoved a hand through his wavy hair. "Very important, Erika. That was my exchange calling. I have a little patient I like to keep very close tabs on. I operated on him two days ago, but he keeps spiking a fever. However, it's now back to normal. The nurses promised to keep me informed."

He was indeed a doctor, but was he the doctor in question? "Little patient" could mean that he was a pediatrician, but not necessarily. He was definitely a surgeon.

Immediately noticing that she no longer seemed to be with him, he wished he knew what had her so darn preoccupied. *Ask her,* a quiet voice urged.

He touched her hand. "Erika, what keeps taking you away from me? One minute we're so connected, the next minute you're so distant. Have I taken too much for granted here? If so, I just want you to know that I'm very single and very available."

She looked at him incredulously. "Now that we know we're both very single and very available, are you the same incredibly talented Dr. Mathis who performed the microsurgery that's been lingering on the grapevine of every hospital on this planet?"

Humbled, he smiled. "One and the same, Dr. Edmonds. I don't know why I didn't tell you I was a doctor. Sometimes it gets in the way of being real. I like to be recognized as a human being, not just a prestigious title. People seem to become preoccupied with occupations, even professionals with each other. Is that what's been bothering you?"

She blew out a gust of breath. "It has me in an absolute state of shock! I can't imagine someone like you wanting to be bothered with a lowly resident. Namely, me."

He suddenly looked disappointed. "You just proved what I was trying to say. Are you going to have problems about hanging out with me? Or can we just be together as human beings and leave our credentials on the office walls? We've had one incredible beginning, you know."

Smiling sweetly at him, Erika propped one elbow on the table and rested her chin in the palm of her hand. "Yes, we have. Now, tell me, does this particular human being I'm sitting here with like to take long walks in the snow and the rain?" she asked, wiggling her eyebrows suggestively.

Laughing, he threw his head back. She could almost feel his deep laughter bubbling in her own throat. "Do you know how long I've searched for a woman who likes to do those romantically crazy, spontaneous kinds of things? If I've found her, you have to be the only one in this city who doesn't worry about getting her hair all mussed. In keeping with the subject matter, are you up to trudging through the snow right now?"

Erika laughed heartily. "If you'll give me time to get a coat, I'd love to trudge through the snow with you. Promise you won't throw snowballs?"

Michael was already out of his seat, preparing to clear off the table. "Do I have to promise that?"

"No, you don't. But let me warn you. I know how to make a killer snowball, and I do know how to hit a moving target!"

Eager to have some fun in the snow, they quickly cleared the table and dumped the trash. Then Michael escorted her to her apartment to retrieve her coat.

Inside her apartment, Erika slid into her coat while he held it for her. As she began to put on her ridiculous blue hat with the red fluff on top, he took it from her hands and gently pulled it down over her head. He then tied the strings snugly under her chin. Two long fingers lifted her chin and his mouth searched hers, leaving them both breathless long after the probing search was completed.

Exiting the dormitory building through a side door, they stepped into the nearly freezing temperature. Giggling like two adolescents, they began their walk huddled closely together, gasping when the cold air smashed against their faces.

The purple, velvety sky appeared inundated with twinkling diamonds while a golden, crescent moon reigned supreme over the nucleus of the universe. The tall pine trees appeared to embrace the starry skies, and the night was sensually alive with the low and distinctive murmurs of nature. Liquid-chocolate eyes explored the depths of hazel ones. Hand in hand, they walked around the campus, totally absorbed with each other in their winter wonderland surroundings. Erika couldn't believe this was actually happening to her.

Michael was keenly aware of what had already happened to him. Could Erika Edmonds possibly be the woman he'd searched the world for? Could she bring him the joy of love that had so far managed to elude him? he wondered, unable to stop his mind from taking a brief spin back in time.

Dr. Michael Mathis had once thought he'd found the woman he wanted to spend the rest of his life with, thought his world had been made complete the day Stephanie Sadler walked into his office carrying a tiny infant girl who looked like an angel. Baby Tamala Sadler had suffered from pediatric AIDS; contracted through a blood transfusion that was necessary at birth.

Michael was as much enthralled with little Tamala as he'd been with her mother. He'd found himself trying to move mountains to keep her alive, but the Divine Power had other plans for baby Tamala. When He called His child home, Michael was there for Stephanie. Though Stephanie was there for him, too, he became extremely restless with their relationship. After several months of helping her work through her grief, he broke off their unofficial engagement.

There was absolutely nothing wrong with Stephanie. She was sensitive, intelligent, and genuinely beautiful from the inside out. But Michael had learned much too late that though he loved Stephanie, he wasn't in love with her. However, it hadn't been a bitter break up, and they'd remained friends. Though she had moved to the West Coast, they stayed in touch. Stephanie was now married, and she often thanked Michael for recognizing his true feelings. She was now madly in love with a man who adored her.

Michael knew he couldn't afford to make the same mistake with Erika, but he had to find out if she was the one he could love with all the power available to him, and then some. He was taking a big risk, but he couldn't afford not to take it. What he'd already felt with her was genuinely amazing. What he'd already shared with her was more than he'd ever shared with anyone, including Stephanie.

He couldn't think about whether he was being fair to her or not. In fact, he found it hard to think at all when she cast that liquid gaze and those deeply dimpled smiles his way, as she was now doing. Her eyes spoke to him in a language he'd never heard.

As they turned back toward the dormitory, Erika scooped up a large handful of snow and tossed it onto Michael's broad shoulders. Her laughter trilling in the air, she took off. When he joined in, the playful skirmish began.

Grabbing some snow in his hands, he ran after her. Catching up to her, he washed her face in it. As he passionately licked the melting white powder from her face, they both slipped and fell to the ground, where they romped in the snow, throwing it at each other playfully.

As Erika rolled a fat snowball around in her gloved hands, Michael jumped up and took off running. Just as she'd warned earlier, she did know how to hit a moving target. "Bull's-eye!" she yelled as the snowball connected with Michael's back. "I told you I make a mean snowball. You can't say you weren't forewarned."

A snowball battle of all battles ensued. The lateness of the hour was the only thing that deterred them from continuing their cold war. Both were soaked by the time they started indoors.

At the door of the apartment Erika and Michael kissed good night, but it was obvious that neither of them wanted the evening to end. It was after nine o'clock, and Michael had early morning rounds. Though Erika's rounds weren't scheduled until the afternoon, she had other mandatory duties on her busy schedule.

Michael ran the back of his hand down the side of her face. "Could I trouble you for a cup of coffee before I go home?"

She laughed. "No trouble at all if I had some, but I don't.

Tea and cocoa are the only things I keep in stock. Care for either?"

Happy that the night wasn't going to end so abruptly, after all, he grinned. "As long as it's steamy hot it makes no difference to me."

Getting the impression that there was a double message in his seemingly seductive statement, she knew the only steamy-hot thing he'd get was the drink, regardless of how much her body ached to be touched by those long, beautiful fingers of his. Michael may be a surgeon, but he had the hands of a concert pianist. Hand in hand, they entered the apartment.

Soon after they got out of their wet outer attire, Michael followed Erika into the kitchen. He laughed, seeing that it was barely big enough to hold them both. He'd never forgotten how tough dormitory-style living had been. Sitting at the oak table, he watched as Erika bent over to retrieve a pan from a lower cabinet shelf. His manhood responded wantonly to her firm, perfectly rounded derriere.

Removing a carton of milk from the refrigerator, Erika poured a generous amount into the pan and added several scoops of dark cocoa powder. Adjusting the gas flame, she covered the burner with the pan.

Turning around, she tossed Michael a dimpled smile that crashed into the essence of his soul. "I'll join you in a minute, but this has to be stirred constantly."

Unable to wait for her to join him, he stood. As she turned her back to him to stir the liquid, he sauntered up behind her, encircling her waist with infinite tenderness. Nuzzling her neck with his nose, he deeply inhaled the bouquet-fresh scent of her honey-brown hair. His tongue trailed a path of heat around the tip of her ear. Tasting her ear, he moaned as he gently blew into it. He craved palming the gentle twin mounds pouting beneath the gray-and-white sweater, but that would have to wait for another time, a time when they both wanted to further explore the intimate pleasures each had to offer.

Not at all immune to his touch, Erika struggled to keep her

hips still, though she really wanted to tease the crotch of his pants by swaying gently against him. That would be like playing with fire, knowing she'd get burned—especially when his heat felt fiery enough to cremate her tender flesh.

"Erika," he whispered, "I think the cocoa's burning." Reaching around her, he switched off the gas.

That's not the only thing that's burning, she thought, feeling helpless, moving a slight distance from his imposing sexual aura. She gulped at the air, needing a gust of fresh oxygen to clear her head. "I don't think the cocoa is a total loss, but it's probably a little singed at the bottom."

He wore a wry smile on his handsome face. "How do you think that happened?" he asked, knowing full well that he was responsible for distracting her.

She swatted him with the dishtowel. "As if you didn't know. Were we being annoying or charming?"

"Annoyingly charming, I guess. Here," he said, pushing her aside, "let me pour it into the cups. You go and sit down. I like waiting on my woman."

My woman. He certainly has taken a lot for granted, hasn't he? she thought, drowning in the sweet sensations that being claimed as his woman had brought on.

While sipping on the hot liquid, Michael began to ask Erika a lot of personal questions, but they weren't personal enough to be offensive. When he asked about her family, without any warning her emotions erupted and she burst into tears, shocking him speechless.

Michael didn't have far to go to clothe her in his arms, deciding to let her cry herself out before saying anything. He really didn't know what to say, since he didn't know what had caused the torrent to spill from her eyes.

When she lifted her head from his shoulder, he took a pink napkin from its holder, dabbed at the corner of her eyes, and kissed the remaining brine from her cheeks. "I think it's time for me to cash in on that rain check. Don't you think so, too, Erika?"

While sniffling and nodding, she had no intention of telling him about her problems, not in a million years. So what was she going to tell him? she asked herself, racking her brain for a passable reason for such a violent outburst of raw emotions. "Erika Edmonds is just plain worn out and tired, and she thinks she needs to go to bed. Her day has been frightening, to say the least."

Looking at her with raised eyebrows, he didn't believe a word she'd spoken. *Well,* he thought, *she could be tired,* and he knew that her day had been rough. However, she was holding back something pretty heavy, and he had every intention of finding out what it was. Even if he had to stay there all night—which he didn't think was the worst idea in the world.

"Erika, if you really have any hope of going to bed this night, you need to tell me what's wrong."

She stared defiantly at him, only to get the same recalcitrant look in return, which caused her to turn from his gaze. "As I told you earlier, the pain is still too close to the surface. Can't you hold the rain check for a while longer? I have no courage where this matter's concerned." Unwittingly, she had now fully piqued his curiosity, making him more determined than before to find out what was going on inside her head.

Taking her hands away from her mouth, he held them to keep her from biting her nails to the quick. "Do you have a blanket I can throw over the sofa?" He didn't offer any explanation, but she didn't need one. She knew just where he'd gone with that question.

She sighed heavily. "I can see that you're not going to let this drop, so I might as well go ahead and tell you so you can get off my back." A million years certainly seemed to have passed by with the speed of sound, she thought. "My mother died recently, and I haven't come to terms with it yet. Now I have to go through the difficulty of selling our family home. Before she died, I had placed her in a retirement home. She suffered from pernicious anemia, and needed specialized care. Though I know it was for her safety, there are times when I'm plagued with guilt." Unable to believe how easy that had been, how much self-control she'd exercised, she sighed with relief.

Kissing her cheek, he drew her close to him. "I'm truly sorry, Erika. And I'm so sorry that I bullied you into that revelation."

Erika put her fingers up to his lips. "No apology necessary, Michael. I'm glad that I told you. It seems to have eased some of the strain I've been under. I'm afraid it's going to take me a bit longer to come to grips with things. I can't seem to get past my grief."

He gently kissed her mouth. "Understandably so. From what I know about the disease it had probably been going on for a long time if she needed to be placed. How long did it go undiagnosed, Erika?"

"Too long, Michael. Too many hard years of never knowing what to expect next. I never knew what it was, or what I was supposed to do about it. I didn't even know how I was supposed to feel about it. And I'll never know what my mother truly felt about what had happened to her." *Unless it happens to me,* she added in her thoughts. Knowing the disease was hereditary, she understood that she might suffer with it, too. That frightened her. "It must have been awful for her," Erika said, her voice cracking. Hot tears born of trepidation rolled from her eyes.

Forgetting all the junk about doctors not showing any emotion, he felt like crying, too. First and foremost, he was a human being. He was also a sensitive man, with a live, pulsating heart housed in his chest. How could he not feel something? How could he not feel deep compassion for the woman sitting next to him, the woman whose heart was a shambles?

He wiped her tears. "Yes, Erika, it must have been awful for her. Do you feel that you did right by your mother? In health and in sickness?"

"There's no doubt in my mind that I was a good daughter. She always told me how good I was to her. I know for a fact that I didn't wait until she was dead to give her flowers. I just wish I hadn't made the decision to place her. She might still be alive if I hadn't."

He looked at her with disbelief "You don't really believe that, do you? Before you answer that, let me ask you something. Had your mother been killed by a car, gotten into a car with someone who brought serious harm to her, or perhaps turned on the gas and forgotten about it, would you feel any less guilt about her death? How would you feel about yourself if you hadn't done everything within your power to protect her from hurt, harm and danger?"

She wrung her hands together. "I see what you mean, Michael. Thanks."

He stilled her hands again. "You have to pull yourself together and get on with living. I'll be here to help you do that. That's if you want me here. It sounds to me as if you gave your mother your best. I can only imagine that she'd want you to do the same for yourself."

Erika didn't know what she'd expected him to say, but she certainly hadn't expected the response he'd given. Neither had she expected him to get involved with her problems, but he seemed determined to do that. Dr. Michael Mathis wasn't dealing from the bottom of the deck, she concluded. He seemed to be dealing straight from the heart.

Michael stayed with her until he was satisfied that she was going to be okay by herself. At the door, they found it hard to say good night again as he kissed her forehead. "I know we didn't get to learn a great deal about each other, but I've learned enough about you to know that I want to keep on seeing you. How about you? Do you want to see me again?"

She smiled. "For as long as it's good between us."

He smiled back. "For as long as we do it for each other?"

Laughing, she flirted with her lashes. "For as long as we're both truly satisfied with what we give and receive from each other?"

Grinning, he pulled her to him. "We could go on like this all night, but we both need to get some sleep. Duty calls early for us doctors. I'd love for you to accompany me to the ballet tomorrow night. That is, if it's not too short notice."

She grinned. "I haven't a thing to do tomorrow night. I'd love to go with you." To deny herself another night in his company would be just plain stupid.

Michael told her what time she could expect him to pick her up. Then, after they shared several staggering kisses, he departed.

Three

Erika arose much earlier than she normally did. She'd slept very well despite the fact she'd been so emotional when she'd climbed into bed. In hopes of making it to Aunt Arlene's house and back before her scheduled duties commenced, she rushed through her personal preparations for the day. After brushing her teeth, she sprayed on some deodorant and combed her hair.

Wrapped in nothing but a fluffy yellow towel, Erika switched on the radio as she passed by the nightstand. The weather report was on and she was glad to learn that no more snow had fallen during the night, which would make driving less cumbersome.

Twenty minutes later, dressed warmly in a thick, navy-blue sweater and gray wool slacks, Erika hurried to the car, tossed her things into the backseat, and slid behind the steering wheel of her aging Toyota.

Much to her annoyance it took several minutes for the car to roar to life. When it did, she lightly rested a foot on the gas pedal to ensure that the engine wouldn't die on her. She was in dire need of a newer car, but that would have to remain a wish for now. Half of the time she couldn't even afford to buy gas, let alone pay on a loan for a new car. She was already paying the note on the home-equity loan Vernice had taken out on the house to help out with her school expenses. She still had eighteen months to go on that. What she needed more than anything was a miracle.

Erika had serious doubts that the house would sell at a price that covered the full amount of the loan, especially in such a depressed real-estate market. The realtor had told her that she'd put the house at her asking price, but that she might have to come down on it. She hoped that that wouldn't have to occur; every single silver dime was needed.

As Erika reached her destination, she could already smell the freshly baked cinnamon rolls her aunt made every Friday morning. A cinnamon roll dunked in hot cocoa was to die for, as far as she was concerned. Very conscious of her ability to gain weight just by looking at one, she attempted to cool her instincts.

The second Erika swung the front door open, the heavenly smells rolled out of the kitchen, sending their delicious scents right up her nose. Inhaling deeply, she moaned, hoping she could control the temptation to eat more than one pastry.

"Aunt Arlene, it's Erika," she shouted, heading straight for the kitchen, where she found her aunt sitting at the kitchen table, sprinkling another batch of rolls with cinnamon and brown sugar. The immaculate kitchen was bright with a flashy whiteness. The blue-and-yellow wallpaper border had the only bright colors in the otherwise sterile white room.

Arlene looked up and smiled with delight at her favorite niece, then glanced at the clock on the stove. "Heavens, girl, what are you doing out so early? It's only a little after five o'clock in the morning."

Smiling sheepishly, Erika plopped down in one of the cane-back chairs. "You already know I came out here to check on you," Erika remarked, giving her aunt a smile.

Arlene smiled back at her niece. "Ah, so the plot thickens. But it's nice to know that you'll be coming around to keep a watchful eye on this old girl."

"I would hardly classify you as an old girl," Erika flattered knowingly.

Arlene folded her hands together and placed them on the table. Without uttering a word, she absently worried her slate-gray hair with steady fingers, lowering her head for a few moments of silent prayer.

Finished with her prayer, she reached across the table and enfolded Erika against her ample bosom. "My dear, sweet child, I just had to thank the Lord for all that he's blessed us with. I couldn't wait a second longer. You're one of those blessings, Erika. Vernice was so blessed to have you for a daughter. I love you and my darling sister very much, which makes me blessed, too. That's why I place everything into the unchanging hands of the good Lord. You must always remember to do the same."

In a powerful voice, Arlene began to sweetly sing "What a Friend We Have in Jesus." The song brought burning tears to Erika's eyes. Once her tears were under control, Erika joined her aunt in the song "At the Cross" and she truly began to feel the burdens of her heart roll away.

Within a few minutes they were talking quietly and nibbling on the sweet rolls. When the subject matter focused on Dr. Michael Mathis, as she told her aunt how they'd met and spent the last evening, Erika could feel her heart take wing. As she talked about going to the ballet that evening, it suddenly dawned on her that she didn't own a single outfit appropriate for such an auspicious affair.

"Oh, Aunt Arlene, I'm going on and on about the ballet and I haven't a decent thing to wear. It looks as if I'm just going to have to pass on this one." Bitter disappointment was clear in her expression.

Arlene stood and walked over to the kitchen counter. Taking the lid off an antique cookie jar, she reached in and dug out a wad of cash. Carrying the money to the table, she handed it to Erika. "Go and buy yourself something real pretty, now. You're a dream in red!"

Erika dropped the cash on the table, looking as though she'd just closed her hand around a hot branding iron. "I can't take your money," she said loudly. "You're on a fixed income as it is. I'd never take money for something so unnecessary."

Patting her thick hips, Arlene chuckled. "Do I look like I'm doing without, child? I've got enough fat stored up to keep me going for years. Besides, Erika, I'm far from broke. Let's just say I'm very frugal." Her doe-brown eyes sparkled with gentle mischief. "You take that money and run. You wouldn't think of insulting me, now, would you? I know you've been raised better than that, child."

Erika knew when she was in a no-win situation, but she wasn't too comfortable with her position. "You're such a sweetheart. Every family should be blessed with a love like you. Thank you, Aunt Arlene." Erika glanced at her watch. "I hate to eat and run, but I've got to go. Is there anything you need me to do for you over the weekend? I'm going to be free as a bird."

Arlene got to her feet. "Just drop by and say hello if you find time. Now let me wrap up some of these rolls for you to take home."

Erika threw up her hands. "Oh, no! I'm determined not to put any of the old weight back on. I've had enough."

Arlene moved on toward the stove. "I think your young man might like to try one or two after your date this evening. Don't you?"

Erika chuckled. "Okay, Aunt Arlene. You win! While you're getting them ready, I'm going to slip into the bathroom." At the end of the hallway, Erika opened the bathroom door and went inside, where she combed and brushed her hair and put on more lipstick. A few minutes later she left the bathroom and hurried back to the kitchen.

"You got the care package ready for me, Auntie? It's time for me to hit the road."

Arlene handed Erika a hefty brown paper bag. "These should get a stir out of your young man, especially if he thinks you baked them."

Erika hugged Arlene's neck. "Michael Mathis is no fool! He'll know that these fine rolls were baked by someone sweet just like you. He wouldn't be fooled for a second."

At the front door, Erika and Arlene affectionately hugged each other. Before Erika got into her car, she once again promised to come by over the weekend. Despite the cold weather Arlene stayed on the porch until Erika pulled off.

It was seven o'clock when Erika let herself into the dormitory apartment. As soon as she'd closed the door, three short knocks sounded against the heavy wood. She opened the door to her best friend and neighbor, Lorraine Poole, who stood there, still dressed in her nightgown and robe. They had agreed to use the knock when visiting each other, but Lorraine often forgot.

"Morning, Lorraine. What did you do, oversleep?"

Lorraine moved inside and darted over to the sofa, where she sat down and curled her shapely legs up under her. She patted the sofa cushion beside her. "I'm not on a schedule today, but that's not why I'm here. You've been holding out on me," she said, her greenish-gray eyes carrying an accusatory glint.

Erika shot Lorraine a perplexed look as she took the seat next to her. "What are you talking about?"

"Oh, *puhleese*, sister! You know what and who I'm talking about. But I'll give you the benefit of the doubt, anyway. Anywho, was that *the* Dr. Michael Mathis I saw coming out of here late last night?"

Erika laughed heartily at her redheaded friend's I-got-to-know curiosity. "It could've been," Erika responded coyly. "Then again, maybe it wasn't. But what if it was?"

Lorraine rolled her eyes expressively. "If it *was* him, then I'd say you got it going on, girlfriend! That is one fine man, and we won't even go into his impressive credentials. How did you meet him?"

For the next fifteen minutes an animated Erika gave Lorraine the four-one-one on her intriguing encounters with Michael Mathis. Lorraine's astonishment escalated with each delicious and interesting tidbit that Erika dramatically made her privy to. During the course of the conversation, Lorraine nearly annihilated one of the overstuffed pillows, punching it whenever Erika told her something she found exciting and beyond belief.

Lorraine gave the pillow one last hard punch. "This is unreal, Erika! Is he really that down-to-earth? I'm having a hard time imagining that one."

Erika grinned. "I didn't see his feet leave the ground once—except when we kissed, of course."

Lorraine laughed. "So, you're going to the ballet. What the heck do you know about the ballet, Erika Edmonds?"

"Absolutely nothing, but you know that I've always wanted to attend one. And I do love to watch the graceful movements of the dancers. Michael told me it's The Dance Theater of Harlem, so you know it's going to be all that and more."

"What are you going to wear?"

Erika frowned. "Big problem, Lorraine. I don't own anything that nice. My aunt gave me money to buy something new, but I feel guilty about using her money for something so frivolous."

"What about that red-hot number you wore at graduation?"

Erika pulled a face. "Do you recall how much I weighed when we graduated? That red dress is perfect for the ballet, but it's a hundred sizes too big. So, there it is."

Lorraine playfully popped Erika on the thigh. "Girl, have you forgotten that I'm the best seamstress this side of the Allegheny? Get the dress and let me see what I can do with it. But if I were you, I would accept your aunt's generosity and be done with it."

"But you're not me," Erika snipped. "As for the dress, I'm not sure it's here. It's probably at my mother's house. I'll check the closet. Come with me."

The two young women trooped into the bedroom and Lorraine stretched out on the double bed while Erika riffled through the closet. The bedroom was as small as the other rooms, but the mirrored closet door lent it some amplitude. The softly shaded, multicolored Princess-style curtains and matching bedspread made the room bright and cheerfully livable.

"Got it," Erika announced excitedly, pulling the dress from a wooden hanger.

"Look at the size of this bad boy!" Erika squealed. "I can wrap this around me twenty times or more."

"You're exaggerating, Erika," Lorraine charged blandly. "I can work wonders with the dress. No one will ever know the difference. Shall I do my thing?"

"By all means."

After rapidly locating her sewing box, Erika slipped into the dress and Lorraine began nipping and tucking the seams, pinning them with straight pins as she went along. Because of the vast amount of weight Erika had peeled off her hips, the dress was now way too long. Lorraine made white chalk marks where she would fashion a new hemline.

Erika bit at one of her nails. "What if this doesn't work, Lorraine? I won't have time to go and purchase a new dress."

"It'll work, Erika. If it doesn't I have plenty of dresses that you can wear. We *are* the same size now."

A wistful gaze shining brightly in her eyes, Erika sighed. "It must be wonderful to grow up with money at your fingertips."

Lorraine laughed bitterly. "Don't you believe it. Money is at the root of all evil, and it can destroy a family. If I could've had my parents love each other and raise me under that same umbrella, I would've been happy to live like a church mouse. My parents' divorce was worse than those awful scenes in the movie *War of the Roses*. At sixteen, I found myself involved in the most bitter custody battle anyone could imagine. My salvation came when my maternal grandmother filed for custody of me . . . and won. My success can mostly be attributed to my sweet Granny-Bee."

Erika looked astonished. "You never told me this before. I

always thought you were the girl with everything, Lorraine. I'm sorry your life wasn't so rosy. But you're on top of it now, kid. You've got what it takes."

"Oscar performances, honey. I faked it until I got over it. But you're right. I'm now on top of it all."

Erika slipped out of the dress and handed it to Lorraine, hoping her friend could in fact work magic with the alterations. "Well, I believe in you, Lorraine. But if it can't be achieved, don't worry about it. I'll just borrow one of those elegant, expensive dresses of yours."

Lorraine kissed Erika's cheek. "Any one you want. You certainly have been a good friend to me. I don't think I could deny you anything, especially when I think of all those nights you sat up with me because I just wasn't getting the hang of this or that course. My medical degree should have your name on it, too."

Erika hugged her friend closely. They'd become inseparable from the onset of undergraduate school. Their relationship could only continue to grow, because they highly respected each other—first as African-American women, second as female physicians.

After Lorraine left, Erika grabbed the things she'd need for her duties and made her way to the cafeteria for a quick cup of hot tea. She thought about the cinnamon rolls she'd put away, but her willpower kicked in and saved her. Her thoughts turned to Lorraine.

Regardless of how close they'd become, Erika understood why Lorraine hadn't gone into her troubled home life. It had shocked Erika to learn that Lorraine had once been miserable. She had her own fair share of carefully guarded secrets, which made it easy for her to understand Lorraine's all the more. Her thinking of dropping out of the residency program was just one of those secrets, which she hadn't shared with anyone but Dr. Baker.

Erika waited in the long cafeteria line, growing impatient with the slow service. All she wanted was to pay for the cup of tea, but it appeared that everyone ahead of her had ordered a full breakfast. *Quick check-out lines would certainly come in handy in this place,* she surmised.

Finally, Erika thought when she reached the cashier. The change was already in her hand, and she gave it to the clerk, hoping the table she'd shared with Michael was empty. As she turned the corner, she saw that the table was occupied. Looking closer, she saw exactly who occupied it. Summoning her with a wave of his hand, Michael stood as she approached the table. Taking the hot cup from her hand, he set it down and wasted no time in tasting drops of heady wine from her moist lips.

Embarrassed, Erika gently pushed him away. "I'm not interested in my life becoming part of the hospital grapevine," she explained softly, praying he'd try to understand.

He laughed. "Don't want to get caught in any nasty briars, huh? My sweet Erika, the grapevine is going to exist from now until eternity. If those who live by it can't find some real dirt, they'll just invent some. How are you feeling this morning? You look wonderful."

Smiling, she sat down. He followed suit. "I'm pretty good, Michael. How about you?"

"Fine, now. I was hoping you were going to wander in here before I had to leave. Your phone number's not listed on the dorm roster. Why is that?"

She blew on the tea before taking a small sip. "Because I don't have a phone. Can't afford one." She shrugged her shoulders nonchalantly.

He was stunned but gracious enough to mask it. "Then you're going to have to give me your pager number."

"What for? I can't phone you back when you page me. I have no phone. Remember?"

"There's nothing at all pretentious about you, is there? However, this hospital is loaded with phones. This place probably has more phones than patients, since the census is so low. Take a look around you. I can't even count them all. Can you?"

"Speaking of phones, I have to get to one. I need to check

on something very important. Will you excuse me for a minute?"

He smiled softly. "No, I won't. I want you to stay right here with me." Reaching into his jacket pocket, he pulled out a cellular phone and handed it to her. "Help yourself, Dr. Edmonds."

She started to object but thought better of it. He already knew the situation with the house. So why couldn't he listen in on the call? "Thank you, Dr. Mathis."

A whiz with numbers, Erika already had the phone number of Randy Mills's office memorized, and her fingers zipped across the phone pad. Randy answered and she let the questions fly, stopping briefly to catch her breath. As she listened to his responses, she chewed on her lower lip. If she'd had any idea what her sensuous actions did to her companion, she would've been highly embarrassed.

A smile, a slight frown, and then a dark scowl stole across her face. Michael studied each facial expression, deeply interested, wondering how one tiny woman could level him so easily. Without any effort on her part, she had taken custody of his heart by storm.

Determined to deal with the high cost of clearing the house, no matter what she had to pawn or sell, Erika squared her shoulders and gave Randy the job. As she attempted to hand the phone back to Michael, her false valor became abundantly clear to him, but he didn't dare think of usurping an ounce of her dignity.

"Keep it. I have a phone in my car and I have a pager."

This was the most unusual doctor she'd ever met, but he was acting totally off the wall right now. "You're the second person in one day who's tried to get me to take something that I feel is totally unnecessary. As you said, there are plenty of phones around here."

"Then why can't you phone me back if I page you? Answer that one for me."

She smiled weakly. "I think there's a little miscommunication going on here. I thought you were talking about paging me late in the evenings. Once I leave my doctorly duties, I try not to come back into this hospital for anything. Nor do I like to use the dorm pay phones unless it's unavoidable."

He grinned. "You've just pleaded my case for me. Good work. You need to have a phone. That's all there is to it. What if someone needs to get you in the middle of the night? What about emergencies, period?"

She may have pleaded his case for him, but he was capable of making quite an impressive case on his own. For now, she was going to concede the argument to him. "I'll keep this phone for the next couple of days, but not a day longer. By then, I'll have one of my own."

Erika had no idea how she was going to pay the bill, but he was right about her needing a phone. Thinking about the money her aunt had given her, she smiled. Knowing she could pay the bill for at least a month or so out of that nice little wad, she was glad she'd refused to use the money for a new dress.

"Good girl. And I'm not being patronizing, so don't take offense. Listen, I've got to run, but I'll be back to pick you up at six-thirty. Do you have time to walk me to my car, since you don't want me to kiss you in here?"

Her smile came easily. "I'll make time." She rose at the same time he did.

His eyes glinted with mischief. "You want me to walk ahead of you so no one will guess that we're together?" he asked, trying to goad her.

She wasn't about to let his goading go without reward. "Behind me will do quite nicely." She saw that she'd failed to give him his just reward when he grinned widely, mischievously.

"Behind you is just fine, especially since I already know the view from back there is going to be so marvelous." They both laughed.

Now, in a super bold mood, Erika easily slipped her arm through his as they cleared the cafeteria exit. Realizing that she wore only a heavy sweater, Michael slipped his coat around her shoulders, pulling her close to him before stepping outside. "We can't have you getting sick. We have a hot date tonight."

She giggled. "That's all well and good, Michael, but what am I going to do for a coat on my way back inside?"

"You let me worry about that. Lady doctor, I'm going to take such good care of you, you're going to get tired of me fussing over you."

She doubted that. She'd been taking care of others all her adult life, and she would welcome any amount of fuss from him.

Michael leaned back against his black Nissan Pathfinder, pulling her close to his growing need. "About that kiss," he murmured against her lips, allowing his tongue to tease the corners of her mouth.

Erika pressed her hands against his chest, returning his kisses sweetly and passionately. Aware of the howling wind that had her shivering, she drew herself in closer to him, sheltering herself in the heat emanating from his body.

His hold on her grew tighter. "Are you sure we didn't know each other in another life? I'd swear I've known you forever, Erika Edmonds." He kissed her again, then walked her back to the door of the hospital, where they kissed good-bye.

"I'll see you tonight, Erika, but I'll be thinking of you throughout the day."

"Same here. Ciao, Michael." She handed him his coat and ran inside.

Erika ran all the way to the classroom, where she was scheduled to sit in on a lecture entitled "False Pregnancy." Dr. Thomas Watson, an obstetrician-gynecologist, was slated as the guest speaker.

Erika took a seat in the front of the room, hoping she could keep her mind off her recent rendezvous with Michael. Dr. Watson was an excellent lecturer, but she would only retain his words if she could will her mind into a receptive state, which was going to be hard after seeing the sinfully good-looking Michael Mathis.

Information pamphlets were located on the arm of each chair. Erika picked up the small booklet and started leafing through it. She closed it when Dr. Watson began the lecture, greeting the class in a professional manner before beginning his presentation.

"False pregnancy is also referred to as phantom pregnancy, pseudocyesis. This is considered a hysterical condition. The female develops many of the signs of being pregnant, including the enlargement of the abdomen. But in reality, she is not pregnant at all . . ."

Dr. Watson went on to explain other aspects of the condition and how it could be diagnosed. He then discussed the methods of treatment. Erika listened with keen interest and curiosity as she jotted down notes and sources of references in her notebook. When the lecture was over, she talked with a few of her colleagues. She then proceeded to the library, where she would participate in a group research project.

Four

Erika *was* a dream in red as she twirled around in front of the full-length mirror hanging on the back of the bathroom door. Lorraine had indeed worked her magic on the dress. The red crepe stunner fit Erika like a second skin. With a low-cut, shoulder-wrap collar, a bodice that hugged the waistline and a hemline flaring out before coming to rest just above the knee, the dress fit better than Erika could've hoped for.

Lorraine clapped her hands with excitement. "Girlfriend, if the good Dr. Mathis doesn't suffer a near cardiac arrest when he sees you, I'm going to eat my stethoscope. Now, here, put these on," Lorraine urged, handing Erika a ruby teardrop pendant and matching earrings. The gems, set in gold, were edged with sparkling diamond chips.

Erika was both astonished and touched by such a loving gesture. "My better judgment tells me not to take these from you, but my sense of style tells me they're a must for this dress and the occasion."

Lorraine affectionately kissed the back of Erika's head. Carefully, she draped the necklace around her friend's neck and closed the dainty clasp. "And a must for enhancing your natural beauty and effervescent personality."

Erika turned to kiss her dear friend on the cheek. "You always know how to make me feel better. I do appreciate all of your kindness, Dr. Poole."

Lorraine's greenish-gray eyes grew serious. "Erika, I sense

that you're going through something right now that's weighing very heavily on your heart. I just want you to know that I'm here to help you get through whatever it is. This is not an attempt on my part to force you to confide in me. I know you'll tell me what's going on whenever you're ready. Solid friendships are just that way."

A halo of respect shone deeply in Erika's eyes as she faced her friend, her fingers lovingly tracing the shape of the delicate ruby. "Thank you for that, Lorraine. I'm glad our friendship is just that way. Whether we decide to confide in each other, or not to, we both have always agreed that it's okay. That's what's so special about our relationship."

Since the front door had been accidentally left ajar when Lorraine entered Erika's apartment, Michael had heard Lorraine's statements and Erika's responses. It moved his heart to know that Erika had such a good friend to turn to, and he hoped she knew she could turn to him, too.

When Michael tapped lightly on the door, Erika smiled knowingly at Lorraine. Walking the few steps to the door, Lorraine followed behind her but stopped right outside the bedroom door, wishing she'd gotten out of the apartment before Erika's date had arrived.

Erika and Michael smiled at each other. Kissing her softly on the mouth, he presented her with a single white rose. Inhaling the rose's heady scent, she gasped at its beauty. "Thank you, Michael."

Michael Mathis was an exotic, erotic male vision of exquisite class. His impeccable tuxedo dripped wealth, and the silk scarf draping his neck was in a rich African design of deep, dark colors, mixed with bold shades of gold and red. The bow tie and cummerbund matched the scarf. Looking like an African prince, he wore his royalty and pride in his heritage like a badge of honor. He looked so wonderful that Erika could barely take her eyes off him.

Feeling the intense scrutiny of another pair of eyes, Michael turned and saw Lorraine leaning against the door. "Hello, there," he greeted warmly.

Lorraine blushed. Michael was so much better-looking than she'd realized. "Hello, Dr. Mathis. I'm Lorraine Poole, Erika's friend." Lorraine quickly moved toward the door.

Michael delayed her progress when he gently took her hand. "It's nice to meet you, Lorraine Poole. You don't have to rush away on my account. We have a little time to kill yet."

Lorraine gave him her best smile. "That's very nice of you, but I do have to be going. You two have a wonderful evening," she said, dashing out the door.

Only seconds had passed when Lorraine popped her head back in. "Nice to meet you, too, Dr. Mathis. If you have any single friends worthy of a great girl like me let Erika know. She'll pass it on to me." She departed again before Michael could respond. Erika and Michael laughed as Lorraine's tiny hand reached back in and pulled the door shut.

Pulling Erika to him, Michael touched her face. Wanting desperately to know if he touched her soul the way she'd touched his, he looked into her eyes. The liquid swirls of chocolate held mystery, passionate wonder and sweet innocence, making him want to experience everything her eyes revealed. "You intrigue me to no end. You light a fire under my skin, Erika. The fiery flames consume me in their passionate heat." He kissed away the tears his confession had brought to her eyes.

Nervously, she played with the buttons on his tuxedo shirt. Her insides quivered, and she expected her legs to give out at any second. If she lit a fire under his skin and he lit a bonfire in her soul, then that could only mean they'd eventually go up in flames, passionately. If it were her fate to be consumed by the heat of his passion, she knew she'd be a willing victim. Michael Mathis made her feel like the most important person in his life. She wasn't about to take issue with something she so wantonly needed.

His lips grazed hers, snapping her out of her reverie. "I

think we should go now. Curtain is at eight o'clock. If I haven't mentioned it, and I don't believe I have, you look ravishing, gorgeous. You're a dazzling siren in red."

He helped her into an expensive, full-length sable coat. It belonged to Lorraine, but Erika wore it as if she'd been born to own it. Being Erika, knowing exactly who she was, she told Michael the jewelry and the coat were Lorraine's.

Once again, her honesty completely astounded him.

Michael led her out to what he referred to as his special outing vehicle, a silver Mercedes-Benz. The car looked as though it had been hand-polished. He held the door as she settled herself into the plush, gray leather seat. Before closing the door, he kissed her again, eagerly anticipating the next opportunity to partake of her sweetness. As he expertly maneuvered the car out of the parking lot, the car phone sounded, causing Erika to jump. He closed his hand over hers to calm her before reaching for the phone.

"Mathis, here," he said, listening intently to the caller's voice. With each word spoken he knew his evening with Erika might not happen. He had an emergency at Children's Hospital and he needed to handle it. Frowning, he cradled the phone.

Erika knew what was happening from the moment the phone rang. That was just the way a doctor's life was lived. When a medical emergency arose, a dedicated doctor responded, quickly and without question. A layperson may not have understood, but Erika did, all too well.

She rested her hand on his thigh. "It's okay, Michael. I understand. If you'll just drop me off at the front door, I can take it from there." Of course she felt disappointed, but she'd never let him know it. The last thing he needed was to feel guilt.

He slid his arm around the back of her seat. "I'm sorry, Erika. Very sorry." He wrapped a finger around a loose tendril of her hair. "Erika, I may only need to assess this patient. It might not take long unless surgery is indicated, but we'll miss the curtain call. Would you mind accompanying me to the hospital? Then we can decide things after I see what's going to occur. At the very least, maybe we can enjoy a late dinner."

She smiled. "I'd like that very much, Michael. I can always take a cab back here if you're going to be there a long time. We'd better hurry up," she advised, resting her head on the seat back.

Michael smiled at her thoughtfulness. "If I'm going to be that late, you can drive the car back here. I'll be the one to catch a cab," he stated adamantly. Without further discussion, Michael turned the car around and headed for the hospital.

On their short drive Michael spoke freely about himself. A native of eastern Pennsylvania, Michael had one brother, Patrick, who was a pharmacist. "My father, Lawrence, is retired from the automobile industry. My mother, Wilimina, is a retired registered nurse. My parents moved to Lebanon right after I entered college. My brother lives in San Francisco. Since my parents had moved to Lebanon, I was delighted when I learned I'd been accepted in Great Western's residency program. I'm thirty-two now and I've accomplished quite a bit. I'm proudest of the research work I'm currently doing in pediatric AIDS. My research project is going really great."

"I knew I wanted to be a doctor at an early age," she said. "My stepfather, Anthony, was wonderful to me. He adopted me as his own. He has a son, but I don't know anything about him. I don't know why I never got to meet him. He wouldn't be my biological brother, but I'd love him as though he were." Erika then shared with him some of the happier memories of her childhood and teen years.

She didn't mention anything regarding her deceased, biological father, Henry Wade. Vernice hadn't told her much about him, or Anthony's son, despite her constant questions.

"I've already mentioned my Aunt Arlene to you. She was our only support system when Dad passed away. She's all the family I have left here in Lebanon since my mother passed. All of our other relatives have moved away."

As their conversation flowed on at an easy, steady pace,

each seemed comfortable with the other while smiles constantly passed between them.

Michael reached over and took her hand. "Have you ever had a serious relationship?"

Erika laughed. "I wish. I haven't had time to nurture any kind of relationship, which is exactly what came between me and Stephen Kemp."

She went on to tell Michael she'd met Stephen in her junior year of undergraduate school. At that time, Erika had thought she and Stephen had a lot in common, but Stephen wasn't nearly as interested in a good education as she was. He seemed to think college was all about partying and having a good time. The brother had stayed in a party mode, without giving a single thought to his academic studies.

"After a few months of exclusive dating, Stephen would get so angry when I couldn't attend this social function or the other. When the relationship started interfering with my studies, among other important matters, I simply dumped him—like yesterday's garbage, according to him. Because of his anger at me, he spread a lot of malicious lies. The one that stung the most was the rumor regarding my sexual preference, which would've been laughable had it not been so hurtful."

Michael didn't comment on her relationship with Kemp, but it stayed on his mind. After he parked the car in his assigned spot at the hospital, he and Erika got out and proceeded toward their destination. Before nearing the double doors, Michael pulled Erika out of range of the door's electronic eye.

His hands smoothed back a loose strand of her hair. "Is Stephen Kemp history, Erika?"

As she sensed that something wonderful might occur, her eyes danced with anticipation. "Ancient history, Michael. Why do you ask?"

Burning into her flesh, his gaze was intense. "I want to make sure the path to your heart is all clear. My heart desires to pursue your heart and it doesn't want to trip over any hidden stumbling blocks. So, are you telling me that your heart is free and clear of any hazardous debris, Dr. Erika Edmonds?"

Pulling his head down, she tenderly kissed his mouth. "My heart is clear and free, Michael. It would be happy to have your heart pursue it. But it's only fair that I ask you the same question. Is your heart free and clear?" If she recalled correctly, she thought they'd already let each other know they were both single and available. Maybe he needed reassurance, she thought, deciding she needed reassuring, too.

"Well, it was. That is, until I met you. I've already begun to move your things into my special place. Maybe we can become permanent residents of each other's hearts. Later, I'll tell you about a woman named Stephanie and a beautiful child named Tamala." Without elaborating further, he guided Erika through the hospital doors. His strides became long and quick as he thought about what might be lying in wait for him.

Suddenly, Erika found herself in a world made of sweet dreams. As she floated through the sterile-smelling corridors on Michael's arm, his words drifted around in her mind. As he directed her to have a seat in the emergency waiting room, she absently obeyed his softly spoken command. Could Michael Mathis really be interested in a long-term relationship with an unsophisticated woman like her?

Yes, a soft voice in her head responded.

As Erika thought of Michael, he couldn't get her off his mind, either, as he flipped through a medical chart. Michael Mathis was hardly looking for sophistication. He'd already found many of his heart's desires in Erika Edmonds: freshness, vitality, sincerity and warmth. What pleased him most were Erika's everpresent veracity and her unpretentious ways. It didn't matter to him that she was a lowly resident, as she'd so bluntly put it. She could be a ward clerk, a member of the housekeeping staff, or a host of other things, and it wouldn't matter to him. Michael could look far beyond titles and credentials.

For him, it was all about looking into the heart of a woman, examining her soul, her spirituality. So far, Erika's heart and soul proved to be worth much more than their weight in precious gold.

Twenty minutes later, Michael, cool and calm, returned to the waiting room, where Erika had been hoping against all odds that she wouldn't have to go through the rest of the evening alone. She smiled when he appeared.

He reached for her hand. "Come with me, Erika. I want you to meet someone."

Assisted by a band of clouds that kept her from swooning at his feet, she mindlessly obeyed his orders as she rose from her seat. They entered another set of double doors and Michael led her to one of the treatment cubicles.

A loud whistle shook Erika from her dream world. Looking in the direction it had come from, she saw a cute, curly-headed black male who appeared to be around twelve or thirteen. Michael introduced him as Vincent Clark.

"Doc Mathis," Vincent enthused, "she sure is some babe! Is she your girlfriend?"

Michael laughed as Erika's café au lait skin turned blush-pink. Playfully, he ruffled Vincent's hair. "She's a girl, and she's my friend. So yes, she *is* my girlfriend."

Vincent sat up in bed, and the sudden movement caused him to wince in pain, but the sharpness seemed to pass rather quickly. "That's not what I meant," Vincent objected loudly. "I want to know if you two are getting it on," he said blatantly, crossing his arms on his chest like a homeboy.

With hers cheeks a burning crimson, Erika turned away from the boy, trying desperately to keep from laughing—especially at the stunned expression on Michael's face.

Michael's eyes gave Vincent a stern scolding. "You stick to basketball and football, young man. Stop concerning yourself with what Dr. Edmonds and I get on, or don't get on," Michael chastised, his tone softer than the stern look he gave Vincent. Michael's younger patients had asked him a lot of astounding questions, but this was the first time one had asked about his sex life. "You get some rest, Vincent. The nurse will contact me if I'm needed again. Now say goodnight to Dr. Edmonds."

Vincent bade the two adults a good evening. Sliding down in the bed, he pulled headphones over his ears. Erika waited in the lobby while Michael conferred with the emergency room physician.

Sweeping her out into the night, Michael held her tightly around the waist. "Sorry about that, Erika. Vincent can be rather forward at times, but tonight he's taken it to a whole new level. I hope he didn't embarrass you too much. He sure embarrassed the hell out of me."

Erika laughed as she squeezed the long fingers splayed against her petite waist. "I was embarrassed enough, all right." Her brow furrowed with genuine concern. "What seems to be the problem with Vincent?"

"He's having acute pain in the right upper quadrant. His white count rules out appendicitis. However, you know how quickly that can change. Since I'm his primary doctor, the emergency room physician wanted me to take a look at him. I recommended twenty-four-hour observation. If surgery becomes necessary, they'll page me. At any rate, Dr. Howard Till is the surgeon on call. So Vincent will be in very capable hands until I arrive. We can try to catch the rest of the ballet. I should be able to get us there before the intermission is over."

Smiling, Erika sighed. "A day in the life of a doctor." She was excited that they'd at least try to make the rest of the ballet.

The hospital was only a few miles from the Lebanon Theater Arts Center and Michael covered the short distance with controlled speed and extreme caution, well-aware of black ice. Erika thought him an excellent driver. As the Mercedes sped through the brightly lit streets, she didn't see any need to entertain alarm.

As they entered the Theater Arts Center, the audiences poured out of the exit doors under sparkling chandeliers and into the spacious, red-carpeted lobby. Women and men lined up at the bathroom doors while others rushed to refreshment bars, draped with red-and-gold awnings.

Erika declined the offer of refreshments and Michael led her to a red velvet sofa, where they sat down. Holding hands, they watched the animated crowd scurry from point A to point B in a somewhat orderly fashion.

While talking quietly, they were approached by a very sophisticated-looking gentleman who appeared to be in his mid-thirties. Besides being tall and lithe, he had smooth, medium-beige skin and twinkling, spice-brown eyes. His good looks rather reminded Erika of her stepfather. When he spoke, his voice carried the same deep lilt, a distinct Anthony Edmonds resonance.

Michael rapidly got to his feet to greet the approaching man, whom he seemed to know. "Richard," Michael exclaimed, "good to see you here tonight, my brother. How's it going?"

"It's good to see you, too, Mikey!" Richard Glover shook Michael's hand, his spicy gaze trained on Erika. He stared at her, as though he'd already met her somewhere.

Michael grimaced at the childhood moniker he'd come to detest. "Had I known you were going to be here tonight I would've brought along the information you asked for." Before Richard could inquire about Michael's date, Michael introduced Erika.

Richard could see that his best friend and client seemed quite taken with his very attractive companion. "Nice to finally meet you, Erika Edmonds," Richard commented politely, eyeing her peculiarly.

Finally? Erika wondered what that was supposed to mean.

She'd only known Michael for two days. Since she was the only one who seemed to take note of the unusual comment, she decided not to probe his response.

"Erika, Richard's my very best friend and my attorney. We go back a long way."

Erika smiled and nodded. "It's nice to meet you, as well."

"Where's Miss Shelly Holland?" Michael asked, inquiring about Richard's longtime girlfriend.

Richard rolled his eyes up to the ceiling. "In the ladies' room, fixing her face. Where else? Her mother's here with us. You know how that goes. Irene still hovers around Shelly like she's a two-year-old, which is the very reason I haven't asked her to marry me yet. Oh, well, that's a subject for Oprah to deal with. I need to find those two. Maybe we'll run into each other after the performance. Nice to make your acquaintance, Erika." Richard looked back at Erika as he strolled into the throng.

Michael took Erika's hand and guided her into the inner chambers of the theater. Very familiar with the layout, Michael steered her to their reserved seats. The lights dimmed and Michael placed his arm around Erika's shoulders, pulling her closer until her shoulder rested against his chest. The red-and-gold curtain went up and the audience fell mum as "Creole Giselle" began.

Although Erika had never been to a ballet, she didn't have any problems translating the graceful movements into what the dancers so beautifully revealed. The love story being told through motion and music was set in 1841 Louisiana. It was about recently freed slaves snubbed by blacks who'd been far removed from slavery.

Tears swam in Erika's eyes as she watched the breathtaking movements of long, willowy legs, arms, and elegant necks. She thought the male dancers just as stunning as their female counterparts. While the dancers blended into one another, like cream being poured into hot coffee, Erika repeatedly gasped in astonishment.

Off and on, all through the rest of the ballet, Erika could feel eyes watching her intently, making her feel icy and overheated at the same time. As she stole glances to the right of her, then to the left, her eyes clashed with the eyes of Richard Glover, who watched her intently.

Their eyes locked briefly, and they appeared to size each other up. Then, from sheer embarrassment, Erika turned away from the concentrated gaze that totally unnerved her. She certainly hoped Michael's friend wasn't flirting with her. That would never do.

With barely enough space between her and Michael as it was, she moved her shoulder closer to him. Guiding her head onto his shoulder, he gently held it in place by resting his hand against the side of her face. Her skin felt velvety to the touch and the slight tremors of her shoulders seemed to suggest that she might be cold. But when he asked if she wanted to put her coat on, she responded in the negative.

The ballet captivated Michael, but Erika captivated him even more. He could see the upper portions of her gentle swells rising sensuously and falling gently with each breath she took. Her lean, shapely legs were a different matter entirely. He thought her firm thighs to be exquisite works of art—especially when he imagined himself nestled between them, snuggled in their strength, and inside the warmth of her blazing, innermost passage.

Unable to help himself, he engaged her in a lingering kiss. The intensity of the kiss caused his blood to boil. Thrilled by the unexpected interruption, Erika slowly ran her hands up and down his inner thigh, stopping abruptly when she got too close to his erect, intimate zone.

Just the outline of his maleness excited her, making her wonder what it would be like to be filled by its breadth and sweetly plundered by its length. No doubt that it would be a mind losing experience, she assessed excitedly. Burning and sweetly torturous thoughts of her and Michael making fiery love left her breathless.

A standing ovation occurred at the close of the ballet. Then Michael carefully guided Erika through the stampeding crowd. Everyone seemed determined to avoid the traffic jam sure to occur in the parking lot. Some of the audience had already departed, but others had been compelled to stay in their seats to savor every drop of the arresting finale.

A half hour later, Erika and Michael were seated in a booth in a cozy alcove of a softly lit all-night diner. As he looked around, he realized their formal attire was a bit much for what might be deemed a greasy spoon, but it made it kind of exciting, anyway.

With his arm thrown loosely about her shoulders, Michael shared the same bench seat with Erika. Each time her thigh made contact with his, he felt as if his skin were blistering right through his tuxedo pants. Her hair had tumbled down from its style, and he just wanted to loosen it altogether and crush its silkiness between his fingers.

The waiter appeared, and Michael ordered the well-done hamburgers and crispy fries Erika had mentioned wanting when they'd discussed where and what to eat. Michael believed Erika deserved the finest cut of steak and all the trimmings, along with the finest champagne, candlelight, and roses, but he desired to give her what she wanted rather than what he thought she deserved or needed. At any rate, Erika didn't seem at all the type who expected glitz and glamour, nor did she expect things to be handed to her on a silver platter. However, he could already tell that she expected a hell of a lot from herself.

Lifting her hand, Michael surveyed the tiny band of gold hearts circling her baby finger. "Your ring is lovely. Someone special give it to you?"

She smiled at the wee inflection of jealousy she'd recognized in his question. "Someone very special. My mother. When she presented it to me, she said, 'these are the types of hearts that never get broken. Daughter, I hope and pray that your flesh-and-blood heart will never be broken by an unrighteous lover.' "

"That was some beautiful speech," Michael praised. "It sounds as though your mother was a very wise woman. I've met your mother—" He stopped dead in his tracks the moment he realized what he'd said. Seeing the perplexed look on Erika's face and knowing why it was there had him cursing himself under his breath.

Every light in the diner seemed reflected in her eyes. "You've met my mother? When? How, Michael?" she asked, her voice soft but anxious. Her tone seemed to belie the suspicious look in her eyes.

Hoping that she'd at least give him a chance to explain himself, he gently covered her hands with his. "Erika, it's not what you're thinking. I should've said that I believe it was your mother I met. Will you let me tell you the story?" With curiosity beaming in her eyes, she nodded.

Using his fingertips, he massaged the palm of her hand. "While I was in Dr. McKinley's office several months back waiting to see him, I think your mother struck up a conversation with me. Once I told her I practiced medicine, all she talked about was her beautiful daughter who was also a doctor. She told me her daughter had wanted to be a doctor ever since she was a small child. I clearly remember the nurse calling her Mrs. Edmonds. As you and I talked about your family earlier, I began to put two and two together." He looked into her eyes for signs of distress. "Do you want me to continue, or am I going to be forbidden to speak to you for not mentioning this earlier?"

Erika admitted to herself that she'd grown wary of him, but after hearing his story she still believed him to be thoughtful and kind. Whatever else he was or wasn't, he was certainly unique. And she wasn't about to blow him off.

She wrapped her fingers around his. "I'd love you to continue, Michael, but first, let me tell you that I think you're very kind and thoughtful. I was a little worried, but now I'm just plain impressed." How many doctors would even sit out in a colleague's waiting room, let alone hold a conversation with a lady who raved on about her lovely daughter?

"Well, during the course of the evening I agonized over whether to tell you out of consideration for your recent loss. Since I wasn't absolutely sure it was your mother, I decided not to say anything. Maybe you can clear it up for me. Was Dr. Duane McKinley your mother's doctor?"

Erika nodded, her lower lip quivering. "Had been for several years. His father was her doctor before he retired. She believed in keeping it in the family. I think it would be a safe bet to say that it was my mother you met." Erika fumbled in her purse and pulled out her wallet, opening it to a picture of Vernice. "Is this the beautiful lady in question?"

Michael's eyes misted as he looked at the lady who'd told him she wished her daughter had been there so he could meet her. "I think you and my daughter would just love each other," Vernice had told him that day. "If nothing else, I know she'd love to have you as a friend." Before he could ask her daughter's name, the nurse had come out and called her.

"Yes, Erika. That's the beautiful lady. Your mother was really sweet, and really crazy about her daughter. This is so amazing. I don't know what to say." Michael then told her the part of the conversation he'd just re-created in his mind. "I now feel like something special was supposed to come out of that long-ago encounter."

Feeling just as amazed as Michael seemed, Erika blinked back tears. "It has. We met. I'm not going to try to analyze it. It's much too deep for me to even try to make sense of." Laughing, she wiped away a tear that had somehow managed to escape. "Now you can tell me what horrible things she said about me."

Michael held her close to him. "She told me her daughter was a treasure, and that her hair was the color of melted honey." Michael laughed. "And all this time I thought there was a fiery redhead under that honey-brown hair." They both laughed. He then told her the rest of the story. "What would she think about me dating her daughter?"

Erika's expression grew soft. "I think she already told you the answer, Michael. Mother loved to be around the young. It kept her feeling young at heart. She especially liked male attention. I can honestly say she'd be pleased we're seeing each other."

He locked his hands with hers. "Not as pleased as I am. I'm glad we ran into each other, gorgeous. Otherwise, we might not be sitting here, and I probably wouldn't have ever known who your mother was talking about. She never gave your name. On second thought, maybe I would have. I think we were destined."

Erika touched his cheek. "You might have something there, Dr. Mathis."

He pointed at the food, which they'd barely touched. "Want to take it out?"

"No. I'm hungry. I'm one of those people who likes to eat out late at night. Did I tell you that I lost a lot of weight recently? More than forty pounds."

His eyebrows raised in surprise. "I can't imagine you weighing any more than you do right now. Congratulations! How are you keeping it off?"

Erika laughed as she picked up a long, fat fry. "Not by eating these. I mostly eat salads and vegetables, red meat once a week. Chicken or fish the rest of the days. I'm determined not to suffer with weight problems any longer. I gained most of the extra weight when my stepfather died. Though I'm going through the grieving process again, I intend to be very careful."

He picked up his hamburger and bit a huge chunk out of it. "Want ketchup for those?"

"Nope. I want to savor the grease," she joked. "The truth is, I don't care that much for ketchup. That's why I ordered mayonnaise. How's your burger?"

"Phat," he responded, using the slang word for anything good favored by some of his adolescent patients. They both laughed at how silly it sounded coming from such an extremely well-educated man.

Upon reaching the front door of Erika's apartment, Michael drew her close to him, kissing her hard on the mouth. He then held her at arm's length. "I'm not going to come in tonight because you've had a long day. But I wonder if I might see you again tomorrow? You mentioned that you'd have the rest of the weekend off."

Erika rubbed his face with the back of her hand and felt the first stubble popping out. "I promised my aunt that I'd come by her place tomorrow, but I could see you after that. I should be back by one o'clock."

He looked perplexed. "Is there any reason that I can't accompany you to your aunt's house? I'd love to meet her."

Erika considered his request for a moment, and couldn't come up with a single reason why he couldn't go with her. Then she remembered the cinnamon rolls that Aunt Arlene had sent to him. "Michael, I'd love to have you come with me, but there's one problem."

"Oh. What might that be?"

"My aunt sent you some cinnamon rolls to try. If you go there with me, she's surely going to ask what you thought of them. So that means you have to come in and get them."

Thankful, Michael looked upward as he took the keys from Erika's hand. *Oh, gorgeous, my prayer just got answered,* he announced inwardly.

Five

At the first brush of light Erika sat straight up in bed. Rubbing her eyes with her fists, she recalled the last thing Michael had said to her the previous night:

"Erika, everything has a beginning, a middle, an end. We've had the beginning. Now I'm looking forward to all that we're going to share in the middle. I hope we'll never have to experience the end."

Erika thought his speech held promise, that his optimism was refreshing, but she could only think about getting through one day at a time. The kiss that followed his speech had nearly knocked her off her feet. Earlier, when she'd watched him savoring every bite of the cinnamon roll she'd given him, she had also wondered if they'd ever have to see the end. If their love affair did come to an end, she had a feeling they'd remain friends.

Jumping out of bed, Erika hurried over to the window that overlooked the park. Everything was painted a dazzling white again. The playground equipment was buried under the snow and the duck pond appeared to be frozen solid. *This weather could cancel our date,* she thought. She didn't want Michael to risk his life on the sometimes treacherous roads. However, Lebanon County's maintenance crew was excellent at taking care of the highways and streets before they had a chance to present a real threat to motorists.

Since it was only six-fifteen, Erika slid back under the covers and dragged a pillow against her chest. Her very next thoughts were of her childhood home. Willing herself to remain calm, she shelved them.

Erika had usually spent Saturday mornings cleaning the house with her mother and taking care of the laundry. Then Vernice and Arlene did their grocery shopping at their favorite downtown market. After all their chores were taken care of, they went down to Miss Bertha's salon to have their hair done.

On Sundays the sisters could be found in the front pew of the Nazarene Baptist Church, the largest black church in Lebanon. Erika had attended church with her family when her schedule permitted, but when she couldn't she made it a point to be present at one of the services held in the Great Western University chapel.

As Lorraine's short, three-rap knock sounded on the door, Erika rushed to answer it. Once Lorraine was inside, she ran back to the bedroom and leaped into bed.

Lorraine laughed as she came through the bedroom door. "Anyone under those covers with you, sister dear?" She dropped down on the foot of the bed. "The way you ran back to this room, I was sure you were running to someone. You know why I'm here, don't you?"

Erika poked her head from under the covers. "Yes, I do. You came here to stick your nose in my business. Michael's absolutely wonderful. The ballet was magnificent, and the kisses were like Lay's potato chips—I'd never be satisfied with just one. How's that for a great evening?" Erika asked, tossing a pillow at Lorraine.

Lorraine caught the pillow and tossed it back. "I'd say you did good, girl. Are you sure you're not leaving out some of the sizzle?"

Erika's response was a pop upside Lorraine's head with the pillow. For the next several minutes, the two women tossed the pillow back and forth, laughing when one or the other got hit. When a pillow sailed by and knocked over everything on the dresser, they decided to call a truce.

"Hey, does your African prince in expensive attire still have his tonsils?" Lorraine asked, placing the items back on the dresser.

"Don't know. I haven't probed that far yet. I'm seeing him today, so maybe I'll find out," Erika responded cheekily.

The cellular phone on the nightstand caught Lorraine's eye. Shuffling across the room, she picked it up and waved the phone in the air. "How can you afford this expensive toy? The last time we talked you hardly had enough money to buy toilet paper."

"It's Michael's." Erika disappeared into the bathroom, where she began drawing a hot bath. "He only lent it to me. I'm going to have a phone installed on Monday," Erika shouted over the noise of the running water.

"That's interesting, since you refused to allow me to have a phone put in for you. Is Michael going to pay your phone bill, Erika?"

Erika came out of the bathroom and glared at Lorraine. "That's not fair. You know I'm not about that. He lent me the phone in case of an emergency. He also wanted to be able to contact me whenever he needed to."

Crossing the room, Lorraine took Erika's hand. "I'm sorry, Erika. I think I'm a little jealous that you have Michael. I only feel this way because I'm lonely. I also miss Joe more than I thought I would."

"Well, we're just going to have to do something about that. Why don't you come to Aunt Arlene's with Michael and me? We're going to have breakfast over there."

Lorraine's eyes sparkled with excitement. "By the way, how's your aunt doing? I haven't seen her in a long time. I forgot to ask you about her yesterday when you said she gave you money for the dress."

No matter how hard she fought it, Erika couldn't stop tears from welling up in her eyes. Just the mention of money was enough to make her want to pull her hair out. It was time to tell Lorraine the truth, she decided. She couldn't keep her financial woes a secret forever.

Putting her arm around her friend's shoulders, Erika steered her over to the bed and asked her to be seated. After they'd made themselves comfortable, Erika spilled her guts—and more tears.

"I didn't have the faintest idea you'd been thinking about dropping out of the residency program. Somehow, it just doesn't seem fair. Are you that far behind in your bills? I've heard you talk about how your school expenses had practically drained you dry, but it never crossed my mind that your finances were in such dire shape. How have you coped with this for so long, without once revealing the enormity of the situation? I would've gone crazy. I knew you had something weighing you down, but I had no idea that your problems were so serious."

Erika hoped that this was the last person she'd have to talk to about her horrid financial picture. There was just no way to say it without drawing a heap of commiseration. But she wasn't looking for sympathy. All she wanted was to find a legitimate way out of this financial nightmare.

After sorting through Erika's financial woes and discussing her joy over what Michael had told her about meeting her mother, Lorraine went back to her apartment to get dressed for the breakfast.

Feeling eerily alone, Erika slipped into the tub of now-cold water. Turning on the hot water, she rested her back against the tub as the water heated up again. As she relaxed, she thought about Lorraine's boyfriend, Joseph Hayes. Joseph was a law student who'd recently transferred to a school in another part of the state. He and Lorraine had had an ugly argument before he'd returned to school, after he'd spent the Christmas holidays in Lebanon.

Lorraine had become upset when they hadn't gotten engaged as scheduled. She had accused Joe of reneging on his promise, but all he'd wanted to do was wait until he could afford to take care of Lorraine in the fashion she was accustomed to. Lorraine had sent him packing, with the promise of finding someone else. Now it looked as though she regretted her childish behavior.

If Erika knew Lorraine the way she thought she did, Lorraine would never ask for Joe's forgiveness and she didn't think Joe was the type to let Lorraine get away with it, without admitting she'd been wrong. Therefore, it looked as if nothing would get solved between them unless a third party stepped in and became the mediator.

Erika sighed, knowing she'd have to be the one to get them talking again. But right now she didn't have the inclination or the energy to involve herself in one more unattractive scenario. She'd had enough, already.

Dragging herself out of the tub, Erika grabbed the towel she'd placed on top of the dirty clothes hamper. Drying herself thoroughly, she then trudged into the bedroom, where she dressed in navy-blue wool slacks and a red hand-knitted sweater. Seated on the bed, she pulled red wool socks onto her feet and slipped them into low-cut, red leather boots.

While brushing her hair, she heard a loud knock on the door. Glancing at the clock, she yelped, realizing how late it had gotten. She had lost track of time while explaining her plight to Lorraine, which meant that Michael was on the other side of the door. Hurrying to finish her hair, she dashed to the door.

Michael looked marvelous in a pair of black wool slacks and a black-and-gray Shaker-knit sweater. The white shirt he wore underneath the sweater looked crisply starched. As he stepped inside, he gave her a hand-written note. "It was taped to the door. A secret admirer, perhaps?" he asked, leaning over to kiss her full on the mouth.

She smiled and kissed him back. "Why don't we see?" She opened the note and read it. "We've just been stood up." He gave her a puzzled glance. "It's from Lorraine. She was supposed to go to breakfast with us. Says she's decided to study instead, but I think not. It's my guess she's not interested in being a third wheel. Lorraine does have her own unique way of doing things."

"Do you want to go see her and convince her to come with us? I don't want her to think we don't want her along."

Erika sighed. "She won't change her mind. Lorraine's got the lonesome blues. But she's not lonesome for just anyone. She's lonesome for Joe." Erika explained to Michael who Joe was. Then she gave him a brief synopsis of their problem.

Michael gathered Erika into his arms and planted a kiss in her hair. "You know her better than I do. Are you ready to leave?" Before she could respond, he kissed her again.

Losing herself in the sensations of his powerful kisses, she wrapped her arms around his neck. Michael molded her against him, his hands gently gripping her hips. Sliding her hand under his sweater, she met with the scratchy feel of the recently starched shirt. His citrus cologne tickled her nose, but she could've cared less. She felt good being so close to him, acutely aware of the fullness of him pressing into her thigh.

As she moaned softly, his tongue probed deeper, his hands roving heatedly up and down her body. Scared of what was happening to her, Erika disentangled herself from his embrace, but her heart just wasn't in it. Briefly, she looked into the depths of his hazel eyes. Flinging herself back into his arms, hungrily, she covered his mouth with hers, pressing herself against the swollen core of his desire.

His breath came rapidly, and he couldn't get enough of the sweet taste of her lips. Growing bold in his exploration of her tenderness, he cupped his hand around a full, ripe breast.

"Erika, Erika," he breathed, "we'd better get out of here while we still can. I want you so much, but I don't want to push you into something I'm sure you're not ready for."

She wanted him as much as he wanted her, but she was afraid of the regrets that might come later. She had no idea how she could get out of this one without coming off like a frightened adolescent.

Sensing her frustration, he reached for the knob and pulled the door open wide. "There, that will keep us honest. Get your coat, Erika. We don't want to keep your aunt waiting," he said, his breathing uneven.

She looked at him as though he had to be kidding. *How could he just turn off like that?* she wondered, yet she saw how labored his breathing was. The cold draft coming in from the hallway did nothing to cool her off, since she felt hotter than a summer in hell.

Slowly, she turned away from him, wanting nothing more than to stay in his arms until the smoldering heat dissipated. Being in his arms would only further fan the hot flames of her desire, though.

"I'll get my coat, Michael."

Erika walked into the bedroom and on through to the bathroom. Turning on the cold water, she stuck a washcloth under it and then put the cool cloth to her head and the exposed portion of her neck. "That's much better," she whispered.

On her way back to the living room, she grabbed her coat from the closet. Michael had leaned his head against the doorjamb, and she could clearly see that his breathing was still out of control. Neither spoke a word as they made their way to the black Pathfinder.

As Michael fired the engine, he looked at her and smiled, his eyes smoldering with seduction. Erika felt their heat penetrate her soul. "I need directions, gorgeous. Better yet, just tell me the address. I know this city inside and out." Erika told him the address and he nodded.

Arlene lived near the rural area of Lebanon. Knowing that part of town very well, Michael steered the Pathfinder in an easterly direction. The conversation was minimal as they headed toward the countryside, both silently addressing what had occurred between them in the apartment.

As the four-wheel drive reached the open spaces, the beauty of the land was breathtaking. The massive fields, white with fresh snow, looked like a large wool blanket. The air felt crisp and much cooler than in the city, and it even smelled much cleaner.

Spellbound, Erika pulled out her sketchpad and began capturing the allure of winter. Her hand tightening around the lower half of the charcoal pencil, she drew and sketched that which caught her mind's eye. Oblivious to everything but the winter wonderland surroundings, Erika got lost in her creation.

Running around to open the door for her, Michael waited for Erika to put her pad and pencils away. As she slid out of the passenger seat, he kissed her again and again. Blushing from head to toe, Erika directed Michael toward the house, hoping her aunt wouldn't pass comment on the telltale signs of passion on her face.

Arlene worked in back of the house, preparing breakfast. Hearing the front door opening, she took off her apron and made a last-minute adjustment to her hair. "Erika," she yelled out, "is that you, child?"

"Yes, Aunt Arlene," Erika responded, entering the kitchen, her hand snugly wrapped in Michael's. "Good morning." She kissed her aunt on the cheek. "It smells like heaven in here, as usual. This is Dr. Michael Mathis. Michael, my Aunt Arlene," she presented sweetly, closely studying her aunt's reaction.

Michael kissed the back of Arlene's hand. Like her niece, she blushed from head to toe. "It's nice to meet you, Aunt Arlene," he charmed. "If you're as sweet as your niece and your cinnamon rolls, I'm in for a special treat."

Grateful for his compliment, Arlene patted him on the hand. "In that case, you're going to enjoy the wonderful feast I prepared in your honor after Erika called and said you were coming. Welcome to my humble home, young Michael."

Arlene indicated for them to sit at the table. She then busied herself putting out the meal. She'd prepared stacks and stacks of blueberry pancakes and mountains of sausage and bacon.

Because of a mild heart condition she always used turkey-based meat products. The platter of homemade biscuits she placed on the table had been topped with natural honey and the maple syrup came from one of the farmers down the road. As if she hadn't cooked enough food already, she had a pan of apple turnovers still baking in the oven.

Arlene finally joined her guests at the table. "Young man, would you please do the honor of passing the blessing on what the Lord has seen fit to supply in such abundance?"

He beamed at her. "It would be my pleasure."

Erika and Arlene bowed their heads as Michael prayed fervently over the food. His prayer spoke to humbleness and thanksgiving, asking for a blessing on the hands that prepared the food and requesting traveling mercies for their return to the city. Before he said amen, he asked the Lord to take watch over Arlene and her home.

As they ate of the sumptuous feast, Arlene talked about the upcoming senior citizens' trip to New York City. The trip wouldn't take place until early spring, but with her enthusiasm it seemed as if it were going to happen the very next day. Aunt Arlene continued to chat nonstop about anything and everything. By the time the turnovers had been served, Michael felt he knew Aunt Arlene almost as well as he knew Erika.

Michael got up and excused himself to call his answering service.

Aunt Arlene raised her eyebrows. "I think your Michael is a wonderful young man. He would be an extraordinary addition to the family."

"Let's not go there," Erika scolded playfully. "I'm not looking for a husband any more than he's looking for a wife. Michael and I are simply enjoying each other's company. Maybe we should just leave it at that."

Arlene clicked her tongue. "Phooey, Erika. Everyone's looking for a mate. As old as I am, I would jump at the chance to marry someone who'd enjoy doing all the things I like to do. It can get pretty lonely at times. After our husbands died, your mother and I were sought out by the majority of the old men that live out in this area, but we just never found the right one."

Erika laughed. "Please, take the pressure off," she pleaded. "You don't want to scare Michael off, do you? Besides, we've only known each other for a few days. I don't see a wedding in my future, at least not my immediate future. But I'll remain optimistic."

Having heard some of their conversation, smiling, Michael rejoined his two companions. "Do you think I could trouble you for another of those mouthwatering turnovers, Aunt Arlene? It surely would be appreciated."

"You just help yourself to whatever you want. We're glad you're enjoying everything. I can't even recall the last time I cooked for a healthy male appetite."

Erika roared. "I do! Don't tell me you're forgetting Mr. Harry Swann. You said that he nearly ate you out of house and home," Erika teased. "Whatever happened to him?"

"As far as I know he's still over in that house by himself. He was nice enough, but he could never stay awake. We'd be watching the baseball game and all of a sudden he'd just nod off. That was okay, but when you're on the dance floor and someone nods off, it's time to put that buddy to bed, permanently. He calls now and then, but I don't give him any encouragement. I can be lonely all by myself."

Michael chuckled as he ate his turnover, hoping he'd never get too old to appreciate the fair sex. He could tell that Arlene had been something in her day, sure that she could still give a man a run for his money. Although he didn't like to admit it, Erika was giving him quite a run for all he was worth. He'd never been so relaxed around anyone. Erika was the kind of woman who made a man do things he'd otherwise never even think of. He'd never done anything akin to what he had planned for them after their visit. However, he was confident they'd both enjoy it.

Although they hadn't planned to stay so long it was near

sunset when Erika and Michael drove away from the Wasler house. Arlene had talked them into a game of Monopoly and then beat the pants off them. Each time they'd prepared to leave, she'd find something else for them to do.

Instead of heading back to the city, Michael drove deeper into the rural area. Erika was half-asleep, so she paid no attention to the direction he'd taken. Eighteen minutes later, after pulling up to a rustic farmhouse, he shook Erika gently. When that didn't rouse her, he kissed her until she was fully awake.

As the sun set behind the mountain range, streaks of bright orange lit up the sky. Magnificent evergreen trees swayed with the wind, and mother earth's heavy blanket of snow had been recently trodden on by the wildlife living in the nearby woods. Off in the distance, sleigh bells could be heard. As an old sleigh drawn by a team of horses pulled up in front of the farmhouse, Erika thought she'd been swept back in time.

"What's going on, Michael? Where are we?"

Smiling broadly, he pulled her close to him. "We're about to take an old-fashioned sleigh ride. Do you have any objections, my gorgeous snow bunny?"

She giggled out loud. "This is amazing. Of course I don't. This is something I've always dreamed of doing." She tugged at his hand. "Let's go."

Michael had a few words with the driver of the sleigh before he and Erika settled themselves into the worn leather seats. Drawing a heavy plaid blanket over their laps, Michael cozied up to Erika, who glowed like a lighthouse in the dark.

As the driver yelled a command to his team, they took off at a steady pace, undaunted by the heavy snow.

This was the stuff fairy tales were made of, Erika marveled, snuggling closer to Michael. Despite the cold winds she'd never been warmer. Michael had a way of heating up the universe and lighting up her life. He was everything she'd ever dreamed of, everything she'd ever hoped for, quickly becoming her everything, period.

Fresh snow began to fall, and their joyous laughter rang out over the countryside. Snuggled in each other's arms, they felt as close to heaven as they could get. As the sleigh carried them deeper into the countryside, they lost themselves to the magnificence of their beautiful surroundings.

Lights suddenly began to appear in the windows and on the porches of the farmhouses, but they were no match for the brightness in Erika's eyes. She was totally mesmerized by the wondrous scenery that stretched for miles and miles ahead of them.

Michael was totally mesmerized by her refreshing innocence. As his mouth crushed hers, she knew that Dr. Michael Mathis was the only one in the world who could make all her dreams and fantasies come true.

Knowing full well that this probably wasn't the time to ask about a woman named Stephanie and the child named Tamala, Erika had a need to know that was overwhelming. Biting down on her lower lip, she studied the engaging masculine profile illuminated by the moon's silvery rays. "I know the timing may be all wrong, Michael, but I'm interested in hearing about Stephanie and Tamala."

No, he thought, the timing was just right. Wanting everything out in the open, he didn't want Erika to have any doubts. "Stephanie and I were supposed to get married, and I was going to become a real father to little Tamala."

Erika immediately regretted opening that particular can of worms. It hurt her terribly to think that Michael had loved a woman enough to want to marry her. Now that she'd inquired, she'd just have to listen.

"However, I learned that I wasn't in love with Stephanie. I loved her, but not the way a man should love a woman he's planning to spend the rest of his life with. Stephanie and I both needed to belong to someone at that time. When she walked into my office carrying a tiny bundle of joy, I thought she was exactly what I'd been looking for. Months after Tamala died of pediatric AIDS, the bright lights went out on our relationship. I think Tamala was the only reason the lights got turned on in the first place."

Michael went on to explain the entire situation. When he was finished, Erika felt tied up in knots, her heart weeping for baby Tamala. But knowing that Stephanie was now married and very happy brought her a touch of comfort and security. Michael had been very open and honest about his previous relationship and had been quick to let her know that it was all in the past. All he wanted to do was concentrate on the present.

Having cleared the air about the past, Michael and Erika lost themselves to the silvery moonlit night. Their impassioned kisses locked out the pain of the past and marked the things they hoped the present would bring. This night would hold a special meaning for them. As they discovered new feelings that made their hearts full, they looked forward to discovering so much more.

The horses carried them back to where they'd begun their journey, but neither of them had wanted the magical ride to end. If they had ridden the countryside for the remainder of the night, they still would've wanted more time to cuddle together in the sleigh.

Erika knew it was just a matter of time before they shared the ultimate in being together. But for now, Michael was content to let her set the pace for what he hoped would be a perfect uniting of two hearts and two souls.

Erika had so many things on her mind that by the time she fell into bed she found it hard to sleep; thoughts of Michael that were traipsing through her head weren't helping matters. After the sleigh ride, he had taken her out for a late supper at a very nice restaurant. He was disappointed when she'd only ordered a large salad. As she explained that all the cinnamon rolls, French fries and pancakes she'd consumed weren't on her weight-loss program, he realized how serious she was about keeping the excess pounds off. Telling her he'd support her in her quest to keep them off, Michael also told her he'd do just about anything for her.

Inside the door of her apartment things had heated up again. Just as he had before, Michael put the nearly out-of-control situation in check. Sighing deeply, Erika turned on her side, begging sleep to take over her mind. But it just wasn't going to happen, so she thought about every time he touched her, how she felt moisture form at the very essence of her intimacy. What was it about Michael that made her want to throw all caution to the wind?

The answer was simply uncomplicated. Michael was intelligent, charming, thoughtful, sincere, a man's man, a gentleman. His sensitivity overwhelmed, his heart was pure. Michael Mathis was the equation, the formula, the missing link that solved the problem. He completed the portrait of the wondrous miracles of life and love she often sketched in her mind but hadn't been able to fully capture on canvas. As she drifted off, she felt sure she could now express all of the wonderful feelings she felt for and with Michael—through the precious gift of art.

During the course of the week Erika was so busy with her medical responsibilities that she barely had enough time to use the bathroom. A lot of her time was spent studying, attending lectures, making medical rounds, and working on and writing reports on the group research projects.

Because of her busy schedule she and Michael were only able to steal a few minutes here and there. Most of their brief encounters took place in the cafeteria. Michael, knowing exactly what was required of Erika as a resident, never once complained about their brief trysts. The deep kisses, the soft caresses, and the laughter they shared gave them both something to hold on to until they could manage to spend another long evening together.

As Erika hurried down the hospital corridor to meet with

her colleagues for rounds, she heard her name blaring over the paging system. Dashing to the nearest phone, she quickly dialed the operator.

"This is Dr. Edmonds."

"I'll connect you with your party. Have a nice day."

When Randy Mills's voice came on the line, Erika was sure her heart had stopped beating. As she wondered if he was going to ask for an advance payment, she took a deep breath, willing her heart to stop drag racing through her chest.

"Dr. Edmonds, good afternoon. Is it possible for us to set up a meeting? I have an opening in my schedule for early next week. I thought we wouldn't be able to move your household for a couple of weeks, but one of our clients just called and cancelled their move."

Anxiety settled in the pit of her stomach. *Oh dear,* she thought, *how am I going to come up with all that money so soon?* Knowing this was something that had to be done, something that couldn't be avoided, she decided to jump in the drowning pool, feet first.

Erika ground her back teeth. "Mr. Mills, unless I can meet with you in the evening, I'm afraid I won't be able to shift my schedule around to accommodate you. I should be free around six-thirty this evening. I could come to your office then."

"No, that won't be necessary. I can drop by the university on my way home. Where shall I meet you?"

"The hospital cafeteria is easy enough to find. I'll see you then, Mr. Mills."

"Fine, Dr. Edmonds. Please call me Randy," he requested before disconnecting the phone lines.

Rushing toward the obstetrics ward, Erika wondered how she was going to deal with her cash-flow problem. She could use her credit card, but she tried to keep it clear for emergencies. Wasn't this an emergency? Perhaps Randy would be kind enough to allow her to make small but reasonable payments on the moving expenses, Erika thought, suddenly feeling the jaws of dark despair clamping down on her again. If she didn't accomplish another thing this day, she was going to try to make Randy Mills understand she could pay for his services but not all at once.

Comfortable with her decision and the fact that there was no other way to handle the moving expenses, Erika rushed on to her destination, slipping into the hospital ward just a couple of minutes before she would've been considered late.

Six

Dr. Baker was busy examining Odessa Blake, a twenty-seven-year-old African-American, who'd been carrying her unborn child for close to ten months. There was a lot of concern for the mother and the infant, but both seemed to be doing reasonably well under the circumstances.

Erika's mind churned with such turmoil that she could barely concentrate on Dr. Baker's comments about Odessa's medical condition as he explained the situation to the residents. When Dr. Baker summoned her, Erika moved toward him at a snail's pace.

"Dr. Edmonds, I'd like you to listen to the baby's heartbeat." When Erika didn't respond, Dr. Baker looked up at her, noticing the faraway, vacant space occupying her eyes. "Dr. Edmonds," he said curtly, "care to join the rest of us?"

Erika's head snapped back, making it evident to everyone that she wasn't in tune with what was going on around her. "I . . . sorry, Dr. Baker, but . . . I . . . didn't catch your last comments," Erika stammered.

Remembering that he'd once experienced the same kind of distraction that now usurped Erika's concentration, Dr. Baker felt a rush of sympathy for her. With a wave of his hand, he summoned her to come closer. Quietly, he repeated his earlier instructions.

Erika placed the tips of the stethoscope in her ears. Before placing it on Odessa's distended abdomen she rubbed the metal part of it against the daisy yellow sweater she wore under her white lab coat. Listening intently for the tiny heartbeat, she heard only the normal bowel sounds of the mother. Moving the stethoscope from one position to another, she frowned when she still couldn't hear the infant's heartbeat. A frown and a slight shake of her head let Dr. Baker know she had a serious concern. Stepping aside, she allowed Dr. Baker to reexamine the woman.

Odessa Blake had initially been sent to the hospital for a fetal stress test, but hadn't yet been hooked up to the monitor. The stress test would've enabled the physicians to monitor the infant's regular heartbeat. Then the heartbeat would've been monitored during induced contractions, which could have been brought on with small doses of certain medications. However, there already appeared to be signs of trouble.

After reexamining Odessa, Dr. Baker came to the same conclusions Erika had reached. Discreetly, he instructed his team to meet with him outside the patient's room. Before departing the room, he lovingly and reassuringly patted Odessa's hands. He then joined his young colleagues.

"Dr. Edmonds, what is your assessment of Mrs. Blake's condition? And how do you think this particular case should be handled?" Dr. Baker asked, peering at her over the rim of his glasses.

Looking over the notes she'd written down while Dr. Baker reexamined Odessa, Erika put a clear-polished fingernail to her left temple. "Fetal distress. I couldn't hear the heartbeat of the infant. If she were my patient, I'd recommend a cesarean section. If the child is already in distress, it's possible that he or she won't be able to withstand the asceticism of contractions. Were you able to hear a heartbeat, Dr. Baker?"

"Barely. I concur with your assessments and recommendations, Dr. Edmonds. However, there are a few matters that have to be determined first."

"Dr. Jamison," Dr. Baker said, "put the OR staff on alert. Dr. Townsend, see to it that Mrs. Blake is immediately hooked up to the necessary monitors. Then make contact with her personal physician," Dr. Baker instructed, looking down at the medical chart. "Dr. Kristina Peters is her OB-GYN."

As the two male residents hustled off to handle their respective assignments, Dr. Baker turned to Erika. "Dr. Edmonds, I want you to inform Mrs. Blake of what's happening here. Think you can handle it, young lady?"

Erika smiled brilliantly. "I can and will. Thanks for giving me the opportunity to make the call. It was certainly a boost for my confidence." Dr. Baker winked at Erika as she backed away from the group and reentered Odessa's room.

Pulling a chair up to Odessa's bedside, Erika sat down. Taking one of Odessa's hands, she placed it in hers. "Mrs. Blake," Erika began softly, "it looks as though you may have to deliver by cesarean section." Odessa gasped, gripping Erika's hand tightly. "It's going to be okay," Erika soothed. "Your personal physician should be here any minute."

Looking panicked, Odessa sighed wearily. "Is the baby going to be okay?"

Erika had no way of knowing for sure, but she couldn't tell Odessa anything to cause her alarm. Before Erika could respond, Dr. Kristina Peters and a staff nurse came into the room. Relieved and happy to have Odessa's own physician there to reassure her patient, Erika briefly discussed the medical findings with Dr. Peters. Turning everything over to the seasoned veteran, Erika vacated the room, praying for mother and child.

Once Erika and her other colleagues were reunited, they went from one hospital room to the next, assessing and observing the patients. Dr. Baker assiduously shared his medical knowledge through his excellent teaching techniques. When medical rounds were finally completed, the team retired to one of the many staff lounges, where Dr. Baker would conduct a staff meeting.

During the meeting, Dr. Baker handed out new schedules. Scheduled to pull duty in the emergency room for the next week, Erika moaned inwardly, but was delighted to learn she'd have three days off before the onset of what she considered to be hazardous duty. Very few residents were thrilled to work the emergency room, with the exception of those specializing in emergency medicine.

Great Western University Hospital wasn't just a teaching hospital. It was also a Lebanon County facility, which meant it received patients from all walks of life. Gunshot wounds and stab wounds had become common—especially among the gangbangers, whose membership numbers had grown by leaps and bounds. The longtime residents of Lebanon were distraught over the rise in gang activity in their small, quiet community, but it appeared that no one had a viable solution for getting the growing problem under control.

At 5:47 P.M., tired and footsore, Erika walked into her apartment, where she immediately kicked off her low-heeled shoes. Stripping out of her work clothing, she made her way to the bathroom. Instead of indulging in her usual, long bubble bath, she turned on the shower and positioned herself under the gentle spray of hot water. Adjusting the showerhead to the pulse setting, she closed her eyes and enjoyed the relaxing sensations the pulsating waters provided. Afterward, dry and relaxed, she slipped into a warm bathrobe.

In the living room Erika set up the ironing board, plugged in the steam iron, and then spray-starched and pressed a white shirt until its collar and cuffs were crisp and the rest of its material was smooth and wrinkle-free.

Standing in front of the mirror in the bedroom, she buttoned the newly ironed blouse. After pulling on a pair of sharply creased, black denim jeans, she laced the loops with a thick leather belt. Brushing all of her hair straight back, away from her forehead, she twisted the long length into a ponytail and secured it with a black-and-white polka-dot hair-wrap band.

Using a wide makeup brush, she applied a few quick strokes of translucent powder to her face and added a hint of terracotta blush to her cheeks. Pleased with her appearance, she grabbed her pager from the desk, secured the door and headed to the cafeteria for the meeting with Randy Mills.

Three glorious days off, she thought cheerfully, nearly skipping to the cafeteria. After those three days were up, she knew all hell could and probably would break loose in the ER. She wanted to make every second of her off-duty time count before that time came. Erika didn't know if Michael would be free and available in that particular time frame, but it didn't stop her from hoping they could spend some quality time together. The slightly fading memories of his kisses told her it had been too long since the last time he'd inebriated her with his lush, passionate mouth.

Of course, three days wasn't all that long. But with the absence of a man who had a way of making her hot and hungry for his exquisite kisses and heated caresses, three days could seem like a lifetime. Sometime during her upcoming three days off, Erika planned to have her way with the incomparable Michael Mathis.

Randy was already seated when Erika strolled over to the table he'd chosen for the meeting. Greeting him warmly, she sat down opposite him. "How are you doing, Randy?" she asked, remembering his request.

Randy pressed his thumbprint into the rim of the Styrofoam cup from which he sipped hot coffee. "I'm just fine, Erika. Thanks for asking." He pulled a business form from his briefcase and studied it briefly. "Well, it looks as if everything's in order. I'll just need you to put your John Hancock on this contract." He handed her the neatly typed document.

Completely out of the blue, Erika slammed her hand down hard on the table, wincing as a sharp pain shot through her palm and up through her wrist. A shocked expression inched its way onto Randy's face.

"Oh, shucks," she lamented. "I'm really sorry for that, but I've got a big problem, Randy. I just don't have the money to pay for this move all at once. Is there any way that I can pay your fee over a short period of time? I'm good for the money and you're welcome to check my credit history. Otherwise, I'm going to have to find a moving company that will extend me a line of credit."

The stress and panicky sounds in her voice concerned her. She'd tried to come off cool and calm, but it just didn't work for her when she talked about her financial dilemma. Though understanding her distress where the money was concerned, she was more worried about the panic attack she appeared to be having. Her stupid reaction had also embarrassed her.

Randy took the contract from her trembling hands and laid it on the table. "Listen," he said calmly, "don't get yourself all worked up over this thing. I'm sure we can work something out. How much can you afford to pay each month, Erika?"

Erika picked up the contract again and looked over the figures, her brain quickly grinding out the arithmetic. "Fifty dollars a month would work nicely. Sixty is about all I can really manage—but that's a stretch. Even then, it's going to take me close to a year to pay you off, which also means a lot of interest." She shook her head in dismay.

Randy smiled. "I'll tell you what. We rarely extend credit for more than three months, but I'll make an exception in your case. You pay me what you can each month, and I won't tack on any interest. How's that for a deal?"

Erika's smile was wry. "You'd better be more specific. If you rely on me to pay what I can each month, you might be really sorry."

Trying to come up with an appropriate response to her comment, Randy studied Erika's soft features. "Well, you're the only one who knows your financial situation, Erika," he finally said. "Just do the best you can. If I ever need medical attention and can't afford it at the time, you can remember my past generosity."

Though unshed tears threatened at the back of her eyes, Erika's generous mouth formed a smile of deep gratitude. "I will. Thank you." Erika took a deep breath. Getting into more debt concerned her more than she wanted to admit, but the house had to be cleared.

Randy simply nodded, feeling sure he could trust her. Erika's honesty about her financial picture had provided him with more than a clue to what she was about. "Does the time that's scheduled for the move meet with your approval?"

Erika's heart was pumping like crazy. Just the thought of all her mother's treasured possessions made her go all soft inside. Sentimental tears leaped into her eyes. "The time is fine, Randy. I'll meet you at the house bright and early tomorrow morning." Her expression grew soft. She no longer had her mother with her, and now the house would go, too, but no one could take her precious memories away. "Thanks so much, Randy."

He smiled warmly at his new customer. "You're very welcome, Erika. Hopefully, everything will go as we've planned. If there are any changes in the schedule, you'll be the first to know. I know how valuable your time is. Speaking of time," he said, glancing at his watch, "I'd better get going." He got to his feet. Surprising himself, he brushed her cheek with a feathery light kiss. "Good luck, Dr. Edmonds."

Erika looked just as surprised as Randy, but they weren't the only ones surprised.

Michael had entered the cafeteria just in time to see Randy's small display of gentle affection. He didn't appear to be thrilled at what he'd just witnessed. He couldn't see the man's face because Randy's back was to him, but it didn't matter to him who it was. Michael simply didn't want any man being affectionate with the woman he'd begun to think of as exclusively his—the woman he'd fallen in love with.

Michael continued to watch Erika and the man, who now faced him. The surprised look on Erika's face was not lost on him. It told him she hadn't expected the kiss. Slowly, he approached the table as Randy exited the cafeteria.

Erika smiled all over when she saw Michael coming toward her. With the intention of kissing his cheek, Erika came face-to-face with Michael. The brooding look he gave her caused her to slightly back away from him. Before she could fully retreat, Michael had her body pressed full against his own. "Going somewhere?"

Unable to respond due to the lump in her throat, she swallowed hard to rid herself of the painful obstruction. "Not here, Michael. You're embarrassing me," she said, despite the urgent desire to kiss him silly.

Pulling her even closer, Michael raised his eyebrows. "Is that so? You didn't appear to be embarrassed when your friend there dusted your cheek with his kiss. Why are you so embarrassed now?"

Noting several pairs of eyes on them, including Dr. Jules Baker's, Erika squirmed in his tight embrace. "The chief of OB-GYN is watching us, Michael. Please," she pleaded through clenched teeth. "I don't want to give him the wrong impression. And as far as *my friend* is concerned, let's not go that route, okay? Can you understand what I'm trying to convey here?"

Michael grinned lazily. "I think so, Dr. Edmonds. But we might have to take this entire matter up later. By the way, what are you doing later?"

Erika couldn't suppress the girlish giggle his question brought on. "I was thinking of renting a couple of movies, but I'm not so sure now." *More to the point, I was thinking of getting you into my bed,* she thought, laughing inwardly. "I don't think I want to spend another evening sprawled on the uncomfortable couch in the dorm's recreation room. I don't own a VCR."

Michael saw that it was close to eight o'clock when he looked at one of the numerous wall clocks. Since he wasn't on call, he decided he'd like nothing better than to solve Erika's entertainment dilemma. "I have a couple of video machines at my place. Can I coerce you into spending the evening with me at my home?" Dropping down into one of the chairs, he gestured for her to do the same. "We can pick up the movies of your choice on the way, but I have to tell you, I own an extensive collection of videos. Some have never been opened."

Erika could hardly contain her excitement, but she didn't want Michael to know how eager she was to spend the evening with him. An entire evening in Michael's company would be a dream come true. "I like old movies, Michael. Do you have *Mahogany* starring Billy Dee and Diana Ross?"

Enchanted by the way she'd seductively breathed Billy Dee's name, Michael laughed softly. "I have most of the black movies made in the seventies. Several black actors lit up the silver screen then, and it looks as if they're about to have another good run. But I'd like to see our people get more involved in romantic and respectable roles. I'm tired, as I'm sure they are, of the violent and substandard roles they've been all but forced to play."

Erika snorted. "If the powers that be weren't so offended and threatened by our people making love on screen, they could get more involved. Why do you think those in power are so threatened by the powerful sexuality of the black male?"

Michael grinned, hoping the subject matter didn't cause a sexual response. "I think you just answered your own question there, gorgeous girl. The old myths about our potent sexuality still run rampant." Thinking of ways he could prove to her the old myths were true, he laughed. "Perhaps it's not a myth at all." Suddenly, his eyes encompassed her in a way she found sweetly seductive and magically alluring. "Do we have a movie date? I'll even make some popcorn. Air-popped," he added, thinking of her diet.

As her dimpled smile took flight in her eyes, he felt the rapid increase in his heart rate. "We do, Dr. Mathis. Do you want to wait for me while I go over to my apartment, or do you want to come with me?"

Michael chuckled. "I want to go with you, of course. Why would I wait here when I can be with the gorgeous woman who causes my heart to frequently run relays?" They both laughed.

With Erika leading the way, they advanced toward the exit, but she stopped abruptly when she neared the table Dr. Baker and several other men occupied. As Erika was about to introduce Michael to her mentor, Dr. Baker rapidly got to his feet.

It became clear to Erika that no introductions were necessary when the two doctors called each other by their first names. The deep mutual respect that Michael and Jules appeared to have for each other was also very clear, which warmed her heart. After a brief conversation and a covert wink of approval from Dr. Baker to Erika, she and Michael exited the cafeteria.

As though she led a double life, Erika turned bubbly and flirtatious all the way to her apartment. While he'd seen a few sides of Erika's personality, he rather liked them all, but the flirtatious side of her was engaging; the side of her that intrigued him the most.

Michael hadn't mentioned living in the rural area of Lebanon when he'd accompanied Erika to her aunt's house, but from the direction in which he was driving she knew there was nothing that far out but vast countryside and densely populated forest areas.

Erika relaxed as the cares of the day slowly seeped from her body. Knowing it would have been a spectacular event, she wished they'd passed this way during the setting of the sun. As they came upon an area that looked like an English hamlet, she gasped. Lights flickered in the cottage windows, and lovely old coach lamps lined the softly lit driveways. It was like a step back in time. She could easily imagine the scene painted on the finest porcelain. Twenty or so miles later, Michael pulled into a circular cobblestone driveway.

Erika was completely blown away by the enchanting, almost medieval-style cottage standing majestically before her. With a sculptured landscape dotted with tiny white lights, surrounded by scores and scores of pines, firs, and other lush greenery, the charm of the elegant cottage was evident even in the darkness of night. The place was rather large to be labeled as a cottage, but amidst tall, stately trees its actual size was dwarfed. The gray, black and white stone exterior made the house a masterpiece of shadow and light.

Inside, Michael took delight in showing Erika around his home, hoping to make her feel comfortable and completely at ease in his space. She squealed with pleasure when they entered the spacious living room.

Camelback sofas were done in a friendly blending of twill, washed damask, and leaves-in-print wrap. Rounding out the look were balloon-back chairs and draped rattan tables. The elegantly structured, large, white marble columns were impressive. Erika was most impressed with the fact that the room looked as if it were situated in the middle of a greenhouse. Greenery was everywhere, amply lit by the remote-controlled skylights. Plenty of fresh air was able to flow in, as well, and Michael said that automatic sensors would close the skylights at the first drop of rain.

As they continued to walk around, Erika was fascinated with the many different statements the decor of the house made with its array of gentle and exciting hues. The pearl-white walls spoke of openness, airiness, and a sweeping spirit that welcomed other nuances into the rooms. The kitchen created a vibrant, energetic mood by tossing warm yellows against icy blues. Soothing sky-blues and sea-greens whispered softly in the rooms used for resting. Deep greens and antique whites seemed to heave low sighs of comfort into the study. Foam-greens and soft peaches hushed the master suite with quiet allure. Erika repeatedly gasped and cooed throughout the tour, making Michael pleased to see how enthused she was over the place he called home.

This was his "rural escape," his curative from the day-after-day conflicts of working and driving into the large steel city. He'd purchased the home not long after his breakup with Stephanie, a turbulent time for him. His mourning the death of little Tamala had made things even more complicated. Amidst a riot of colors invoking comfort and pleasure, he could readily select the atmosphere that best fit his presiding mood.

After making a roaring fire, Michael settled himself on the plush rug in front of the native cobblestone fireplace. Tenderly, he drew Erika into his arms, gently tasting her lips. Then his mouth crushed over hers with a hunger so fierce that it momentarily frightened her. As his need to devour her lessened, his kisses became soft and tantalizing. Melting against him, she satisfied his hungry cravings.

Holding her slightly away from him, he got lost in the spectacular show of firelight taking place in her eyes. Michael felt himself drawn into the depths of their magnetic powers, helpless against their strength. Erika closed her eyes and begged for his kisses with a whisper against his trembling lips. His soft moans mingled with hers as their mouths willfully and sweetly collided.

Erika wanted Michael, wanted him snuggled inside her pool of heat, inside her heart and soul, desperately wanting all of him. His ardent kisses and tenderly roaming hands told her that he wanted her, too, wanted to passionately love every part of her.

But Michael wanted so much more than her body, including exclusive rights to her heart and soul. Did he have the right to ask all that of her so soon? he wondered, positive his feelings for Erika were nothing like the feelings he'd thought he felt for Stephanie. But how could he be one hundred percent sure? Knowing he couldn't be, he wasn't going to run away from someone who could actually turn out to be his soul mate. He already felt soulfully connected to Erika, but now he needed to find out if she felt, or could ever feel, the same way about him.

The next passionate kiss she hit him with tossed all his thoughts out the window. Michael groaned loudly as he buried his tongue deeply in the sweet nectars of her inner mouth. Shoving her hand under his sweater, Erika worried the nipple hardening right beneath her fingers. She allowed her fingers to travel through the thick chest hair and down to where it formed a triangle and disappeared. As his warm hands sought out her erect nipples, she gasped, slightly grinding her hips against his pulsating maleness.

Erika and Michael knew they were treading in dangerous territory, but couldn't drag themselves away from the heated contact. Both were adults, and it seemed they both desperately wanted and needed what was happening between them.

When Michael began to unbutton her blouse, Erika did nothing and said nothing to dissuade him. In fact, her eyes encouraged him to continue. As his mouth closed over one creamy breast, she arched herself fully into him. This time the grinding of her hips against him wasn't so subtle, and the seductive swaying of her body nearly drove him insane.

While his smooth tongue trailed a line of hot, moist kisses up and down her bare abdomen, he licked at her navel until she squirmed with pleasure. As his hands slowly undid her belt buckle, a pool of flaming heat rapidly rose in her inner core. The opening of her zipper revealed a pair of black silk bikini panties, which caused Michael's heart to hammer away at what was barely left of his composure.

Adroitly, his fingers snaked inside the black silk, tenderly stroking her moisture-laden core. Erika moaned so softly that he just barely heard her. Slowly dragging the jeans down off her hips, he tossed them aside. Now he could do all the things to her that he'd dreamed of doing. Only if she'd let him.

For Erika it wasn't a matter of letting him take her; it was more a matter of when he was going to allow himself to have her. She'd already made up her mind to take all of what the good Dr. Michael Mathis had to offer. From the feel of his erection she knew there was one thing he had plenty of to offer, and she wanted every inch of him to aggressively but tenderly assault the lake of fire raging between her thighs.

As though he'd read her mind, he swept away the wispy triangle of silk. His head dipped down between her legs, smothering her with the intense fires of his mouth and gently probing tongue. Over and over Erika screamed, causing Michael's excitement and manhood to expand even more. Out of her mind now, she heard her screams turn to soft, desperate utterances.

Knowing his own attire restricted his movements Michael quickly stripped down to his cotton briefs. He wanted Erika to have the pleasure of removing them, which would make him certain that she wanted him to make love to her. However, he didn't have to wait that long to find out the answer.

"Michael, I need to feel all of you," she moaned as she helped him out of his briefs. "Make love to me, Michael. Please, Michael," she begged, her softly whispered words telling him just what she wanted and needed from him.

Praying he wasn't just imagining her sweet words, which told him she needed him as much as he needed her, he slammed his eyelids shut. Again, he heard the very same words tumbling from her lips in a gasp of wantonness.

"Oh, yes, Erika," he breathed against her parted lips. "I'm here to give you all that you want from me," he moaned softly, guiding her hand to his rigid maleness, wanting to show her how much he desperately desired her.

Closing her hand around him, she gently stroked him up and down. As he turned onto his side, she ran her hands over his firm buttocks. Etching circles of fire up and down his strong back, she marveled at the feel of his Indian-brown skin, which was as smooth as satin. His sexuality felt as though it had been carved from stone.

The flames in the fireplace shot upward as he hovered over her, poised to give her everything she needed from him. Slowly, she drew him down closer, closer, until she could feel his breath. Invitingly, she slowly parted her legs. Michael wanted to draw the moment out, wanted to savor the delicious sensuality of it all, wanted to be in her forever. As his fingers slipped inside her, she tightened her muscles, causing him to imagine what it would feel like to have her wrap herself around his manhood in much the same way.

It was the last thing he had to imagine as he tenderly filled her with his plunging length and throbbing breadth. Not wanting to hurt her, he slowly edged his way into her, stopping at intervals to allow her to adjust to the length and the thickness of his organ.

His moving over her with tantalizing, circular, thrusting motions made her cry out from the sweet sensations cascading through her. Just as he'd imagined, when she locked her inner muscles around him, it was the sweetest, deadliest imprisonment he'd ever known. The impenetrable lock not only imprisoned his manhood—it imprisoned his heart and soul. His entire being belonged to Erika Edmonds and he could only hope she'd one day become his permanent cellmate.

As they rode the waves of passion and the storms of fiery heat, they came together as one. The protection he wore was the only thing between them, and they both hoped the day would come when protection would no longer be a necessity for them.

His deep thrusts grew in intensity, and Erika was in a frantic state as she raised up to meet each frenzy driven, mind-drugging blow. The need to be utterly fulfilled was overwhelming, yet neither of them seemed ready to plunge into the waiting depths of sweetly violent shudders and soft screams. The raging needs of their bodies could no longer stand being denied the ultimate in pleasure as the last sweet thrusts swept them over the edge of desire and to the heights of utter fulfillment.

Satisfaction was fully achieved, yet they couldn't find the strength to pull themselves apart, nor did they have the desire to be apart. Erika felt as though a shooting star had just landed in her midsection, turning her insides into a hotbed of smoldering flames.

Michael, proud of the way he'd made her beg for more of his unfathomable passion, was absolutely amazed by the way she'd so zealously fulfilled his every fantasy. The emotions she'd evoked in him still ran rampant through his body. The leaping flames in the fireplace had nothing to do with the burning and aching in his loins and in his throat. If he didn't get some water quickly, he believed he'd surely perish.

Seeing the speeding tears coming from Erika's eyes, Michael forgot all about his own needs as he pulled her further into the sanctuary of his heartfelt compassion. "Oh, God, Erika, did I misinterpret everything? Didn't you want us to go this far? What have I done?" he questioned huskily, nearly choking on a painful moan.

"No, no," she gasped, trying to catch her breath. "No, Michael, I wanted this as much as you did. So much so that it has me frightened and a little shaken. I've never—" His mouth hushed her with a kiss, making her desire for him return in full force.

Michael had heard all he needed to hear. Knowing that he hadn't misread her was all he needed to know. They had desired each other in the same urgent way, and had each completed the fantasy they'd so often dreamed, which made everything they'd experienced right for both of them. Neither one had any regrets.

Pulling a crocheted blanket from one corner of the sofa, Michael wrapped it around Erika's nude body, telling himself he didn't want her to catch a chill. The truth was he couldn't stand to look at her without wanting to possess her all over again, and they needed to fully recuperate from their frantic lovemaking.

There'd been times when he'd wanted to ease the wild, impassioned fury with which he'd taken her. In no uncertain terms her body language had insisted on him keeping up the feverish, tender but forceful pressure.

He kissed the tip of her nose. "I have a mean batch of chili simmering in the Crock-Pot. Want some?" he asked, stroking her cheek with the side of his forefinger.

She smiled lazily. "Mmm, sounds good. Can it be served by osmosis?"

Laughing from deep within, he glanced at the clock. *It's already after ten o'clock,* he thought, *and we haven't even watched a single movie.* The thought of taking her home wasn't at all pleasant.

"It won't take me that long," he finally responded. "You can use the master bathroom if you want to freshen up while I get everything ready. We also have a movie to watch," he reminded her, hoping she wouldn't express a desire to leave. He wasn't disappointed when she merely nodded her approval, watching as she padded down the hallway, wrapped only in the blanket.

Seven

Hurriedly, Michael pulled on his pants and went into the kitchen, where he washed his hands in the sink before removing a couple of yellow ceramic bowls from the polished, honey-oak-stained cabinet. Placing the empty bowls on a long, extra-wide rattan bed-tray, he added pale-yellow, linen napkins and shiny flatware boasting clear yellow handles.

Something funny suddenly came to mind, and he laughed. Pulling open one of the utility drawers, he reached inside and came up with a handful of colorful balloons. Once he'd drawn a happy face and her name on a bright yellow balloon, he drew a huge smile and penned his own name on a sky-blue one. After blowing each one up, he tied them to the corners of the serving tray, hoping Erika would find pleasure in his artistic talents, as he did in hers.

Michael made a mad dash to the master bathroom. As he entered the romantically lit room, he saw Erika stepping into the shower, and he stepped in right behind her. She giggled and threw herself into Michael's arms, kissing him deeply.

The shower was brief, but exhilarating. As Erika stepped out of it, Michael held out a thick terry robe for her to slip into. As he snugly tied the belt around her waist, his tongue flicked at the soft column of her neck. Lowering the collar of the robe, he sprinkled her shoulders with butter-soft kisses.

Grabbing another plush robe from the back of the door, he wrapped it around himself. Carrying her into the bedroom, he turned down the bed and settled her in the center of the cool, flowery fields of fresh percale linens.

He brushed his lips across hers. "Be right back. Don't fall asleep, either."

Erika closed her eyes but had no desire for sleep. Michael made her feel awake, alive. She didn't want to miss any of whatever might come next. So far, he had surpassed all her expectations and she rather suspected she'd surpassed his, as well. Yet she believed they were capable of ascending to an even higher plateau.

Neither of them was the type to play with the emotions of others, she decided. They had made mistakes in the past, but that didn't necessarily mean they'd have a repeat performance. Something deep inside her told her Michael Mathis was exactly what she needed in a man, exactly what she wanted in one!

Back in the kitchen Michael filled the bowls with steaming chili and placed them on the tray, along with a pack of saltine crackers. After pouring two glasses of iced lemonade, he carried the tray to the bedroom, hoping the balloons wouldn't pop from the chili's rising heat.

She laughed. Just as he'd hoped, Erika was delighted by his artistic creations. "Oh, Michael, you're so thoughtful. I feel like a silly teenager."

He grinned. "I feel like one, too." Michael set the tray on the nightstand and put the *Mahogany* movie into the VCR.

Settling himself in the bed, he reached for the tray and placed it over their laps. Picking up the remote control, he flipped on the VCR. They watched as the previews rolled. Reaching for a spoon, he dipped it into the steaming chili and held it up to Erika's mouth. Their eyes locked in an impassioned embrace as he fed her and then himself from the same bowl. She sipped the lemonade while he held the glass for her.

When she said that she'd had enough of everything, he set the tray aside.

He lowered her head against his chest. "Are you sure you've had enough of everything?"

Clearly understanding his underlying meaning, she pouted seductively with her lower lip. "Stick around and you just might find out," she responded cheekily, deliberately turning her attention to the movie.

Erika and Michael laughed at the parts of the movie that were funny, and while Michael held her close, Erika cried through the parts that touched her deeply. She was a sentimental jerk, she thought, and she couldn't help herself—any more than Michael could keep himself from falling in love with her and who she was. When the movie was over, he dreaded the time when she'd ask to be taken home, but Erika wasn't thinking about home at that moment. Her eyes were so heavy she had no choice but to give in to the sleep strongly forcing itself on her.

As she scooted herself farther down in the bed and rested her head on his bare stomach, he sighed contentedly. Reaching out to remove her hair from the restraints of the polka-dot hair-wrap, he stroked her hair until he felt the evenness of her breathing fanning across the hair on his stomach. Resting his hand on the side of her lovely café au lait face, he watched her as she slept.

Michael couldn't take his eyes off the gorgeous woman whose shiny hair was splayed across his stomach. As he thought about what she'd come to mean to him, he wondered if they'd rushed things. Yes, he knew that she'd wanted him as much as he wanted her, he told himself, but he still had to wonder. Whatever was going to happen, he thought, they had from now until she awakened. Right now, that was enough for him.

It was nearly two A.M. when Michael became worried about the lateness of the hour. As far as he was concerned, she could sleep all night, right there by his side, but he wasn't sure if that was her intention. When he shook her gently, she cried out, bolting upright in the bed.

He gathered her to him. "What is it, sweetheart?" he urged softly.

It took her several minutes to realize where she was. "Oh, Michael, I'm sorry if I startled you. I'm afraid I was dreaming about the house. I'm worried about being able to sell it."

Tears began to stream from her eyes as she thought about all the debt she'd incurred and the precarious situation she'd placed herself in with Randy Mills. She couldn't help wondering if Randy was going to expect something other than monthly payments from her.

He somehow felt her inner turmoil. "Don't cry, gorgeous," Michael pleaded. "Remind me not to give you any more chili before you go to sleep," he teased, trying to lighten her mood.

She laughed softly. "What time is it, Michael?"

"It's ten minutes after two. You were sleeping so well I didn't want to disturb you, but I decided I should since we hadn't discussed you spending the night."

She looked up at him. "Do . . . you . . . want me to go back to the city, Michael?"

He kissed her on the mouth. "I want you right here where you are. I'll take you home in the morning. Okay?"

She nodded. "I'd like to have the alarm set for five-thirty." Cuddling up to him, she began to tell him all about the scheduled move.

Michael was happy that she had finally come to terms with moving her mother's things from the house. He sympathized with Erika for having to give up the house she'd grown up in, and he also understood the financial burden of keeping it. To say the least, he knew it was eventually going to be an emotional eruption for her.

"Would you like me to be there when the furnishings are moved, Erika? It might make it easier for you."

She pondered his request. "Maybe I should do this alone.

I've got to make peace with it sooner or later. But you being there for me is a comforting thought."

He tenderly brushed her hair back from her face. "Let's do this, then. I'll make my rounds first. Then I'll come over to the house to see how things are going. If everything is going okay for you, I'll just leave. If not, I'll be there for you. Besides, I need to keep my eye on your moving man," he teased. "He seems smitten with you."

Tears sprang to her eyes. Michael was so darn sweet and thoughtful. She couldn't believe her luck in finding him, especially at a time when her life was so bleak and full of dark uncertainties. Was he an answer to a prayer? Was he really as genuine as he seemed? She was still so stunned by his total lack of arrogance.

She kissed his cheek. "Michael, I like who and what you are. It'll be a blessing to have you to turn to after the move."

He kissed her back. "I'll do anything I can to make things easier for you and your aunt. I know about losing a loved one. Tamala wasn't my daughter, but I couldn't have loved her more. We need to find time to do some of the things with Aunt Arlene that she and your mother used to do together. I know it won't be the same, but it'll keep her from feeling alone. Together, we'll help save her from boredom."

"I hope so. I'm looking forward to us spending a lot of time together. We can still do all the things we did together when mother was alive." Erika bit down on her lower lip. "Michael, I just might need you to help me with something that's become awfully important to me."

He rolled up on his side. "Let's hear it, gorgeous."

Erika took a minute to think about how she could use him to put her plan into action. "I'm trying to come up with some ideas on how to educate our people about pernicious anemia and other important health care issues. A lot of people have never even heard of the disease. I think it's also important for the elderly to learn preventive medicine techniques. It would be a great benefit to seniors in the black communities. Certain statistics prove that, compared to other races, blacks are more likely to receive inferior medical care. We also have to take into consideration how disproportionate the economic factors are between the different groups. I'm beginning to feel it's my duty to help bring about a change, or at least try. Can I count on your support?"

He was impressed by her willingness to help others. "A one-woman crusade, huh? You know you can count on me. Have you come up with any ideas?"

"Many. What do you think about getting the hospital to let us do free screenings for pernicious anemia of those who live in the community? We could also do a series of free health lectures. I'm sure there are many doctors who would love to be involved in such a worthwhile project. Before the lectures, we could serve the people who attend a meal at a reduced rate."

He seriously thought about her suggestions, already knowing they were good ones. But would the university hospital board of directors think the same way? "You have great ideas, Erika, but I'm not sure you're going to get the type of backing you want. The board's way of thinking is still somewhat antiquated."

She smiled lazily. "That's where you come in," she said hopefully. "You could make the presentation. I think they'll be more likely to listen to someone of your status. You're highly respected, you know," she praised knowingly, hoping to sway his decision. "Me, I don't stand a chance with the hospital board."

Knowing she'd set him up like a clay pigeon, he smiled. He was putty in Erika's hands, but he wasn't going to concede so easily. "Don't go underestimating yourself. This may sound sexist, but those old fogies are hardly immune to a beautiful face. When they get a glimpse of the extraordinary mind behind the gorgeous face, I don't think you'll have any problems convincing them. I am willing to help out, but only if we meet with them together. Deal?"

Erika threw her arms around his neck. "Deal!"

Not that she thought she had to, but to show her appreciation of his kindness and goodness Erika wrapped herself around him. In response to his earlier question, she showed him that she indeed hadn't had enough of everything.

Michael's heart raced as she molded herself against him. This time the pace of their lovemaking was much slower, less frantic, but the eager anticipation and the exquisite intensity remained the same. Knowing she'd be there all night afforded him the opportunity to explore her intimacy more thoroughly, without worrying about time. In this case, time was no longer of the essence. Erika was all his for the rest of the night, and he was all hers. He hoped no emergency would change that.

Molded tightly together, they began an impassioned journey, a journey they both foolishly hoped would never end. Erika felt as hot as before, and Michael was a human inferno. While thrashing wildly about in the huge bed, they found exotic pleasures in loving each other with all the passion that burned inside of them.

They'd made love on the floor in front of the fireplace, and now the massive bedroom had become their erotic haven. A fire burned in the fireplace in the bedroom, too, but they were too busy kindling their own roaring fires to pay it any attention. Heat came from everywhere, but they were lost to the thrilling, fiery sensations racing at breakneck speed through their nude bodies.

An eternity later, as they exploded together in a diamond-shattering climax, they felt the earth rotating on its axis.

The drive into the city was an amicable, quiet one. Erika was lost in her thoughts about the move and all the chaos sure to accompany it. Michael reflected on all he'd shared with Erika, hoping they'd share so much more, feeling they were good together and good for each other. Erika allowed him to relax, and he could be exactly who he was with her. So many other women had been so in awe of his profession that they'd treated him as though he were some type of god, always making him feel as though he was on display for their friends and families.

While he'd also dated other female physicians, they turned out to be worse than most. They'd made him feel like a prized trophy instead of a human being. Some doctors felt that marrying another doctor was the socially correct thing to do, and it didn't seem to matter to them whether love was involved or not. It was all about prestige for some. But Michael wasn't interested in any of that, and he sensed that Erika wasn't, either, which was another reason she so intrigued him.

As they turned onto the street where her dorm apartment was located, Erika looked over at Michael. She missed him already. How could that be? He sat only a few inches from her and he'd promised to be there, whenever she needed him. But she didn't want to be away from him for a measly second; she was that much in love with the good Dr. Michael Mathis. Feeling like a silly teenager with totally unmanageable hormones, she felt tears begin to spill fast and furiously.

Seeing her tears and heaving shoulders, Michael quickly maneuvered the Pathfinder into a tight parking space and cut the engine. Leaning across the console, he gathered her into his arms. "Shh, sweetheart, crying is only going to make you feel worse. Maybe it's not going to be as bad as you think. My offer to stay with you is still open. All you have to do is say the word," he soothed, handing her a tan checkered handkerchief.

Taking the handkerchief, Erika wiped her eyes. So many things passed through her head that she felt as though her brain suffered from whiplash. "Thanks, Michael." She sniffled. "But I still think I have to do this alone. I have to come to terms with this entire ordeal." She rested her trembling hand on his thigh. "I need to stop focusing so much on my feelings. I've tried to tell myself that I have to do this, but it does nothing to dispel the anguish I feel over parting with my home.

I know the house hasn't been sold yet and there are times when I'm not sure it'll sell at all, but it feels as if a large part of me is being ripped away. For some reason that terrifies me."

He kissed her forehead. "It's okay to feel terrified, Erika. This is a tough situation for you. Just remember that I'm going to be here for you. That's a promise."

Before getting out of the car, Erika leaned into him, spreading her fingers through his silky, maple brown waves. "I will keep your promise close to my heart." She kissed him softly on the mouth. "See you in a little while?"

He tossed her a heartwarming smile. "You bet, gorgeous. If I'm not there by the time everything is out of the house, page me. Okay? Good luck, Erika."

Erika nodded and kissed him again. Before she was able to get out of the car, he was there to open her door. He escorted her to the dorm entrance. As she was about to enter, he kissed her deeply and walked the short distance back to his car. When he turned to give her an encouraging smile, she waved and smiled back.

The apartment was just the way she'd left it. The ironing board was still up in the living room; thank goodness she'd pulled the plug on the iron, she thought. After folding the board, Erika stored it in the broom closet. Wrapping the cord around the iron, she placed it in the cabinet under the kitchen sink. Walking back to the bedroom, Erika opened a dresser drawer and pulled out a faded pair of blue jeans and held them up. Who in the world purchased brand-new jeans with the knees and the front and back of the thigh areas slashed to ribbons? "Lorraine Poole," Erika said, remembering that the very generous redhead had given them to her.

Shaking her head, Erika laughed as she pulled a nicely tailored, oversize, light blue denim shirt from the closet. Quickly, she stripped off the clothes she'd worn the previous evening, tossed them on the bed, and dressed in the outfit she'd removed from the closet.

The shirt wasn't long enough to hide the designer slashes, she noticed right off. She actually blushed when she saw her exposed flesh through the slightly seductive slits. "Now these are what I call comfortable working duds," she remarked, surveying her tattered image in the mirror. "Oh, well, if nothing else, I'm fashionable."

Once she'd locked the apartment, Erika took the stairs instead of the elevator down to the first level. Tossing the denim jacket around her shoulders, she rushed out to the parking lot, where she got into her Toyota, praying that the engine wouldn't stall out again.

As she pulled into the driveway of the family home, Randy was just edging his small van up to the curb. Right behind him was an extremely large moving van. After the driver of the van parked, four muscle-bound men leaped out of the back. The two men in the cab emerged and walked over to Randy.

It looked to her as though Randy was holding a small meeting with his employees, and she stood by patiently waiting for her chance to speak with him. A few minutes later, smiling, Randy looked over at Erika and summoned her to the small group meeting.

"Good morning, Dr. Edmonds," he greeted, his tone very professional. "Looks like we're right on schedule." Erika smiled as she nodded. "If you don't have any objections, I'd like you to park your car on the street. We're going to back the van into the driveway to save us a heap of unnecessary steps, especially when we're removing the heavier items," he explained, flashing her a bright smile.

"No problem." Erika turned back toward her car.

"Wait a minute, Eri—Dr. Edmonds. I want you to meet my crew. This is Todd," he said, pointing to the largest of his employees. "Steve, Clarence and Thomas," he added, presenting each man with a slight hand gesture.

"These are the best of all my guys," he continued. "They're hard workers who believe in getting the job done, expeditiously, but they require plenty of liquids. Think you could brew up some coffee for us? We have plenty of mineral water and soft drinks stored in the cooler in the back of the van."

Her smile was softly innocent and welcoming. "It would be my pleasure. Let me move my car, and then I'll make the coffee. Here," she said, handing Randy the keys to the house, which were separate from her car keys. "You all can go inside and get started. It's pretty nippy out here," she offered with a full, dimpled smile.

Before going to her car, she took special note of the powder-blue, short-sleeved work shirts the crew wore. Each shirt was personalized with a first name over the right pocket. "Mills Incorporated" was embroidered on the left side. Navy-blue pants and black, steel-toed boots completed the company uniforms.

Putting the car in reverse, Erika backed out of the driveway and recklessly swung into a curbside parking space, astonishing the two men who hadn't yet made their way into the house. Laughing at their stunned expressions, Erika shrugged her shoulders. She then got out of the car and locked the doors. As she strolled toward the front door, she couldn't stop herself from looking all around the area, which she would always think of as home. Wiping fallen tears away with the sleeve of her jacket, Erika entered the house and walked straight through to the kitchen. Believing coffee would stay fresher longer, Vernice had always kept the ground coffee in the refrigerator—the same place Erika now kept it.

Only a short time elapsed before Erika called the workmen into the kitchen for freshly brewed coffee. Not a real genius with the fancy new coffeemakers, Erika hoped she hadn't made it too weak, or too strong. As the guys trooped into the kitchen, she began to pour the coffee into large Styrofoam cups.

When Randy lifted his cup and said, "Just right, Dr. Edmonds," Erika let her concerns fly free. The other men seemed to be enjoying the hot brew just as much as Randy.

At a loss for what to do, Erika wandered around the large house, looking at everything she already knew by heart. If she went blind, she'd still be able to find her way around the old place, she thought warmly. Seeing the furniture being carried out brought her no comfort, so she slipped out the back door.

She brushed the snow from the porch swing before sitting down. Allowing her eyes to reacquaint themselves with different delights of the backyard—the vegetable and flower gardens, two large maples and a stately buckeye tree, all of which were now barren—Erika remembered the conversation she'd had with Vernice after she'd picked her up from the doctor's office on the day Michael had spoken about several nights ago. When Michael mentioned he'd met her mother, she'd forgotten about the conversation.

Vernice's statements astonished Erika as she recalled them: *"Erika, when I first saw this young man, I could only wish that you were there to see him, too. He was so handsome and so genuine. I was amazed to find out that he was a doctor."* Erika'd had no idea who the young man was. Her mother hadn't known his name.

Amazed at how her mother had always managed to remember things about the opposite sex, even when her memory was at its worst, Erika smiled. Michael must have had a profound effect on her that day, Erika speculated, which had made it important for Vernice to remember everything about him.

"I hope you can meet him one day," Vernice had continued, smiling sweetly. *"I just know that he's something special. His spirit spoke to me in a quiet way, much like your dad's did the day I first met him."*

As she was warmed by the thought that her mother had approved of her Michael long before she herself had even met him, Erika's deeply dimpled smile competed with the sun's bright rays. But as she thought about the conversation between her and Vernice, she still found it hard to believe. Vernice had actually picked out the man she'd eventually fall in love with. And it had occurred before Erika ever came to know Michael on a personal level, though she'd heard of his professional accomplishments. The whole thing was uncanny.

Then, as she thought about what was taking place in the house, she trembled. As she pulled her jacket snugly around her, she could feel her somewhat composed demeanor beginning to fall apart. She fought the urge to dissolve into tears, and told herself to be optimistic.

Maybe it's not going to be so bad, after all, she told herself. But it was more than just moving her mother's things, more than selling the house, she told herself as she grew highly agitated. It wasn't about any of that, she surmised sadly. It was her finances.

If only she could take on a part-time job, she just might be able to get herself out of this financial bind. *Don't go setting yourself up for disappointment,* she thought. She had no extra time, not if she was going to finish her residency.

"You are in financial ruin, sister. You have no one to blame but yourself."

The house was almost completely empty, with the exception of a file cabinet she was going to take to her place and a few other odds and ends. She could now see how large the place was, how difficult it would be for one person to take care of it alone.

Even though she'd helped Vernice with the cleaning and the basic upkeep, she now understood that tending to this house had been more than a notion. When Vernice had taken ill, Erika'd had a hard time convincing her that her health would no longer permit her to care for the place. Then, when Vernice started wandering off and getting into cars with strangers, Erika'd had to do what she thought was best at the time. Yet the guilt of that decision still plagued her night and day.

Yes, she thought, as she continued her walk through the house, within these four walls were invaluable memories,

memories she would always carry in her heart. There was no reason she couldn't let go of the house and still retain all the loving memories the family home had provided her with. Her security didn't have to be compromised. Her security had come from two loving parents, not from a lifeless structure that only came alive because of the family that had occupied it.

Yes, Anthony and Vernice were deceased, she told herself, but their memory didn't have to be left behind with the house. They would always be with her. No matter what, her memories could never be taken away. Through her heart and mind, Anthony and Vernice would always be part of her life, along with numerous family pictures.

Erika started to realize that giving up the house was not such a bad thing, after all. Yet it still hurt. Once it was sold, a new family would fill its interior with warm love and joyous laughter, the same kind of love and laughter her family had reveled in. There had been bad times, too, but the good times had far outweighed the bad. It would be selfish of her to try to hold on to a place where laughter no longer abounded, a place devoid of a whole family like the one she'd been fortunate enough to have all of her life.

Deciding to tuck away her memories for safekeeping, knowing she could summon them whenever she desired, Erika left the back of the house, feeling confident that she could successfully let go. Let go and let God.

When she walked to the front of the house, Randy had just come through the front door.

"Oh, there you are," he remarked. "What happened to you? You suddenly disappeared."

Involuntarily, her lashes hooded her eyes, as though they tried to shield her vulnerability from Randy's probing gaze. "Just having a last-minute rendezvous with some very special memories," she said, unable to keep her emotions out of her response. As Randy slipped his arms around Erika and pulled her too close for comfort, Michael had just started down the hallway.

Confused, Erika hadn't seen Michael, yet she felt his torturous gasp rip right through her own lungs. Recognizing her confused state of mind, Michael slipped forward to make his presence known.

Cursing himself for doing something so utterly foolish, Randy let his arms immediately fall away from Erika and drop to his sides. Mumbling under his breath something that Erika didn't catch, Randy skulked off, leaving her feeling a bit more bewildered.

As she turned to Michael, he tossed her one of his infectious smiles. Eagerly, she smiled back, wondering how long he'd been there and how much he'd seen. Randy had only offered her a comforting shoulder, and she hoped Michael saw it for what it was.

Michael greeted her with a tender kiss. "Progress has certainly been achieved within these four walls. I can't believe the movers are actually finished." He looked deeply into her eyes. "Feeling any better about things?"

Glad that he wasn't going to make an issue of Randy's innocent offer of comfort, she looped her arm through his. "Much better. I've been so silly where selling this house is concerned. I realize now that I'm not selling my memories, just the house they were built in. My memories are my own, vividly beautiful ones that are forever mine." If what she'd been saying was true, then why did she feel like crying her eyes out? She didn't want to cry in front of Michael. Desperately trying to ward off mounting tears, she clutched at his arm, allowing him to lead her to the front door.

Erika suddenly felt as if she might pass out. As cold as it was outside, she felt as if she were in a blazing furnace. Her palms were sweaty, and it felt as though white-hot flames had burst loose in and around her heart. She moaned. "Michael, I don't feel very well." Everything around her grew fuzzy, then very dark.

Due to the wan coloring Erika's skin had rapidly taken on, Michael had already anticipated the possibility of a fainting spell. As Erika slumped against him, he gently lifted her and carried her over to the car, where he carefully deposited her in the passenger seat. Lowering the seat back into a prone position, he hurried to the trunk of the car. Opening it, he took out his medical bag and groped inside for a blood pressure cuff and a stethoscope. Quickly, he returned to Erika and took her blood pressure and pulse.

At more than one hundred beats per minute, the pulse was abnormal, but when he listened to her heart he could tell that her pulse rate had begun to calm down. He was pretty sure all the moving excitement was responsible for her sudden illness, but he thought he should take her to the emergency room, anyway.

Erika stirred, slowly opening her eyes. "I'm okay, Michael. It's just emotional stress. I want to go home now."

Michael tenderly cradled her face in his palms. "I think I should take you to the hospital. You should be checked out just to make sure that everything is okay."

She shook her head gingerly. "No. It's not necessary. Sometimes this happens to me when I'm under extreme emotional stress. Can I go home, please?"

Michael was still concerned, but he thought it would be best to comply with her wish. "I'm going to take you home, Erika, but after I run an important errand I'm coming back to check on you. Would that be okay?" When she agreed to his request, he put his medical gear in the trunk and then settled himself in the driver's seat.

Erika's apartment wasn't that far away from the family home, so Michael was able to get her there quickly. She said that she could make it into the building by herself, but—aware that she could have another anxiety attack—Michael wasn't about to take any chances.

Michael rather suspected that Erika was more emotionally fragile than she knew, and he planned to be around to help her get through this tough time. Why was he so attracted to vulnerable women? Stephanie had also been very vulnerable.

Was there a void inside him that could be filled only by championing women in emotional turmoil? He'd always been a champion of the underdog. Helping people was his main reason for becoming a doctor. He was a nurturing soul and would lend support even to an enemy.

He'd mistaken his feelings for Stephanie, who'd needed a lot of nurturing. Was he now making the same mistake with Erika? Michael had to admit to himself that he'd sensed a deep sadness in Erika the minute he'd first laid eyes on her, but there was so much more about her that he'd found himself attracted to. Besides her gorgeous face, Michael believed that Erika possessed a real soul and a heart of gold. Yes, she was vulnerable, as Stephanie had been. But Erika Edmonds was a woman that he couldn't stop himself from falling in love with, nor did he want to fight the sensational feelings that came with it. Whatever was happening to him, he was going to enjoy it to the fullest extent, he promised himself as he walked her to the door of her apartment.

Eight

It was only a little after ten A.M, but Erika was so weary she felt as if the entire day had already passed her by. Seeing how tired she looked, Michael encouraged her to lie down until he returned from his business appointment. Once inside the bedroom, he helped her out of her clothes and into a loose nightshirt. Covering her up, he sat on the side of the bed.

Michael nibbled lovingly at Erika's ear, combing through her hair with his fingers. "You going to be okay until I get back?"

Lifting her head from the pillow, she placed it in his lap. "Yes. I just need to close off my mind for a short time. It's exhausted."

"I know, gorgeous," he sympathized. Lowering his head until his lips met hers, he brushed his mouth across the fullness of hers. "Mmm," he moaned softly, "you're so deliciously sweet, Erika."

His touch caused her inner needs to rise. Pulling his face closer to hers, she ran her tongue across his lips, causing his manhood to strain against the crotch of his denim jeans. Their need for each other was so strong it was overpowering. Without giving it a minute's thought Michael quickly undressed and slipped between the cool sheets with Erika—exactly what she'd been hoping for.

As his fingers made contact with her inner core, he could feel the scorching heat of her passion. She already felt hot and slick with moisture, which let him know how much she really wanted him. Her readiness and his growing need for her were nearly Michael's undoing. His fingers teased and manipulated her inner sanctuary, causing her to writhe from the sweet ecstasy his touch produced.

Wanting him to feel the same ecstasy that nearly drove her insane, Erika slid her slightly closed hand up and down his rigid shaft, gently rubbing her thumb across the smoothness of its crown. "Does this feel good, Michael?" He moaned. "What about this?" she asked, drawing circles around his manhood with the tips of her fingernails. His moans were muffled, but his body language told her of the pleasure he received.

Red-hot shocks of pleasure rolled through their bodies. As Michael's tongue flicked in and out of her heat, wave after wave of ecstasy quickly drove Erika into an uncontrollable frenzy. Erika really wanted to taste him, too, but she was much too shy to initiate that type of provocative intimacy, especially without any prompting from her mate.

Once the protection was in place he blanketed her with his body. Michael entered her with slow, sweet deliberation, his erotic movements full of purpose. Hoping to leave an indelible memory deeply imbedded in her soul, he wanted to captivate her entire being. Michael wanted all of Erika's love and was willing to do whatever it took to win her heart. Little did he know that she wanted no less from him. From the moment they'd first made love, Erika knew she'd never want to share herself with anyone else. Her heart was already exclusively his.

Michael tenderly immersed himself deep in her inner sanctum. "Let me love all of you, Erika?" he pleaded. "I want to love you until all my strength is depleted."

Tangling her fingers in his hair, she tightened her legs around his waist. "Yes, Michael. Love me, Michael," she urged breathlessly, rising up to meet him. So close to a climax, Erika discovered that she could barely breathe from the anticipation of falling off the edge.

Michael wasn't in any better shape. His maleness was ready to experience the dynamic blowout he knew Erika was capable of causing. Before he could have another thought Erika's reckless movements beneath him caused him to involuntarily match the wild rhythms of her shuddering body.

As he undertook the challenge she presented, along with his own need to satiate her, he ground into her with a tender but constant force, making her body jerk and tremble. As his own heat mingled with hers, he pounded into her with the most tender and sweetest fury. Nothing short of exotic and exquisite pleasures coursed through them, turning them into quivering masses of languid jelly.

Panting loudly, he rolled away from her and pulled her on top of him. "What am I going to do with you, gorgeous? As the teenagers would say, you have me whipped, girl! But it's the most sensuous whipping I've ever had," he teased lightly, rubbing his nose back and forth against hers. Hungry for the taste of her sweet mouth, he satiated his voracious appetite.

With a sudden feeling of shame taking hold of her, Erika buried her face in Michael's chest. She wasn't sure what Michael thought of her willingness to sleep with him so quickly—not once but twice—nor did she know how to tell him what bothered her.

When he tried to lift her head to make eye contact with her, she resisted, making him suspect that something wasn't quite right. "Hey," he whispered, "what's going on with you?" he asked, attempting to lift her head again.

Keeping her head on his chest, she turned it toward him. "I hope I haven't given you the wrong impression of me. I'm not a promiscuous woman, Michael. But you do have a way of making me want to do the unthinkable. There's nothing casual in my making love to you. I do care deeply for you, Michael. And if my confession scares you off, then so be it, but I'm not taking it back."

Michael gently stroked her hair, finding it difficult not to shout out the joy he felt at her remarks. Refusing to allow her to look away from him, he rolled her onto her back. His hazel eyes pierced her soul. "Erika, you have definitely made an impression on me. I care just as deeply for you. There are no negative connotations attached to us giving ourselves to each other. It's something we both wanted. Are you finding it hard to respect me since I gave myself to you so freely?"

Erika was genuinely astounded by his question. "Of course not! It's usually not the woman who loses respect in these situations. Michael, I'd never disrespect you because we chose to make love. That's a guy thing."

He lifted her chin. "I know, but the disrespect issue should cut both ways. I haven't known you any longer than you've known me, so that puts us on a level playing field." He sighed. "Erika, all I'm trying to get you to see is that I'm not like the men who get what they want and then put the woman down. This is no casual thing for me, either. I respect you as much now as I did before we first made love. I'll continue to respect you. You're a highly respectable woman. I'm a highly respectable man. We made love to each other because it was what we both wanted. No more, and no less." He ended on a deep sigh.

Erika grinned from ear to ear. "You are something special, Michael! Just like my mother said. Her husband, my stepfather, was something special, too. Thanks for sharing your enlightening views on this sensitive issue."

She wanted to tell him that she made love to him because she loved him, but she decided she'd like to keep it to herself until she got used to the idea. Besides, she wanted to say it at a time when she thought it would carry the most weight. Maybe during their next very special time, she thought, sure there was going to be a next time.

Remembering what Erika had told him Vernice had said about him, Michael smiled broadly, looking totally bewildered. Shifting his weight, he propped himself on one elbow. "I can't stop thinking about what your mother said about me, Erika. Are you sure she'd approve of me?"

Erika rolled up onto her side and moved her arm across his bare stomach. "Yes, she would. I didn't know who she was talking about when she told me she thought you were very special. As I've already told you, I didn't even remember our conversation when you told me you thought you'd met her. She'd be ecstatic to know that you and I are seeing each other. Michael, both my parents would definitely approve of our relationship. I'm sure they're sharing in my joy," Erika said, close to tears.

Michael was flattered and pleased. "That makes me feel good, Erika. I'm glad they'd approve. Speaking of our relationship, gorgeous, do you think that I can have exclusive rights to your company?" Her eyes grew rather large. "What I'm trying to say here is that I want mine to be the only male name penned in your social calendar."

Erika blinked hard, trying to fight the tears. "Well, I don't know," she said. "I have a lot of male friends, and we do go out from time to time, but there's no intimacy involved." She thought about all the male friends she did have, and she couldn't imagine giving any of them up. *Except for Marlon Hale,* she thought, laughing inwardly. And she wouldn't even give that X-rated comedian the boot.

He shook his head from side to side. "I don't want to cut you off from any of your friends—male or female. I just want to be the only one that you kiss and hug, among other sweet intimacies," he suggested, still not sure he had the right to ask her to be exclusively his. He squeezed her hand. "I want to be one of your best friends, but your only lover, Dr. Erika Edmonds. Am I asking for too much?"

Erika couldn't help smiling all over. He didn't want anything that she didn't want. "Why didn't you just say that in the first place? It's a done deal, honey," she drawled lazily. She crushed her mouth over his, sealing the vow she'd just made to him. "One more thing. Do these exclusive rights cut both ways? Are you going to be exclusively mine?"

He hugged her tightly. "Absolutely and irrevocably," he exclaimed, sincere and full of promise. Both vows were sealed with another staggering kiss.

The timing was all wrong for him to speak about leaving, but he knew he had to go. He had to pick up some information for a lecture series Richard Glover was going to present to his pediatric AIDS research group. A strong supporter of AIDS research, Richard was always there to offer his assistance to those who needed it.

Michael gently gripped her waist, pulling her in closer to him. "Listen, I know the timing sucks, but I've got to get to my appointment." He glanced at the time on the clock radio. "My attorney's only going to be in his office until one o'clock. I should've been there long ago. Am I still welcome to come back here after my appointment?"

Nodding, she smiled. "I'll be counting the seconds."

"Good! Now you lie here and get some rest. I'm going to clean up in the bathroom. Then I'm out of here." He kissed her deeply.

Jumping out of bed, he gathered his clothes from the floor and dashed into the adjoining bathroom. Erika scooted over to the center of the bed, placed a pillow behind her head, and hugged another one to her chest. With all the blankets on the bed, why did it suddenly feel so cold? She knew the answer. Michael had kept her warm with his passion and his steaming-hot body. The fire in his touch was hot enough to burn the entire building down, she thought, laughing inwardly. Knowing that Michael cared for her as much as she cared for him warmed her all over again. Her arresting thoughts were disrupted when he reappeared.

He leaned over to claim her lips. "Keep the home fires burning for me, gorgeous," he requested, taking off before she could respond.

As the doorlatch caught, she buried her head in the pillow and cried. Even though she had come to terms with selling the house, moving everything out had been as bad as she had anticipated. If she'd been a little more optimistic, maybe she wouldn't feel so poorly now. She had allowed negativity in, and look what had occurred.

Erika usually addressed her pain, gave voice to it, allowed herself to feel it, and then moved on. But now she seemed to be stuck in one place, the same place she'd been in when she'd first placed her mother at Golden Age Retirement Center. She'd only gotten deeper in the mire after her mother's death. Guilt, shock, disbelief and denial were all the places she visited every single day—day in, day out. As the tears dried on her cheeks, Erika's turbulent thoughts grew silent. Finally, she slipped into a badly needed, long-overdue peaceful rest.

Michael entered the high-rise building located in the heart of downtown Pittsburgh, slipping into the elevator that would take him to the seventeenth floor. As he leaned against the metal railing, his mouth turned up in a huge smile. Sweet thoughts of Erika were the reason for the bright smile and his effervescent mood. The woman was a miracle worker, he quietly reflected. And she had worked her miracles on every part of him, especially his heart.

Stuffing his hands deep into his pants pockets, he exited the elevator and walked to the end of the long corridor, where Richard Glover's office was located. Richard was in the reception area when Michael entered.

Smirking, Richard looked down at his watch. "You're almost a day late and a dollar short, pal, but glad you could make it. Another ten minutes, and I would've been out of here," Richard said, gesturing for Michael to follow him into his private office suite.

Although Michael had been in Richard's office on numerous occasions, he still marveled at the massiveness of the suite as he looked around to see if any changes had been made. Richard was always adding something new to his private space, but everything looked the same.

Gleaming mahogany furniture and brass accents graced the

large room. Mahogany bookshelves lined one entire wall, and were loaded with fine, leather-bound books. Smoked glass covered the top of the antique desk. In one corner of the room sat two burgundy leather sofas and four matching chairs.

Richard handed Michael a manila folder that held several typed sheets of paper. "Here's what you need for the programs. I've just about completed my writings for the lecture series. Once they're typed, I'll turn them over to you, as well. I'm really looking forward to holding this seminar for your research group."

Michael looked at the contents of the folder, which included a brief on Richard's personal and educational history, as well as his professional accomplishments. The information was needed before the secretary of the research team could have the seminar programs printed.

Richard was a highly respected attorney. His support of AIDS research and of those afflicted with the disease made him the perfect candidate to speak to the research team. He had also won several major law cases for AIDS victims who'd been discriminated against by their employers. His caseload had nearly doubled due to the widespread publicity that had come as a result of the nature of the cases and the large number of resounding victories.

Michael closed the folder and laid it on the dark mahogany coffee table, making himself comfortable in one of the leather chairs. He looked over at his friend, who poured coffee into ceramic mugs. "Your works are very impressive, man. I'm glad I asked you to do the lecture series. The group is going to love you."

Richard had a distant look in his spice-brown eyes, and it suddenly dawned on Michael that Richard hadn't heard a word he'd said. When the coffee overflowed from the cup, Michael's suspicions were confirmed. Richard's face bore a heavy scowl as he realized the mess he'd made. Looking embarrassed, he wiped up the spill in a hurry.

Michael saw that his friend's eyes still carried a blank stare, eyes that were normally lit with a gleeful twinkle. "What's up with you, bro?" Michael asked worriedly. "You seem to have something deep on your mind."

Richard snapped out of his preoccupation and focused his attention on Michael. He shook his head. "I've got something to tell you, man. It's pretty heavy." He crossed the room and handed Michael a cup of coffee. Instead of taking a seat, he stood over Michael. "It involves the woman you're currently seeing."

Michael jumped out of his seat and stood toe-to-toe with Richard. "Erika? You just met her. What could you possibly know about Erika that's so heavy?" Fearing what Richard might say, he prayed it wasn't something he'd be offended by.

Wearily, Richard dropped down on the sofa. "Have a seat, man. This could take quite a while."

Looking uncomfortable, Michael returned to his original seat. "Let's have it."

Crossing his legs, Richard took a long gulp of his coffee and looked directly at Michael. "I know more about Erika Edmonds than you think." Richard swallowed hard. "I happen to love the girl very much, Michael." Michael's jaw dropped and the tendons in his neck began to pop out. "I love her, Michael, because she's my sister." Richard's hands closed into tight fists as he struggled to appear unaffected.

Unable to believe what he'd just heard, Michael leaped out of his seat again. It had to be a lie or a bad joke. By her own admission, Erika was an only child. "That can't be, Richard. Erika doesn't have any siblings. Have you lost your mind, or what? We grew up together, remember? If what you're saying is true, why didn't you mention this when you saw me with her at the ballet?" Michael had another ten questions ready, but realized he needed to give his friend the chance to answer the ones already posed.

"Michael, it can be, and it is. Erika and I share the same father. Although I don't carry his last name, Anthony Edmonds was my biological father. My middle name is Anthony. Anthony was involved with my mother long before he knew Erika's mother. I didn't mention it to you at the ballet because the opportunity never presented itself. I was stunned to see you with her. You hadn't told me about her yet. I almost blew it when I said something about it finally being nice to meet her. She looked puzzled by that."

Once Michael assimilated the information, he began to laugh, realizing Richard had his facts confused. Apparently he didn't know that Anthony Edmonds was Erika's stepfather, who later adopted her. "Man, I can clear all this up for you. Anthony is Erika's stepfather, not her biological father, though he did adopt her. So you see, she's not your sister by blood," Michael explained carefully. "And she does know that her stepfather had a son."

Richard looked irritated as he got to his feet. "No," Richard thundered, *"you* see. Anthony is Erika's biological father. She just doesn't know it. No one bothered to tell her. I don't know all the facts surrounding her birth, but I do know that she's my sister. I wanted you to know it, too, before you got any notions about sleeping with her."

Michael was dumbfounded. A lightning bolt striking him couldn't have rendered him any less helpless. Pacing the floor like a caged animal, he knew how much this revelation could mess Erika up. He was positive that she didn't know any of this, that she didn't even have the slightest clue. She only knew that Anthony Edmonds had a son she'd never met.

When she spoke of Anthony, she sometimes used the term stepfather, he recalled. But she couldn't have loved Anthony any more if she'd known he was her biological father—which now appeared to be the case. This was going to be another cruel blow to her already damaged defense mechanisms. The news of Richard's birth father was just as shocking. Michael had always thought that Todd Glover was Richard's natural father.

"Michael, what I just told you can't ever leave this office. According to my father, Erika's mother was adamant about her never finding out. I don't know why. I promised my father that I'd never tell her as long as her mother was still alive." His eyes filled with disbelief, Michael looked at Richard as though he had two heads. "I need your word, Mikey," Richard pleaded, hoping he wasn't alienating his best friend.

Michael was at a loss for words, completely torn in two. How could he not tell Erika about what he'd learned? How could he keep something so important from her? Wasn't that betrayal? It seemed that the people she loved most had been too busy practicing desperate deceptions to stop and think about what it could do to her if she ever found out. He'd be guilty of the same thing if he chose to say nothing. Desperate deceptions were a distressing burden for the innocent to have to carry. Richard had just put him in the most precarious position he'd ever been in and he wished he hadn't.

Michael rubbed his hands across his forehead. "Ah, man, don't ask me to deceive Erika. This girl means so much to me, Richard. I'm in love with her, man." Michael could see that he'd shocked Richard. "She and I are so good together. How can I keep something like this from her? She has a right to know."

Richard wasn't impressed with Michael's confession. In fact, he was angry about it. Somehow he had equated Michael's love for Erika with sex. "Are you sleeping with my baby sister?" he asked pointedly, immediately going on the offensive. Seeing the murderous look in Michael's eyes, Richard balled up his fists, but he held them rigidly at his sides.

Michael shot him an unpleasant hand gesture, which was totally out of character for him. "That's none of your damn business, big brother. I love and respect Erika Edmonds very much. Let's just say her virtue is safe with me," Michael spat out angrily. "Don't you think that I'd ever be disrespectful to her, or intentionally hurt her in any way."

Regretting the unenviable position he'd placed his good friend in, Richard impatiently shoved his hand through his neatly cut hair. At the age of ten, when he'd moved to Philadelphia from Lebanon, Michael had been the first friend he'd made. He had moved to a new city, and had just gotten a new father. Things had been tough for him back then, but Michael's friendship had made moving to a strange place much easier to cope with.

Richard approached Michael cautiously, flinging his arm around his friend's shoulders. "Let's not get so angry here," he said, knowing he'd gone on the offense. "I had no right to question your integrity. I know you're a damn good man. I apologize. I shouldn't have said any of those things to you." Knowing they had to figure out what to do about this entire mess, which neither of them had created, both men sat down.

"Michael, man, I do need you to keep this secret—at least, until I can figure out how to handle this without causing too much trouble. I want to be a part of my sister's life. Can you do that for me? Just give me some time, man?"

Michael locked his fingers behind his head and pressed forward. "Oh, how I wish you hadn't told me any of this. I'm going to feel awful for every second that I have to practice the same desperate deceptions the others have. Did you know that Erika's mother died recently? That Erika's now faced with selling the family home? By the way, did you even know her mother?"

Stunned, Richard opened his eyes wide. "No, I didn't know about her mother or the house. I didn't know Vernice, but I talked to her on the phone a couple of times, after we'd moved back here from Philly. Our conversations were very brief. I didn't go to their house, because Vernice didn't want Erika to ask too many questions about me. My father always came to see me. Of course, had I gone there, they would've had to lie to Erika. But didn't they realize they'd already done that? They also lied to themselves. But my father loved Erika and would've loved for us to have gotten to know each other. His wife wouldn't permit it. There was something deeper going on there, but my father never revealed what it was."

Richard got up and walked over to his desk, where he retrieved a notepad. He returned to his seat on the sofa. "Tell me all about Erika. Then I want to know about what happened to her mother. I want to know everything you know, Michael. It's important to me to learn about my little sister. All communication about her was cut off when my father passed away. I need to know how she's doing, Mikey."

"Weren't you at your father's funeral? Why didn't you talk to Erika then?"

Richard put his head in his hands. "I can't begin to tell you how I felt the day I saw her at the funeral. My mother and I stayed completely in the background. We had no desire to cause Anthony's family any discomfort. Losing him was enough to deal with as it was. I felt pretty much the same way the night I saw her at the ballet with you. I knew it was Erika because my father used to send me pictures of her. But coming face-to-face with her evoked emotions that I can't even describe."

Unwittingly, Michael beamed with pride as he talked about Erika to Richard. When he gave blow-by-blow descriptions of how they'd met, how he'd quickly fallen for her, Richard smiled, admitting to himself that Michael cared deeply for his sister. He himself couldn't have chosen a better man for her.

Michael discussed everything he knew about Erika, but he kept all the intimate details of their relationship to himself. What he and Erika shared intimately was between them. No one else was entitled to know the details of their private affairs, not even big brothers or best friends. He saw that Richard already knew a lot about Erika through his father, but he seemed so eager to learn even more. Then the conversation turned from Erika to Vernice, before it shifted to include Aunt Arlene.

"That's incredible. It must have been fate. I can't believe you met Erika's mother long before you met her."

Michael grinned. "I find myself thinking about it all the time. I just have to believe we were meant to be. I found Vernice to be in high spirits that day. I sense that she had a heart of gold to go along with her spirit. Erika described her as a bit domineering and tough-skinned, but my guess is those characteristics were just a small part of who she really was. Erika said Vernice seemed to operate in a state of denial most of the time, which concerned her a lot. She feels guilty about placing her mother in a safe environment, but I think I can help her out with that issue. I'm going to work hard at it. She needs to understand she had no alternative."

Michael then talked about Erika's nearly destitute financial situation and the new expenses she'd recently incurred with the moving company.

Richard found Erika's situation startling. "I find it hard to believe that in this day and age Erika doesn't have a telephone!"

"I don't think I need to remind you of the financial struggles we had while we were fighting our way through medical and law school, Richard. It was hard as hell."

"I'll concede that one to you, pal. But why is she selling the house? Why doesn't she move out of the dorm and back home if money's so tight? That seems like an answer to both problems."

"It's so much more convenient for her to live on campus, because of the hours she has to put in at the hospital," Michael explained. "Her pride won't allow her to accept outside help, mainly from me."

By the time Michael finished filling Richard in on the life of his sister, Richard's mind was turning like a spinning wheel. It hurt him to know his sister lived on such a limited income. He didn't understand why she had to. He thought their father had made sure that Erika's future would be financially secure. There should've been an insurance policy on Anthony listing Erika as the sole beneficiary. Anthony had told him he'd been paying the premiums on a policy for her, just as he'd done for him. At the request of Anthony, Richard's mother had kept his policy in her possession. But where was Erika's? Or had she already used up the money?

Knowing the name of the agent who'd issued the policies, Richard made a written note to check into the one Erika should've received. Mackenzie Bailey should be able to easily clear up this matter. He would know if the policy had been cashed in. Richard was determined that his sister's needs would be met, come hell or high water. He would see that she had sufficient money. No sister of his was going to be left destitute.

Erika awakened, feeling better than she'd felt before her nap. As she hugged the pillow to her, she could smell the lingering scent of Michael's sandalwood cologne. Hugging the pillow even more tightly, she deeply inhaled the sexy scent of Michael, which was mixed in with the sandalwood. A few strands of his wavy hair were scattered about on the sheet. She laughed, wondering if she'd tugged at his hair hard enough to dislodge it from his head. She certainly remembered tangling her fingers in its thickness and tugging on it when his exquisite strokes had delved deeply and wildly into her liquid heat. Their lovemaking had surely rocked the foundation of the building she lived in. Trembling with longing, the sweet memory of their earth-shattering climax came to mind, making her drunk with desire.

Getting out of bed, she walked over to the small desk, where she picked up the stack of monthly bills that hadn't yet been paid. Pulling out the straight-back chair, she sat down and pulled a calculator out of the center desk drawer. As she took out the bills, one at a time, she entered the amounts due into the calculator. After comparing the total amount due against what she had left in the bank, she knew she was in big trouble. She was three hundred dollars short of what was actually needed to cover all the monthly bills, including the moving expenses.

But how could that be? she thought, fearful, pulling out her checkbook. Flipping through all the entries on the ledger, she spotted the problem. Two hundred ninety-eight dollars were paid to Smitty's Garage for car repairs. When she'd calculated the figures, before she'd given the first installment check to Randy Mills, she hadn't included the car repair.

Erika looked through all the bills again to see where she might be able to cut down a little on payments, but no matter how she crunched the numbers she still came up short. Even if she used the money that Aunt Arlene had given her for the new dress, she'd still be deficient—and without a phone. Thank God she hadn't had the time to have the phone installed.

The money that was once in Vernice's savings account had all been used for the funeral. Before that, she'd used some of the money to keep the equity loan payments right on schedule, not to mention what she'd used for emergencies. A large part of Erika's stipend went for her rent at the dormitory. Was she going to have to move back home? She'd agreed to list the house for six months—it had only been on the market for two. She couldn't remember what the penalty would be, if any, if she were to take it off the market prior to the contracted time length. She made a note to check it out.

Moving out of the dorm was the last thing she wanted to do, but it might be the only option. Practically living inside the hospital was not only convenient—it was almost a necessity, especially when she had to work all night. But moving out would sure beat dropping out of the residency program. Was she just creating reasons to hold on to the house?

Nine

A familiar knock sounded on the door and Erika's cheeks became infused with color. She didn't want Lorraine to see her in nightclothes at this hour of the day. Besides, she hadn't showered since her last rendezvous with Michael. His natural body odor mingled with her own scents were loud enough to shout to the world their delicious sins. A plan suddenly came to mind, and Erika rushed into the bathroom and turned on the shower. Dashing to the door, she let Lorraine in. Before Lorraine could utter a word, Erika was off and running.

Lorraine laughed as she entered the apartment. Amused, she wondered what that was all about. Lorraine traipsed through the tiny rooms and stopped outside the bathroom door, where she could hear the shower running full force. *A shower in the middle of the day?* she wondered thoughtfully, knowing most of Erika's habits. *What could that mean?* Lorraine was inquisitive by nature. Erika's actions had made Lorraine a little more suspicious than she might otherwise have been, but Lorraine was every bit as perceptive as Erika gave her credit for.

Plopping down on the bed, Lorraine took special note of the sloppy state of rumpled sheets. Then she spotted a gray T-shirt—a man's T-shirt, possibly. She thought it rather large to be Erika's. Then again, everyone wore oversize clothes these days. But when she picked up the shirt, she smelled the manly scent of cologne or aftershave.

Lorraine's green-gray eyes twinkled with devilment, thinking it would be fun to test Erika's reaction to what appeared obvious. If nothing else, it appeared that Erika and Michael had shared the same bed.

Erika was towel drying her hair when she emerged from the bathroom, having covered her nude body with a navy-blue, knee-length sweatshirt. Washing her hair was as good an excuse as any for being in the shower in the middle of the afternoon, she thought smugly.

Immediately, Erika noticed the devilish glint featured in Lorraine's eyes and the cat-ate-the-bird grin on her generous mouth. "What?" she questioned indignantly, feeling her color rise again. "Why are you looking at me that way?"

Lorraine's facial expressions didn't change as she picked up the T-shirt and twirled it around on her forefinger. "Is this yours?" she asked, a taunting tone explicitly clear in her voice. "I've never seen you wearing it."

Impatiently, Erika clicked her tongue against the roof of her mouth. "I have a lot of clothes that you probably haven't seen. What are you getting at?"

Lorraine balled up the T-shirt and threw it at Erika. "I haven't been *getting* any since Joe left. Looks like you're the one *getting* it all! Was the brother good, girlfriend? That's all I want to know."

Her cheeks burning like fire, Erika wished that she could disappear into thin air, and Lorraine's taunting laughter annoyed her to no end. She tossed the T-shirt on the bed. "It's not what you think. But go ahead and have your fun. Don't let me stop you. I'm the only one who knows what did or didn't occur here."

Lorraine laughed loudly. "I doubt that! I'm sure the good Dr. Mathis has some clue as to what went on in this bedroom." Erika shot Lorraine a scathing look, one that told her to mind her own business. "It's okay, Erika. You don't have to tell me the details. I love playing guessing games. At any rate, I just dropped by to tell you I'm going to break down and call Joe. Can't stand this rift another day."

Erika smiled lazily. "Good! Then you won't have time to be all up in my business," Erika said, laughing. "Tell him I said hello, and that I hope he comes back here and gives you just what you and I both know you need."

As if to prove things could get worse, Erika heard another familiar knock on the door—the strong, firm one belonging to none other than the good Dr. Mathis. Erika groaned. "Will you get that on your way out, Lorraine?" she requested, making her suggestion very clear.

"It's like that, huh? Okay, girlfriend, I got you loud and clear." Letting each other know neither of them had taken any of this seriously, both women laughed. "Love ya, Erika Edmonds," Lorraine cooed.

Erika winked at her nosy but loving friend. "Love you, too, sweetie. See you in a bit."

Lorraine opened the door and quickly greeted Michael. Then, in a flash, she was gone, leaving Michael wondering if he had bad body odor. Michael popped his head outside the door, but Lorraine had already disappeared. Shaking his head, he walked back to the bedroom.

The bewildered look on his face was incredibly boyish. "Does she always blow in and out of here like that? I hope I'm not the reason she keeps disappearing. I'm beginning to wonder about my personal hygiene."

Holding her arms out to him, Erika smiled. "Your manly smell is divine to me." Looking into her eyes, he embraced her with a tenderness that brought tears to her eyes. "I missed you," she whispered softly. "I'm glad you're back."

He kissed her passionately, his way of thanking her for all the compliments. "We missed each other, gorgeous. Did you get some rest?" Guiding her out to the living room, he dropped down onto the soft cushions. Taking her down with him, he felt as if he could use a good nap himself.

Erika snuggled up to him. "I took a short, restful nap. In fact, I'd just awakened a few minutes before Lorraine showed up. She was only here a short time. So, did you get all your business taken care of?"

He'd gotten more business than he'd bargained for, he thought sullenly. Though he'd agreed not to tell Erika about Richard—until Richard could figure out the best way to approach her with everything—he wasn't at all comfortable with his decision. Michael just wasn't used to being dishonest. In fact, he loathed dishonesty. Richard would eventually talk to Erika, but Michael saw the potential for danger staring him right in the face.

She playfully tweaked his ear. "Are you going to answer me? Better yet, did you even hear me?"

He nestled his nose in her neck. "I heard you, sweetheart. There was more business to handle than I'd originally thought, but we got through it."

A worried look settled in her eyes. "You're not facing a malpractice suit, are you?"

He thought that might be easier than being emotionally blackmailed into betraying the woman he loved. "Nothing like that, Erika. Really, it's nothing to worry about. Richard and I had to discuss the lecture series that he's giving to my research group. I also had to pick up his personal information, which will be included in the printed programs." He kissed her cheek. "Can I talk you into coming back to the house with me? I have somewhere I'd like to take you later. I'd also like you to stay the night with me." He received the full effect of why she was referred to as "the doctor with craters for dimples." There was nothing dietetic about her smile. It dripped with sweetness.

"Oh, I'd love that, Michael. Are you sure I'm not going to wear out my welcome? I don't want you to get tired of me."

If she knew what he knew, he thought, that would be the least of her worries. "Just make sure you don't get tired of *me*. Get your things together? I'm going to lie right here and wait." Without needing any further prompting, Erika kissed him and left the room.

* * *

Loving the feel of being centered in the middle of Michael's greenhouse room, Erika curled up on the sofa and closed her eyes. He called it the garden room, but it was actually the great room. The air was fresh with the smell of live plants and delicately scented flowers, and the entire room had a very relaxing, out-of-doors atmosphere.

Michael was in the master bathroom taking a shower. Before leaving Erika by herself, he had turned on the stereo to keep her company. He'd chosen to play the new compact disc he hadn't yet had a chance to listen to, which helped to relax Erika even more. "The Wind Beneath My Wings" was now wooing her delicate ears.

Piano By Candlelight featured popular inspirational and love ballads arranged exclusively for the piano—no words, just tinkling, melodious mixtures of ebony and ivory. He'd ordered the CD by phone after seeing it advertised on television.

When Michael finally joined her, he wore a pair of fresh, dark brown jeans and a brown fleece V-neck sweater. Erika had on forest green jeans and a wool, ribbed-knit sweater the same color as her jeans, which was what had prompted him to put on similar attire. Although he was taking her out later, their clothing was appropriate for what he had in mind.

Michael stretched out beside her. Resting his head in the well of her arm, he looked up at her as though he stared into the face of an angel. "How do you like the music? From what I've heard so far it sounds very romantic."

She made a demonstrative showing with her eyes. "It's heavenly. Yes, it's very romantic. This is the kind of music I could go to sleep to every single night, among other wonderful things."

"Hmm. I think I know what you mean." He moved his leg across her hip. "Remind me to play it before we go to sleep tonight. I'm for whatever turns you on."

Michael would like nothing better than to make love to her

all night long, but not tonight. He wanted her to know that he wanted more out of their relationship than just sex, wanted to feel her next to him, to hear her heartbeat, to smell her sweet breath as it fanned his lips and cheeks.

With Erika by his side, he wanted to feel and see the joyous colors of love, to hear the melodious sounds of her tinkling laughter and her sexy, northeastern drawl, to touch all the wild emotions that being with her brought to his body and soul. The love he felt for her had nothing to do with sex. It had everything to do with the sensitive woman she was. Making wild, passionate love to her was simply an added benefit.

Erika brushed his damp hair with her fingers. She didn't know too many black men who wore their hair that long, but it looked good on Michael.

As she pressed her lips against his hair, the clean, citrus-shampoo smell of it filled her nostrils. "Where are we going this evening? I rather like the thought of staying right here curled up in the security that your strength brings to me."

Loving the way she so openly and beautifully expressed herself, he smiled. "The security of my strength will always be with you, whether we're here together or somewhere else—most of all when we're apart. As you find security in that, I find security in your gentleness. It's very nurturing." He'd avoided answering her question on purpose; she'd just have to wait and see where he was taking her.

Touched by his sincerity, she felt bright, unshed tears in her eyes that revealed that to him. "That's so nice to know, Michael. Now we both know that we can find security in each other. I, for one, need to feel secure. My world has been crumbling around me for the past several years. Before you came along, I was buried alive under the suffocating debris. Thank you for saving me. I hope I don't ever do anything to make you regret it."

Michael felt his chest muscles constrict. Here she was worrying about doing something to make him regret saving her life, but he was the one who'd done something that could possibly end with him losing his own. Losing the kind of life he'd always hoped for. Losing the woman he loved. Losing her would mean sudden death for his ability to live through loving someone so completely.

Why had he allowed himself to be emotionally blackmailed into deceiving her? Richard was a good friend and he loved him like a brother, but Erika was the only woman he'd ever truly loved, the only woman he wanted to share forever and a day with. Would she want the same thing with him after she found out about all the desperate deceptions? Somehow he doubted it. Just the thought of losing her made him feel sick all over.

Erika noticed that Michael wasn't himself. Sensing that something bothered him, she hoped he wasn't already regretting asking for an exclusive relationship. "Do you want to let me in on what's troubling you? You haven't been yourself since you returned from seeing your friend. Let me help you, Michael," she pleaded softly.

Her soft plea wreaked havoc on his conscience, but he couldn't tell her the truth. Not yet, anyway. "Sweetheart, just your being here is help enough. Don't ever go away. Everything is going to be just fine."

His evasiveness frightened her, and so did his thinking she might go away. She'd only just found him, just found the one person who eased the burden of her struggles, who made coping with life a whole lot easier, who made her want to dance, sing and shout to the world that she was in love.

Michael Mathis was the one person who could help her to help herself just by being there for her. Could getting himself tangled in her problems be troubling him? But being there for her was his idea, not hers. No matter how grateful she was to him she didn't want her problems to come between them. She didn't want the things that bogged her down and her inability to cope with them alone to become a source of irritation to him. She suddenly felt she shouldn't lean on him so much, but she had to regain the strength she'd somehow lost to her grief.

Yes, she'd have to be very careful about appearing so helpless and so needy. If needing him too much meant losing him, then she'd have to bury those needs when she was with him.

"Michael, maybe I shouldn't stay here tonight," she uttered with regret. "You seem to need some space. I don't want to crowd you. Would you mind taking me home?"

He stared at her incredulously. Hadn't he just asked her to not leave him? "Yes, I do mind. I don't need any more space than what's between us right now. But if you really want to go home—I hope you don't—I'll take you after we go out."

As Michael pulled up in front of a large Presbyterian church, Erika telegraphed him a puzzled look. "We're going to church? Is this the date you had in mind?"

He laughed at her expression. "What's wrong with that? I think it's a great place to go and release all the tensions of the day. But that's not what we're here for. There's a special program I think we should attend. It'll be good for both of us." Without offering any more explanation, he got out of the car and walked around to open her door.

Inside the church, Michael led Erika to a room located in the basement. Several people sat around in chairs forming a circle. Michael directed Erika to a couple of empty chairs, and they sat down. Simultaneously, everyone welcomed them to the group as a tall, slender woman got up and stood in the center of the circle.

"Hi, my name is Marianne. As the chairperson, I'd like to welcome everyone to our support group. To our newcomers, we'd like you to know we're all here for one another. When I had to place my father in a nursing home, I had no support whatsoever. Because of the burdens and the guilt that often accompany the decision to place a loved one, I felt compelled to start a support group for people like myself. This group is for people who felt they had to do the right thing no matter how unpopular the decision was—to ensure that their loved ones got the proper medical attention, to do whatever was necessary to ensure the safety of those loved ones."

With understanding shining brightly in her eyes, Erika looked over at Michael. How could one man be so caring? she marveled. As tears sprang to her eyes, he squeezed her hand, giving her a reassuring smile.

As Marianne launched into her story, Erika listened intently, wondering if Marianne had somehow placed a hidden camera somewhere in the house she'd once shared with Vernice. Marianne described the very fears Erika had lived with. It was eerie, incredible.

"There were days when I didn't know what to do for my father. He was stubborn and he didn't want any help from me or from anyone else. He suffered a broken hip the last time he fell, but he refused to go to the convalescent home. A few weeks ago he fell and broke his right arm. I couldn't go to work and leave him alone, but he didn't want me around, either. One minute he's kind and gentle. Then he tries to take my head off. My dad's always been fiercely independent, and he doesn't realize he can no longer do all the things he used to do.

"So, I had to take matters into my own hands. To say the very least, my father was not at all happy with me." Marianne took a deep breath. "I finally got the courage and the guts to place my father where he'd be safe. He's now safe and sound, and he seems much happier, but I haven't learned to deal with all the shame and guilt that came as a result of my decision."

When Marianne broke down and cried, one of the other members jumped up and guided her back to her seat. As everyone thanked Marianne for her story, Erika saw that there wasn't a dry eye in the room.

A fragile-looking, middle-aged man came forward. "My name is James. My forty-five-year-old wife is now living in a nursing home." Erika was stunned by the age of the woman.

"My wife, Arnell, was the most vibrant and independent woman I knew. She was a schoolteacher until she suffered head trauma in a car accident, which left her disabled and unable to teach. I tried taking care of her at home, but Arnell became irritable and hard to communicate with. She would try to do things she knew she couldn't do, but that was her way. I'd come home from work and find her in the middle of the floor crying her eyes out because she'd burned the meal. I'd wake up in the middle of the night to find her sobbing uncontrollably." James, too, had to stop and compose himself.

"One day Arnell disappeared into a dark, inner hell, becoming totally uncommunicative. After several months of her unrelenting silence, I realized I could no longer care for her on my own. The accident has destroyed two lives. Arnell was my world, and now my world no longer claims me," he practically wailed.

Erika wanted to say something, too, but she couldn't seem to summon the courage to talk in front of these strangers. Michael whispered something to her, and she prayed that she could find the courage to move forward into the circle before the meeting was over.

Looking at Michael, Marianne summoned him to the podium. As he drew near, Marianne said, "This young man here is very active with our senior groups and our youngsters. He's also one of the best doctors in Lebanon, one of only a handful who still makes house calls. Let's give Dr. Michail Mathis a warm round of applause before he addresses our group," she requested, making way for Michael at the podium.

"Marianne, you're too kind," Michael remarked sweetly. "You're the one who should be applauded," he offered, smiling brightly at the woman with the streaked gray hair and rosy cheeks. He then thanked the committee for allowing him the opportunity to say a few words.

Michael cleared his throat out of nervousness. "This committee has made great strides," he began. "When it was first formed, we only had three or four members, and now we're about seventy strong. We could do with about seventy more. I brought a special friend along with me this evening. Like me, she's a very dedicated physician. Dr. Edmonds," he called out, "could you join me at the podium so everyone can see who you are?"

Embarrassed by all the eyes turned on her, Erika felt her cheeks color as she moved toward the podium. To put her at ease, Michael put his arm around her when she stood next to him.

"This young lady may be an OB-GYN resident at Great Western University, but she also has a tender spot in her heart for our community seniors. Like the members of this committee, she's been thinking of ways she can help make life a little easier for those who need it. Don't you all think she should become a full-fledged member of our group?"

The applause was hearty as Michael encouraged Erika to share a few of her experiences regarding Vernice. Erika wanted to kiss him right then and there, but decided to save it for later. Michael was one of a kind, the only kind of man she wanted in her life.

"Hello, everyone," she said softly. "My name is Erika. I'm afraid I'm not prepared to give a speech, but I can tell you that I'd be honored to become a member of your most wonderful share-and-care committee." Another round of applause followed her remarks. Fleetingly, she touched Michael's hand. Momentarily, he grasped her fingers.

"As Michael stated, I'm very interested in our community seniors. I've had some of your same experiences as a caregiver, so I can relate to the stories I just heard. I also had to make the decision to place a loved one—my late mother, Vernice Edmonds. Before her death, my mother was a resident at Golden Age Retirement Center. She suffered from a blood disorder called pernicious anemia. The disease destroyed my mother's short-term memory. Then it went to work on her long-term memory." In short, Erika explained the important things she knew about pernicious anemia, along with methods for treatment.

"When mother was placed in residential care, guilt became my new roommate. I often tried to put myself in her place. It became too painful to stay in that place for very long. But I knew that I had to be there before I could even begin to understand." Erika licked her lips. "I had to imagine what it would be like to no longer be able to live in my very own home, or be around my belongings, personal and otherwise. I had to imagine what it would be like to have certain freedoms taken away, like driving and going to the beauty shop at will. I made myself think about being unable to go to all the places I once could've gone to blindfolded. It was awful for me to even imagine, so I know how awful it must've been for her to live it.

"I say to you that it is awful, but it doesn't have to be the end of the world. There are residential care facilities that devotedly cater to the needs of their residents. I know, because I was fortunate enough to find such a wonderful place for my mom. As so many people told me, receiving the best care would only richly enhance the quality of my mother's life.

"I was also told she'd thank me one day for ensuring her safety and she'd be grateful for the day-to-day assistance, but I never bought into that," Erika said, laughing along with everyone else. She took a sip of water from the glass Michael handed to her. "Folks, it's hard, but sometimes we have to take the bull by the horns, which means taking charge, or even taking a charge from the bull itself. If you need some assistance, don't put it off, especially when there are people out there who are professionally trained to do it so much better than we can. However, I do suggest that you shop around for the best in care, regardless of financial situations. Our loved ones are our most valuable national treasures."

Back in her seat, Erika didn't want to stay and hear anymore heartwrenching stories. But she had to. It was expected.

Tears fell from Erika's eyes for the next hour, and Michael

kept his arm firmly planted around her shoulders. Erika had been told about support groups, but she'd never found enough time to attend one. From now on, she told herself, she'd make time. In fact, everyone who had to place a loved one in a safer environment should make time to attend support-group meetings. It was vital to maintaining one's sanity. Had Michael not been so caring, she wouldn't be sitting here with all these people who hurt as much as she did.

After the last person finished speaking, Erika found herself moving into the circle once again. There was something else she needed to say and while she was so high on courage she'd better take advantage of it.

As a common courtesy, she gave her name again. "We've all talked about our loved ones and the devastation we've experienced because of their illnesses. It took me a while, but I began to realize that the devastation wasn't all about me. It's not what we think, what we feel, or even what we want. The real devastation lies deep within the hearts and minds of our loved ones." Erika took a sip of the water, which she'd carried back to the podium with her. She then glanced briefly at Michael. When he winked and nodded in approval, she found the courage to continue.

Letting the tears run down her cheeks unchecked, Erika began to tremble. She found no shame in wearing her heart on her sleeve, found no shame in mourning the things her mother had lost due to her illness, especially her life. "No matter how much we're hurting, we must always remember that our loved ones are the true victims of their particular circumstances. Thank you."

A standing ovation followed Erika's eloquent speech, the loud applause continuing until she was back in her seat. Prayer followed. Then the meeting was adjourned. There were refreshments, but Erika desperately needed to feel the cold night air on her skin. She and Michael said their farewells, then rushed up the stairs and out into the night.

As Michael slid behind the steering wheel, Erika threw her

arms around his neck. He grabbed a handful of her hair as her lips crashed down hard against his mouth, her kiss fraught with desperation and her touch awkward. As her trembling hands flitted over his face, she gulped at his breath, her own coming rapidly and raggedly.

Michael could feel her emotional pain seeping out of every pore of her body. Her whimpers were like those of a small child who'd just been punished by a parent. But Erika was dishing out her own punishment, Michael reflected, punishing herself with a powerful weapon—guilt.

Michael held her away from him. "Erika, Erika, you have to get hold of yourself, sweetheart. You're trembling all over, not to mention tearing yourself apart."

Erika screamed, looking all around her as if trying to locate where the screams had come from. The sheer sound of terror in her scream pierced Michael's soul like that of a sharp knife. Hysteria claimed her remaining sanity as she began to cry and laugh at the same time. "Michael, I want my family back again," she cried in anguish. "I need them back, Michael. I want everything the way—"

Pulling her head toward him, he buried it against his chest. As he tried to muffle her desperate cries, she continued to wail like a wounded animal. Then, she stopped, as suddenly as she'd begun. With a blank stare shrouding her eyes, Erika lifted her head and looked at Michael. The raw, naked pain he saw deep in her eyes sent him reeling.

Pulling her head back against his chest, he sucked in a jagged breath. "We're going to get through this, my love. I love you, Erika Edmonds. I love you, Erika." His tears fell into her hair as he clung desperately to her convulsing body.

She'd heard him, loud and clear, but she couldn't respond just yet. She needed to savor this most exquisite moment. Erika had wanted to wait to tell Michael that she loved him when it carried the most weight. Now was the time. This moment couldn't carry any more weight. Her heart was already so heavy with her love for him.

Lifting her head again, she allowed her eyes to connect with his soul. It was dark in the car, but she didn't need light. Her eyes were filled with illumination, the illumination of love.

She cupped his face between her hands. "I love you, Michael," she confessed breathlessly. "I love you, too."

Michael's breath caught. As he stared at her, laughter bubbled in his heart. His dream had come true, the dream that she'd someday love him the way he loved her. "Oh, gorgeous, I've been hoping you'd fall in love with me, but I never dreamed it would happen this soon. I was willing to wait for as long as it took. I don't have to wait any longer. I can't tell you how good this makes me feel. Erika, no matter what else happens, please remember that I love you."

The fear of her discovering his deception was overwhelming, but knowing that she loved him, too, gave him the confidence to at least hope she'd understand and forgive him. He kissed her tenderly. He kissed her passionately. Then he kissed her until he swept her breath away, leaving himself breathless in the process.

Michael released her and turned on the interior lights. He fumbled in the console until he came up with a box of lightly scented wet-wipes. Removing one from the box, he tore the packet open and gently washed her tear-streaked face. Reaching to the backseat for her purse, he pulled it up front and handed it to her, asking her to remove her makeup bag. She pulled out a compact and a bushy makeup brush, which he took from her hand.

Opening the compact, he swept the cosmetic brush across its contents and dusted her face with corn silk. She giggled as he tickled her nose with the end of the brush. Once she'd dug the other cosmetics out of her purse, he dabbed her lips with lip gloss and brushed her cheeks with blush, all of which was very sensuous to her.

Michael kissed away the strawberry-flavored gloss and applied more. "Now, you're all ready to meet my family. Where's your hairbrush?"

Erika was amazed that he wanted to take her to meet his family. *Another weighty moment,* she thought happily. "Are you sure, Michael?" She handed him the hairbrush he'd requested.

"Sure as I'll ever be, gorgeous. This will be a night I don't want you to ever forget."

He brushed her hair with tender, firm strokes and then pulled down the sunvisor, where a lighted mirror was located. "Look at how beautiful you are," he said, turning her face toward the mirror. "If it hadn't been for all the tears streaking your face, you wouldn't have needed any makeup. You're a natural beauty, Erika."

Erika blushed. "And you're a natural charmer! But you can charm me anytime, anywhere, Dr. Mathis."

As Michael pulled out of the church parking lot, Erika gathered the cosmetic items and placed them back in her purse. Reclining the seat one notch, she relaxed. Michael drove deeper and deeper into the rural area. Several miles later he pulled up to a farm, the same one where they'd begun the sleigh ride.

Erika glanced at him out of the corner of her eye, then back at the rustic farmhouse. "Don't tell me! This is your parents' house, isn't it?"

His laughter was deep and rolling. "I thought you just said not to tell you." She narrowed her eyes at him. "Okay, you win. It is. And while we're on the subject, I have a confession to make. My father was the sleigh driver!"

Erika's mouth fell open, her eyes wide with disbelief. "You've got to be kidding. Why didn't you tell me that night?"

Michael grinned widely. "I didn't want you to think I was moving too fast. Believe me, my father understood. He was young once, too. They're waiting to meet you. Shall we go inside, gorgeous?"

Ten

The farmhouse was just as rustic on the inside as it was on the outside. The furnishings were simple, but very well constructed. Maple, oak, pine and other hardwoods were evident in the decor. The front rooms looked as though Ethan Allan might have decorated them. Warm autumn colors added a nice touch to the house's rustic state. And, much like in Michael's place, green plants were in abundance.

Erika felt welcome in the Mathis home from the moment Wilimina, a petite woman with golden-brown hair, hazel eyes, and a medium-tan complexion, embraced her as if she were greeting a long lost friend. "My dear, we're so happy to have you visit us. Of course, Michael has told us a lot about you. Please come into the family room," Wilimina requested sweetly. "Michael's father is in the back."

Looping her arm through Michael's, Wilimina kissed her son. Michael hugged his mother affectionately, kissing her on the forehead. Taking the hands of the two women he adored, he escorted them to the back of the house.

The large family room held a wicker sofa, chair and chaise lounge, all of which were padded with loose-pillow backs and rolled arms. The pillows, decorated with rather large blossoms, were hand-painted in rust, olive green and gold. A matching ottoman was situated in front of the chair. Solid through and through, a hand-carved, sand-washed pine armoire and sand-washed pine tables completed the rustic decor.

An extremely tall, handsome man stood by the stone fireplace sipping on a hot drink, his smoky silver waves thick and neatly trimmed. When Lawrence Mathis smiled broadly at Erika, she saw a replica of Michael's smile imprinted on his full lips. His skin was also Indian-brown.

Lawrence stretched his arms out to Erika as he moved toward her. Without hesitation, she slipped against the warmth of his broad chest. Her stepfather immediately came to mind. Lawrence released Erika from the bear hug, but kept a tight grip on her hand.

"My, my, we're going to have to get my son some eyeglasses," Lawrence boomed in a heavy voice. Lawrence directed Erika to the wicker sofa and sat down beside her. "Michael said you were gorgeous, but in my estimation that's an understatement. I was told to 'chill out' the night I took you all for that sleigh ride. Michael was afraid of chasing you away," Lawrence teased, winking one hazel eye at his son.

Smiling at his loving father, Michael sat in the chair as soon as Wilimina was seated on the chaise lounge. "She already knows that, Dad. I also warned her about your sense of humor."

Erika quickly began to understand why Michael was such a kindhearted, loving individual. His parents were extraordinary people. They already treated her as though she were a member of the family. Like Michael, they seemed to give freely of themselves.

Learning they hadn't eaten for hours, Wilimina took Erika into the brightly decorated, old country-style kitchen, where she pulled a large pot of homemade beef stew from the refrigerator for warming. "I made this stew early this morning. It's a family favorite." Erika sat at the table, while Wilimina busied herself warming the meal and setting out the dinnerware.

Needing no prompting, Erika got up from her seat. "I'd like to help set the table," she offered. "That is, if you don't mind?"

Wilimina smiled. "I'd love for you to help, dear. You'll find the dishes in there," she said, pointing to an upper cabinet. "I keep the silverware in this drawer," she directed, touching the drawer with her fingertips, "and the napkins are on the lower shelf in the pantry."

After retrieving all the things needed to set the table, Erika folded the napkins in triangles, then she placed one at the side of each plate, with the eating utensils on top of it. As Wilimina ladled the beef stew into a large, ceramic serving bowl, Erika saw that the stew was loaded with large chunks of white potatoes, carrots, pearl onions, celery and plenty of tender-looking beef.

Wilimina uncovered a basket holding dozens of yeast rolls. "I also baked all of these rolls this morning—and the desserts over there." She pointed to a glass cake server that held fudge brownies laden with walnuts. Next to the glass server was a freshly baked apple-raisin pie. Once the food items were all placed on the table, Wilimina called her husband and son into the kitchen.

Michael kissed Erika when he came into the room. As they stood around the table, holding hands, Mr. Mathis blessed the food. Then everyone took a seat. During the early-evening supper, the conversation was lively and quite interesting, to say the least.

Michael and Lawrence debated Clinton's overall performance as commander in chief, both being Democrats. Lawrence told Michael he had some strong doubts about the party's ability to deliver on the majority of its campaign promises. Michael felt they couldn't possibly undo all the damage that had occurred during the previous two administrations. Wilimina talked to Erika about her days as the director of nurses at the old Methodist Hospital.

"I have occasion to practice my profession by volunteering my services at the local chapters of the Sickle Cell Foundation, the Lupus Foundation and the American Red Cross. Lawrence and I are both involved in several community service organizations. Michael tells us you're an OB-GYN resident. Are you an advocate of women's issues, as well?"

Erika grinned. "I am. But I'm more of an advocate for anyone who has special needs, especially our senior citizens. Michael and I just came from a support-group meeting. I'm afraid I've been feeling guilty about placing my mother in a nursing home before she passed away. However, the meeting was just what this doctor needed. Being able to share with others who are faced with situations similar to my own helped me tremendously. It was so thoughtful of Michael to take me there. You two have a very kind son," Erika said, beaming at Michael.

Wilimina patted Erika's hand. "Thank you, Erika. We think he's kind of special. I'm very sorry about your mom. If Lawrence and I can do anything to help you get through this difficult time please don't hesitate to call on us. Like our son, we're great listeners. As you can see, Lawrence has some pretty broad shoulders. I won't mind sharing one with you."

Appreciating the extended kindness, Erika smiled. "Thank you. That's very generous of you both. I promise to take you up on that offer when I need comforting."

Midway through supper the doorbell rang, and Michael excused himself to answer it.

Seconds later Michael returned to the kitchen with Richard Glover close on his heels. Not knowing why, Erika tensed up the second she laid eyes on Richard. She had no idea why this man unnerved her, but he did. For some strange reason, she was also very curious about him.

"Hey, Mom and Dad. How are you this evening?" Richard asked, bending over to give Mrs. Mathis a big kiss on the cheek and hugging Mr. Mathis.

Erika's eyebrows raised sharply when he referred to the Mathises as Mom and Dad. It was easy to see that Michael's parents were especially fond of Richard, as well. No one had to offer him dinner since he was already busy helping himself.

Erika noticed that Michael appeared to be tense, too. He'd been so relaxed before Richard's arrival. Once Richard was seated at the table, she caught the uneasy glances periodically passing between the two friends.

Did Michael's earlier pensive mood have something to do with Richard? It was after their meeting that she'd first noticed his preoccupation. Because Michael had once again promised to be there for her, she no longer felt he regretted getting involved with her personal problems.

Whatever strange feelings Erika had about Richard, she was gracious enough not to let them show. When he directed questions at her, she politely answered. Before long, Richard had her laughing, along with everybody else. Whether she was ready to admit it or not, he was really witty, and very charming. Erika actually found herself feeling sorry for him when he sadly revealed that he and his longtime girlfriend, Shelly, had had an amicable parting of the ways.

As Lorraine's lovely face popped into Erika's mind, she quickly scolded herself for even thinking of introducing him to her best friend. She didn't even like him. Or did she? She was no longer sure how she felt about Richard Glover. He hadn't done anything offensive to her, despite his strange behavior at the ballet. No matter how she tried to ignore it, Richard reminded her a great deal of her stepfather. Anthony had been a rare gem.

Michael sat quietly as he reflected on how furious he'd been when he'd found Richard on the other side of the door. Richard had known he was bringing Erika home to meet his parents. He felt that he'd purposely shown up for that reason.

But could he really blame his friend for wanting to get to know his own sister?

Carefully, he watched Richard interact with Erika. It was a tough situation all the way around, and he didn't like being placed in the middle of it. He understood where Richard was coming from, but he couldn't wait till the truth came out.

After dinner Lawrence broke out the dominoes. The three men settled themselves around the leather card table, each one eager to claim victory.

As Erika watched the three grown men act like spoiled children, she felt as if she were sitting in the middle of World War Three. This was the only time she'd had occasion to see Michael's arrogance. She didn't find it at all offensive. In fact, she thought it rather intriguing.

It appeared that Wilimina was quite used to all the fuss the three males put up. She calmly crocheted a baby blanket. "If my son Patrick were here, things would really get raunchy," she told Erika. "Patrick is a riot." Wilimina laughed. "Patrick Mathis believes he's responsible for putting the dragon on the back of the domino bones. He's also a sore loser," Wilimina revealed.

"I've often wondered what it might be like to grow up with a house full of siblings," Erika said, "what it would be like to have a bunch of sisters who loved to fight over clothes and makeup."

Regardless of the shouting and the feuding, these three males were having the time of their lives. From the smile that lit up Wilimina's face, Erika could see she enjoyed her men enjoying themselves.

The evening came to a close shortly after Lawrence declared victory. Michael and Richard claimed to have let him win because of his senior status, knowing what they'd claimed was a crock, since it was rare for either of them to best him. Patrick was the only one who could beat Lawrence repeatedly, especially when they played one-on-one. Wilimina reminded Michael and Richard of this.

Erika hated to see the evening come to a close, having enjoyed herself tremendously, but she was dead tired. It had been a long and exhausting day for her, not to mention the drain on her emotions. Erika was given a standing invitation to the Mathis home, with or without Michael, which seemed to please him greatly. He was also extremely pleased with the way the evening had turned out despite Richard's surprise visit.

Erika came to the conclusion that Richard had to be a very special person, especially after she saw how much he was loved by the Mathises. Until she got to know him better, which was sure to happen since he was Michael's best friend, she wasn't ready to label him a friend or a foe.

Warm hugs and farewells were easily given at the door. After Richard walked Erika and Michael to the car, he returned to the Mathises' porch, watching the car widening the distance between him and his sister.

Michael turned up the heater as soon as they entered the house. The outdoor temperature had once again dropped, leaving the house feeling slightly chilly and damp. While Erika rushed off to take a shower, he went into the kitchen to make hot drinks.

After turning on the teakettle, he went into the bedroom and lit the fireplace. Returning to the kitchen, he poured the hot water into a ceramic teapot and added a couple of herbal tea bags. Erika was still in the shower when he placed the bed-tray on the nightstand.

As he entered the bathroom, he pulled a plush towel off the towel-bar. When she stepped out of the shower, he was ready and waiting. Wasting no time, he rubbed the towel over her nude body, drying her with tender care. Then he carried her into the bedroom and laid her down on the bed. Using a remote control, he turned down the lights. With another touch of the remote, piano music from the new CD drifted lazily from the bedroom speakers. Erika smiled. How could she ask for more? Michael seemed to be able to anticipate her every need, which made her feel so loved and cherished. As the roaring fire caressed her skin, he climbed in next to her.

Reaching over to the nightstand, he took a tiny vial from the tray. Pouring a generous amount of the warm oil into his hands, he slowly dripped it over her entire body, taking the pleasure of massaging it into her delicate skin. Erika softly cooed and moaned as Michael's hands moved expertly over her body, kneading and massaging every inch of her flesh.

As she fell limp, she relaxed her head against the pillow, allowing herself to bask in the glorious feel of his strong hands. The tenderness with which he rubbed her inner thighs made her want to scream out his name. After turning her onto her stomach, he firmly stroked her buttocks, his fingers gently pressing into the areas around her spine, causing a trail of desert heat to race up her back. It was heavenly. It was divine. But she wanted so much more. She wanted to feel his manhood entombed in her liquid heat.

Turning over onto her back, she pulled his head down, allowing her lips to rove hungrily over his. "I want you inside of me. I want to feel you in the depths of my passion," she murmured softly against his parted lips.

Michael moaned with regret, remembering the promise he'd made to himself. As hard as it was going to be, he was going to keep it, but it didn't mean that he had to deprive her of being utterly fulfilled. "I'm going to love you, Erika. I'm going to take you to the top of the mountain and drop you off the highest cliff. I'll be here to catch you when you fall into rhapsody," he moaned, grinding his hips against her trembling thighs.

Michael lowered his head and parted the pathway, giving himself easy access to Erika's molten treasures. She arched her back as his fiery tongue made contact with her inner thigh. Writhing uncontrollably, Erika moaned as he loved her in a way she couldn't begin to fathom. His tongue was everywhere, and what it left untouched his fingers adroitly covered.

An inferno already burned inside of her, but Michael was hell-bent on taking her to heights never before attained. The room swirled crazily before her eyes. As the roaring fire appeared to take on a life of its own, she was sure it had leaped from the fireplace.

The fire now burned itself deep into her already sizzling flesh, and then she saw the majestic mountaintop. With one final thrust of his tongue, she toppled over the edge. Ripples and ripples of torrid heat consumed her inner core before Erika fell deep into the chasm of the rhapsody he'd promised earlier. Michael was there to catch her as she floated into oblivion.

The look in Michael's eyes was arresting. Though he hadn't been inside her, he had felt everything she herself had felt, which still blew his mind to bits. During his erotic manipulations, the delightfully agonized expressions crossing her features and the involuntary, maniacal thrashing of her body had made it clear to him that he successfully carried out his mission.

Erika drew his head down to rest on her bosom. "I've been to the mountaintop," she recited, using the famous words of the late, great Dr. Martin Luther King. "I've seen the Promised Land!" No disrespect was intended toward the black civil rights leader. Erika had nothing but the utmost respect for his brilliant mind and tireless dedication to his people. And she felt every bit as much elation as he must have on the day he saw the Promised Land. The circumstances were certainly different, but the everlasting impressions were the same.

Michael surprised her when he recited parts of the "I Have A Dream" sermon. Then, from beginning to end, he recited the "I've Been to the Mountaintop" sermon. Tears came to both of their eyes as he finished with the words, ". . . free at last, free at last! Thank God Almighty, we're free at last!" Michael sang out loudly.

Silent, they both wondered if black people would ever be free.

Erika put her head in Michael's lap as he stroked her hair. "That was a wonderful thing you did for me this evening, Michael. Hearing the others' stories made me see that I wasn't alone on this guilt trip. Guilt is a laborious journey when you have to travel it all alone." She looked up at him. "I loved my mother very much. If I could've taken care of her myself, I would've leaped to the challenge. If I could've met all her needs, special or otherwise, I wouldn't have hesitated. Michael, please tell me that I did the right thing."

Michael stroked her cheekbone with his thumb. "Without a

doubt. Your motives were pure. Your heart was in the right place," he remarked, laying his hand over her heart. "You don't need me to tell you about all the terrible things that could've happened had you not taken the necessary steps to keep her safe. Erika, hindsight's always twenty-twenty. But in this case, what you chose to do back then was the only choice, the right choice. Your mother's at peace now, and she would want no less for you. I'm going to help you find that peace, Erika Edmonds. You deserve to have it."

"Michael, I have found peace. In you, in your strength, in your courage."

Erika fell asleep wrapped in Michael's arms, wrapped in his courage. As he watched the rise and fall of her beautiful breasts, to him it looked as if she had indeed found some peace.

Michael lay awake long into the night, wondering what might happen when she discovered that Richard Glover was her biological brother. How was she going to react when she found out he'd known about it and hadn't informed her? What was going to happen to the love she'd confessed for him? What would happen to the relationship they'd so carefully built? Would his deceit cause yet another crack in her delicate armor?

Michael's thoughts turned to the meeting he'd scheduled with the hospital administrators. Erika had been so excited when he'd told her the powers that be were willing to listen to her community-service proposal. Michael wasn't sure the committee of stuffed shirts would approve such an expensive proposition, but he had faith in Erika.

Erika was working on a plan that she hoped would defray much of the cost to the hospital. Michael knew how much this idea meant to her. Therefore, he had to trust her. He had put himself out on a fragile limb, but Erika was worth it. The cause was worth it. Whether the administrators went along with the program or not, he knew Erika Edmonds was going to find a way to educate the community-at-large about pernicious anemia, as well as any and all preventive medicine measures that would benefit Lebanon's seniors.

Somehow he got the feeling that this worthy project was only the beginning of her one-woman crusade. Delivering babies and healing ailments of women just wasn't going to be enough for Erika, with her staunch belief that an ounce of prevention was worth a pound of cure.

Practicing medicine carried a lot of responsibility and tons of liability, and the profession was in dire need of dedicated physicians who cared, physicians desiring to make a difference, physicians just like his gorgeous Erika.

Putting his worries to rest, Michael snuggled up to the sleeping woman sharing his bed. Erika loved him, he loved her. . . . He had to put all his faith and trust in their love. She was a woman he wanted to share more than his bed with. She was the only woman he wanted to share his entire life with.

The emergency room was unusually calm. Every treatment room was empty. Doctors, nurses and other medical technicians stood listlessly around the nurses' station, exchanging previous emergency room war stories.

Erika, for one, was glad that everything was so quiet, though she rather suspected it was just the lull before the storm. The last several nights had been torturous. During her last few shifts she'd been on her feet from the onset of the shifts until they were over. On a couple of those occasions she'd had to stay on duty way past her normal hours.

The previous night's emergencies had just about run the gamut. An elderly lady suffering from severe chest pains had been brought in by ambulance. Once stabilized, she was moved to the intensive cardiac care unit. A seven-year-old boy had fallen from a top bunk bed, fracturing his arm in two places. Once the X rays were read, the on-call orthopedic surgeon had to be contacted. And the two-year-old who had ingested her mother's sleeping pills had to have her stomach pumped and was admitted for observation. There had also been a patient who arrived DOA.

During the course of the night there had been twenty-one patients admitted. Two had been transferred to other local hospitals, and one had been airlifted to a hospital that housed a special head trauma unit, Erika recalled with a slight shudder.

Though Erika didn't normally drink coffee, she needed something to keep her awake and alert. If this evening was going to be anything like the last few, she'd need to be on her toes. After pouring a cup of coffee, she informed one of the nurses that she'd be in the doctors' quarters. University Hospital had several rooms reserved for the emergency room physicians on duty. Besides a telephone, the tiny room's furnishings consisted of a sofa, a bed, a small desk and an old reclining chair. An end table and lamp were stationed at the end of the sofa.

As Erika passed the desk, she removed the novel *Beloved* by Toni Morrison. Seated in the worn leather reclining chair, she opened the book, only to put it down a few minutes later. Moving over to the bed, she threw herself across it. Several days ago, something pretty strange had occurred, and she couldn't stop thinking about it. The strange occurrence had come after the last night she'd spent with Michael.

Michael had fixed her a healthy breakfast that morning, she recalled, before they'd taken a brisk walk around his property and into the forest beyond. It had been freezing cold, but, as usual, she'd found warmth from the strong arms that encircled her waist. Michael's entire being emanated warmth. He'd asked her to spend her last day and evening off with him, but she had so many chores she'd left unattended. Knowing she had to begin her emergency room coverage the very next evening, she'd had to beg off, regrettably so. After Michael had dropped her off at home, she'd gathered all the dirty clothes and taken them down to the dormitory laundry.

Once the clothes had been washed and put away, Erika had sat down to tackle the bills. Because of the shortage of money in her checking account, she'd gone to the bank to have money transferred from savings. Erika had later dropped by the moving company to pay the monthly bill. When Erika had handed Randy Mills the monthly installment check, he informed her that the bill had been paid in full. Randy told her the check had arrived by messenger, and had already been deposited in the bank. It had been a cashier's check. Since he'd assumed that it had come from her, he'd had no reason to make a copy of it.

The question was, who would've paid such a large sum of money for her moving expenses? She suspected Michael of being the generous benefactor, but she hadn't gotten the nerve to confront him. His paying her bills was totally unacceptable, and she had every intention of telling him just that. Aunt Arlene had already denied shelling out the money. Michael was the only other person she knew who'd make such a sincere show of generosity.

Before she could entertain another thought, the phone rang. Leaping off the bed, she picked up the receiver. "Dr. Edmonds, here."

"We need you out here," the desk clerk shouted. "We've got a woman in the parking lot who's in labor. She's in the car with her husband. T.J. and Erma have already wheeled a gurney outside."

Erika rushed out the door and ran all the way to the emergency room. Just as she traveled through the double doors, Erika saw T.J. and Erma pushing the gurney into one of the treatment rooms.

T.J. waved a hand. "The baby's head is almost out, Dr. Edmonds," she yelled excitedly.

Erika snapped into action. She washed her hands thoroughly and slid them into latex gloves. The young black woman was puffing and blowing with signs of excruciating pain written all over her face. Her poor husband looked as if he were in labor, too, Erika observed. T.J., a black nurse in her early twenties, did what was necessary to make the woman more comfortable.

Busy shouting orders, Erika positioned herself at the end of the table, ready to assist the new baby into the world. Erika's lips moved rapidly as she mouthed a silent prayer. She'd assisted in many deliveries, but this would be her first solo one. The emergency circumstances warranted it. Erika put her hands under the back of the emerging infant's head, which indicated to her that the baby had been in a vertex position in the uterus, the most common and normal position.

"Okay, push," Erika instructed. "Do your breathing exercises. That's it. Good! Okay, okay, push again." April Thomas let out a bloodcurdling scream. "It's going to be okay," Erika soothed, instructing April to push again.

April panted, blowing out steady streams of deep breaths as she pushed down hard. The shoulders were out now, and Erika adjusted her hands to offer the baby more support. In the next instant she scooped the baby up in her hands.

"It's a boy," she announced gleefully to the parents, handing the baby to Erma for her to administer the necessary suctioning. After motioning for Mr. Thomas to come closer, Erika handed him the sterile surgical scissors and began to instruct him on how to cut the umbilical cord.

Mr. Thomas laughed. "I know exactly what to do," he stated with pride. "This is only our fourth child."

Sighing, Erika removed the surgical cap and wiped the sweat from her brow. She grinned. "Now I understand why the delivery took place so easily and so quickly." She sighed again. "I'm glad it was so easy, since this is my first solo delivery."

Erika tended to the mother's needs. After the afterbirth had been discharged, she had a few words with the proud parents. She then moved aside so the other staff members could do their jobs. Nurses from the neonatal unit were already in place to transfer the baby to the nursery. Needing a good cry to celebrate the successful delivery, Erika slipped out of the treatment room, only to learn that her private celebration would have to be put on hold. Stitches were needed in treatment room four.

After getting rid of the soiled latex gloves, Erika washed her hands again. Walking into the treatment room, she smiled at the mid-thirties Latino man who wore a bloodsoaked dishtowel wrapped around his left hand. She looked over the medical chart she'd been handed. "Hello, Mr. Vasquez," she greeted cheerfully, slipping a fresh pair of latex gloves onto her hands. As she gently removed the towel from his wound, she saw the gash was deep, but the bleeding appeared to be under control.

"How did this happen?" Even though it was written in the chart for her to see, she liked to hear from the patients themselves.

He looked abashed. "I was using a knife to open a locked metal box I had lost the key to. The knife slipped and went through my hand," he explained, his Spanish accent heavy. "I thought it was going to be okay, but it kept bleeding. That's why I came here."

"You did the right thing," Erika remarked. "Well, for sure, you're going to need a few stitches. Then we'll see about getting you out of here. When was your last tetanus shot?"

He scratched his head. "I don't know," he said politely, appearing embarrassed.

Erika gave Mr. Vasquez a friendly pat on the back. "It's okay, sir. We'll go ahead and give you a booster shot as a precautionary measure." Poking her head around the curtain, she caught the eye of one of the technicians. "Travis, I need a suture kit in here please. Mr. Vasquez is also going to need a tetanus shot." Travis acknowledged her request with a nod.

She'd been correct in assuming that the once quiet state of the emergency room had just been a lull before the storm. A steady stream of patients had begun to show up for treatment. Some were real emergencies, and others could've waited to see their private physicians during normal office hours. By four A.M., Erika was dead on her feet. Luckily, the emergency room was once again quiet.

Erika dragged herself to her assigned room. Without bothering to remove her clothing, she fell into bed, hoping she wouldn't be called on for the remainder of her shift. Medicine was a hectic profession, but she had to admit she loved taking care of those in need. It was such a rewarding career. With all of its ups and downs, she couldn't imagine herself doing anything else, nor did she want to. The only thing she regretted was not being able to help her parents when they'd taken ill. But she firmly believed in the Almighty, the Miracle Worker—the Master Physician who never lost a case.

Dead tired but restless, Erika tossed and turned in the small bed, which was a far cry from Michael's king-size one. Even in her own double bed she could toss and turn without the fear of falling off the edge. Erika sat up, punched the pillow, and placed it back under her head. As she lay awake the large sum of money that someone, probably Michael, had just shelled out for her was still a thorn in her side.

Michael was a very sensitive man, and she knew that discussing her dislike of his covert method of operation, no matter how generous it had been, would have to be handled with loads of sensitivity and patience. The whole idea of him giving her monetary support made her feel like a kept woman. Erika Edmonds wasn't the type that could be bought and paid for by anyone, least of all a man, not under any circumstances.

Erika again began to seriously contemplate putting her specialized training on hold—at least, until she could get her finances straight. She could practice medicine in an already established practice, or possibly get a staff position with University Hospital, or even another local hospital. The Pittsburgh area was loaded with medical facilities. She could move back into the family home until it was sold—an inconvenience, but at this point there weren't any other available options to be considered.

Erika finally drifted off to sleep, but it wasn't long before her rest became less than peaceful. Sweet dreams of Michael quickly turned nightmarish. Loud voices began to invade her unconscious state. . . .

Michael stood over her, jeering. Then he began to yell at her. "I don't want you going out tonight. You need to stay at home, Erika."

"But, Michael," she cried, "Lorraine and I are only going to the movies. She and I haven't been out together since you and I got married. What's wrong with me going to the movies with my best friend?"

His face grew gray with anger. "Must I remind you of who pays the bills around here? You're so ungrateful, Erika. I give you everything, and all you do is whine and complain. If you go out with Lorraine, I'm going to cut off all your expense accounts. I hate to keep reminding you that you're bought and paid for, in full. When you dropped out of the residency program and began to rely on me for everything, you gave up your rights to any independence. Have I made myself clear, Mrs. Mathis . . . ?"

"Damn you, Michael," she shouted, nearly falling out of the bed. Awakened by the near spill, Erika realized she'd been having a nightmare, and she wiped sweat from her face. Groaning loudly, she scooted over in the bed until her back was close to the wall, pulling the pillow over her head. Nightmare or no nightmare, the entire scenario had a very unsettling effect on her.

Eleven

Several minutes had passed when Erika looked at the clock. Her shift would be over in another hour. She'd been asleep a lot longer than she'd realized, but due to the nightmare she felt as though she hadn't slept at all. Getting out of bed, Erika sat at the desk and picked up the phone. As she dialed Michael's home phone number, she hoped he was already up. When he picked up the phone, sounding alert and chipper, she gave a sigh of relief.

"Good morning, Michael," she greeted, forcing cheer into her voice. The foggy sound of her voice revealed her fatigued state.

"Morning, gorgeous," he asserted cheerfully. "You sound exhausted, Erika. Tough shift?"

"The last several nights have been tough, Michael. And I am exhausted. However, I delivered a baby last night," she informed him excitedly, momentarily forgetting the real reason she'd phoned him. "It was a boy! And there were absolutely no complications. This was only their fourth child, of course," she said, laughing.

"Congratulations, Dr. Edmonds! Too bad it wasn't a girl. Then they could've named her after you. How's your schedule for this evening?" he asked, hoping they could steal a little time together. They hadn't seen each other in several days, and he wasn't sure how much longer he could stand it. He thought about her every waking moment.

Erika took a deep breath. "This is my last shift, Michael. I get off in less than an hour, but I only have twenty-four hours off. We need to talk before I go back on duty," she stated adamantly.

"This sounds serious, Erika. Is there something wrong?" he asked, hoping she hadn't gotten wind of anything to do with Richard.

She closed her eyes. "I don't want to talk about it over the phone. What time will you be available this evening?"

"This sounds like something that shouldn't have to wait. I have medical rounds this morning, then office hours until noon. My office is only open half a day on Wednesdays. What if I come by your place around one o'clock?"

"That's fine with me, Michael. Would you like me to fix some lunch?"

"No, you get some rest. I'll bring lunch. Something healthy. I love you, Dr. Edmonds!"

"I love you, too," she said, even though he'd already disconnected the line.

She loved him more than he could ever imagine, but would he still love her after she told him to butt out of her private affairs? Erika had a fiery temper, and she hoped it wouldn't surface during their discussion. Her temper was not a pretty sight.

Erika dragged her tired body out to the emergency room, where she deposited herself behind a gunmetal-gray desk. Pulling out the medical charts of the patients she'd seen during the shift, she began to peruse them, making sure she entered all the pertinent notes into the charts.

Wanting to save the staff the trouble of having to track her down for her signature, Erika made sure she'd signed all the charts. All medical charts needed to be signed by the attending physician. Not only was it important, it was necessary, and a part of the standard operating procedure—one that many doctors often failed to adhere to. Erika waved to the new shift of medical personnel as she went back to the room to gather all of her belongings. On the way to the dormitory she ran into Marlon Hale, the last person she wanted to see.

"Hey, Doc," he called out loudly. "You look like you just emerged from a war zone. ER duty!"

She smiled at his knowing response. "You guessed it. I'm doing my best to get to my apartment before I fall asleep on my feet."

He stroked his chin. "When you gonna let me take you for a ride in my new BMW, better known as 'Break My Window' or 'Black Man's Wheels'?" he joked, reluctant to hear what excuse she might use this time.

Erika's laughter was strained. " 'Black Man Working' sounds better to me. You brothers and your buppie status symbols," she insulted teasingly, not wanting to address his question. Her answer might hurt his feelings. "I've got to get to bed, Marlon. Talk to you later," she said, hoping he'd catch the hint.

"I see. It's like that, huh? You go ahead and get some rest. But be warned, I'm not giving up on you, sweet thing."

Rolling her eyes, Erika sucked her teeth. "Whatever, Marlon. See ya."

Ten minutes later, Erika had reached her apartment without any other annoying encounters. She'd barely closed the door when Lorraine's familiar knock hit the door. "Oh, boy! Am I ever going to get to bed?" Erika muttered, throwing the door open.

Lorraine looked fresh and well-rested. Her denim jeans and black shirt were pressed neatly, and her red hair was twisted in a knot on top of her head. "Hey, now," she greeted as she spun into the room. "You look as though you've been put through the wringer." Lorraine's bubbly demeanor suddenly grew somber. "I need to talk, girlfriend. Can you give me just a few minutes, please?" As tired as Erika felt, there was no way she could turn her friend away. Tears welled in Lorraine's eyes, causing Erika deep concern.

"Come on, sweetie. Let's go sit down." Erika dropped her

belongings on the desk and walked over to the sofa, taking off her shoes before sitting down next to Lorraine. "What's up?"

Wringing her hands, Lorraine bit down on her lower lip. "It's Joe, what else? I called him the other night to see if we could get our relationship back on track. His answer was very evasive. I suspect he's seeing someone else. How could he do that so soon?"

Pursing her lips, Erika pondered Lorraine's question. "I hate to remind you of this, but you did tell him you were going to find a new man. Maybe he took you seriously this time. Why do you think he's seeing someone?"

Lorraine shook her head. "I kind of sensed that someone was there with him. His answers were so evasive and noncommittal. It seemed as though he couldn't answer the way he wanted to. He told me he'd have to get back to me later, but he hasn't called yet. I'm worried, Erika," she moaned.

"Try not to worry, Lorraine. Wait until you hear what he has to say. I'm confident that he'll call you. But if you really want him back, you need to stop threatening him with other men. No man likes to hear that from the woman he loves. You shouldn't keep saying it—especially if you don't mean it."

Lorraine frowned. "Maybe you're right, Erika. I have to stop acting like a spoiled brat. Joe's been so good to me in the past and all I do is give him ultimatums. Ultimatums that he's probably sick and tired of hearing."

Erika nodded her head. "I agree with you one hundred percent. I know you don't expect me to be anything but honest with you. Joe knows you come from a wealthy background, Lorraine. I don't see anything wrong with him wanting to wait to marry you. He just wants to offer you the same type of life you've been used to."

Lorraine looked defeated. "Yeah, I know. I just hope it's not too late. Listen, I'm going to run so you can get some sleep. But before I go, how's that handsome doctor you've been spending all of your free time with?"

Erika contemplated telling Lorraine about the troubling money situation, but decided against it. Lorraine had enough to deal with right now. "He's wonderful! He's the most wonderful man I've ever had the pleasure of knowing. He's in love with me," Erika announced casually, not wanting to show how excited she was over Michael's confession.

Lorraine's green-gray eyes widened with wonder. "He told you that? He actually said he loved you?"

Erika smiled smugly. "He did, Lorraine. And I love him, too. I just pray this relationship never fizzles out. He's sooo good!"

Lorraine felt a twinge of jealousy over Erika's good fortune, but it didn't put a damper on her being genuinely happy for her dear friend. "You go, girl," Lorraine exclaimed, trying to fight off a swarm of tears. "No one deserves to find love more than you do, Erika. Now, I'm getting out of here before I break down and cry." Lorraine kissed Erika and dashed toward the door, but tears already gushed from her eyes.

Erika cried too, knowing she *did* deserve love. She deserved happiness, too. Michael deserved the same. But would the money issue cause a rift between them? Was their love strong enough to overcome this very real obstacle? Would he really understand why she couldn't accept his monetary support?

Michael was all that and more, but would another side of him surface? Could her nightmare become a reality? Deciding to save all the questions for Michael to answer, Erika took a quick shower.

Having dried off, she dressed in a frilly, lavender nightshirt and climbed into bed. Fully relaxed, she buried herself under the blankets. The sheets smelled fresh from a sachet-scented fabric softener she'd used for the first time, making them smell like a bouquet of spring flowers. Falling into a serene place, she hoped she'd awaken before Michael's familiar knock sounded on the door. She certainly didn't want to miss out on seeing him. To make sure she didn't oversleep, she set the alarm clock.

* * *

As Michael passed through his reception area, he smiled. One section of the area looked like a miniature toyland. The colorful foil wallpaper was cheerfully decorated with balloons, clowns and numerous circus scenes. Miniature chairs and tables were lined up against one wall, and a rack filled with children's books hung over a large table. Stuffed animals and other toys were crammed into an old-fashioned toy chest.

Although Michael specialized in pediatric surgery, he had adult patients as well and he also shared office space with Wynton Sharpton, a pediatrician who was not a surgeon. A good many of Michael's pediatric surgeries were referrals from Dr. Sharpton. Michael sat down at the desk inside his private office to finish dictating a few discharge summaries.

An hour later, he turned off the microcassette recorder and donned a white lab coat to wear during medical appointments. He had three more patients to see before calling it a day.

Leaving his private office, he stepped into the corridor. Stopping at room number one, he removed the medical chart from its holder beside the door, scanning the nurse's handwritten notes as he entered the room.

Four-year-old Jabarri Wilkes was recovering from a herniorrhaphy, the surgery Michael had performed to repair Jabarri's umbilical hernia. The hernia had caused the navel to protrude, which had caused the child a lot of pain and discomfort.

Michael chatted with Mrs. Wilkes for a few moments. Playing with the child, he hoped to get him to relax. Once the child felt comfortable, Michael anesthetized the surgical site with Novocaine and gently removed the stitches. Using a cotton swab, he cleaned the area with a sterile solution.

"He's doing just fine, Mrs. Wilkes. I'd like to see him next week. See Darlene before you leave." Reaching into his pocket, Michael pulled out a red lollipop and handed it to Jabarri. "You deserve this. You're a real hero, little man."

Jabarri giggled as he tore the wrapping off the candy. Remembering his manners, he thanked the doctor in a shy, tiny voice. Before leaving the room, Michael ruffled the top of the child's head.

Immediately, Michael entered another treatment room, where he greeted Mr. Carlton with a firm handshake. Walking over to the treatment table, he lifted six-year-old Derrick off the table. "Hey, pal, how you doing?" Michael asked, sitting the child back down carefully.

Derrick grinned, showing off his missing two front teeth. "I'm okay, Dr. Maffis. I've been eating a lot of ice cream. It makes my froat feel real good."

"That's great, Derrick! Now let me have a look at your throat."

Removing a tongue depressor from a glass jar, Michael instructed Derrick to open wide. Using a penlight-like instrument, he examined the back of Derrick's throat.

"It looks good, Mr. Carlton. He's healing nicely."

Due to Derrick's frequent bouts with tonsillitis and constant streptococcus infections, Michael had performed a tonsillectomy. Tonsillectomies weren't performed as often now as in days past. The tonsil's exact function was still not known. But in Derrick's case it had been very necessary.

"Mr. Carlton, make an appointment for Derrick to see me in ten days. I'll have Darlene give you a back-to-school form. I believe he's ready. If he experiences any problems, don't hesitate to call the office. But everything should be just fine."

Michael turned to face Derrick. "You keep on eating that ice cream, young man, but don't stuff yourself. See you in ten days." Michael tousled Derrick's sandy-brown hair on his way out the door.

Vincent Clark was Michael's last patient. The teenager had ended up having an appendectomy the day after Michael had seen him in the emergency room. His white blood count had soared during the night, and his right quadrant pain had increased considerably. Vincent's stitches had already been removed, but he'd come in for another post-operative check.

Michael laughed and joked with Vincent before he examined him. Michael couldn't stop his heart from taking flight when Vincent inquired about his "hot-looking" girlfriend. As a flashback of their passionate couplings momentarily clouded his vision, he smiled.

As Michael examined Vincent, he noticed a yellowish pus leaking from the incision site. More of the pus oozed out as he lightly pressed down on the area. The yellowish substance had a foul odor, which indicated to Michael the strong possibility of an infection.

Looking down at Vincent, Michael pressed on the area again. "Does this hurt you when I press down?"

Vincent shrugged his shoulders. "A little bit. Sometimes that area feels really tight. What's that yellow stuff, Dr. Mathis? It sure is funky!"

"There may be an infection in your incision, Vincent. I'm going to clean it up, then have Patty draw some blood. Until I know for sure what's going on here, I'm going to put you on another type of antibiotic. I also need to have this substance cultured. However, I don't think it's something we need to worry too much about. Where's your mom?"

Vincent frowned heavily. "She's in the waiting room. I'm too old to have her in here with me. She thinks I'm still a baby, but I'm not. I'm a man," he announced, hitting his chest with his fist. "I can tell her what you've said."

Michael laughed. "You can, Vincent, but it's my professional obligation to discuss your case with her. Your parents are responsible for you, not the other way around. Get my meaning, pal?"

Vincent scowled. "Yeah, I guess I do. I sure hate missing all those basketball practices. I'll be glad when I can get back into action. I can't wait to slam-dunk a ball!"

Michael patted Vincent on the back. "Patience, my young brother, patience. I'll see you back here next week. I'm going to send Patty in, then talk to your mother. I'll give her the new prescription I plan to write for you. Take care of yourself, Vince."

"Hey, doc, wait a minute. How old is Nurse Patty? She looks really young."

"Too old for you, Vincent. And don't give her a hard time. She's capable of dissing you real bad," Michael joked, speaking in terms Vincent understood best.

Smiling to himself, Michael entered his private office, sat down behind his desk and wrote out a prescription for Vincent. Using the intercom line, he asked Darlene, the receptionist, to send in Mrs. Clark.

Once Mrs. Clark was seated, Michael explained his medical findings to her and handed her the written prescription.

He answered all of her questions, told her when he wanted to see Vincent again, and asked her to call his office if Vincent spiked a fever or experienced any other complications. Mrs. Clark thanked him and returned to the waiting room.

It was close to two o'clock by the time Michael reached Erika's door.

Erika, dressed in a pair of pale yellow sweats, kissed Michael as he stepped inside the door carrying two large brown bags. Taking one from his hand, she led the way into the kitchen, where they opened the bags and set the contents on the table.

Plastic containers held a variety of food items: salad greens, thick slabs of baked chicken and turkey, shredded cheese, boiled eggs and thick rings of sweet, red onions. Another container held celery, carrot sticks, cherry tomatoes, red radishes, and black and green olives. Two fat dill pickles were packaged in Saran Wrap. A plastic sectional platter was filled with a variety of fresh fruits cut into chunks and slices. The last items to be placed on the table were two containers of deli-fresh salad dressings.

Erika thought the table looked like a fruit and salad bar.

Everything smelled so fresh. The vegetables looked crisp, as if they'd just been plucked straight from the garden. With barely enough room left for anything else, Erika pushed the containers to the middle of the table as she set out the dishes and silverware.

Standing on tiptoe, she pulled Michael's head down and kissed him in the center of his forehead. "I'm sure the deli owner smiled at his good fortune. You must have spent a small bundle in there. Everything looks great. Shall we partake of this healthy feast?"

"Dessert first," he remarked seductively, pulling her into his arms, blistering her lips with a staggering kiss.

Pulling out a chair for her, he seated himself, and they filled their plates. Then Erika went to the refrigerator and pulled out a glass pitcher of mixed, unsweetened fruit juices. Talking amicably, they munched on their salads, hoping to temporarily delay the conversation that had them both on edge.

While talking about the patients he'd seen in his office, he especially enjoyed relating the comments Vincent had made about her. To say the least, the six-foot-plus hunk of firm but pliant steel sitting across from her was distracting. The need to get her concerns out in the open all but dissipated as she listened to the man capable of driving her insane by a mere touch of his hand.

An unsettling thought suddenly occurred to her: in just a few minutes she could be biting his head off. They could become embroiled in a shouting match, her accusing him of trying to take over her life, him vehemently denying the charge. She hoped he *would* deny it, but only if he was being totally honest.

He put his arm around the back of her chair. "What planet are you on, gorgeous? You seem to have forgotten me," he said, feeling a little left out.

Oh, no, she hadn't forgotten him, not by a long shot. She doubted she'd ever be able to forget him. More than that, she hoped she'd never have to try to forget.

"I'm sorry, Michael." She sighed. "I guess it's time for us to have that talk." Looking bewildered, she hesitated for a moment. "Someone has paid the entire bill for my moving expenses. You can imagine how shaken I was, especially after I learned that Randy thought the check came from me. It appears that an unknown benefactor has donated a large sum of money toward the move. Do you know anything about this, Michael?"

He looked genuinely surprised. "Why would I, Erika?" He had no idea she suspected him of being the mystery benefactor. "Have you talked to Aunt Arlene about it?"

She closely studied his features and body language, and neither appeared to signal any discomfort or guilt. She was left with no alternative but to get straight to the point. "Did you donate the money, Michael?"

The question caught him totally off guard. "Me? Of course not," he exclaimed, sounding slightly offended. "I'd never do something like that without discussing it with you first. It's true I've wanted to help you financially, but I knew you wouldn't even consider that type of help from me, or for that matter, anyone else. I thought you knew me better than that, Erika." He felt disappointed that she thought him capable of tampering with her dignity.

She put her hand across her forehead. "Oh, Michael, if not you, then who? I can't think of anyone who would pay out that kind of money for me. Aunt Arlene has checked with my aunt and uncle who live on the West Coast, and neither of them know anything about it."

Michael shifted uncomfortably in his seat, which wasn't lost on Erika. It had begun to dawn on him that he did know who would do something like this, and he didn't like where his thoughts had taken him. If Richard was responsible for this, he was going to wring his bloody neck and hand it to him. How could he make such a conspicuous blunder?

Getting up from his seat, Michael walked over to the kitchen window. Frowning heavily, he looked down at the parking lot. After a few seconds of serious pondering, he turned to face

Erika. "This is all so crazy, Erika. I don't know what to make of it." He really didn't. He wasn't positive Richard was the responsible party. "Do you believe it wasn't me?" His question was fraught with urgency. He needed her to believe him. If she didn't, what would the future hold for them?

Erika walked over to him and put her arms around his waist, pressing his back into the windowsill. "Yes, I believe it. I'm sorry, but I had to ask. I'm relieved that it wasn't you, but I guess I'm a little bit disappointed, too. Now I'm going to have to find out who's behind it and why. If it had been you, then it could've been easily settled. But now, I don't know where to begin," she said, offering her lips to him.

It was an offer he couldn't refuse. Bending his head, he took her mouth lightly, plying a gentle pressure that soon became urgent and demanding. He wanted to kiss all of her doubts away, wanted her to know she never had to doubt him. His intimate points were well-taken, and she kissed him back feverishly.

But if Richard *was* responsible, he'd presented him with a much bigger problem than he'd initially believed. If Erika learned Richard was both her brother and her benefactor, she'd probably assume that Michael knew both, as well. It was going to look as if he'd deceived her on two counts instead of only the one he was actually guilty of. How many other things would he have to keep from her before Richard got around to telling her everything? Richard had dragged him into something that threatened his very existence. Without Erika in his life he'd have no meaningful existence, he thought fearfully.

The fear of losing her intensified his need to hold on to her as he sweetly plundered her mouth. His need to completely possess the woman he just might lose made him crazy. His lips smothered her face with kisses, tracing the soft column of her neck. When her fingers twisted in his hair, he reached up to lace his fingers in hers.

Cupping her face in his hands, he held her head away from him. "Come home with me, Erika," he practically pleaded, looking deep into her eyes. "I don't want to be alone. I promise to take care of you."

Feeling how tense his shoulders and neck had become, she backed slightly away from him. "Michael, what's wrong with you? You're coiled like a spring, and you sound so darn fearful." Concern furrowed her brow.

Pushing his hands through his hair, he laughed nervously. "It's not really fear that you're hearing, Erika. I just want us to be together. Our schedules are so hectic that I just feel we should steal every moment available to us. Besides, I'd like to cook dinner for you."

A smile touched her eyes as well as her lips. "I'd like to go, but I planned to see my aunt today. I want to get out there before she has dinner, which is usually around five or so. Maybe I could drive over to your place afterward."

He placed a kiss on her chin. "I'd like to go out to the house with you, Erika. I just want to be with you. May I escort you there? I did promise your aunt I'd be back to see her."

Erika grinned. "Certainly, if you're sure. I'd like her to see us together. My aunt seems to like you an awful lot. But don't get upset if she starts asking questions about our relationship. She doesn't mean any harm. She just worries about me feeling all alone."

He hugged her. "I know she doesn't. I enjoy being in your aunt's company. I may be pushing the envelope here, though I hope I'm not. I'd like you to spend the night with me. I'll bring you home before I go to the hospital. I have a surgery scheduled for eleven A.M., which means we won't have to get up too early."

She grew apprehensive. "Michael, I want to spend every waking moment with you, but I don't want to wear out my welcome. Nor do I want you to tire of me."

He shook his head. "We've been over this road before. I want you to stop worrying about wearing out your welcome or my tiring of you. It's not going to happen. If I thought there was a remote possibility of you saying yes, I'd ask you to move in with me. How's that for wearing out a welcome?"

She was both flattered and disappointed by his statement. And he was right—there wasn't a chance in hell that she'd move in with him. But had he offered a more permanent arrangement. . . . *Oh, boy,* she thought, immediately erasing the wishing well in her mind.

"Let's just play my spending the night by ear. I need to change my clothes, and then we can go." She looked over at the messy condition of the table. "First, I'd better clean up in here." She moved toward the table.

Grabbing her around the waist, he thwarted her forward progress. "You go get ready. I'll take care of cleaning up this mess." When it looked as though she was going to protest, he playfully swatted her on the behind. "Go," he gently commanded.

Knowing it wasn't going to do any good to protest, she smiled brightly. "Just rinse the dishes off and stack them in the sink. I'll do them later," she tossed over her shoulder in parting.

In her bedroom Erika opened the closet and pulled out a fuchsia-colored wool pleated skirt and the matching double-breasted jacket. The pleated skirt was a miniskirt, a length she wouldn't have considered wearing when she was overweight. The jacket boasted a shawl collar and large gold buttons.

After removing a bone knit sweater with cap sleeves from a dresser drawer, she laid the clothes out on the bed. Erika stripped out of the sweats, pulled on a pair of neutral-toned tights and slipped her feet into bone-colored, ankle-cut leather boots. There was still enough ice and snow on the ground to warrant safe footwear.

Seated on the bed, Erika bent over and laced up the boots. She slid the sweater over her head, then pulled on the skirt. After a run-through of light cosmetic applications, she checked herself in the mirror, noticing how bright her eyes looked and the healthy color of her cheeks. Despite the long working hours she'd put in, she looked fresh and glowing.

It's the look of love, she decided. Michael's love had put the stars in her eyes, and the blushing color in her cheeks. *What's love got to do with it?* she questioned.

It has everything to do with it, replied a soft voice in her head.

The kitchen was sparkling clean when Erika returned to the tiny room. There weren't any signs of the meal they'd just consumed. Neatly folded, the brown paper bags were the only items left on the table.

Michael was hanging up the dishtowel as Erika slipped up behind him and wrapped her arms around his waist. "You are one hardheaded rover," she accused teasingly, using the expression that her stepfather had often used with her.

Turning around to face her, he caught her lower lip between his teeth. "Yeah, I guess I am. But if you're going to bother to rinse the dishes, you may as well go ahead and wash them. Besides, you don't need to come back to a bunch of dirty chores. These hands," he said, holding them up, "are so capable."

She rolled her eyes up to the ceiling. "Yes, I know," she breathed, recalling how capable they were of igniting a fire under her skin. He kissed her thoroughly before guiding her to the door. Erika stopped abruptly. "Don't you think we should take all the leftovers to your house? I'll never be able to eat all of them."

"Don't worry. You won't have to. I plan to come back here to help you. They will stay fresh for a couple of days. Let's go. We're wasting precious time."

On the way to the house, Erika asked Michael to stop at a store so she could purchase some candy to take to Aunt Arlene, who loved Reese's Peanut Butter Cups and York Peppermint Patties, which had also been Vernice's favorites. Erika planned to get several of each.

As they neared their destination, Erika's heart started racing.

Stroking the back of her hands, she tried to calm herself down. If Aunt Arlene brought up the subject of marriage, Erika just knew she'd die from embarrassment. Marriage was the last thing on Michael's mind, and she didn't want her aunt to pressure him in any way. But her aunt had a way of getting all in the Kool-Aid without even knowing the flavor. To marry Erika off to such a wonderful man as Michael would make Aunt Arlene very happy.

Erika had already called ahead to say they were coming, which would've given her aunt enough time to think up all sorts of things. She could just imagine Arlene rushing around to make herself presentable. Like Vernice, Arlene was like a schoolgirl when in the company of a good-looking man. Had Vernice's sassy sister been a few light-years younger and not related by blood, Erika thought with a mischievous smile, she might've had some serious competition on her hands. It wouldn't surprise her one bit to learn that quite a few other attractive women secretly vied for the attention of the man she herself loved so dearly. *Ah, too bad,* she thought audaciously. *Sorry, ladies, he seems to want only me!*

Twelve

Erika and Michael found Arlene in the huge family room, where she entertained another female guest. As Erika had expected, Aunt Arlene was dressed to the nines, looking lovely in a pair of navy slacks and a white, button-down cardigan. Erika could see that her aunt had made a recent visit to the hair salon.

Arlene rushed over to her niece. "Oh, I'm so glad you came, Erika," Arlene enthused. "I had a feeling you'd be coming out today. I was going to call you, but you called here first," she explained excitedly. "I'm really glad to see you, too, Michael."

Warmly embracing her, he kissed Arlene's cheek. "It's good to see you."

Erika smiled brightly. "And I'm so happy to see you, Aunt Arlene," Erika rejoiced, bringing Arlene close to her side. "I was here a few days ago, but you were out on a senior trip. I'd like to hear how your outing went."

"It was really nice, Erika. Our little group did some shopping, and had lunch later," Arlene said, patting her hair. "The group also took in a movie, and we had a short coffee break afterward. I've been missing you, love."

Erika smiled, and hugged Arlene again. "Well, I'll see to it that you don't have to miss me very much. I'll try to come here as often as I came when Mom was alive and we'll try to do all the things we did before. Nothing is going to change between us, Auntie. Outside of missing me, how are you doing?"

"I couldn't be better. Come on over here. I want you to meet my good friend." Arlene took Erika by the hand and directed her to the woman who sat on the sofa.

"This is Helena Deavers. Helena, this is my niece, Erika. She's a doctor," Arlene announced with pride. "And this fine, young man, Michael Mathis, is also a doctor."

Helena was a classy-looking Caucasian woman. Her mixed-gray hair was cut in a pageboy, and her bangs were cropped short. Her icy-blue eyes busily summed up Erika and Michael, yet her manner was warm and friendly.

Helena extended her hand to Erika. "Your aunt has told me a lot about you, young lady. You two make a striking couple," she offered with a genuine smile. "Your children will be absolutely beautiful," she said—the last thing Erika had expected to hear.

Michael easily recognized that Erika's discomfort was for him. As he pulled her close to him, his eyes told her not to worry. "We haven't gotten quite that far," he advised Helena, smiling. "But I'd have to agree with you. Our children would indeed be beautiful." Blushing heavily, Erika lowered her lashes, totally embarrassed by their comments.

Once everyone was comfortably seated, Erika handed Arlene the small, brown paper bag she'd carried into the house. "These are for you, Aunt Arlene. A couple of your favorites."

Arlene opened the bag, and a huge smile caressed her face. "I can't remember the last time I had a piece of chocolate candy. Thank you, Erika. You're always so thoughtful." After offering a piece to Helena and Michael, who both politely declined, Arlene opened a Peppermint Pattie and bit into it. "The candy is so refreshing, and it tastes so good."

Arlene ate the candy, then took a Reese's cup out of the bag and tore off the wrapping, inhaling the scent of peanut butter before breaking off a piece. "Erika, I want to ask you something. Has anyone come to look at the house?"

Wondering where this line of questioning was going, Erika rubbed her hands together. "No, not yet. Is there a reason you're asking?"

Arlene met Erika's intense gaze. "I know you don't want to sell the place," she said, tilting her chin upward. "I think I'm beginning to understand how you feel about it. If you want to hold on to it, I'll help with the payments until you can lease it out. Would that make you feel better, Erika?"

Erika moaned inwardly. "Why don't we discuss it later?" she suggested, not wanting to talk about it while company was around. Arlene nodded her understanding and excused herself to go into the kitchen.

A few minutes later, when Arlene called out to Michael from the kitchen, he quickly heeded her summons. Left alone with Helena, Erika engaged her in a conversation about current events. Vernice had loved to watch the news and read the newspapers, Erika remembered with fondness. Her mother had kept up with everything that went on around the world.

Carrying a tray of refreshments, Michael reentered the room. As he glided toward her, Erika felt her hands go all shaky. The man simply did it for her, no two ways about it. Everything about him spoke of confidence and elegance. A fine, suave, debonair, African prince—that summed up Michael Mathis quite nicely. For right now he was all hers, but she was just selfish enough to want forever with him.

After setting the tray on the coffee table, Michael bent over and kissed Erika on the cheek, causing her color to rise. His eyes seemed to tell Erika that he couldn't wait to have her all to himself. Though the visit was going very well, Erika couldn't wait to leave, either, couldn't wait to be alone with Michael, couldn't wait to be in his arms once again. His strong, tender arms were her haven, a serene port safe from the storms of her life. Those wonderful arms held the master key to her very security. Was it Michael Mathis that held the golden key to her personal future?

Her blood ran hot, surging through her ears, filling her head with heady explosions. Looking over at Michael, she smiled winsomely. The expression in her eyes spoke of her intense need for him, a need burning white-hot in the essence of her femininity. While his tongue outlined his lips in a provocative way, he winked, smiling back at her. When he ran his palms down his muscular thighs, her eyes smiled.

As her color continued to rise, Erika was glad Arlene and Helena were engrossed in conversation, a conversation she couldn't have joined in if she'd wanted to. She had no idea what topic was being discussed. But the soundless topic of conversation in her and Michael's suggestive expressions came through crystal clear—in short: "Can't wait until we're alone."

Finally reaching the house, they watched as the sun slowly cascaded down behind the forest, where they heard and saw the evening come alive with all the vibrant sounds and signs announcing that nightfall lay dead ahead. The winds rustling through the trees sang a lullaby to the creatures of the forest community, and they responded by humming their own style of music as they scrambled to their shelters for the night. Knowing the evening was their special time to hunt for food and play, the night creatures crept from their hiding places. An owl could be heard hooting from its home high among the trees.

Michael hugged Erika to him. "Want to walk a bit before we go inside?"

She smiled up at him. "I'd love to, sweetheart. This is such a special time of the evening and I love strolling through nature with you."

Michael took her hand as they walked to the gate leading to the backyard. They walked through the yard and through another gate at the end of the property, which led into the forest. Taking the beaten path, they walked into the forest until they reached a clearing.

Sitting down on a wide, felled tree stump, Michael pulled

Erika down on his lap. "Listen, gorgeous. Just be still and let the sounds of nightfall seep into your soul. Let's claim this as our very own special place. If I had a penknife with me, I'd carve our names in this stump. Remind me to bring it the next time we come here." She nodded, laying her head back against his chest, listening to the sounds of nightfall, as he'd instructed.

Several minutes later, they resumed their walk, continuing until the gentleness of night fell around them. Looking upward, they saw the first star of the night appear in the hazy, purple sky. The atmosphere was bathed in serenity.

When unexpected showers started to fall, they only huddled closer together, neither of them minding the rain spattering on them. Michael kissed away the raindrops as they splashed against Erika's lovely face. She saw rain as just a way of nature bathing itself, she told him. Michael believed the rain cleansed the universe of all its impurities, making everything sparkling clean and brand-new—another way of expressing the same thing Erika believed. Erika liked the way they seemed to be in tune with each other's thoughts and emotions.

Lightning suddenly striking near them caused them to run for shelter. If lightning hit one of the trees, they knew it could prove disastrous for them. As their laughter rang through the forest, they ran for the back porch.

Just inside the second gate, Erika lost her footing, but Michael was right there. Smiling to herself, she realized he'd been there to break her fall from the first moment they'd laid eyes on each other. Valiantly, he'd been doing that ever since.

Instead of turning on the lights, Michael walked all through the house and lit a variety of scented candles, along with both fireplaces. In a matter of minutes glowing warmth permeated the entire house. Soft music added a romantic ambience to the glowing, candlelit rooms.

Once he and Erika discarded their wet attire and donned thick robes, they went into the kitchen, where Michael began to prepare the meal, using only candlelight and the flames from the gas stove for light. The flashing lightning added a touch of heightened drama.

Erika watched the moving shadows playfully dancing across the walls. From her seat at the table she felt hypnotized, watching Michael's strong physique fall in and out of the shadows as he moved about the kitchen with quiet determination.

Soon the air was filled with the delicious smell of broiled steak. As fresh vegetables steamed in white wine, lemon juice and a pat of herb butter, Michael made a light salad dressing of virgin olive oil, ground oregano and Parmesan cheese. He then tossed the salad greens.

Erika sniffed the air and her taste buds caught fire. Once again, Michael proved to have a pair of very capable hands. A beautiful, sensuous man cooking by candlelight was a devastating sight to behold, a sight that stirred up powerful images in Erika's mind. In her opinion, Michael Mathis was an artistic masterpiece, perfection in motion.

By candlelight, they dined. By the light in their eyes, they exchanged sweet words of love. By sheer magnetic draw, their lips met between bites of the exquisitely prepared feast. It was easy for them to agree on one specific point: It didn't get any better than this.

These were the very moments they'd looked forward to all day. Tonight they would touch, kiss, speak of magnificent dreams and snuggle together throughout the evening. As the dreamy music compelled them to slow dance, they entwined in a loving embrace.

He pressed his cheek against hers. "I love the way your eyes shine in the candlelight, Dr. Edmonds. I love the way you make me feel. In fact, I love everything about you. I'm stupid, crazy in love with you, gorgeous."

Smiling, she looked up into his eyes. "Is that so, Dr. Mathis? Why don't you show me how much?" Her fingers were tangled in his hair. "I need reassuring," she flirted, batting her eyelashes seductively.

Tugging at the collar of the bathrobe until he brought it

down around her shoulders, he kissed her collarbone. "How much reassuring?"

"Lots."

"Physical or emotional, gorgeous?"

"Both, handsome."

Drawing her lower lip between his teeth, he sucked gently, kissing each side of her luscious mouth, kissing her deeply. "How do you want to be reassured?"

The corners of her mouth turned up in a slight smile. "Hmm, that was certainly reassuring. Another dozen kisses just like that one might do the trick."

Slowly, his mouth closed over hers. Finished tasting her lips, he tasted her neck and earlobes. Tilting her head back, he kissed her throat until she moaned. As his hand slid under her bathrobe, caressing her naked flesh, she moaned louder.

Savoring his heated caresses, Erika looked up into his eyes. "I want you to make a promise to me, Michael. Our relationship has grown strong and I don't want to do anything to upset this balance we seem to have developed between us. I want you to come to me if you see any problem areas developing in our relationship so that we can discuss your concerns. Can you promise me that?"

He cupped her face in his hands. "Gorgeous, you don't have to worry about something like that. However, I promise to do as you ask. But if it's left up to me, our relationship is only going to get stronger. We've come along so nicely. I can only pray that I've been as good for you as you've been for me. And I promise to be nothing less than wonderful to you."

Much, much later, as they curled up in bed, no problematic situations were discussed, but they did talk about the special meeting scheduled for the next day, regarding Erika's ideas on special community service projects for the neighboring seniors.

Snuggled up to each other, they talked only of bright promises and of future days and nights they'd spend loving each other in each and every way. Michael had never been more content in his life, and Erika couldn't remember ever feeling so at peace. They seemed to bring out the best in each other and neither was foolish enough to expect they'd never have to see the other at his or her worst.

The entire day had been positively wonderful. But this was a night for discovery; a discovery that placed their trembling fingers on the pulse of each other's thundering heartbeats.

Erika felt strange sitting around a conference table with nothing but men, though it was something she was used to. The fact that they were all men had little to do with the way she felt. These were men who outranked her in every aspect of the word: men who were powerful figures in the medical community, men who'd been practicing medicine long before she was even born, men whose status was highly revered, men who could make or break a young resident.

But Michael was there, she reminded herself. He was the stabilizing force that would get her through this awkward meeting of ingenious minds. She knew he'd at least be heard, because of the respect and admiration he received from his senior colleagues. Jules Baker was present, too, and had assured Erika that she had his vote. If she and Michael failed to sell the community service ideas to the powers that be, there was an excellent chance that Jules could, and probably would.

The meeting was called to order and Michael took his place at the podium. Although he'd just gotten out of surgery, he looked refreshed. His fashionable attire could hardly be described as businesslike. Anything short of flawless would've been a gross understatement, Erika thought with a smile.

As he respectfully recognized his colleagues and began to state his case, Erika noticed that everyone appeared to hang on his every word. She'd heard Michael had a way of mesmerizing groups, just as he mesmerized her. Unlike the tone in which he spoke to her, though, his voice was now powerful, his words exuding confidence.

Utterly entranced by his professional demeanor and his composed air of authority when he finished his speech, Erika could see clearly that he'd captivated his audience, too. When Michael summoned her to the podium, she wasn't sure she could stand up, let alone make it to the front of the room. Her legs felt like rubber and her knees knocked together.

Dr. Jules Baker saw the panic in Erika's eyes as he stood up and pulled out her chair. Gripping her shoulder, he put his head close to her ear. "These are just flesh and blood men, Erika. Don't see them as anything more than that. Take control," Dr. Baker whispered, hoping to boost her confidence. "Your anemia-screening proposal is worth every ounce of your energy."

Erika squared her shoulders and smiled, through the podium seemed to be a mile away. Michael was there waiting for her, she reminded herself, which made it much easier for her to run the gauntlet. As she reached the podium, Michael presented her to the board members after giving a brief history of her background. Quietly, he stepped slightly behind her. Erika basked in the security Michael's presence afforded her, knowing he'd be right there to catch her should she stumble and fall. She'd come to expect that from him.

Looking directly at the board members, Erika acknowledged each one by name. Michael smiled knowingly. Erika had won their rapt attention. She could've easily addressed them as a whole body, but she had taken the time to memorize each of their names and faces. It was a smart move on her part. He was impressed.

Erika cleared her throat and continued. "Out of respect for your valuable time, I'm not going to give a lengthy speech. However, I am going to address some of the concerns you may have about these community service projects," she said, smiling endearingly.

Without further ado, Erika plunged into her presentation, carefully prepared and ready to go over the topics they'd be most interested in hearing about: funding, manpower, security, advertising sources, and other pertinent issues. Fully composed, she gave them a brief history of her mother's illness.

Taking the issues one by one, Erika laid out her strategies in painstaking detail. Leaving no stone unturned, she cleverly answered each of the burning questions she thought might be asked of her.

"Funding," she remarked. "I know these are expensive endeavors, but we intend to hold several fund-raisers to offset laboratory costs and other operational expenses the hospital might incur. I have several people who are now working on ways of finding legitimate money for our projects. As for manpower, at last count, I had thirty volunteers who have committed. There are many others who have expressed a desire to get involved in these worthwhile projects. Many laboratory technicians are willing to donate their off-duty time."

Erika turned to look at Michael. "Advertising. Dr. Mathis has been kind enough to volunteer to undertake this essential assignment," she offered enthusiastically, hoping the love she felt for him wasn't too terribly obvious. "Several office suppliers have already agreed to donate the necessary supplies needed for making and distributing fliers, which Dr. Mathis and I will design on the computer. We also hope to use children from the community for distribution. We hope to eliminate postal fees, to further help keep the costs down. Gentlemen, I hope I've addressed the majority of your concerns.

"Oh," she said, laughing softly, "Officer Easton from the local police department is going to assist us in getting off-duty officers to help out with any needed security. He once told me that I could use him in any way I saw fit, but I'm not too sure he meant it quite like this." Everyone laughed at her effervescent humor. "Since it's for our seniors, Officer Easton couldn't find it in his heart to turn me down, as I hope you won't be able to, either. Thank you for your precious time. It has been an honor to stand here before you. I'm prepared to answer any questions you might have."

Tall, coffee-black, impressively built for someone older than sixty, Elam Templeton III, the hospital administrator, got to his feet. Before speaking, he took a brief glance at each of his colleagues to see if they were as impressed with Erika's presentation as he was. Although he was greatly impressed, he knew the others would expect him to play the devil's advocate.

"Thank you, Dr. Edmonds, for such a brilliant presentation. It was very enlightening. I have one very important question to start with. You have our every sympathy where your mother is concerned, but I have to ask—has this crusade you're on come as a result of guilt? Are you doing this because you feel you didn't do enough to help your mother when she was alive?"

Feeling Michael's anger bristling behind her, she silently asked him to calm down by flattening her palms against the air in a downward gesture. While she also resented the question and the implication of negligence on her part, she was almost glad about it. Taking the time to look each board member dead in the eye gave her a chance to rein in her emotions to a manageable level. The silence seemed interminable, but she knew she was gaining the edge because the men looked totally uncomfortable.

She placed her hands on the podium. "I'm not going to stand here and tell you that I was the perfect daughter, that I met my mother's every need, that there weren't times when I grew impatient and frustrated with the entire situation. One of the saddest parts about this is that I am a doctor. I became one because my mother sacrificed and did without for my education. But I couldn't save her life. I had no clue as to what was happening to her, and neither did some of the best doctors around.

"Now, to answer your question. Do I feel guilty about my mother's situation? Hell, yes, I feel guilty. I'm weighted down with guilt, but not for the reasons you've alluded to. I feel guilty because I couldn't do more for her, didn't know how to ease the pain of what was happening to her, wasn't able to assure her it was going to be all right—because I wasn't sure it ever would be.

"Was I a good daughter? If you could ask her that question, I think she would tell you I was one hell of a damn good daughter. Did I do everything for my mother that was within my power? Did I allow her to smell my gifts of roses while she was alive? Did I love my mother in the way she deserved to be loved? With every fiber of my being. With every breath in me!

"How much more guilt do I have to bear? How much guilt are we all going to have to bear?" Several eyebrows raised at that question. "I can see that many of you want to know what I mean by that. Are we, as medical doctors, willing to continue to ignore this very real threat to people's lives when we can do something about it, starting with education? How many people are we going to let die before we act on the facts we now have in our possession? How much longer are we going to let modern medicine embrace the theory that any one disease is exclusive to one race of people? There's evidence of amalgamated bloodlines from practically the beginning of time. Would I be doing this if my loved one hadn't been affected by pernicious anemia? Probably not, simply because I didn't know anything about it before my mother was diagnosed. Isn't that how most diseases are brought to the forefront? When a loved one is struck down—with something no one knew about, or didn't understand if they did—is when most crusades start."

Feeling she'd said enough, perhaps too much, Erika decided it was time to surrender the podium. "Gentlemen, I again thank you for your valuable time. I'll be more than happy to address any other questions."

Elam Templeton looked slightly abashed as he got to his feet again. "Thank you for your outstanding presentation, young lady. However," he grumbled, "I don't see this board approving free screening tests for everyone in this community.

That would be much too expensive. But I must admit you've certainly presented a total package."

Erika sucked in her bottom lip as she met Templeton's steely gaze. "It's not our intention to screen everyone in the community. The fliers will list the symptoms pertaining to pernicious anemia and any other diseases we decide to feature. The screening will only be for those who meet the qualifying criteria. We're also working on ways to communicate other preventive medicine procedures to all the citizens of Lebanon. We'd like to reach as many seniors as we possibly can. Our senior citizens are at risk."

Pleased as punch, Michael stepped forward and slipped his arm loosely around Erika's shoulders. "Gentlemen," he said, "we do understand your concerns, but we need to start somewhere. If we can reach just one pernicious anemia sufferer in time, alert one person to symptoms of other unheard of diseases, we will have done a great community service. I can guarantee you we'll work out all the kinks, but first we need to have your full approval."

Templeton excused himself so he could confer with his colleagues.

Erika and Michael watched and waited patiently as the men put their graying, judicious heads together. When Jules Baker commandeered the conversation, Erika couldn't hear what was said, but she knew it would be favorable to their cause.

Michael gently nudged Erika's waist. "You were impressive, to say the least, but don't expect to get an answer today. These old coots like to have people play the waiting game. I know how they work. Don't worry. We did what we came here to do. I'm positive of it."

Laughing, Erika touched his hand briefly. "I was delightfully engaging, wasn't I? But putting that all aside, I'm not as sure about them as you are. They terrify me. I can't believe I'm in the same room with so many head honchos, and I can't believe how I took them to task. Did you ever feel this way?" she whispered. "I'm as nervous as an atheist in church."

He chuckled. "Yes, only ten times worse. As a first-year resident, I don't think I would've had the guts to take these guys on. These finely tailored suits dine on interns and residents on a regular basis. I never would've voluntarily placed myself on their dinner plates," he joked, smiling wryly.

"I always thought you were the fearless type," she teased. "Oh, Michael, here we go," she exclaimed when Templeton stood up to address them again, his stern gaze drawing their immediate attention.

He folded his hands in front of him as he began to speak. "Dr. Mathis, Dr. Edmonds, as you both know, these are major projects for our hospital to undertake, though we all agree they're worthwhile. Therefore, we cannot make a hasty decision without taking a little more time to discuss the pros and the cons. We'll have an answer for you within the next week or two. This meeting is adjourned," he said, deciding not to elicit any more comments from the project sponsors. Dr. Erika Edmonds had already given more than a corroborating earful.

Disapproving of Templeton's premature adjournment, Erika's heavy sigh of disappointment was audible. "It looks as though we've been dismissed," she complained to Michael. "That was pretty rude of him, don't you think?" she inquired, gathering her written notes from the podium.

Michael laughed as he placed his hand under her elbow, directing her toward the exit. "You'll eventually learn how to play the game, my sweet, naive Erika. I wouldn't draw any negative inferences from their actions. As I said before, they like to play the game. At any rate, we don't have to rely solely on them to effect the outcome we want."

Erika nodded her head in agreement. "Well, for sure, the message is going to get out there, one way or another. I'm committed to this venture. Mother's death won't be in vain."

"That's the spirit! Let's have a late lunch while we discuss our other options," Michael suggested, leading the way to the cafeteria.

After paying for chunky chicken salads and hot drinks, they

found their way to their special table, where Michael seated himself across from Erika, offering a short prayer of thanks over their meal.

Erika took the clear wrapper off her salad and added a spoonful of bleu-cheese dressing to the crisp greens. "I'm going to talk to Aunt Arlene about doing a few health lectures at the senior citizen center she frequents. Then I'm going to try to make some other worthwhile contacts for future lectures. Can I count on you to help me out?"

Michael swallowed the food he already had in his mouth and ran a napkin across his lips. "Sure thing. Our options are practically endless. But, Erika, I don't want you to wear yourself too thin. You already have a heavy schedule. Everything's going to fall into place. Do you believe that?"

"I have to believe it, Michael. It's important to educate as many people as we can. Thanks for all your help."

He smiled at the woman he loved. "Anytime, sweetheart. What do you have on your schedule after we finish lunch?"

"I have a few personal errands to run," she hedged, not wanting to reveal the nature of her plans. "What about you?"

"I'm going to make hospital rounds. Then I need to go in to the office. I don't have any patients scheduled, but I have tons of paperwork to finish. Will you call me later?"

"Your every wish is my command, Dr. Mathis."

An hour after her lunch with Michael, Erika sat in the reception area of the law firm of Lightner and Gooding. When Randy Mills had gone to his bank to inquire about the mystery check he'd deposited, on a stroke of good luck he'd found out the check hadn't been processed yet. He was able to get a copy, which he'd kindly given to Erika. Erika learned that besides the check issued for the moving expenses some of her school expense accounts had been paid in full, too.

She'd been outraged. Having someone messing around in her private affairs was daunting, not to mention the thousands of dollars shelled out on her behalf. She wouldn't stop until she found out who possessed such exasperating nerve. Abel Lightner was with a client, and Thomas Gooding was in court, she was told. Erika opted to wait for Mr. Lightner, rather than make an appointment for the next day. Getting to the bottom of the mystery donor was a must for today. She simply couldn't wait through another twenty-four hours.

Waiting, Erika leafed through the latest issue of *Essence* magazine, featuring the newest lines in spring fashions. Several stunning outfits caught her interest, especially the evening attire. She had always liked to dress up, but her meager finances didn't afford her the luxury of dressing the way she'd love to. A minuscule white dress with a sheer neckline and sheer sleeves was by far her favorite. Pastel sequins dotted the sheer material. The bodice hugged the waistline and the straight miniskirt had a seductive slit up the back. A pair of white linen shoes matched the dress perfectly, decorated with the same pastel sequins. Just for something to do, Erika wrote down the names of stores that stocked the dress and the shoes.

Realizing that someone was standing over her, Erika looked up at a forty-something black man with a dusky brown complexion. Totally bald, he possessed arrow-straight, gleaming white teeth. Erika thought his ebony eyes were too large for such an angular face. His athletic build indicated a regular workout regimen.

Abel Lightner extended his hand, which Erika touched briefly. Once the introductions were made, he directed her to an inner office with the finest in furnishings. Everything was plush, right down to the leather office chair situated behind the expensive mahogany desk. Once she was comfortably seated, Abel sat in the high-back leather chair.

He stared at her with cool, calculating ebony eyes. "What can I do to assist you, Ms. Edmonds?" he asked, keeping his chilly eyes fastened on her.

When speaking to the receptionist, Erika had purposely left off her professional title. It often intimidated the opposite sex.

But Abel Lightner didn't look like a man who could be easily intimidated.

Erika removed a sheet of paper from her purse. "This," she said, walking over to his desk and handing him the copy of the check. Without commenting, she returned to her seat.

He waved the paper in the air. "What about this?" he asked pointedly.

His arrogance stunned her, grating on her nerves at the same time. "I thought you could tell me. That is the name of your firm on the check, is it not?" Her tone was less than patient.

He tossed the copy aside. "You came here to see me, so I think you should get right to the point. I'm squeezing you in as it is. I do have paying clients to see."

Erika bristled. "This check was issued to pay an account for my moving expenses. Although I don't have copies, I've been given reason to suspect there are a few more such checks floating around out there. I would like to know who is shelling out all this money, and why. Have I now made my point?"

Abel clapped. "Now we have something to discuss. Then again, maybe we don't. Under the law, at the request of my client, I can't reveal the information you're seeking. But I would think you'd be grateful for the assistance. I've always been told to never look a gift horse in the mouth. Maybe you shouldn't either, Ms. Edmonds."

Anger staining her cheeks a blood-red, Erika rapidly got to her feet. "I am not a charity case, Mr. Lightner! Pass that on to your client. I will pay back the entire amount for the moving expenses, but it's going to take time—a year, possibly less. However, I can't begin to imagine how I'll ever pay all the other money back. All I can do is insist on the school returning the funds. That is, when I learn who it is they should return them to."

"Good luck, Miss Edmonds," he offered with a sneer. "But I'm afraid you're on your own as to finding out the identity of your more than generous benefactor."

"Well," she ground out, "I can't thank you for your help,

since I didn't receive any, but I thank you for seeing me. Have a good day, Mr. Lightner," Erika managed through clenched teeth, marching right out the door, slamming it hard behind her.

Thirteen

Out in the hallway, anger and frustration gave way to tears. At the elevator she slammed the side of her fist onto the DOWN button. When the car took too long to come, she decided to walk down the two flights of stairs. Just as she reached the door leading to the stairwell, she heard the elevator bell ring. As she looked back at the elevator, her hand froze on the doorknob.

Looking like a model just stepping off the cover of *Ebony Man* magazine was none other than Richard Glover, attorney-at-law.

Quickly, she turned her head so he wouldn't see her face. Breathless, she waited until he started down the hall. When he entered the offices of Lightner and Gooding, she began to smell a big rat. Her first thought was that Michael had lied to her. Michael had solicited Richard's help to deceive her. But that somehow didn't seem quite right. Why would Michael get Richard involved in something like this? It didn't make sense. She didn't know one way or the other, but she would have to play this scenario out. She needed some answers.

Walking back to the office, she opened the door and went inside. Richard was not in the reception room, but she had a pretty good idea where he'd gone. When she saw that the receptionist was away from her desk, Erika suddenly knew just what she had to do.

Making a beeline to Abel Lightner's office door, she was

about to enter and tell Abel she wanted to see if she'd left her keys behind, but the sound of raised voices halted her movements. Straining to hear the conversation between the two lawyers, she stood stock-still, training her hearing on the words coming from behind the closed door.

"Ms. Edmonds was very angry and upset, Richard. Though I tried not to show it, I felt rather sorry for her. I guess we didn't figure on her getting a copy of one of the checks. Erika Edmonds is pretty clever in spite of the fact she's a woman," Abel joked. "She knows about the other checks, too. This Edmonds woman must have a golden—"

"Watch your sexist mouth, Lightner. Get your mind out of the gutter."

Erika would have liked nothing better than to storm in and take Abel Lightner down a peg or two, but she was more interested in finding out what was going on with him and Richard Glover. Richard was up to his eyeballs in this mess, she now knew. But why? If Richard was involved, then Michael had to be. There was no other reasonable explanation. Richard didn't know anything about her or her family. She'd never heard of him until Michael.

"For your information, Erika Edmonds is my biological sister. And she's a brilliant doctor! Anthony Edmonds fathered not one, but two very intelligent children. Erika just doesn't know it yet. She thinks our old man is her stepfather," Richard informed Abel.

A look of horror crossed Erika's face. Backing away from the door as though bullets had been fired through it, she felt a sharp pain crease her heart. Slipping past the reception desk, she ran out into the corridor.

Leaning against the wall for support, she fought the waves of nausea threatening to make her toss her lunch onto the carpet. Fearful that Richard would come out of the office and find her there, she ran for the stairwell and didn't stop running until she felt cold air stinging her face. The tears on her face began to freeze as she gulped at the fresh air. The nauseous feelings began to subside, but she couldn't stop the pain from repeatedly striking her heart like a torrent of cyanide-tipped bullets, nor could she stop thinking about the deceptions her parents had practiced—if what Richard Glover had said was the truth.

Seated behind the wheel of her car, Erika was a nervous wreck, yet she started to laugh. She hadn't really heard Richard say she was his biological sister, had she? Some of his remarks had been muffled, she told herself. Stress had a way of doing funny things to people, of making them hear and see things that weren't real. That was it. There was just too much blasted stress in her life, more than enough to make any sane person go crazy.

Michael coming into her life had caused her to stop dealing with all her personal problems. She'd just stuffed them somewhere deep inside her. Now they were starting to manifest in other ways. She had made herself believe love was a cure-all, but it wasn't. It was just a temporary relief from insane circumstances. Now all the insanity was back. Perhaps it had never gone away.

Richard Glover just couldn't be her brother. If that were true, someone would've told her long before now. Anthony couldn't be her biological father. If that was true, then it carried the heavy weight of numerous undesirable implications. Yet Richard reminded her so much of Anthony. Maybe Anthony was Richard's father. Maybe Richard didn't understand that Anthony had adopted her. She had known Anthony had a son. But if Richard was her brother, why hadn't she been told more about him? Why hadn't Anthony acknowledged both children as his own? Why hadn't her parents ever allowed them to meet each other?

So many new questions faced her. No answers would be easily attained. Both Anthony and Vernice were deceased. Vernice had never answered any questions concerning Erika's so-called natural father, she recalled. So what would make her think her mother would give her answers now, if she were alive? Vernice never did anything she didn't want to. Erika had never really had the courage to confront the woman, who could be very formidable, especially when faced with something she didn't want to deal with.

Erika considered talking to Aunt Arlene, but what would she say to her? Since she wasn't even sure that what she'd heard was true, it made no sense to start making waves, especially without having any proof. Besides, she still wasn't so sure she hadn't misunderstood what Richard had said. There had been a closed door between them, she reminded herself. Was she cracking up, or what?

By the time Erika made it home her mind felt totally worthless. Stopping at one of the pay phones located in the hallway of the dorm, she put in a call to her aunt. Much to Michael's dismay, she had returned the cellular phone to him, and the money situation had kept her from having a phone line installed.

"Hello," Arlene greeted wearily. She sounded tired, Erika noted.

"Aunt Arlene, it's Erika. How are you doing today?"

Erika listened to her aunt make a few minor complaints. "I'm sorry you don't feel well. I called to find out if there's anything I can do for you." Erika heard Aunt Arlene take a deep, ragged breath.

"Erika, child, I could say no, but there is something. Do you think you could ask Michael if he would mind moving some of my old things out to the storage shed? It's just too much for me to handle. Your moving man offered to move some things for me at no extra charge, but at the time I hadn't decided what things to keep and what to get rid of. I really can't use some of these things, but they're too good to just throw away."

"What sort of things, Aunt Arlene?"

"Mostly clothing. They're in good shape, but I'm just tired of them," Arlene said, laughing. "There's quite a bit of decent furniture available, too, since you gave me Vernice's newer pieces."

"Why don't we just have a yard sale? Spring is just a short time away. They can be moved to the storage shed for now, and then we can bring them back out for the sale. What do you think about that idea?"

Arlene sighed. "I don't know, Erika. I'm just getting too old to exert that much energy on a yard sale, especially when I'd much rather be playing bingo or gin rummy. But I'll give it some thought. Is there anything else you want to talk to me about?"

No, she didn't want to talk about this latest twist to her "poor me" saga, at least not this very minute. What would she say to her, anyway? Auntie, have my parents been keeping major secrets from me? Unfortunately someone else is airing out the dirty linen for them—and it doesn't look as if it is going to come clean.

"Auntie, I'll talk with you later," Erika responded reluctantly. "I'm not feeling all that well, either. I need to lie down."

Arlene sensed that Erika was trying to spare her from something unpleasant. She had heard an unusual sadness in her niece's voice from the moment she came on the line. "What is it, child? You know you can tell me anything. You sound as though you're hurting. Is it physical or emotional?"

Erika forced a laugh. "I can't keep anything from you, can I? I'm still upset about the mystery money I asked you about. I can't help wondering if Michael's been lying to me," she said, knowing she was guilty of doing the same thing with her aunt. Well, she wasn't exactly lying, but she wasn't telling the entire truth, either.

"Listen, sweetie, I can't believe Michael would just lie to you. He doesn't seem the type. Before you go accusing him of something he may have nothing to do with, you'd better be one hundred percent sure he's guilty. You two seem so happy together. I can't imagine he'd risk losing you over money, of all things. Michael is so very smitten with you, but it sounds as though you don't trust him one iota."

Erika gasped but kept her composure. "Oh, I do trust him, but . . ." She just couldn't find the right words to finish her sentence. How do you say you trust someone, then add a word like *but?* "Aunt Arlene," Erika said on a shudder, "I'm sorry for dumping on you. Take care. I'll call tomorrow to see how you're doing."

"Okay, sweet child. All we can do is pray. Michael seems to have a lot of feelings for you. You need a good man in your life, especially right now. I'm here, too, whenever you need me. I love you, niece."

"Thanks, Auntie. I love you, too. Stay well."

Erika hung up the phone and picked up her keys from the metal base.

She hadn't been inside the apartment for more than five minutes when the four walls appeared to be closing in on her, making her feel like screaming at the top of her lungs. As thin as the walls were, she knew every dorm resident at home would be at her door expressing concern. Reaching behind the sofa, Erika pulled out her art supplies.

Sitting down on the sofa, she began to sketch the profile of a woman. She sketched the eyes and eyebrows, then the nose and mouth. After adding shoulder-length hair, she shaded it in with a light brown pencil. As she sat back to observe what she'd done so far, she frowned. The large eyes in the drawing were filled with a liquid sadness she could almost touch. The full lips lacked the warmth of a smile. The entire profile symbolized a woman in pain.

She had sketched her own emotions.

Erika Edmonds was a woman in pain, the kind of pain the love of a good man hadn't been able to erase. Erika Edmonds was the woman in the rough sketch. If she'd sketched this earlier, she suspected that the outcome would've been totally different, recalling what she'd seen in the mirror only yesterday.

Just yesterday she'd observed eyes bright with the look of love, cheeks flushed with fresh, healthy color and a smile bright enough to light up the universe. Where was that Erika Edmonds now? Where was the woman who'd felt so good just a short time ago? Who was this new Erika Edmonds? Maybe she wasn't at all who she'd thought she was.

Erika Edmonds was suddenly a stranger. . . .

More than half the day was gone, and not much had been accomplished in the way of real productivity. Going to the firm of Lightner and Gooding had only brought on more grief, the last thing she needed. She'd already had enough grief to last her a lifetime. Deciding to just rest and, she hoped, get some sleep before her last shift in the emergency room, Erika undressed. Then she put on a silk bathrobe and climbed into bed.

Anthony, the sweetest husband and the best stepfather a child could have, was the first person who crossed her weary mind. Erika had no knowledge of when Anthony first came into Vernice's life, but he'd always been in hers. She couldn't remember a day when he hadn't.

Her first vivid memories of him were of his taking her to kindergarten every morning. She'd been four years old then. He'd also taken her to have her picture taken at a much younger age. She still had the picture of her taken with the panda bear he'd bought for her, but couldn't remember if she'd been one or two at that time.

If Richard was about the same age as Michael, then he had to be at least five or six years older than she was. She wondered if Anthony had been married to Richard's mother. She'd never even considered that Vernice might be his mother. She knew Anthony had a deceased ex-wife, but she was positive there hadn't been any children from that union.

Thinking back on the conversation she'd overheard, Erika grimaced. If what Richard said was true, then a lot of lies and deceptions had been practiced. Why would Vernice lie to her about who her natural father was? For that matter, why would Anthony deny her the rightful position as his daughter? Why would either of them strip her of her birthright and birth name? Sure, she carried Anthony's surname, but it was only on the adoption papers, not on her birth certificate. Henry Wade was listed as her natural father.

Erika thought about the personal papers kept locked in a metal file box now in her possession. Could the answers lie inside that box? Did she dare pry into Vernice's personal papers? How else would she know if something in there could answer all these puzzling questions? She couldn't make up her mind to open it.

Vernice wasn't the sort of person Erika could've questioned or demanded answers from. So many questions, she thought, tired, so many burning questions, questions she'd asked long before she'd even known there was a Richard Glover in the world. It seemed she'd been playing *Twenty Questions* all her life, and she'd been the loser because Vernice had refused to play the game. Now Vernice was winning again, because she was no longer around to confront. She simply won by default.

Where did Michael fit, if he did at all, into the scheme of things? Erika just couldn't allow herself to think he might know something about Richard's claims. To think like that would somehow tarnish her image of him, his overwhelmingly favorable image.

He was kind, sensitive, honest and thoughtful. And he was in love with her, which would render him incapable of deceiving her. Michael didn't know about the money. Therefore, he didn't know about Richard claiming her as his sister. It seemed logical to her.

At the moment she had no choice but to believe in his innocence. Michael's love for her was the only thing that made sense anymore. And if that love was somehow destroyed by lies and deceit she'd have no sense of purpose left, especially if she learned that he'd deliberately lied.

When an unfamiliar knock sounded on the door, Erika wondered who it could be as she padded to the door, walking on the heels of her slippers. She opened the door to a neighbor from down the hall.

Reggie Glass smiled at her. "You have a phone call, Erika. Should I tell the caller to hold on?" he asked, scanning her disheveled appearance.

Erika looked down at her clothes, too, and frowned. "No, I'll come now," she said, dismissing her messy state. "Thanks, Reg."

Smiling again, he raised his eyebrows. "See you later, Erika." She walked right behind Reggie, following him the few steps down the hall.

As he moved on, she stopped and picked up the phone. "This is Erika."

Soft laughter flowed from the phone. "Hi, gorgeous. I'm happy you're in. Do you mind if I drop by for a visit? I'm here at the university. I've been consulted to see a patient who's been admitted here."

"I'll be waiting. Have any idea how long you'll be?"

"I'm on my way. I've already seen the patient."

"In that case, the door will be unlocked. See you in a few." She hung up the phone and returned to the apartment.

Dashing into the bedroom to change clothes, Erika untied the robe, a mischievous smile playing on her lips. Keeping the robe on was suddenly more appealing to her. If Michael was only going to be there for a minute, why get all dolled up? she decided, knowing she had other things on her mind.

Standing before the mirror, she touched up her hair and put on a hint of lip color. All the tears had done some damage, but he'd have to look closely to see it. Erika opened her robe and looked at her nude body in the mirror, seeing that her pouting breasts stood firm and her nipples had already peaked to a fully erect state. Her abdomen was flat and hard; there were no traces of the fat that had once made it flabby and soft. The exercise regimen had paid off. Her thighs were firm, and the café au lait skin over them looked creamy and soft.

Dropping the robe to the floor, she turned her back to the mirror. Looking over her shoulder into the mirror, she surveyed her tight, round buttocks, which used to be indented with deep dimples and ugly cellulite pockets. Erika smiled, pleased with the new body she'd worked hard to attain. It was a body that any woman would love to reside in, a body Michael loved to have in his bed morning, noon and night.

Looking at her body in the mirror made Erika feel exuberantly alive and sexy. After putting the robe back on, she lay across the bed, eagerly anticipating the arrival of her handsome lover. She could almost feel Michael's heated flesh searing into her own. Acting totally out of character, she discarded the robe and slipped between the sheets, leaving one shapely leg exposed. Hearing the latch catch, she mussed her hair and lowered the top sheet to give Michael a peekaboo look at the gentle swell of her breasts. Erika knew her seductive efforts were quite effective when she heard his sharp intake of breath, and the seductive smile he sent her way made her hot all over.

"Hello, gorgeous," he said softly, keeping his eyes trained on the exposed leg. He could only guess that she was totally nude under those sheets, which pleased him greatly. This wasn't something he would've expected from his sweet innocent, but he found her seduction routine to be a delicious work of intrigue.

Moving toward the bed, he loosened his silk tie. Sitting on the edge of the bed, he stroked her leg, seducing her lips with his mouth. "You're purposely driving me insane. Am I right?"

She grinned. "I plead the fifth."

As he took possession of her mouth again, Erika fumbled with the buttons on the cassette player, pressing PLAY. "Body and Soul" by Anita Baker flowed from the speakers. If the words of the slow love song weren't an invitation, then he didn't know what was. When her fingers fumbled with the buttons on his shirt, the invitation to love her was all but handed to him on a silver platter. As she unzipped his pants, he knew exactly what she had in mind.

"Oh, Erika," he breathed, helping her to disrobe him, "I hope you know what you're getting yourself into." Naked, he joined her under the sheets.

"I think you got that wrong, Dr. Mathis," she challenged. "It's what *you'll* be getting yourself into. Let me warn you. It will be dangerously hot!"

Lowering her head against his chest, she licked at one nipple, then the other, making his body jerk and tremble under her touch. Groaning, he pushed her back against the pillows, his hands cupping her breasts. Then his tongue replaced the warmth of his hands.

"Yes," she moaned, twisting her fingers in his hair.

The inside of her thighs ached for attention. As though he sensed her need to have him caress her there, his hands moved downward, tenderly stroking her inner thighs. As his fingers nestled in the curls already damp with feminine moisture, he stroked her until she cooed with deep pleasure.

Michael hadn't made complete love to her in several days, but he now declared the drought over. Her gentle flower was bathed with fresh dew and he allowed his fingers to glide through the creamy moisture. As though a magnet drew his fingers to her inner core, he probed inside. As she tightened her muscles around them, he probed deeper and deeper.

"Michael, Michael," she called out, her voice thick with lust. "I love you, Michael."

Lifting his head, he momentarily studied the dazed look in her eyes. "I love you, too, Erika." Ready for what was coming next, he reached for protection.

Wildly, he crushed her lips under his. Rolling onto his back, he held her close, keeping her mouth locked onto his. Using her buttocks for leverage, he lifted her and sat her on his chest, allowing her legs to straddle him. As he manipulated the tiny, smooth but hard nub, she threw her head back violently, causing him to slightly decrease the pressure on the tender spot.

Once again he lifted her, placing her above his manhood, drawing her slowly down over him. As she sank deeper and deeper onto his heated flesh, he raised up to meet her. With one deep thrust, he buried himself inside of her pool of hot, creamy dew. Her lovemaking was sweet torture, arresting ecstasy, as she'd grown more and more passionate since the first time. Off and on, Erika and Michael swapped control, each enjoying the other's role as the aggressor. There was something more demanding in Erika's passion and Michael felt it right down to the core of his heat.

When she was in control, she became even more demanding, but he didn't mind meeting all of her desires. She was also more vocal about telling him exactly what she needed and wanted from him. Her explicit words of passion excited him more than he would've ever thought possible. Not that she hadn't more than satisfied him before, but the responses they now elicited from each other had become dangerously exciting.

As the world around her blurred, Erika tightened her grip around his waist. As she cried out and fell limp against his chest, his own sweet release flooded through him with such force he could barely suck in enough oxygen to keep himself alive. With neither of them having enough strength to speak, the room grew dreadfully silent.

Erika rolled away from Michael, only to lay her head on his chest moments later. She looked up at him. "I don't feel so all alone anymore, Michael. Thanks to you." She cleared her throat. "My stepfather loved me, you know. He loved me as though I was his very own. It's too bad that I wasn't," she said, a flood of tears gushing from her eyes.

The jagged edges of her sobs tore at her throat and she hiccuped and trembled until Michael's soothing touches brought her spasmodic breathing under control. The look on his face was strained. Had Richard already talked to her? Was she now in denial? No, he thought, Richard certainly would've told him before talking to her. He wiped her tears away. "Erika, I'd be surprised if he didn't love you. You're an easy person to love. But not every child is so lucky. I can't tell you how many cases of child abuse I've had to report. Most of the children were abused by their natural parents. I'm glad you don't feel alone anymore. If I have my way, you'll never have to feel alone again," he said, burying his face in her hair.

"That's a comforting thought, Michael," she said tearfully. "Do you have to go back to the office?"

"No. I'm through for today. Why do you ask?"

"Can you stay with me until I go on shift at eleven o'clock? If you can't, it's okay."

He kissed the top of her head. "I have nothing important waiting for me. I need to store some information in my computer, but I can do that over the weekend. Is there something you want to do?"

"No. I have to get some sleep before too long. I know it's crazy, but I just can't be alone with myself right now. I remember a time I loved being alone. It gave me time to think, sketch and do whatever else I wanted to do. I just don't think I know who I am anymore. That scares me. I'm not used to being afraid, Michael, nor do I like it."

His brow furrowed with concern. "Something is going on here that you're not telling me about. You can share anything with me. I want to help you with whatever it is," Michael offered sincerely, growing as fearful as she had talked of being.

"Thanks, but I have to work a few things out before I go spilling my guts. Knowing you're going to be here helps a lot. Do you think I'll make it through the residency program? I keep worrying about having to drop out. I don't want that to happen, Michael. It would be so undignified, not to speak of downright embarrassing."

He stroked her hair. "I can't see any reason why you won't. Your dedication will pull you through. I have every faith in you. Do you believe in miracles, Erika?"

"I believe in God, Michael. And with God miracles are possible. The miracle of God's love is what keeps me going every day. I'll make it through if it's His will. I try to never second-guess Him."

She placed his hand over her heart. "I know I've needed a lot of reassurance from you lately, Michael. It's not that I doubt you—I'm just feeling so vulnerable right now. I've lost the two most important people in my life, the only people I could truly depend on, and I haven't learned to cope with those devastating losses yet. I just hope you can bear with me. I'm not a weak woman by any definition, but I'm a very vulnerable one at the moment. But as my mother used to say, 'this too shall pass.'"

"It's very wise not to second-guess Him, Erika. Hold on to that thought with all your might. All things are possible with Him. You take all the time you need. There's no statute of limitations placed on grieving. You'll learn to cope. Don't rush it." He kissed her forehead. "Are you hungry?"

"Not really. But if you are, there's plenty of food in the refrigerator. I haven't touched the leftovers we stored. Why don't you go and fix yourself a plate? I'm just going to lie here and rest."

"Is it okay if I bring it in here?"

She nodded before her eyes drooped shut. Michael kissed her as he got out of bed and pulled on his pants. In the bathroom he washed his face and hands. Erika was asleep when he walked through the bedroom on his way to the kitchen. Smiling at her curled-up figure, he thought about how much he loved her. But was his love enough to take away all the pain he'd seen in her eyes? he wondered. He certainly hoped so.

After pulling out all the leftovers, he took a plate from the cabinet and filled it with vegetables and meat. When he didn't see a breadbox, he searched the cabinets for a loaf of bread, then finally found one in the refrigerator. It was a diet version of rye, but he pulled it out, anyway. Making a sandwich of turkey, chicken and cheese, he drowned it in Weight Watcher's mayonnaise. He would've preferred the real thing, but Erika didn't have any of that, either.

Once everything was piled high on his plate, he sat at the table. He'd decided not to go back into the bedroom for fear of disturbing her while she slept, knowing what it meant to pull ER duty. No matter how much sleep you got it never seemed to be enough, especially when you had to be on duty all through the night.

As he mulled over the comments Erika had made to him about her stepfather, he knew something was going on inside her head. But what? He'd tried to reach Richard earlier, but he hadn't returned his call. Michael vowed to see him as soon as Erika went on duty. A confrontation with Richard was no longer avoidable. Richard had some serious explaining to do.

Michael was very careful as he slipped back into bed. Huddling in one corner, he tried not to disturb her but it was for naught. Turning over, she slid up behind him. Throwing her leg across his hips, she draped her arm across his abdomen. "Did you get enough to eat, Michael?"

Turning to face her, he grinned. "I made a pig of myself. Are you sure you don't want something? You have to keep your strength up."

"I'm fine. I'll take something with me when I leave. Are you going to go straight home when you leave here?"

The suspicious tone in her question surprised him. "I was thinking of stopping off to see Richard. I haven't seen him since the night he came to my parents' house. However, we've talked a time or two. But I won't be out too late. I have a busy schedule tomorrow."

"Oh," came her soft reply. "Why do you have to see him so late? Is there something wrong?"

"No, not really. I'd just like to see and talk to him. You don't like him, do you?"

She frowned. "Why do you say that?"

"I can tell by the way you act when we're around him. Why does he rub you the wrong way?" Knowing this was a dangerous line of questioning, he hoped to God she didn't turn the tables on him. He just wanted to find out where she was coming from.

"Who says that he does?"

Oh, boy, he thought. She wasn't going to give anything up without him having to pry it out of her, something he wasn't about to do. "No one said it. And what we're discussing is really not all that important. Let's talk about something else. Besides me, what's your favorite dessert?"

"Why are you so anxious to change the subject? Is it getting too hot for you? Are you afraid I might ask you something you don't want to answer, or can't answer?"

Wow, this is getting dangerous, he thought, propping himself up on one elbow. He stared at her intently. "You're really having a bad day, aren't you? But I'm not going to let you pick a fight with me. Isn't that what you're trying to do, Erika?"

She looked as though she felt ashamed of herself. "I can see that you're on to me. I'm sorry. I'm just not myself today. Will you forgive me?"

"If you kiss me like you mean the apology you just gave me. You have to show me that you're *really* sorry. No half-stepping!"

"No half-stepping." Pushing his head back into the pillow, she climbed on top of him and kissed him breathless, releasing him only long enough to let him capture his breath again. "Is my apology accepted?"

"Yes, yes," he responded breathlessly, pulling her head down onto his chest.

Minutes later, Erika was asleep in the spot she had quickly become accustomed to, his arms. Gently, he wiped away the single tear resting at the corner of her right eye. He couldn't take his eyes off her. Even in sleep, she appeared to be in pain. He couldn't help but wonder what had happened to make her so vulnerable and suddenly so unsure of herself. There had always been a fair amount of vulnerability surrounding her, but somehow it had increased tenfold. Erika was not at all her normal self.

Something had hurt her deeply, and it had occurred since they'd shared lunch in the hospital cafeteria. When they'd awakened that morning, she'd been perky and saucy and they'd laughed and joked all the way into the city. Ever since the anonymous check had come into play she'd been somewhat different. But was the money issue really the culprit? Was it the only culprit? Something had turned his gorgeous lady into a mass of defenseless chaos.

As much as he wanted to dismiss it, he wasn't naive enough to believe Richard had nothing to do with all of this. One thing was for sure—the very next time they were together, if Richard hadn't talked to her he was going to tell her the truth himself. He was going to let Richard know that tonight. In fact, he now thought that he should be the one to tell her.

If she had to find out from Richard, whom she didn't seem to like, there would probably be hell to pay. She loved him and he had betrayed that love. It was up to him to right a wrong. Yes, he had to let Richard know he'd be the one to tell Erika the truth about her brother and stepfather. He was the only one who should tell her.

When Erika turned over and scooted to the far side of the bed, Michael sat up and looked around the dimly lit room, remembering when he'd lived in the same type of cramped resident quarters. He'd been as broke as Erika was now. Like her, he'd been determined to succeed as a doctor, working several odd jobs to keep himself afloat.

He was now one of the youngest and most revered surgeons in the state of Pennsylvania, yet he hadn't bought into all the hype when used by God as an instrument to save that baby's life. And he hadn't allowed all the grandiose attention to change him on the inside. He was too comfortable with himself for that. His parents had raised him well. The words *to thine own self be true* had been drilled into him, and to let his conscience be his guide.

Thank God he had a conscience, even though that very conscience might help his relationship with Erika work out, or break them far apart. Whatever the outcome, he had to follow his conscience, and it was telling him to right the wrong he'd allowed himself to be drawn into. It bothered him to know he'd wittingly placed his relationship with Erika in severe jeopardy.

No matter how cold it sounded, Richard had nothing at all to lose. Erika already knew that Anthony had a son somewhere in the world, but she hadn't mentioned even knowing his name. Richard Glover only existed for Erika as Michael's friend and attorney. But Michael had so much more to lose. Erika had become as much a part of his life as breathing. She was the only one who righted his sometimes upside-down world.

With his mind firmly made up to tell her the truth, he laid his head next to hers on the pillow. Her breath fanned his cheeks and he smiled. If he knew nothing else, he knew for sure that he wanted to share a pillow with her for the rest of their lives. When he finally fell asleep, he did so with a contented smile on his handsome face.

Fourteen

When Erika awakened to dress for work, the smile was still visible on Michael's face. As she studied his sleeping profile for a few minutes, her heart swelled with love and pride in the man lying next to her. The temptation to kiss him was overwhelming but she didn't.

Climbing out of bed, she tiptoed across the room and into the bathroom. Gently, she closed the door behind her. While the shower water heated up, she washed her face in the sink. Opening the shower door, she stepped inside, where the swirling steam immediately relaxed her body and mind.

After pouring a generous amount of shower gel into her hands, she began to rub it over her body. Another pair of hands appeared out of nowhere and Michael began rubbing her body tenderly but vigorously. Molding her against his body, he winked. She relaxed into him, letting him work his magic.

All the foreplay in the shower had her rushing to get dressed. Michael watched her as she ran around the bedroom like a chicken with its head cut off, thinking how adorable she was when in a tizzy. When he told her so, she rolled her eyes at him, causing him to burst into laughter.

With very little time for primping, Erika shoved her body into green hospital scrubs, then ran into the kitchen to fix a snack to take with her. When she opened the refrigerator, she howled with glee. Michael had prepared a brown bag lunch for her. *Erika's Lunch* was written on the bag with a black marker.

Her laughter brought him scurrying into the kitchen. "You like that, huh? It's only the leftovers, but I dressed them up real nice. Think of me when you take your first bite."

"Something tells me I won't be able to do anything *but* think about you throughout my entire shift. Can I poke you with a hypodermic needle to see if there's really red blood in your veins? I kind of suspect the only thing that'll come into my syringe is liquid brown sugar, since you're the sweetest. Thank you! Do you treat all your women this good, Dr. Mathis?"

He grinned. "That answer is simple, since I only have one woman in my life. Yes, I do. She deserves to be treated good, real good."

Since their love affair was now the juiciest bit of fruit on the hospital grapevine, anyway, Erika had allowed Michael to walk her over to the emergency room. Once her belongings were stashed in the doctors' quarters, she walked him to the rear door.

Lifting her off the ground, he kissed her passionately, her feet dangling in midair. "That should hold you for a little while. Don't work yourself too hard. I'll be in touch, gorgeous."

She blew him a kiss. "I like the sound of that," she cooed, walking away. He watched her until she was completely out of his sight.

Sprinting all the way to his car, he jumped in and fastened his seat belt, thinking about calling Richard on the car phone. He quickly changed his mind. A surprise attack was more to his advantage, if Richard was even at home.

Michael broke every traffic safety rule on his way to Richard's. Thirty minutes later, as he pulled up in front of the large, showy house, he looked to see if there were any lights on. The front of the house was bathed in soft lighting, which probably meant Richard was having a cozy rendezvous, but Michael didn't let that deter him from his mission. This discussion was long overdue. Nothing short of death could stop him from confronting Richard Glover on this cold, cold night. Pressing his finger into the doorbell, he heard melodic chimes signal the announcement of a visitor.

Wearing wine-colored silk lounging attire, Richard answered the door, looking as though he might have been asleep. Michael saw that his hair was in disarray. "What are you doing here this time of night, homeboy? It's near midnight!"

"I know exactly what time it is," Michael snapped, pushing past him to gain entry. "We need to talk. You've got a lot of tall explaining to do, *homeboy!*"

"Wait a minute, man. I got company. Give me a break, will you?"

"Not tonight. The only break I have on my mind is the one I'm going to level against your neck! What have you been up to since we last spoke?"

"Well, if you're going to insist on having an argument, let's go into my den. My company does not need to hear this."

"Shelly's heard us argue before," Michael hissed.

Richard gestured for him to be quiet. "Shh, man! Are you trying to blow my cover? You know my relationship with her is history."

"Is it really? How many times in the recent past have you tried to make her history? But that's another story. I'm not here to talk about your love life, or lack thereof. I'm here to talk about Erika Edmonds—your sister."

Richard raised his eyebrows. "That little girl sure has rocked your world. I've never seen you this agitated about anything," Richard marveled, directing Michael into his lavish den. As Richard sat down on a teal-colored leather sofa, Michael deposited his tall frame on the plush matching chair. "Now. What are you carrying on about at this time of night, Mikey?"

Michael glared at him, his eyes sending a message of clear

and present danger. "Did you send a check to Randy Mills to help pay off Erika's moving bills?"

Richard punched at his thighs with closed fists. "I thought I was helping, man. Now I know it was a big mistake. What would you have done if someone told you your sister was having financial difficulties, especially knowing you had enough money to relieve her of that stress?"

Michael moved to the edge of the couch. "I would've had the decency to talk to her about it first. Didn't you know this was going to open up a can of worms that you yourself said you weren't ready to deal with?"

Richard glared back at Michael. "I said I made a mistake. What do you want—blood?"

"That'll do for starters," Michael shot back. "Do you have any idea what this is doing to her? She's starting to doubt herself, which gives me reason to think you've done more than just pay out a few measly bucks for her. Have you?"

"Not intentionally."

Michael's eyes darkened with anger. "What the hell's that supposed to mean, Rich?"

Richard looked chagrined. "I've also paid off some of her school expense accounts. I went to my attorney's office this morning and was told that she'd just been there to inquire about the anonymous payments. Abel said she was as hot as a forty-five when she demanded to know who had footed her bills."

Michael looked thunderstruck. "Do you blame her? How do you know she didn't see you there? Maybe she saw you go into his office, and was able to put two and two together. Of all the mindless things you've done, this one takes the cake. Not only have you put the possibility of your ever having a real relationship with Erika in serious peril, you've put me in the same damn predicament. I should've never agreed to any of this. What were you thinking when you decided to have your attorney send out those damn checks?"

"That I wanted to help Erika out. Beyond that, I guess you

could say that I didn't think. What are we going to do about it now?"

"*We* aren't going to do anything. But I intend to tell her the truth. Tomorrow! I'm not going to have this ghastly situation backfire in my face. It might already be too late. She definitely suspects something. With you being my best friend, you had to realize the repercussions for me. Or didn't that even cross your mind?"

Richard sighed with discontent. "Mikey, I think you should let me clean up this mess. I got us into this, and I should be the one to get us out."

"No! I'm going to clean up my own mess. You can do what you want later—that is, after I tell her the truth. I strongly advise you to stay away from her until I've done so."

Richard looked agitated. "Whatever, man! I'm truly sorry about this. It's too bad that the two people who are really responsible for all this damn havoc can't be held accountable."

Michael shoved a hand through his hair. "Listen, I've got to get out of here. I'm sorry for losing my temper, but it couldn't be helped. By the way, I'm going to ask your sister to marry me. Do I have your blessing?"

Richard grinned broadly. "Man, I got to give it to you. You don't waste any time going after what you want. I've always envied you for that. It takes me forever to find out what I want, and then it takes me forever to go after it. But I have to play the devil's advocate here."

Richard stood up and walked over to sit on the arm of Michael's chair. "You pursued Stephanie in much the same way—and we both know what happened there. Are you sure you aren't doing that again? You seem to have this thing that makes you want to rescue the fair sex. Is that what's going on here? Do you just want to rescue Erika from all her problems? If that's the case, it's not going to work out this time, either. Knowing what little I do of my sister, I only guess that she wants love—not salvation."

Michael sighed. "I've asked myself those same questions.

I know I plunged headlong into the relationship with Stephanie. By the grace of God, it all worked out for the best. She's happy now, and I want to be. Erika Edmonds is what I want and need to fulfill my own happiness. I love her. Unequivocally!"

Richard embraced his friend. "You have my blessing."

There were several patients in the emergency room waiting to be seen, but none of their emergencies was deemed life-threatening. However, a few cases were of concern to the medical staff.

Erika walked out to the nursing station. After speaking to one of the nurses, she quickly went back into the treatment room she'd just left. The female patient was obviously in a lot of pain, Erika saw from the entrance. The young woman was writhing on the small bed as she wrung her coffee-brown hands together. Erika read the symptoms and the complaints written in the patient's medical chart, but knew she couldn't order any pain medication until she had an idea of what was going on medically.

Erika walked over to the bed and introduced herself to the patient. She then began an examination on the lower right side, the area the patient seemed to favor the most. "Mrs. Lowe, have you ever seen blood in your urine?"

Trying to get her pain under control, the young woman sat up, rocking back and forth, her face bathed in perspiration. "No, but it hurts when I urinate. My lower right side and my back are killing me. Can I please have something for the pain?" she pleaded. "I can't take this much longer. I have two small children, and my labor pains were nowhere near as painful as what I'm experiencing now. Doctor, can't you do something to help me?"

Erika gave her patient a sympathetic glance. "As soon as we get you over to X-ray and back, I'll order something for your pain. Unfortunately, the pain medication can sometimes mask the problem, so we need to have you wait until you've been X-rayed. The technician will be here any minute now."

Mrs. Lowe groaned. "What do you think's the problem?"

"It's too early to determine, especially in the absence of laboratory results. However, there's a possibility it could be kidney stones. Have you ever had them?"

Mrs. Lowe shook her head. "No, never, but my father's suffered with them for years. I've never had this type of pain, either."

"I'm sorry you're hurting so much. I need to check on something. I'll be back." As Erika started to go and find out what was delaying the X-ray technician, he came running through the door.

"Sorry it took so long, Dr. Edmonds. I had a problem with a piece of my equipment, but everything's okay now. I'll take your patient over to the X-ray department now."

Erika smiled. "Thanks, Rodney. Please bring me the films as soon as you have them developed. I need a KUB. We're looking for a kidney stone." She shrugged her shoulders. "It's all on the X-ray order sheet." Erika assisted Rodney in getting the IV pole situated in its slot on the wheelchair before she walked back to the nursing station.

Smiling, she watched the animated head movements of Terry Jean—T.J.—and Erma as they discussed something amusing. Erika felt blessed to have them on her shift again. They were excellent nurses who had a lot of compassion and understanding packed into their full-figured frames. She could always count on them in any emergency situation, finding them personable and very professional toward the patients.

Walking up to Erma, Erika slung her arm around her shoulders. This was a little awkward for her since Erma was more than half a head taller than she was. "Have Claire page Dr. Benson, please." Claire was the on-duty admissions clerk. "I'm going to need his assistance in reading the X-rays on Mrs. Lowe. Two heads are always better than one. Kidney stones can sometimes be hard to detect."

"Sure, Dr. Edmonds, right away. I just called the lab to see what's holding up the urinalysis. The results should be here in a few minutes. Everything seems to be moving so slow tonight," Erma said wearily.

"Only because it's our last shift," T.J. offered. "We all know how that goes, don't we?" she asked, rolling her eyes up so only the whites showed. All three women laughed.

"Thanks, Erma, for checking on the results. I'm sure the urinalysis will be positive for blood."

When Rodney wheeled Mrs. Lowe back to the room, he helped her into bed. He then went out to the nurses' station and handed Erika the films. Before he went back to his department, Erika thanked him for the expeditious way in which he'd handled the case.

Taking one film out of the jacket, she held it up to the overhead lights. There appeared to be a large stone lodged in the ureter—the tube leading from the kidney to the bladder—but she wanted a second opinion. When Dr. Jeremy Benson came along, they put the X-rays under the viewing lights. It didn't take Dr. Benson long to concur with Erika's assessment.

Dr. Benson pointed out the stone. "There's your baby, Dr. Edmonds. In my opinion, Mrs. Lowe needs to be admitted. The ultrasound tech will be here in a few hours, but I don't think an ultrasound is going to tell us much more than what we can already see. But it's your call."

"Thanks, Dr. Benson. I'm going to phone the on-call urologist. I believe it's warranted. He can better decide what other tests need to be run. But right now that lady needs some pain medication. Thank you for coming to the rescue. See you around."

"Anytime, Dr. Edmonds." He waved as he left the area.

Erika stopped by the nursing desk. "Give Mrs. Lowe seventy-five milligrams of Demerol and twenty-five of Vistaril. Please make sure she doesn't have any allergies, T.J.—I know you've asked once, but it won't hurt to ask again."

"Should I give it to her through the IV tubing?"

"Intramuscular. I'm still not comfortable with the IV injections, but I'll ask the urologist about it when I talk to him."

A few hours and several emergencies later, Erika dropped down onto the bed in her assigned quarters. While she was removing her snack from the brown bag, a small envelope fell out. She smiled brightly. Michael had added a little note in the lunch he'd prepared for her. It tickled her to death. After reading it, she realized that it was a written invitation.

> Dr. Michael Mathis requests the honor of Dr. Edmonds' effervescent presence at Christopher's Restaurant, high on top of Mount Washington. Dr. Mathis also requests that Dr. Edmonds bring a romantic spirit, a healthy appetite, and happy feet. Your carriage will arrive promptly at six o'clock this evening, my gorgeous Nubian queen. Please RSVP.

Erika clutched the invitation to her heart. She had a romantic spirit and a somewhat healthy appetite, but she wasn't so sure about the happy feet. At the moment her feet were killing her. *A good soak would do wonders for them*, she thought, unwrapping each of the small food packets.

When she saw that each packet had a little message taped to it, she burst into laughter. *I love you. I miss you like crazy when we're apart. Your loving was too, too hot! Let's do it again—soon!* The last one made her blush. Still laughing, Erika removed all the messages and folded them neatly, wanting to preserve them to read over and over. Michael had taken a lot of time to prepare these delightful surprises, and she was going to cherish them just as she cherished him.

As soon as the shift was over, Erika went to her apartment and changed into clothes comfortable enough for lounging about. She then made herself a cup of hot tea. Hoping to find some concrete answers to many of her questions, Erika carried the tea into the bedroom, where she would retrieve the metal box kept in her mother's filing cabinet. The idea of probing into her deceased mother's private affairs was unsettling and frightening. Unsettling, because it was a breach of privacy. Frightening, because of what she might discover.

The bedroom was silent as falling snow when she entered. Dust had already settled on the filing cabinet. To remove the dust she ran a tissue across its surface, but couldn't bring herself to open it. Feeling nervous, her body hot all over, she decided that fresh air would solve at least one of her problems, and she walked around opening the windows.

As she raised the bedroom window, she shivered from the sudden blast of cold air blowing in from the outside. Trying to get the courage to look at Vernice's personal papers, Erika dusted the furniture for the better part of an hour and vacuumed each of the tiny rooms in the apartment. Standing back to take a look at her handiwork, she smiled with satisfaction.

After putting the cleaning solutions in the cabinet under the kitchen sink, she went back to the bedroom. Erika stood in the doorway, fighting back tears. The bed was neatly made. The clock radio had the correct time but was otherwise mute. The closet door was slightly ajar. There, peeking out from under the bed, were what Vernice used to refer to as her old comforts—her fluffy blue slippers. She'd worn practically all the fur off them.

Walking over to the closet, Erika slid the door all the way back. Giving herself easier access to the cabinet stored way in the back of the closet, she pushed the clothes along the bar in opposite directions. Removing the key she'd taped to the back of the cabinet, she opened the file to remove the metal box. As she lifted up the box, she saw a manila folder wedged between the hanging folders and the back of the cabinet. With the intention of putting it back in the right place, she pulled it free and looked at the filing label.

Surprised to see her name printed neatly on the upper right hand corner of the folder, she carried it over to the bed and opened it. She was even more surprised by its contents, which smelled musty, but felt dry to the touch. It appeared to be an old insurance policy. When she pulled it out of its clear plastic jacket, she saw a folded sheet of paper.

Laying the policy on her lap, she took out the sheet of paper and began to peruse it. Holding her hand over her heart, she gasped. It was a letter from Anthony, penned in his own hand.

Dear Erika,
If you are reading this then I have gone home to be with the Lord. There are so many things I should've said to you, but never did. For reasons I don't quite understand myself, I missed so many golden opportunities. But in spite of all the things I should've told you and didn't, I never let a day pass without telling you how much I loved you. I love you, my beautiful daughter. Whatever you do, wherever you go, whatever the future reveals to you, please remember that Daddy loves you.

Erika traced Anthony's scrawled signature with numb fingers as the phrase *whatever the future reveals* burned deep inside her bewildered mind. Had this been his way of telling her he was her natural father, without actually writing the words? Or was she just reading something into the lines that wasn't really there, something she desperately needed to believe? Either way, it appeared he'd missed another golden opportunity to tell her exactly what was on his mind.

While looking at the insurance policy, she gasped again, seeing that she was the sole beneficiary, left a tidy sum of money. She couldn't believe they'd overlooked the policy when gathering up all the important documents right after Anthony's demise. Considering where she'd just found it, she realized how easy it would've been for them to overlook.

As hard as it was to do, Erika held her emotions in check.

There were many other papers to look over and she needed to keep her wits about her. Before all was said and done, she knew, the discovery, if any, could leave her an emotional cripple. Without her parents around to hold her up, she didn't know what she'd use for a crutch. For sure, not Michael. She'd leaned on him hard enough already. She'd lost count of all the many times he'd cushioned or broken her fall.

The discovery of the policy was amazing enough, in as much as it would help get her out of her financial difficulties. Given her druthers, though, she would take a living, breathing Anthony and Vernice Edmonds over any sum of money. At any rate, Erika wasn't even sure if the insurance company would still honor the policy. A lot of time had passed since Anthony's death.

Going back for the metal box, she retraced her steps to the bed. With shaking fingers, she finally opened it. The first document she removed was the original copy of her birth certificate, but she set it aside. It couldn't have changed since the last time she'd looked at it. Henry Wade would still be listed as her birth father, and all the other pertinent information would still be the same. Erika also knew what the adoption papers contained, though she read them, anyway.

However, Vernice and Anthony's marriage certificate was a different matter. It wasn't at all what she'd thought it would be. Instead of the date reflecting that their marriage had taken place three months after Erika was born, it was dated a year and three months after her birth. Yet the adoption papers were dated six months after she was born, which could only mean they hadn't been married at the time of the adoption. But how could that be?

She didn't think the court would've allowed unmarried couples to adopt children back then, but apparently they had. Had her adoption come under unusual circumstances? Erika felt something wasn't right. Maybe Vernice and Henry Wade's divorce papers would shed some light on this brainteaser.

Erika searched the files for the divorce papers, but they were nowhere to be found, which she thought was awfully strange. They'd been there at one time, she knew. She'd seen them, but she'd never read any of the details. Erika read through some other documents, but they weren't relevant to what she hoped to learn.

After putting everything back in the file cabinet, she locked it and put the key back in place. While walking around the apartment, she allowed old memories to fill her full of joy. The sorrow came soon after.

So many wonderful events had taken place in their old house. But there had been some unpleasantness, too, she recalled painfully. The house was now lonely and lifeless. Ever since Aunt Arlene had broached the subject of Erika keeping it with her help, Erika had known she'd never really wanted to get rid of it. Her desire to keep the old place was now stronger than ever.

The money Anthony had left her would help her keep the house up, and she could pay back all the money that had been paid out for her school expenses. She'd love to toss the whole amount, in cash, right in Abel Lightner's lousy lap. But she could only seriously weigh such possibilities after she learned if the insurance policy was still valid. Vernice had once suggested they lease the house. Leasing it out suddenly seemed a very attractive option. Erika still believed in God's miracles. She bowed her head for a moment of thankful prayer.

After closing the windows and securing the locks, Erika grabbed a jacket and left her tiny apartment. In her car, she placed the folder containing the insurance policy and Anthony's death certificate on the passenger seat. The address of the insurance company was on the policy. It would be her very first stop.

Erika was ushered into Mackenzie Bailey's private office.

A short, balding black man with a pleasant smile and too much weight for his small stature, he extended his tawny-brown hand to her. "Have a seat, young lady, so you can tell me what I can do for you."

Once she'd explained her mission, she handed him the policy in question and sat back in the chair while he made himself familiar with the case. Looking around the office, she decided its decor was comfortable but nothing to write home about. Family pictures, which hung on the walls in brass frames, lent a colorful touch to the otherwise drab room. Five sons and a daughter, Erika noted, laughing inwardly. Mackenzie Bailey had certainly been busy in his youth. All the children, whom she guessed to be much older now, looked very close in age. The family portraits had obviously been taken many years ago, when he had a full head of curly hair.

Mackenzie looked up and smiled. "You're the second person in less than twenty-four hours who's inquired about this policy. There was a young man in here to see me, and I assumed he was your attorney. I've been able to find out a few important facts since then. You've saved me some legwork. I was going to come and see you."

Erika raised her eyebrows at the mention of an attorney, disliking the implications. *Richard, no doubt,* she thought darkly, yet her hint of a smile seemed to speak of amusement.

"Miss Edmonds," Mackenzie continued, "after this policy was written it was mailed to a post office box. About five years ago, when the premiums stopped coming, we sent lapse-in-policy notices but they kept coming back. We later learned the post office box had been closed, but no reason was ever cited. We had no forwarding address. When your father died, this policy was probably overlooked because of the two different addresses."

"I don't understand, Mr. Bailey."

"The computer can only scan the information we feed into it. When we paid on the other policies, we just didn't put everything together for some reason or other. But I've been able to clear everything up. Since the death certificate is here, we can issue you a check within the next thirty days or so. Have I covered everything for you, Miss Edmonds? By the way, I need a copy of your driver's license."

Erika opened her wallet and handed Mr. Bailey the license. "I need to ask one more question," she uttered, watching him as he made copies of all the documents. He gestured for her to continue. "Do you remember the name of the attorney who came to see you?"

"Oh, yes, ma'am! His name was Glover. He left me his business card. Real nice fellow. Are you saying he's not your attorney?"

"I'm not saying that at all, but his coming here figures. He's my brother," she responded, smiling. It surprised her to hear how proud she sounded, how acknowledging Richard as her brother hadn't left a bad taste in her mouth.

Mackenzie grinned. "I should've figured it out myself. He seemed a little too protective of you to just be your attorney. I even wondered if maybe he was your boyfriend," he said, chuckling merrily.

"Well, now you know he's not. But he is my boyfriend's best friend. I have to be going, Mr. Bailey. Thanks for your kind assistance, sir."

"As soon as your check is cut, Miss Edmonds, you'll hear from me. Good day, young lady."

Erika settled into her car. The proof that Richard was her brother was mounting. She guessed Anthony had told him about the insurance policy. How else would he have known? While some pieces had fallen into place, others still didn't fit into the puzzle. The date on the marriage certificate was just one of many. She still wanted to wait, though, to talk to Aunt Arlene, whom she figured to have some of the missing pieces—if not the answers to the entire puzzle.

Though she felt sleepy and tired, she had one more stop to make. She didn't need a new dress for her date with Michael, but she wanted one, deserved one. She hadn't charged anything on her emergency Visa card in months, but it wasn't going to have a zero balance for much longer.

Even if the insurance policy hadn't existed, Erika would've purchased a new dress. She would've later worried about how she was going to pay for it. She'd made the decision to buy a dress right after she'd read the inspiring invitation from Michael.

Michael, she thought warmly. Dear, sweet Michael, the only man who could turn her heart inside out with a simple smile.

Fancy Free Boutique was located far from the normal shopping lanes. Erika had often admired the clothes in the display window, but today she was going to go inside to admire all they had to offer. As she drove the few miles, she tried to decide what color dress she'd like to purchase. Owning nothing dressy in basic black helped her make up her mind rather quickly.

Something black, daring, sexy and elegant would fit right in with the chic jet-setters who frequented Christopher's, a mountaintop retreat, a favorite rendezvous for lovers of all ages. . . .

Fifteen

The second Erika entered the boutique she was offered assistance. Politely declining the help, she was left alone to wander through the shop at her leisure. The boutique was noted for having only one or two copies of the wearing apparel it stocked. It was unlikely that two women walking down the street would ever be wearing the same Fancy Free outfit. That pleased Erika, as she desired to be totally original this evening.

Michael was so special he deserved to have something special in return. Tonight, she would pay close attention to her attire, hair and makeup. Erika hoped to find the perfect dress, one that would knock Michael's socks and shoes right off his feet.

A dazzling slip-dress in black caught her eye, but nothing was basic about its elegance. From the shop's original cocktail collection, layered with tiers of filmy chiffon, the dress was slinky, and it sparkled with golden glitter. A matching bolero-style jacket was designed to keep the chilly air away, but she liked the dress better without it. Erika could already imagine herself in it. Taking it from the rack, she closely looked it over, carrying it into the nearest dressing room.

Minutes later she twirled around in front of the three-way mirror, loving the billowing movements of the chiffon tiers. She pushed her hair high up on her head in a style that was a perfect complement to the already perfect dress.

It suddenly dawned on her that she hadn't looked at the

price. Looking down at the tag, she whistled as she read it, her spirits quickly sinking. There was no way she could afford such an expensive dress. Stepping out of it, she quickly donned her own clothes. Taking the dress to the rack, she hung it back up, looking regretful.

Smiling, a saleslady approached Erika. "Don't you like the dress, dear? It's one of a kind."

Erika frowned. "I love it. I just can't afford it."

"It is on sale, you know. Maybe we can knock off a few more dollars if you're really interested in it."

"Is that the sale price on the tag?"

"Oh, no! The discount is taken at the register. I'll check the sale price for you. It'll only take a minute."

Erika walked around looking at other dresses still hoping that one would end up affordable. This time she checked the tags. The saleslady returned and gave her the sale price. Erika frowned. "I don't know. It's certainly better than before, but I'm still not sure I can manage it. Maybe I should continue to look around." When the saleslady came down thirty more dollars, Erika stuck out her hand. "You have a sale. I may not be able to eat for the next month or so, but I'll worry about that later. Could you ring it up for me?"

"I'd be delighted to, dear. Are you paying cash?"

"Are you kidding? Plastic is all I have on me." Erika dug into her purse and came up with her Visa card, handing it to the friendly clerk.

The clerk tried to interest her in a pair of shoes that perfectly matched the dress, but Erika wasn't going to go that far overboard. Lorraine would have to bail her out again. Lorraine had more shoes in her closet than the law should allow one person to own. There was no doubt in Erika's mind that she'd have just the right shoes to complement the new dress. If not, she'd just have to make do with an old pair of black patent-leather shoes from her own closet.

* * *

There were hundreds of words Erika could've used to describe the mountaintop restaurant, but she chose only a few: elegant, romantic, breathtaking. On approach, via the glass elevator, the panoramic view had been spectacular.

Someone else may have spoken of white linen tablecloths, candlelight, flower centerpieces, fireplaces and music selected as though only lovers dined here. Well, for sure, she and Michael were lovers, which seemed obvious to all the heads turning as the hostess directed them to the table Michael had requested.

A magnificent view loomed before them and romance seemed to charge the atmosphere with magical currents of electricity. Erika felt as though the music and the candlelight were purposely seducing her, making her feel sensuous.

The black dress billowed and swayed as she walked. Enjoying the view, Michael dropped slightly behind her to further appreciate the tantalizing sway of her hips and the firm, shapely legs he loved to stroke at every given chance. Before pulling out her chair, not caring that the hostess was still present, he plundered Erika's mouth with an urgent tenderness.

The hostess blushed almost as much as Erika when Michael turned his attention her way. "Thank you. This is perfect."

"Thank you, sir. Your waiter will be here shortly."

"There's no rush. My companion and I love to take our time discussing what we're going to have for dessert later." He gave the hostess a knowing wink. Blushing, she hurried from the table.

Erika gave him a scolding look. "You were incorrigible, Michael. That poor woman was blushing like an adolescent. Maybe she finds you as sexy as I do. Your fabulous body and that stunning tuxedo tell a girl all she desires to know."

He lifted her hand and pressed a kiss into her palm. "Maybe so, but your opinion of me is the only one I care about. Earlier, you were so excited about our mode of transportation. Have you recovered yet?" he asked, recalling her animated screams and screeches when she first saw the white stretch limousine.

"Your invitation said a carriage, but I never dreamed it was going to be a limo. I'm rather partial to the Benz, but I can't tell you what went through my mind when I saw that stretch. Baby, you keep outdoing yourself!"

He grinned. "I'm glad you were so excited about it. Are you going to have a glass of wine before dinner, or do you prefer one of those sissy cocktails?"

"That depends on what you're having, Michael."

"Since we have a chauffeur, I'm going to have a Scotch on the rocks. I can't imagine you downing a Scotch. It's smooth as silk, but still too hard for someone so soft."

Erika threw her head back and laughed. "I can't imagine it, either. A zinfandel will be just fine." Summoned, the waiter appeared, and Michael gave him their drink orders, hoping he'd take his time getting back.

This evening wasn't going to be rushed. Michael knew that what he had to tell Erika later wasn't going to please her in the least. He wanted to enjoy as much pleasurable time in her company as possible before that time came, wanted to put off the inevitable for as long as he could. Forever would work nicely. More than anything, he just loved being in her presence. If he could, he'd keep the dawn from raiding the heavens by adding several more hours to the velvety night. Sipping the drinks, their heads drawn closely together, they talked intimately.

Erika didn't bring up the insurance policy or any other information that had to do with Richard being her brother. She had convinced herself that Michael didn't know any more than he'd already revealed. Once she had all the answers, she'd fill him in on all the details. Then, he could help her put her life back together, a life almost certain to fall apart.

They ordered lobster tails, cracked crab and grilled prawns, along with shrimp cocktails and fried mozzarella for appetizers. Michael asked to have their salads served with the main course because Erika preferred it that way.

The meal was as exquisite as the atmosphere. Erika thought

the restaurant served entirely too much food, but she wasn't going to have any problems asking for a people bag. Michael had mentioned taking some of the food home, so her asking wasn't going to embarrass him.

Once Michael had taken care of the check, he escorted Erika into the lounge, where a small combo played music they'd enjoy dancing to. Before suggesting they dance, Michael ordered another wine for her and a Scotch for himself. He would draw the line at two. He had doubts about Erika's ability to handle a second glass of wine. Her eyes already looked bright and glassy.

Michael pulled out her chair. With his arm possessively around her waist, he guided her onto the dance floor. Floating into his arms, she nestled her head on his broad chest. As they swayed to the romantic music, his grip around her waist grew tighter with every step they took.

He tilted her chin upward. "I'm in heaven," he whispered. "Where are you?"

Softly, her eyes met his. "I don't know, but I'm not in this world as we know it. I feel so much peace here."

Out of the blue, she got the strangest feeling that her peace was going to be shattered beyond repair. Fear struck her eyes. Trying to ward off the odd feeling, she shook her head. *No, I'm not going there, not tonight.* "Hold me tight, Michael," she whispered shakily.

Back in the limousine they settled in for a ride around the brightly-lit city. Pittsburgh was magnificent at night, she mused as they rode past a few of the city's finest attractions: Center for the Arts, Civic Arena, Heinz Hall, Station Square, Market Square. The driver eventually lazed by the Golden Triangle, the junction of three rivers: the Monongahela, Allegheny, and Ohio.

On the ride to Michael's place Erika and Michael did everything but make love. Erika had often wondered what it would be like to make love on the plush leather seats of a limo, but she was too much of a lady to request that they do just that. Had she known her asking would've thrilled and delighted him, she might've reconsidered. The driver wouldn't have known—at least she didn't think so—but she would've.

She could only imagine how embarrassed she would've been to face the chauffeur when they arrived at their rural destination. That would never do. She'd just have to put it on her list of future fantasies to be fulfilled.

By the time they reached the house she looked as though they had made love. Her face was flushed with a gentle blush, her lips swollen, the dress crumpled, and her hair falling from its majestic place on top of her head. And she was hot enough to start a fire by merely touching her finger to dried brush.

Michael looked just as disheveled as his gorgeous lover.

Instead of going into the house they took their usual stroll through the property. Despite the cold weather Erika couldn't cool down. She wanted Michael so much she could taste the desire and the need to have all of him. Her desires burned inside her stomach like hot acid.

She stopped as they reached the back porch. "I want to do something crazy and daring, Michael, something I've never done before. I want to make love under the stars!"

His jaw dropping in disbelief, he was astounded by her tenderly spoken request. "It's rather chilly out here, don't you think? Spring will be a perfect time for us to make love under the stars. Do we have a date for the first day of spring? It's just a short time away."

Feeling rejected, she pouted. "I don't want to wait until the first day of spring. I want you here and now," she demanded childishly, putting out her lower lip.

He couldn't keep from laughing. "Erika, you're acting like a spoiled brat, but if you want to catch your death out here, who am I to deprive you? You obviously know what you want.

But I'm going inside to get a couple of blankets. Coming with me, gorgeous?"

A sheepish smile crept onto her lips. "If you'll promise me we'll *come* together later!"

A wide grin spread across his mouth. "And you called *me* incorrigible? After hearing that comment, I don't think so!"

After unlocking the door, he lifted her and carried her back to the bedroom. Pulling out two sets of clean sweats, he tossed her one. "Put these on. I don't want you to freeze outside."

"For what?" she inquired haughtily, "you're only going to take them right back off. Besides, you got all the heat I need, baby," she cooed mockingly, her hands on both hips.

He gave her an I-need-to-get-you-in-check look. "You let me worry about taking them off. You just put them on. Trust me. You'll be glad you did. You may see me as a furnace, but Brother Hawk won't give a hoot about my heat when he comes tearing through that back porch. If I'd known you were going to turn out to be so daring, I would've taken you out to the barn at my parents' place. Shall we make a date for a night in the barn? My parents will be going away soon. They always take a trip around this time of year."

She lowered her eyelids. "I'm not so daring, Michael. But when I'm with you, I simply lose my mind, and all my ability to reason. Have I disappointed you?" she asked, her eyelids fluttering involuntarily. "I was a little brash with my come-on, wasn't I?"

"Brash? Hardly, sweetheart. You are refreshing! I wouldn't change one thing about you, except your ability to beat me at most of the board games we've played. Come here, gorgeous. If there's any doubt about how I feel about you, let me show you how deep my feelings run." It didn't take long for him to totally convince her of the depths of his love for her.

Michael carried her and several blankets out to the back porch. Standing her on her feet, he covered the chaise lounge with two of the blankets. Erika wasn't going to admit it, but she was glad to have on the sweats. Michael hadn't made any understatements regarding Brother Hawk, who was already blowing her body to bits. After lighting a kerosene heater, Michael placed it in the corner, away from the wind but close enough for them to benefit from its heat.

He held his hand out to her. "Your love nest awaits you, beautiful. Are you sure you want to go through with this?"

Crossing her arms behind his neck, she kissed him softly on the mouth and ears. "Yes, I'm sure. And I want to go out to the barn one night. I want to make love to you in every place that our imaginations will take us. I want to make love to you on all four corners of the earth. Is that too tall an order, Michael?"

Looking deeply into her eyes, he laced his hand into her hair. "There's nothing you could ask me that I wouldn't try to do for you. No, it's not too tall an order, Erika Edmonds. Now, let me tell you what I'm going to do for you tonight." When he tickled her inner ear with his tongue, she laughed so loudly the night creatures scrambled for safety. Lowering her down onto the chaise lounge, he covered them, fulfilling Erika's fantasy of making love under the stars.

Their lovemaking was slow, easy, tender and oh so infinitely sweet. Michael had underestimated the power of his own heat, because Erika had never felt hotter in her entire life. The kerosene heater was no match for Michael's radiating heat. It warmed her down to the soles of her feet. But most of all, it warmed her heart.

While the sweats got lost somewhere in the blankets covering them, even Brother Hawk couldn't penetrate the fortress of heat their lovemaking had created. Erika had gotten her wish. Making love under the stars was awash with sensuality. While making love, they'd taken the time to survey the stars twinkling against the purple velvet sky, which made their union all the more romantic.

The brilliant stars had the appearance of diamonds set on a backdrop of lush purple velvet. *The crown jewels would look like glass against the crown of jewels created by the Divine*

Power, Erika thought. *Queen Elizabeth, eat your heart out,* she added cheekily.

Michael kept his promise of their climaxing together, so powerfully, so explosively, so erotically. For a long time afterward, they just lay in each other's arms, drowning in the peace nature bestowed upon them, a peace surpassing their wildest expectations. Erika had earlier thought her peace was going to be shattered beyond repair, but those frightening thoughts had gotten lost in the wind, as it had swept the cobwebs from the corners of her mind.

Michael eventually got up from the chaise lounge and turned off the kerosene heater, but he left it in the corner. Not bothering to dress, he draped himself and Erika in a blanket. Escaping into the house, they ran straight to the bathroom and into the shower.

Steaming hot water gushed out, yet Erika still believed Michael's body heat was the hottest she'd ever bathed in. Even the sweltering Pennsylvania summers held no comparison.

Toweling her body and massaging it with hot oil had become a ritual—a ritual he loved to execute. Tonight, Erika decided to return the pleasure. Taking control, she massaged him until he thought he'd died and was floating somewhere between heaven and earth.

Much later, when Erika looked as though she might drop off to sleep, Michael knew he couldn't let her. As much as he'd like to wait until morning to talk to her, he couldn't. He'd already put the discussion off for too long.

Making love to her hadn't been in his original plans, but he couldn't refuse Erika anything she desired. Tonight, she had wanted to make love under the stars. He had indulged her in her death-enticing whims, fearing he might never get the opportunity to do so again—so sure she was going to be furious with him after he told her what he'd known all along about Richard. It was the very same fear that had caused him to make so many reckless decisions over the past week; lying to her had been the most reckless.

Now, more than ever, she was going to think he'd made an utter fool of her and had enjoyed doing so. This scenario had all the ingredients of a sizzling daytime soap opera. Unfortunately, this was real life and he didn't like the starring role he'd been asked to play.

Feeling guilty for rousing her from her state of sweet euphoria, Michael nudged her gently. She stirred, curling herself up against his body. "We have to talk, sweetheart. I have something I need to get off my chest. Think you can stay awake long enough to hear me out?"

Frowning, eyes half-closed, she looked up at him. "I guess, but I sense I'm not going to like what you're going to tell me. But go ahead. I'll try to stay awake and quiet." Waiting for Michael to begin, Erika made herself comfortable, propping her back against the headboard.

Michael took a few deep breaths. "You're right about what you just said. You're not going to like what I have to tell you, but I have to say it anyway. I've learned something about you that I've been asked to keep a secret. I agreed to it, but I know it was the wrong thing to do, even then. I want to right that wrong." Feeling uneasy, she swallowed the lump in her throat. The strange feelings she'd had earlier seemed to wrap themselves around her once again.

"The morning I left your place and went to Richard's office, he told me something I never would've dreamed possible." Michael gulped hard and continued. "Richard believes you're his biological sister. In fact, he knows you are. Anthony told him a long time ago. He was in constant contact with your father. Anthony is your biological father, not your stepfather." He grew silent, allowing her to take everything in. She appeared calm on the outside, but he was sure her emotions were warring.

Erika kept her eyes sharply focused on him. "So, you knew about the money, too. You chose to lie about it, Michael. Why?"

He shook his head. "No! I only learned the truth about the

money recently. When I told you I was going to see Richard, I was very angry with him over this whole mess. Erika, I am guilty of keeping one secret, but I'm innocent where those checks are concerned. It was because of the checks that I'm telling you all this. I couldn't do this anymore. You mean too much to me. Richard had promised to tell you himself, but I couldn't wait any longer. Besides, I thought I should be the one to tell you."

Briefly, she looked away. Then she turned back to face him. "I already know Richard is my brother. I overheard him telling Abel Lightner the morning I went to Abel's office. I don't claim to understand any of it . . . I'm not sure I ever will. The answers to all my questions are buried with my parents and I don't have the heart to confront my aunt yet, who I believe knows the whole story."

Leveling Michael with a look of distrust, Erika got out of bed, only to climb right back in. "Michael, I wish you had cared enough about me to tell me this when you first learned it. You've deceived me just as my father and mother did. I don't deserve this from you. And as far as Richard's concerned, he can go straight to hell. Since he's your best friend, maybe you should join him." The anger in her suggestion was clear.

Gripping the sheet tightly, he blew out a ragged breath. "I guess I deserved that. But I need to say something else to you. Then I'll let you decide our fate. I love you! And I need you to think about a few things. Whatever reasons your parents had for not telling you the truth, we'll never know. But know this. They were there for you. They resided in the same house with you. They took care of all your needs. They loved you, Erika. And I know you love them. It's written all over your face every time you mention their names, or recall some fond memory of them. It's written on your heart every time I look inside of you."

He took her hand. "Not many children get to live under the same roof with both parents. Nor do they always find love there. I don't condone their methods, but I can't judge their reasons, either. They may have been very valid. Again, that's something we'll never know. I hope you continue to cherish the love and acceptance you received from them. You can't change what's happened, but you can learn to accept it. Embrace the loving memories, Erika. Don't blot out all the blessings love has already granted you. Don't block all the blessings love has yet to offer. Love is what opens doors, and love never allows them to close on you."

Her laugh was derisive. "I still think you would've made a great lawyer, Michael, since quite a few of them are liars. You've once again pleaded a good case. However, I'm sorry to inform you you've lost this one, brother counselor. Since this case is officially closed, I'd like to go home."

Michael moved closer to her, but was scared to touch her, scared of the rejection surely to come. "I'm sorry to hear that, sorry you feel that way. But I have something else to say." He got up and retrieved something from a dresser drawer.

Returning, he knelt down beside the bed. "I love you, Erika. I don't want you to feel alone or betrayed ever again. I don't want to ever be without you. And I know my timing is lousy, but love won't let me wait. Will you marry me, Erika Edmonds?"

Her mouth fell open in incredulity. This was the last thing she had expected, yet the one thing she'd hoped for since the day she'd fallen in love with him. Completely losing her composure, she lowered her chin to his head, pushing her fingers through his thick waves. "Oh, Michael," she cried, "less than an hour ago I would've given anything to have you ask me to marry you. Then, I would've accepted. But this is now. You're right, the timing is definitely all wrong. I'm a very confused woman. Right now I don't know what I want, but I do need space, enough space to figure this all out. I'm sorry, but I can't accept your proposal."

He was crushed, devastated, but she hadn't completely closed the door, he told himself. Somewhere in her statements she'd left open a small window of opportunity. "Are you saying you can't accept it right now, or that you can't ever accept it?" Michael asked, drawing in a deep breath and holding it.

"I don't know the answer to that, either. I can't even think about it right now. I don't want to think about it, Michael. All I want to do is go home and be alone with my thoughts. Will you take me?" Not one tear fell from her eyes, but her pain was clear. He heard it in her voice and saw it in the way she moved her body.

He pressed the perfectly faceted three-carat trillion-cut diamond ring into her hand. "Regardless of your decision, I want you to have this ring. It was purchased with you in mind, only you. I'll take you home now."

Squeezing the ring in her palm, she wondered if it was all she was ever going to have of Michael. Though she'd never wear it, she wouldn't give it back, either, not right now. She loved Michael—and would never add insult to injury. They were both deeply injured, and there was no reason for either of them to have to endure any more pain.

In a daze, committing everything in his house to memory, especially the bedroom, she got dressed. This was the room where they'd hoped, dreamed, whispered intimate secrets, and made sincere promises to each other—a room her presence might never again grace.

Michael had betrayed her, deceived her, lied to her. And she just couldn't accept that from him. Knowing she couldn't get used to having a sordid image, she opted to rely on the sweet memories she had, the memories they'd made before desperate deceptions had robbed her of the man she so ardently loved.

Upon their arrival at the university Erika wouldn't permit Michael to walk her inside. As she heartlessly pushed him away, he didn't know if he'd ever see her again. Without the slightest objection, he let go of her. Allowing her to maintain her dignity was important to him.

Pulling Lorraine's sable coat tighter around her, she walked away from him. Wanting to take one last look at him, she didn't dare to, fearing she'd end up back in his arms, compromising her principles.

Crying inwardly, Michael watched the woman he loved with everything in him disappear from his sight, blinded by his tears.

Instead of going to her apartment, Erika took the inside walkway linking the dormitory to the hospital. There, she took the elevator up to the roof, wondering why she and Michael had never gone up there together.

The large deck on the roof was outfitted with benches, chairs and tables. Because no smoking was allowed inside the hospital, all the smokers escaped to the roof for cigarette breaks. It was still a mystery to her how people in the medical profession could smoke tobacco, especially with the wealth of information available to them about smoking-related diseases.

It was bone-chillingly cold outside, but Erika didn't seem to notice. Before sitting down, she made sure the chair was clean. She couldn't afford to have Lorraine's fur coat cleaned, she thought, forgetting the money she'd just inherited. Maybe Richard would have it cleaned for her, she mused cynically. Maybe she should just take him to the cleaners, period. He seemed to like to flaunt his wealth and status.

No longer able to hold back the tears, she let them flow, hot and heavy. Why was life such a chore? Why did pain seem to be her closest friend? Maybe she'd let it get too darn comfortable with her over the years. Now, her friend, pain, ruled her life.

"Daddy, dear Daddy," she cried out morosely, "why didn't you ever tell me I was your very own flesh and blood?"

Reflecting on the years that she'd spent loving him and trusting him was painfully sweet. Daddy had rocked her to sleep at night, taken her to school in the mornings and been there for her when she got home. Prepared by him, breakfasts, lunches and dinners were always ready on time. With Vernice at work, they'd shared all their meals.

Daddy had held her hand at the dentist's office, held it when she'd cut herself with a knife and had to have stitches. He'd been there when she was happy and when she felt blue. When she was old enough, he'd taken her downtown and shown her how bills were paid. On those long walks downtown, he'd also held her hand. Anthony had been like her shadow, always there.

He'd been so good to her. Why was she so darn mad at him? Why did she feel so betrayed by him? What could've been so bad that it caused him to deny her his legacy? She was angrier with him than at Vernice, she realized.

It was hard to admit, but maybe she was angry with Anthony because she'd relied on him more than on Vernice. He'd certainly been more predictable than her mother had and his spirit had been a peaceful one. Vernice had once been at war with herself and everyone else around her.

Anthony had always shown his love for Erika. It had been there in his smile, in his hugs, in his warm brown eyes. It was different with Vernice, which was something she rarely admitted to herself. She'd never been sure of her mother's true feelings for her, especially when she was much younger. Erika was an adult before Vernice ever told her she loved her. Even now she didn't understand why it had taken her mother so long to profess love to her only child. Had Vernice been capable of loving back then? she wondered, no malice intended.

You had to love yourself before you could love another. Erika wasn't convinced Vernice had loved herself back then. Perhaps it was simply because she hadn't known how to.

There had been a few things about the relationship between her parents that puzzled Erika in her youth, but she'd never asked questions. Their closed-door arguments had been rather loud at times, yet they'd always made up rather quickly. Erika had often sensed that there were deep secrets between them, but she would've never guessed Anthony being her biological father was one of them, a well-kept one. They'd kept her in the dark about that—and for so many years.

It was a horrendous thought, one that made her sick to her stomach, that if Michael hadn't been Richard's best friend she would've never known the truth—not unless Richard had come looking for her. It certainly seemed he'd known about her existence. A worse thought was where would she be had Michael never come into her life?

God, she screamed inwardly, denying herself the pleasure that just the thought of Michael brought forth. She couldn't allow herself to think of him, not until she sorted everything out.

Walking to the edge of the roof, she looked up at the moon and the stars, making a wish on the brightest one. Then, crying bitterly, she rushed to her apartment, feeling lonelier than she'd ever felt in her life.

Sixteen

After completing several hard shifts and several sleepless nights, Erika sat quietly at the kitchen table, waiting for her aunt to join her. As usual, Arlene was baking something that smelled awfully good, but Erika's appetite had been a no-show for days.

Arlene turned off the oven. Carrying two cups of hot tea, she joined her niece, setting one of the cups in front of Erika. "I'm all finished for now. What did you want to talk to me about, child?"

Erika fumbled with her car keys and then laid them on the table. "I want to talk about something that happened twenty-seven years ago." She waited for a reaction from her aunt, but none came. "I knew Anthony had a son long before he met Mother, but did you know?"

Arlene sighed. "It had been mentioned. I believe his name is Richard. Why do you ask?"

Erika gritted her teeth. "Because he's claiming to be my biological brother. That would make Anthony Edmonds my biological father. Is that so, Aunt Arlene?" Erika asked, already knowing the bittersweet truth.

Arlene showed a little discomfort, but she'd known this day was going to come, was surprised it hadn't come sooner. "It is so, sweet child. Anthony was your natural daddy. I'm sorry, Erika, but they didn't want you to know. To be real honest, your mother was the one who wanted it kept from you." Arlene steeled herself for the next question.

"Why?"

Studying Erika intently, Arlene took a small sip of tea. "Erika, it's a long story, so you'd better sit back in that chair and relax. If your mother were alive, I wouldn't even think of discussing this with you. But I always felt you had a right to know the truth." Arlene took another sip of her tea. "Relax, child. I can already feel how tense you are." Arlene looked concerned about the unhappiness she saw on her niece's lovely face.

"Your mother was unhappy for some reason or another. Whatever she believed were the problems in her marriage, she eventually allowed them to take her interest elsewhere. She met Anthony at a baseball game. Later, she ended up having an affair with him. During that affair she became pregnant—the worst thing that could've happened since she was still married to Henry Wade and living under the same roof with him." Erika gasped at the revelation of what she never would've guessed.

Arlene patted Erika's hand to soothe her rattled niece. "It was an awful time for her back then, but she did her best. In my opinion, though, she was never able to handle it. Anyway, she went to Henry and told him her situation. He didn't like it one bit, but what was done was done. Since she was still married to him she asked him if she could use his name on your birth certificate. He agreed, a very noble and gracious thing for him to do. A lot of men would've turned her down cold."

Erika wiped the tears from her face. "Is that why they got divorced?"

Arlene nodded her graying head. "Partly. Bitterness was in her marriage before she ever met Anthony. The marriage ended badly. In those days this type of situation was heavily frowned on. Vernice took a lot of ridicule, and it took her a long time to recover. You once said you thought your mother lived in a state of denial. Now you know why."

Arlene massaged the back of Erika's hand. "You also said you thought something from her past contributed to the anger she often displayed. I believe you were right. Vernice lived in denial for such a long time. She was angry at her circumstances, not you or me. Bringing this up now can only do you more harm, but it's better for you to know. Have you met your brother?"

Erika blew out a ragged breath. "I have. He just happens to be Michael's attorney and his best friend." Arlene looked surprised. "Talk about coincidences! Remember the checks I told you about?" Arlene nodded. "Well, Richard is my wealthy benefactor. Richard showed up after I'd seen his attorney on the day I went to the address on the check. I overheard him telling his attorney I was his sister. I've gone through hell ever since, wondering if it's true.

"Michael confirmed it for me a few days ago, but deep inside I already knew it. Michael has known it all along, but Richard asked him not to tell me. I'm furious with Michael for deceiving me. He also asked me to marry him a couple days ago, but I think not. One deception is one too many. I don't plan to ever see him again," Erika exclaimed bitterly, hating the ominous finality in the tone of her voice, hating her unwillingness to forgive.

Arlene sharply raised an eyebrow. "Does that mean you're never going to see me again, either? I'm as guilty of deceiving you as he is," Arlene announced.

Erika looked stunned. "Of course not! You were asked not to tell me," Erika reminded her aunt ardently.

"So was he, Erika. It's my guess he was trying to protect you. What would he have gained by keeping it from you? When I objected to your not being told, I was told to stay out of it. I did. As much as I wanted to tell you, it wasn't my place to do so. For what it's worth, your daddy wanted you to know, too. He talked to me about it many times. Your parents lived with broken hearts, and they died the same way. Each had separate burdens to bear. No child was ever loved by her parents more than you were. Anthony loved his son, too. He couldn't bring him home, but he didn't let it stop him from going where he was. He saw him every chance he got. But when Richard's mother married and took him to Philadelphia with her, their times together became few and far between," Arlene recounted dolefully. "According to Vernice, Anthony always did the right thing by his son."

Erika's eyes watered up again. "Why couldn't he have done the same for me? Why didn't he take a tough stand on this issue? It sounds like my father wimped out. How could he let someone control him like that? How could he let anyone keep him from claiming his own flesh and blood? He should've claimed me the same as he did his son. He was as deceitful as Mother obviously was. Apparently they deserved each other."

Arlene stood straight up, wagging her finger back and forth in Erika's face. "Erika Edmonds, don't you ever let me hear you talk about your parents like that again. It's downright disrespectful! It's okay to be angry. You should be angry. Just find a more constructive way to vent it. You're never too old for a good spanking, young lady."

Erika slammed her fist on the table. "I'm not angry," she remarked, feeling as if she might explode from all the pent-up frustration of her anger. Still, she forced back the bitter tears, forced back the need to rant and rave like an angry, uncontrollable maniac.

Arlene leveled a steady gaze at her niece. "Who are you trying to fool? You've never been angrier than you are right now, dear child. Your body language speaks for itself. You must go ahead and release the rage burning in those chocolate-brown eyes. You'll stay angry until you do let it go. Anger can be healthy, but only if it's released before it festers inside of you. Stop lying to yourself, my dear child."

Erika blew out a gust of shaky breath. "Okay, so I'm angry.

What do you want me to do? Go to my parents' graveside and vent all over them? That's certainly not going to ease their consciences, since they won't hear me. Besides, even if they were alive there's no way I could ease their consciences. For sure, not with my anger. Knowing that someone could eventually get hurt by all this deceit, I don't know how they lived with themselves."

"Don't tear them or yourself down over this. You go home, sit down, think about all the things they did for you, and take a brisk walk through your life. Then come back here and talk to me. For every step you take on that walk, you'll find your parents right there beside you. Your mother went through a lot of things you'll never know about—she's gone through the fire. It should make you feel good to know your mother never allowed herself any peace, never forgave herself for anything. That's more than enough punishment for any one person to bear. Apparently you don't think so. Perhaps you'd be happier if you thought she was burning in hell as you sit here in judgment of her."

Erika gasped. "That was so unfair, Aunt Arlene! I never wanted her to be miserable about anything, don't want her punished . . . and I'm not judging her. In fact, I prayed on my knees daily for God to grant her peace when she was alive. I now pray daily for her eternal peace."

"What you've been spewing is unfair, child. I'm glad to know my harsh statement didn't bring you any comfort. And speaking of unfair, you're being real unfair to Michael. From what you've been telling me, he's been behind you every step of the way. If you give him up it'll be the biggest mistake of your life, girl! There's one thing we should always remember. Humans make mistakes. Vernice and Anthony were human. Look to the Father above for your salvation, not to any one person living in the flesh, including the preacher man."

Erika looked puzzled. "I do know that, Aunt Arlene. I've made tons of mistakes already and I'm not yet thirty. But am I supposed to up and forgive Michael for lying to me? Am I supposed to act as if it never happened? I've been taught to never compromise my morals or principles. Knowing that Michael compromised his own integrity, are you telling me I should start compromising mine?"

Erika got up from the table and walked over to the stove, where she refilled her cup with hot tea. After filling Arlene's cup, she went back to the table.

"Michael Mathis is a lot like your daddy. That's why he was so easy to fall in love with, whether you want to admit it or not. Your daddy was a good man—a man who went through his own private hell. Yet he stayed. He could've just walked away from it all. That doesn't sound like a wimp to me. Henry Wade was a good man, too. And I believe he died still loving your mother," Arlene said, tears welling in her eyes.

Angrily, Arlene brushed the tears aside. "Your mother was torn by two lovers. Stubbornness and pride played a big hand in her divorce and in her remarriage. Putting that aside, Vernice Edmonds had a heart. A broken one, but nonetheless a heart. A giving one."

Erika didn't bother to wipe her tears. "I know Mother had a wonderful heart. She was just so unhappy with herself most of her life. I don't mean to put her down. I love her. If only she'd known how to love herself, I'm sure she would've done so. Most of us are products of our own environment. I believe that a long time ago someone drilled into Mother that she wasn't worthy of happiness. Someone along the way made her feel she wasn't valued, discounting her feelings in the process."

Arlene looked surprised by Erika's statements. "Vernice was a person who took everything to heart. She tried to hide the fact that she was mighty sensitive, that her feelings got hurt real easy. At any rate, your mother helped a lot of people, child. She would have given her last dime to someone in need. Vernice was only guilty of being her own worst enemy. If she could've gone back and changed everything, I'm sure she would've. But she couldn't. So you continue to love her in the way I know you do.

"True love is unconditional. There are times when we do have to compromise, especially when it's something worth it. Just learn to separate the bad compromises from the good ones. And remember that you were also taught about forgiveness. Though your mother taught you to be forgiving, she was never able to forgive herself for the mistakes she made."

Erika smiled weakly. "I've taken everything you've said under advisement. Now I want to talk about Richard. Do you think I should talk to my brother?"

Arlene smiled with empathy. "That has to be your decision. But if he were my brother, nothing would stop me from embracing him with all the love in my heart," Arlene said, reaching out to Erika. "After all, he's your flesh and blood, too. You don't want to be guilty of the same injustices you're accusing your parents of, now do you? Richard is as innocent in all this as you are. There aren't many people who'd pay out such a large sum of money for someone they barely know. It seems that Richard has some of the same wonderful qualities as his father. If he accepts you as his sister, then perhaps you shouldn't hold any ill feelings toward him." Carefully pondering Arlene's words of wisdom, Erika knew her to be right in everything she'd said.

"Remember, he's a victim, too. Think how he must have felt, being deprived of seeing his only sibling. The things he's already done for you say he wants to know you."

Erika didn't even try to hold back the tears. There were so many things she would need to consider before coming to any final conclusions. It was clear she was going to need to reassess the decision she'd made regarding her relationship with Michael Mathis. She just wasn't capable of doing so right now. As she recalled the devastated look on Michael's face when she'd refused to allow him to walk her inside, she felt sick all over. It was true. Michael had always been behind her, had the same quiet spirit and the same gentle ways as her father. Apparently, Richard did, too.

Arlene handed Erika some tissue, gathering her niece closer

to her warmth, rocking her gently. "You go ahead and cry it all out, child. This won't be the last of your tears, but they are the first step of your healing process." Before leaving her aunt Erika found the address to Richard's office in the yellow pages of the telephone book.

Without wasting another minute thinking about it she drove into downtown Pittsburgh, trying to think of all the things she wanted to say to Richard Glover, her brother. Aunt Arlene had been right. Richard was a victim, too. In fact, he'd been deprived of his father more than she had. At least she'd grown up having him at her disposal twenty-four hours a day. Richard had had only stolen moments here and there. It had to have been a raw deal for him anyway you sliced it, Erika thought somberly, approaching the entrance to Richard's office suite.

If Richard's success could be measured by the size of his office and the expensive furnishings in the outer offices, he was quite successful, Erika thought, giving her name to the receptionist. Taking a seat, she wished she could see the look on Richard's face when he learned she was there to see him.

Richard made a quick appearance. Looking somewhat apprehensive, he smiled nervously at her. "Hello, Erika. I guess we have a lot to discuss. Will you come into my private office? Or perhaps you'd rather go to a more neutral setting?" he offered kindly.

She stood up. "Your office will be fine." Her tone was somewhat clipped. She hadn't intended to sound that way, but she was just as nervous as he was.

"Mia, hold my calls, please," he instructed as they passed the reception desk. The receptionist smiled and nodded.

Inside Richard's office, Erika sat on the sofa and Richard drew up a chair, making sure he and Erika faced each other. For a few dreadfully tense moments, they only stared, each trying to find a trace of family resemblance in the other. Erika had already decided he had a lot of Anthony Edmonds in him.

Richard thought he had the most beautiful sister a brother could ever hope for, thinking Erika had Anthony's skin coloring as well as his hair color—that is, before he'd turned completely gray. Her other delicate features were uniquely her own, beautiful to behold.

Clearing his throat, Richard was the first one to break the interminable silence. "Erika, I know I've gone about this all wrong. When Michael introduced you at the ballet, I was stunned out of my gourd. There, before me, was the sister I'd longed to meet and have a relationship with, yet I wasn't sure you even knew I existed. It hurt like hell. All I wanted to do was take you in my arms and smother you with affection, but I couldn't. I'd been forbidden to see you for so many years that I just reacted to the way I was conditioned. I'm sorry."

He took her hand. "For what it's worth," he continued, "Michael didn't want any part of this from the very beginning. I convinced him to keep my secret until I got up the courage to face you on my own."

She scowled. "I don't want to talk about Michael, not right now. This is between you and me. This is about family," she said shakily, tactfully withdrawing her hand from his.

"Michael *is* family to me, Erika, but I'll honor your request. Is there anything in particular you'd like to ask me?" He laughed. "Now that was a dumb question!"

Erika laughed, too, shifting her body as she tried to relax her tense muscles. "There are so many things I want to ask, but there's only one burning in my mind right now. How did you take being denied by our father?"

Richard pondered her question carefully. "I never felt denied by him, Erika," he said steadfastly. "Of course I was hurt by not being able to go to his house, to feel that I was a part of his family, but I know he would've changed all that if he could've." He cleared his throat. "I don't want to come down on your mother," he said cautiously, "but I think she feared me—for a reason I'll never know. There was something heavy going on between her and our father, but he never told me what it was." He looked puzzled. "I didn't ask, but I always felt there was a deep, dark secret between them. Things just never added up for me. Do you have any idea what was going on between them?"

Briefly, she focused her attention on the leather-bound books on the bookshelf. Then she turned her attention back to Richard. "I didn't, but I do now. My mother was still married to her first husband when I was conceived. She and Anthony were involved in what could be called an illicit affair. Just before I came to see you my aunt told me the entire story. It explains a lot, but I think things could've been handled very differently.

"My mother may have feared you because she guessed that Anthony had told you I was your sister—that's if she didn't already know it. So many people have been hurt by their deceptions. For sure, you and I. Where would you like us to go from here?"

Feeling very comfortable now, Richard moved over to sit down next to her, easing his arm around her shoulders. "I would like us to get to know each other, of course. I'm not asking you to love me. Just give us a chance to find out if we can build a sister and brother relationship. What would you like to see happen, Erika?"

Surprising him, she laid her head back against his arm. "Richard, the fact is, we *are* brother and sister, of the same flesh and blood. I have to say you unnerved me when you kept your eyes trained on me at the ballet, but now I know why. I was angry as hell when I learned you were the one sending those large checks out for me."

Raising her head, she looked at him. "I wanted to strangle you and Abel Lightner when I overheard you telling him I was your sister. His rude remarks had me wanting to knock down his door and hit him upside the head with it." He laughed and she liked the sound of it. It reminded her of Anthony's deep laughter.

"So, you were still there when I went into his office," he

remarked sheepishly. "I hope you heard me call Lightner on his sexist remarks. A big brother can be very protective of his only little sister."

She smiled. "I know. Mackenzie Bailey told me you were very protective of me when you came to see him."

"You're quite the little detective, aren't you?" he commented, laughing. "When did you go see Bailey?"

"After I found the insurance policy Daddy left for me."

Richard was amazed by how she'd put things together. "So, he found out it wasn't already cashed in. Will they honor it?"

"Yeah, they will, but I'd rather have Daddy," she said, tears filling her eyes. Quickly composing herself, she went on to explain what Mackenzie had told her.

Richard wished he could remove all her pain. "I'm glad, Erika. Dad wanted to secure your future. He took care of me, too. That's just the way he was. We may not agree with how he chose to do things, but we can agree on one fact. He loved his kids and he did the best he could. At least, I think so. I love him. He was a damn good man."

In awe of his sensitivity, Erika cautiously touched his face. "I love him, too. And you're not so bad yourself." He kissed her gently on the cheek. With tears in her eyes, she placed her hand on his head, pressing his lips deeper into her skin. It felt so good, so right.

Turning ever so slightly, she threw her arms around his neck, pressing her own lips against his temple. "Do you mind if your little sister wants to tag along behind you from time to time?" she asked, bursting into tears.

Fighting hard to restrain his uncontrollable tears, he locked her in a tight embrace. "This big brother would love to have his little sister tag along, not behind him, beside him. He wouldn't have it any other way. It's one of the things he's lived for." Holding her away from him, he wiped her tears. "Shall we make some silly pact? Perhaps lock our pinky fingers together? Or should we draw blood——and mingle it?"

She laughed. "I think a big hug and a kiss will be enough

to seal our commitment. I'm a doctor, but the sight of blood still has a way of making me a little queasy."

Kissing and hugging, both felt they'd found one of the most important parts of themselves. Richard had found the part of him missing for a long time. Erika had found a part of her she'd never known belonged to her.

Richard got up from the sofa. "I have something to show you." Opening a cabinet door, he pulled out a large green folder and carried it back to the sofa. "Take a look at these." He handed her the folder.

Erika was flabbergasted. "Oh, my God! These are all pictures of me. And look at these old newspaper articles about me. You have kept a close eye on me, haven't you? It's such a shame I never knew you were there. Did Daddy give you all these school pictures?"

"He did. Some of the newspaper articles, as well. He was proud of you. He knew you were going to be successful in your quest to become a doctor. He would've bet the farm on it—and won, I might add. It's too bad he didn't live to see it for himself. He was at most of the important events in my life. When I passed the state bar, on my first try, he was there to help me celebrate. Erika, we had a father who cared. Don't judge him or your mother too harshly. About these pictures, I'm going to purchase frames for them and display them in this office and at home. Okay?"

Erika frowned. "If I can choose the ones I won't mind on display. Some of these pictures are atrocious. Think I can get a picture or two of you?"

"I don't have any recent ones, but I'll have some made. Maybe we should get one taken together. When can you come to the house?" he asked enthusiastically. "We can go through all my old photo albums. I think I can stand to part with a few old pictures of myself. I'm sure you'll enjoy seeing some of the old ones I have of Dad. Can you come soon?"

"Just say when, big brother. I'll be there. Unless, of course, I have to be on duty."

"What about tomorrow evening? I'll fix us a great meal."

"He cooks, too," she exclaimed. "Daddy loved to cook. I can be there around six o'clock. Write down the address for me with detailed directions. When driving in strange territory, I'm like a compass without a needle. Useless."

Hours later, when Richard walked Erika to her car, he leaned against it, drawing her into his arms. "I can't tell you how happy I am, Erika. I hope this is the beginning of a lasting relationship. I can honestly say I already love you. I hope one day you'll feel the same about me. Another thing—have a telephone installed. I'll take care of the expenses. The sister of a prominent attorney should not be without a phone," he joked.

She kissed his cheek. "I think loving you back will be a piece of cake—and just as sweet. At any rate, families are supposed to love one another. A phone will be installed, but I'm going to pay for it. I'll see you tomorrow. Good-bye, Richard Edmonds."

He smiled broadly. "I like the sound of that. Maybe I should start using my legal surname. I'm sure my stepfather will give me his blessing. When I was growing up, it was easier using the same last name as my mother. Dad understood. I never saw a real reason to revert back—that is, until now." Richard looked down at the ground and then back at her. "I know I agreed not to mention Michael again, but I feel compelled to do so. Sis, you won't find a better man, or one who can love you more than Michael does. Don't close the door on him. Don't shut him out of your life." He kissed her and then walked away, hoping she'd think about what he'd said.

All the way home Erika did think about what Richard had said. His words and Aunt Arlene's kept echoing in her head. She didn't need them to tell her what a great person Michael was, or how wonderful he was, how genuine he was. She already knew. However, the fact that he'd deceived her remained. What was she supposed to do? Pat him on the back and say, "Nice job, Michael. I love being deceived. I really get off on being lied to. I'm gone on being made a big fool of." Why should she reward deception?

If she fell right back into Michael's arms, that's exactly what she'd be doing, rewarding him for deceiving her. How could she maintain her self-respect if she gave in to her desperate need for him? Besides, he'd allowed her to strip her soul bare before him, had made love to her knowing he was going to break her heart later. For Pete's sake, she thought, the man was a doctor. He was supposed to mend hearts . . . not break them. He was supposed to heal, not make people emotionally and mentally ill. Had he forgotten the Hippocratic oath?

It suddenly began to dawn on her that she was more angry at Michael for making love to her, knowing what he was going to tell her later. The whole idea of it rankled right down to her bone marrow. It seemed as though he'd totally disregarded her feelings as he sought all the pleasure he could get from her. He had wined her, dined her and seduced her. Then, as if her life didn't have enough chaos in it, he'd had the nerve to ask her to marry him.

A little voice inside her head told her she'd been the seducer. In fact, she'd insisted on him making love to her—under the stars, no less—yet she still debated with her conscience. He'd known he was going to break her heart before the evening was over. He'd known from the start, even before he'd written that darn dinner invitation.

As far as she was concerned it had all been a cold, calculated act. If Michael thought she could just up and forgive him, he was sadly mistaken. No man would ever do something so cruel to her again. Love or no love, Dr. Michael Mathis simply wasn't going to get away with the crime he'd so brazenly committed. He was guilty of breaking her heart. No crime, however big or small, should go unpunished.

Before she could insert her key into her apartment door lock, Lorraine was right there beside her. "It's about time you got home. Dr. Mathis sure keeps you on a tight rein," Lorraine teased.

Without commenting, Erika opened the door, allowing Lorraine to go in first. As she went into the bedroom to put away her things, Lorraine followed right behind her, draping herself across the bottom of the bed.

Sighing with displeasure, Erika looked at Lorraine. "I can see that I'm not going to be able to keep any secrets from you, so I might as well tell all. Make yourself comfortable, Lorraine."

Stretched across the bottom of Erika's bed, Lorraine was all eyes and ears as she listened to Erika spin a tale that grew more fascinating by the second. Erika having a brother she'd never met astounded her, and that she thought of throwing Michael over because he'd kept it a secret from her was downright insane. She planned to tell Erika exactly that when she finished with her unbelievable saga.

"I saw Michael earlier at the hospital. Unaware of what was going on, I told him how worried I was about you, told him you were walking around looking like one of the cadavers all us medical students have the misfortune to encounter. I honestly thought it all had to do with your financial woes. Michael said nothing to make me think otherwise."

Erika shrank inside. "Don't you ever mind your own business? How could you talk to him about me like that? He probably thinks I'm lovesick over him. And he's right. This isn't some sort of silly infatuation. I am in love with that man, crazy in love." She sighed with discontent. "So you see, Lorraine, you never know what you're going to find in the darkness of a closet. Skeletons come in all sizes and shapes. They have a way of taking on a life of their own. They may get banished to the back of the closet for a period of time, but skeletons will eventually come to life, when you least expect it."

"When I talked to Michael, he didn't even hint that you two were no longer seeing each other. His eyes flared brightly with the look of love the second I mentioned your name. But now, looking back on our brief encounter, I remember Michael did seem somewhat detached. He looked tired. In our profession, looking tired is par for the course, so there wasn't any valuable discovery there."

"I feel betrayed by him. I just can't . . . refuse to . . . let Michael's evil deeds go unpunished."

Lorraine cheered. "That was nicely put. I couldn't have said it better myself. Now, let's get right down to the real nitty-gritty, sister. Why are you blaming Michael for something your parents are responsible for? Are you willing to forever banish him to the darkness of the closet? If so, expect him to come back and haunt you, when you least expect it. Are you ready to deal with that real possibility?"

Erika's body language expressed impatience with Lorraine's statements—even if in part they were her own words. "I really don't want to get into the issue of Michael. I'm not ready to deal with anything concerning him. I love him and miss him like crazy, but he's the one who should've weighed all the possibilities when he was making the choice to deceive me. Case closed, Lorraine. Dead issue!"

Lorraine threw up her hands. "Okay, girlfriend! Have it your way. I still contend that throwing Michael over for wanting to protect you is insanity. You need to check yourself." Erika tossed her a dagger-sharp look. "Okay, okay. I'm through with it. Tell me about this brother of yours. Is he handsome?"

Erika's eyes turned buttery soft. "Very much so! He's also a very successful attorney. Richard is tall and slender and has the hottest, spice-brown eyes you've ever seen. We're having dinner together tomorrow evening. We're going to go through his old photo albums. It should be fun. How are things with Joe?"

Lorraine's joyous expression quickly fell from her face. "It's over. He's seeing someone else. I'll get over it. In your words, case closed. Dead issue."

"I'm sorry, Lorraine. Perhaps it wasn't meant to be. Would

you like to meet my brother? He just ended a longtime relationship, as well. He'd really make a good friend."

Lorraine suddenly perked up. "Sure, why not? When?" she asked eagerly.

"You could have dinner with us tomorrow evening. Of course, I'd have to clear it with him first. Interested?"

Lorraine scowled. "That might not be too cool. You guys are just getting your family together. Maybe next time."

"You *are* family, Lorraine. Before you say no, let me see how he feels about it. Okay?"

Lorraine shrugged her shoulders. "Okay. I'm going on home now, but let me know something as soon as you find out. You know I have to have loads of time to make myself gorgeous!" Lorraine slid off the bed, hugging and kissing Erika before walking out of the room.

"You're always gorgeous, Lorraine," Erika yelled after her friend. Instead of a response she heard the front door click shut.

It was an interesting word Lorraine had used, Erika thought as she sat down on the bed. Gorgeous! How many times had Michael called her that? Too many times to count. In fact, it was the first name he'd ever called her. "Where's the fire, gorgeous?" he'd asked that day. *In your touch,* she'd responded inwardly.

Interestingly enough, those words still rang true. In her dreams Michael's touch was as fiery as it had been on that glorious day—so fiery she'd awaken soaked through and through with perspiration. Thinking about his touch always produced the same body temperature: hot, hot, hot. Shoving her torrid thoughts of Michael to the back of her mind, she lay back on the bed to allow herself the freedom to think everything through.

Seventeen

The morning ushered in a bright, sunshiny day to warm the city, but failed to hit one particular spot—the frozen one in Erika's heart. Though she'd been up and about for hours, she hadn't slept the entire night. The telephone company technician had come and gone, having installed the much needed phone. Using her newly acquired telephone, she dialed Richard's office number, liking the reach-out-and-touch-someone feeling.

The moment she learned who the caller was, Richard's receptionist, Mia, immediately connected the siblings.

"Hey, little sis," Richard greeted lovingly. "Please don't tell me you're calling to cancel our date. My heart couldn't take it."

"Not at all, big brother. I'm calling to ask if I can bring along my best friend. She's having man problems, and I thought it would be nice if you two could meet."

Richard chuckled. "You wouldn't by chance be trying to play matchmaker, would you? I'm not ready to get involved with anyone right now, but you have my permission to bring her along. By the way, does your best friend have a name?"

Erika grinned. "Lorraine Poole, M.D. A very outspoken, stunning redhead. She possesses the most beautiful, greenish-gray eyes, a fiery temper and a great sense of humor. She's always been a great friend to me."

"She sounds delightful! I'll be looking forward to meeting her. Do you drink wine? If so, what's your preference?"

"I drink it on occasion, but I have to get up early tomorrow. Lorraine likes sparkling wines, such as Spumante. She's on a shift break right now so she can have a sip or two."

"I'll see what I can hook up. See you this evening, baby sister. Bring that lovely smile of yours along. It'll brighten the atmosphere," he charmed.

"You bet! See you later, Richard Edmonds."

Smiling at her use of his legal name, savoring the last remark, he hung up the phone. Twirling around in his office chair, he stared out the large, plate-glass window overlooking the city and the junction of the three rivers. He couldn't help thinking about trying to bring Erika and Michael together. If he invited Michael to dinner, too, they'd be forced to face each other. But would Erika see that as just another deception leveled against her? Probably so.

This relationship with his sister was on new ground, fragile ground. The possibility of alienating her was a major concern. As much as he wanted her and Michael together, he also wanted her to learn to love and trust him. Forcing her to see Michael might do more harm than good, he decided. Not daring to give it any more thought, he buried himself in his work.

Michael had buried himself in his work, too. After performing an early-morning surgery and having seen more than twenty patients during office hours, he was ready for a break. After seeing the last patient of the day, he changed out of the lab coat and into his suit jacket. Saluting his office staff, Michael left the office.

Getting into the Pathfinder, he drove toward home, but the empty house was the last place he wanted to find himself alone. It hadn't been the same without Erika there to bring it to life. Her laughter echoed in every room and the bedroom was especially devoid of the sizzling excitement she'd brought to it whether they were making love or just nestled closely together.

Erika had become a large part of the character of the house.

In her absence the house was just an empty, lifeless shell, a constant reminder of what could've been, how it should've been filled with their love. Later, after they'd had time to really settle down together, the house should've been filled with the patter of the feet of tiny replicas of Erika and a miniature Michael or two.

Driving past the turnoff to his house, he drove on, only stopping when he reached his parents' home. Seeing lights on in the back of the house, he guessed that the occupants were watching television or just relaxing in each other's company, something they took great pleasure in doing.

Lawrence and Wilimina Mathis were extensions of each other. No one knew where one began and the other ended. It had always been that way, as far back as he could remember. They'd once told him that they were angels with only one wing each, and could only fly when they embraced. Long after fusing their wings in holy matrimony, the Mathises continued to embrace their theory; when one took flight, the other was always there to navigate.

Using the key he carried in his wallet, he let himself into the house, following the sounds of the music leading him to the back of the house. Michael found Lawrence and Wilimina curled up together on the sofa, looking as though they'd found the key to eternal happiness. "Hi," he said from the doorway. "Am I interrupting a Hallmark moment? You two look mighty cozy."

Lawrence and Wilimina looked up at the same time. "Michael," Wilimina enthused. "What a nice surprise! Please come and join us."

"Hello, son," Lawrence welcomed cheerfully. "Not that we're not ecstatic to see you, but what brings you out here this evening? And where's that lovely lady friend of yours?"

Michael's expression turned from joy to painful sorrow. "To put it mildly, I've been dumped. I'm afraid I didn't handle our relationship the way I should have."

Wilimina felt immediate sympathy for her eldest offspring.

"Come, Michael, have a seat. We'd like to hear what happened. That is, if you want to share with us."

Dropping down in the chair, Michael put his feet up on the hassock. While explaining everything from beginning to end, he looked as though he'd lost his only true love, his best friend. In his opinion, he had.

"Oh, what those poor children must be going through. I'm not going to stand in judgment of their parents' decision, because it's not for me to judge, but I am concerned for Richard and Erika. Their spirits must be absolutely broken. I know mine would be. Has Erika totally slammed the door on a future with you?"

"I see it in a totally different way," Lawrence said, before Michael could respond to his mother's question. "Even with both parents deceased, Erika and Richard can still be a family."

Michael rubbed his hands up and down his thighs. "I hadn't thought about it that way, but that doesn't help my situation. As for your question, Mother, pretty much so. I sensed that she'd left open a small window of opportunity for us, but I haven't heard a single word from her since she walked away from me. She has a right to be mad at me. I *am* guilty of deceiving her. I'm guilty of the one thing she may never be able to forgive—deception."

Lawrence scowled. "Deceive her? Or protect her the only way you knew how? Given enough time to come to grips with everything, I believe she's going to realize your honorable intentions, son." He put his hands together. "Just think about it. Erika has just learned her true identity. Now she has to accept it and become comfortable with it. If she truly loves you—I believe she does—she'll be back. Would you like something to eat or drink, son?" Lawrence asked, though he guessed food and drink were the last things on his son's mind.

Michael raised a flattened palm. "No, thanks, Dad. My appetite hasn't been the best lately. I keep worrying about how Erika is dealing with everything. She learns that the man she believed to be her stepfather is actually her biological father.

At the same time she learns she has a brother she'd never met. To top it off, she doesn't even like Richard. For some strange reason he rubbed her the wrong way from their very first encounter. It seems there are no victors in this unfortunate situation. But Erika is the only woman who dots all my *I's* and crosses all my *T's*."

Lawrence got up from the sofa and stationed himself at Michael's feet on the hassock. "No son of mine has ever given up on something he desperately wanted. Don't start now. Wage a fierce battle to win her back. Bombard her with every sweet weapon known to man. Use candy, flowers, balloons and any other romantic notion you can think of to cause her to rethink her decision. I've only been in her company briefly, but I get the feeling she's worth fighting for. Go for it, son. At this point, what have you got to lose? Nothing," Lawrence added before Michael could reply. "What do you have to gain? Everything you've ever dreamed of in a female companion, from what you've told us."

A quarter of an hour later, Michael left the country house, feeling a renewal of hope and excitement. Yet he still didn't want to go back to the loneliness he'd find at home. Driving around aimlessly for more than an hour, he ended up in front of Richard's house. Hoping he could talk to his friend about Erika, he parked on the street. There was a fancy sports car parked in front of his car.

After ringing the bell, he stuffed his hands in his pants pockets and waited. When the door finally opened, he could hear music and laughter coming from inside, but Richard's strange expression belied the joy coming from inside the house.

"Mikey, man, you're starting to pop up all over the place. What's on your mind, brother?" Michael started to enter, but Richard took a step forward, blocking his entry.

Michael looked puzzled. "Is this a bad time for you? Sorry, I guess I should've called first." Michael looked and sounded dejected and full of dark despair.

Richard now knew what it felt like to be torn between two

people he loved. Anthony must have had the same feeling. It was an ugly, painful one. "It's not that, Mikey. You're welcome here anytime, but tonight there's a little complication. I'm having dinner with my sister and her friend, Lorraine Poole."

Michael didn't try to hide his narcosis. "You and Erika have connected? And she's not angry with you?"

Richard shook his head. "We have. I guess I can say she's no longer angry with me, though she sure in hell was. She came to see me in my office yesterday. After a long conversation, we decided we wanted to try to have a relationship. Honest, I was going to tell you, man. I just didn't get to you before you got to me. I'm sorry I've made such a mess for you."

Amazed, Michael opened his eyes. "Well, it's probably the best thing that could've happened for both of you. You two need each other. I'll just move on, but I want you to call me later. I need to talk to you, need to know that Erika's okay." Michael turned to walk away.

Richard stilled him with a hand to his shoulder. "Come on in, man. I can't turn you away like this. If Erika gets upset, we'll decide what to do then. But right now I want you to come in and have some dinner. I made barbecued ribs."

Michael shook his head. "No, it would be a mistake. Erika would think you engineered this whole thing. I don't want that."

At that precise moment Lorraine stuck her head out the door, gasping when she saw Michael. "Now I see what's been keeping you, Richard. I thought you might be sick or something. Forgive my intrusion. Michael, it's so good to see you." She felt terribly uneasy as she went back inside and closed the door.

The two friends said their farewells and Michael started toward his car. He hadn't quite reached it when Lorraine resurfaced, calling out to him from the porch. "Please wait a minute, Michael." He walked back to meet her. Grasping his hand, she squeezed it gently. "Come inside. Erika knows I came back out here to ask you to join us. She didn't object. I swear to you."

Michael looked leery. "I don't know, Lorraine. I don't want Erika to get the wrong idea. I don't want her to feel betrayed again. There's been enough of that already. She's finally finding something good in these unfortunate circumstances. I don't want to spoil that for her, nor do I want her to believe this was some elaborate scheme Richard and I cooked up."

Lorraine's smile was sympathetic. "She knows this wasn't planned. Richard's talking to her now to make sure she understands. Come on in, Michael. You and Erika have a wonderful friendship, and there's no reason why you two can't be on good terms with each other."

Wanting so much to see Erika, her beautiful face, perhaps a smile or two—to feel her warmth even at a distance, Michael stroked his chin thoughtfully. "You might have something there, Lorraine. I'll come in for a few minutes. If I sense any amount of discomfort in Erika, I'm out of here. Agreed?"

Lorraine smiled tenderly. "Agreed."

Erika felt Michael even before he stepped into the room. Immediately, she folded her hands, hoping to stop them from trembling. Just seeing his handsome face again made her rejoice inside, but she tried desperately not to make an outward showing.

Although he wore just a simple, crisp white shirt open at the collar and black linen slacks, he looked great to her. Draped on his magnificent body, his clothes had a way of making a profound statement all on their own, Erika thought, feeling dizzy from the stress.

Taking a quick, admiring glance at the casual but sexy pantsuit Erika wore on her petite frame, Michael sat on the loveseat facing the sofa where she sat. "Hello, Erika. It's nice to see you again." Her wool-enriched, camel-and-brown plaid jacket and brown trousers were nice complements to her skin color, he thought, liking the way the jacket skimmed her sleek body, how her camel, ribbed-knit sweater hugged the upper portion of her torso. "You look really good, Erika. Are you doing okay?"

She smiled, answering at least one of his prayers. "Thank you, Michael. You look great yourself. And I'm doing just fine." *If you believe that lie I'll tell you another and another,* she thought, *anything to keep you from knowing how miserable I am without you.* "How about yourself?"

"Pretty good, Erika."

Damn you, Michael, she screamed inwardly, having hoped he was even more miserable than she was, and then some.

Seeing how tense Erika and Michael looked, Richard came forth to ease the tension of the moment, feeling responsible for the whole mess. He had to find a way to clear it up, he decided, placing an open palm on Michael's shoulder. "Okay, Michael, name your poison."

"Just a club soda with a twist of lime. I'm on call tonight."

"One club soda, coming right up."

"So, Michael," Lorraine said, "how's the pediatric field?"

Michael smiled warmly. "Kids are a treasure, a delight to be around. They never fail to say the unexpected. And they're painfully honest, and so trusting. I never know what's going to come out of their mouths next. They certainly keep me on my toes, especially the adolescents."

Erika smiled inwardly, recalling the things coming out of young Vincent's mouth the night of the ballet. She couldn't help wondering if Michael remembered, too.

This is no good, he thought, wishing his pager would go off, rescuing him from the unbearable situation. All he really wanted to do was to sweep Erika out into the night, to take her home with him, to never let her out of his sight again. What he didn't want to do was to sit and hold a polite conversation with the woman he loved with a maniacal passion. At the same instant he made a second quiet supplication, his pager went off.

Looking down at the pager positioned on his belt, he pressed the button lighting up the tiny viewing screen. He got to his feet at the same time Richard brought his drink. "I need to use your phone, man, to respond to the page I received from Lebanon Presbyterian."

Richard nodded. "Help yourself, man. You'll have more privacy if you use the one in the den."

Erika looked at Richard and Lorraine, who appeared to be holding their breath. "This is tougher than I imagined. The pressure of seeing Michael again is too much. Pray tell, how do I sit so close to the man I love deeply and deny myself the pleasure of touching him? One of you please tell me what to do. My desire for the feel of him against my body is burning white-hot."

Lorraine stood behind Erika, massaging her shoulders. "Take a deep breath. Everything's going to be just fine. You just need to listen to what your heart—" Lorraine cut her gentle advice short as Michael came back into the room.

Michael frowned heavily. "Sorry, but I've got to go. I'm going to have to pass on that drink, Rich. This emergency sounds as if it may end up in surgery."

Lorraine gasped. "A child?" Michael nodded.

Dumb question, Lorraine, Erika thought. *He's only the most revered pediatric surgeon in the state.*

Richard approached Michael, extending his hand. "I understand. Your drink will be here when you get back. I'd hoped we could get an interesting game of bid whist started. Maybe next time. You will try to come back, won't you?"

Michael laughed. "I don't think there's a remote possibility of that happening. I'm already tired after a full office schedule. But I promise to call if it's not too late. Thanks for inviting me in. Sorry I couldn't stay longer."

Erika felt relieved and saddened at the same time. She didn't want Michael to go, but under the circumstances she didn't think she could stand the pressure of having him so near. Having him so near yet emotionally so far away was a heavy burden for her heart. Out of sight, out of mind didn't necessarily work for her, either. In fact, the more he stayed out of sight, the more she thought of him. Still, she had so much to work out with herself. There were things she needed to have answered before she could even think of her future, let alone decide it.

"Good night, everyone. Have a good time." He looked over at Erika. "Good night, Erika. I'm glad you've met your brother, and that you two want to have a relationship. Good luck."

Erika silently begged her tears to stay away. "Good luck at the hospital, Michael." Richard stayed inside with Erika while Lorraine walked Michael out to his car.

Lorraine rested her hand on Michael's arm. "I might be out of line here, Michael, but you've got to put up a better fight. Erika misses you as much as you obviously miss her. She loves you. That hasn't changed one iota. Don't give up. Don't throw in the towel yet. Don't give her time to get used to being without you. I think you know what I'm trying to say here."

Lifting Lorraine's hand, he kissed the back of it. "Thanks, Lorraine. You're not the only person who's telling me not to give up. I have to go now, but I take your words of wisdom with me. Good night, Erika's best friend." Lorraine stood on the porch, watching as Michael drove away. Feeling sorry for her brokenhearted friends, she went back inside.

Lorraine found Erika and Richard involved in what appeared to be a serious discussion. Figuring the discussion had to do with Michael, she left them alone and began to clean off the table. While stacking the dishes, she found herself thinking of Richard in an intimate sort of way. He was handsome and sexy, and she couldn't stop herself from wondering what it would be like to have her arms and legs wrapped around his muscular body. She could only imagine it would be an awesome experience!

Richard walked into the kitchen. The corners of his mouth turned up, leaving an endearing smile on his face. "I see you've been really busy in here, Lorraine. I didn't expect that you'd clean the kitchen."

She laughed. "Why? Do you think cleaning is beneath me? I may have had a pampered upbringing, but I was still taught how to be responsible. I helped to create this mess we made."

"No, Lorraine, I didn't think that," he said softly, conjuring up an image of what it might be like to have her beneath him in bed; her red hair a tangled but lovely mess, her arms wrapped tightly around his neck. "Thank you for cleaning the kitchen—which is probably what I should've said from the start."

"You're welcome, Richard! Shall we go back to Erika?"

Smiling, he boldly reached out for her hand. "We shall. But let me warn you, Erika's in a bad mood. Don't take it personally."

"My dear man, Erika and I never take each other's raunchy moods personally. We're best friends, remember?" Richard and Lorraine returned to the dining room, where Erika moodily picked at a slice of cherry cheesecake.

She looked up as they entered the room. "Hey, you two. What were you guys doing in the kitchen so long? Whipping up a new recipe?" Erika taunted. "Or were you discussing Michael and me?"

"Neither," Richard responded. "Lorraine and I were just trying to find out a little more about each other. I hope you're not being paranoid, baby sister. Are you?"

Erika gave him a smug smile. "No, I'm not. I'm just a little tired. I wish I had driven my car, as well. Then you and Lorraine could spend as much time together as you wanted. Seeing Michael here has me questioning my sanity. I should've at least walked him out to his car." She moaned. "He probably thinks I'm an ungrateful witch."

"A witch, yes—because you've bewitched him—but I don't think he believes you're the least bit ungrateful. He understands your pain, Erika." He cleared his throat. "Are you really ready to go home?" he asked, hoping she'd stay a while longer.

"I'm afraid so, but I don't want to spoil the evening for

you two. You both seem to be having such a good time. Would it be okay if I lie down somewhere? I could use a short nap."

"Erika, I'll take you home," Lorraine interjected. "Richard and I will see each other again. Won't we?" she asked, turning to face him.

Mesmerized by the sound of her sweet voice, he nodded. "I think that's a safe bet, Dr. Poole. But I have another suggestion. If I may?" Lorraine gestured for him to continue. "I can follow you two in my car. Then, if you'll agree, Lorraine, we can go have coffee somewhere close to the university."

Erika's smile encouraged Lorraine to take the offer. She'd like nothing better than to have Richard and Lorraine get together. She felt the chemistry between them—and was sure they felt it, too. With Lorraine's eager nod of approval, everyone got busy putting Richard's fabulous house back together.

Richard escorted his guests to their fancy transportation before getting into his own. Once he backed his champagne-colored Mercedes-Benz out of the garage, Lorraine steered her sports car away from the curb, heading toward the city.

Lying in the darkness of her bedroom, Erika could see prisms of moonlight coming in through the window as she thought about her brother. The evening with Richard had been good, special, rewarding. In such a short time they'd come to grips with so many things. While their relationship was taking off—to go as far as it would lead them—her relationship with Michael had crash-landed in midflight.

In her discussions with Richard it had dawned on her that she, too, had been partly living in a state of denial, if not total denial. She had ignored or refused to deal with a lot of issues since she was old enough to learn how to hide her pain behind a facade of forced smiles and nervous laughs.

Why did people measure love by what they did or didn't get from someone else or by what someone had or hadn't done for them, especially from a parent to a child and vice versa?

Love between a parent and child should be as natural as sunlight, she thought wistfully. Neither party should ever wonder if they're loved. Nor should there ever be any forced acceptances between them.

Love was a mystery forever being told, rarely ever solved. Where a parent and child were concerned, no mystery should exist. But in her world it had existed, remained something of a mystery—a mystery she was determined to solve.

She'd been loved by both parents, but had it come naturally? What should've been the purest of all loves had been tangled up and covered up in a web of ugly lies and deceit. Now those same lies had made themselves known, causing those most harmed by them to stand up and pay attention.

If she were blessed with children, they'd never have to wonder if they were loved. Her love for them would be apparent in every breath she took, in every kiss she planted, in every little tender spot she showered with affection. She would administer painstaking care to the souls of her children. As their gardener, she would give each of them their fair share of moisture, of warmth and of light. She'd read somewhere that the soul of a child is the loveliest and most precious flower in the Garden of God.

As she entertained memories of Michael, it became abundantly clear that his love for her was as natural as the sunlight, had been transparent in every breath he took. He had showered her with more than her fair share of moisture, warmth and light. Michael had been protecting the garden of her soul. Restless, knowing she wasn't going to sleep, Erika slid out of bed and went into the living room, where she retrieved her art supplies from behind the sofa.

Looking at the sketch she'd created while waiting for Michael that first night in the cafeteria, she saw it was unfinished, as unfinished as her relationship with Michael, as unfinished as her life was without him. Erika began working on the sketch. When it was finished, the two lovers would be surrounded with tiny replicas of themselves. *A family,* she thought joyfully. A family she would love and cherish; even beyond her death.

Why hadn't she gone out to Michael when she'd learned that he was at Richard's door? Why hadn't she listened to all the people who'd said she was making the biggest mistake of her life? Anger, she told herself. She'd let anger eat her up from the inside out. If she kept it up, she would possibly devour any chance for true happiness. Anger was destructive, and it took too darn much energy. She'd just have to figure out all these things for herself. Erika would readily listen to advice, but the ultimate decision had to be her own.

Through learning of her parents' somewhat checkered past, she'd been forced into accepting things because she was unable to confront either of them. Had it been possible, she would've confronted them, telling them exactly how she felt about everything.

Instead, she'd taken it out on Michael, whom she had made a victim of *her* circumstances. Instead of two innocent victims there were now three. If she had her way, they'd no longer be victims of someone else's past mistakes. The three of them would somehow get beyond all this, she prayed, far beyond the desperate deceptions.

Standing at the window that overlooked the duck pond, she watched as the dawn stole across the sky. While sipping on tea, she wondered what Michael was doing at that very moment. Was he still asleep? Or was he up and about? It was still too early for him to be making hospital rounds, but he liked to get up early and take a brisk run through the forest. Afterward, he liked to indulge himself in a long, hot shower—more so, when she was there to join him. Just the thought of showering with Michael brought a generous smile to her lips and delicious warmth to her feminine treasures.

Oh, Michael, my love, will we ever be together again? Will we ever be as one?

Eighteen

Erika showered before dressing in brown wool stretch pants and an ivory-beige, bulky-knit sweater. The outdoor temperature was still quite chilly, but spring was quickly shoving its way in. She couldn't wait for the warm weather to make an appearance. In just a few days spring would be officially announced.

Grabbing a jacket from the hall closet, she picked up her purse and left the apartment, hoping Aunt Arlene would already be up and about. Maybe they could have breakfast together. For sure, they were going to have a heart-to-heart discussion about Michael.

Grabbing a hot drink from the hospital cafeteria to nurse on the way out to the countryside, Erika saw very few people about. It was still very early, and the shift change hadn't yet occurred, she realized, looking at the wall clock. As Erika headed for the cashier, she ran into Dr. Jules Baker, smartly attired in a dark blue leisure suit and a pale pink silk shirt. Erika had become very fond of Dr. Baker, whom she truly thought of as her mentor.

Dr. Baker smiled brightly as they stood before each other. "Good morning, Dr. Edmonds." He beamed. "Are you here for breakfast, too?"

Erika laced her fingers with his long, slender ones, letting go after his heat warmed her heart. "No, I'm not. I'm just going to grab something hot to drink. I'm on my way to see my aunt. How are you doing on this fine morning?"

Dr. Baker sighed, a slight mist glazing his eyes. "I'm good, Erika. But I'm as tired as I've ever been in my life. Just when I think I'm used to this hectic pace I find I'm not. I'm afraid my beautiful Jada is being severely neglected by me. Though she understands my professional obligations, I don't like us being away from each other so much." He appeared thoroughly distressed over his busy schedule. "Do you have a couple of minutes to sit and chat?"

"For you, yes," Erika responded, sensing his need to vent. Taking hold of Erika's hand, Dr. Baker led her over to one of the cafeteria tables, where they sat down. Helping Erika out of her jacket, he hung it around the back of her chair.

He grinned. "I was really glad when you told me you weren't going to pull out of the residency program," he began. "I take it things are better for you financially."

Pursing her lips, she pressed them together. "They will be, very soon. I'm still waiting for that insurance check to clear the bank. For now I'm still pinching my few pennies. As you know, I also have a very generous brother to rely on."

Dr. Baker winked. "It'll all work out, Erika. How was your first date with your brother?"

Erika's eyes brightened. "It went very well, thank you. I learned a lot of things about our dad that I didn't know. My brother's a very intelligent man. Charming, too. He reminds me so much of our father. I believe Richard and I are going to have a very meaningful relationship. We've warmed to each other quite a bit in such a short time, but I guess that's only natural. After all, we are siblings."

Happy for her, Dr. Baker smiled. "Well, considering what you've already told me about him, I kind of thought you and your brother would get along famously. Have you made any decisions about a future with Michael? Tongues of those who've guessed you two were romantically involved are wagging out of control now that you aren't seen together."

For a brief moment Erika looked wounded. "Nothing final. But I do know that I love him very much," she cried, folding her hands in her lap. "I also know Michael thought he was protecting me from getting hurt. With Richard as his closest friend, he probably felt he had to protect him, too. So he did what any real friend would do under the circumstances," she explained with a shrug. "I still have to put a few things together. Then I'll try to see if he and I can at least talk. Michael has been a good friend to me, as well. I owe him a lot."

Dr. Baker frowned. "Knowing Michael as a colleague and as a friend, Erika, I don't think he's looking for gratitude from you. He's one of the most unselfish doctors I know. He never makes anyone feel beholden to him. It's my guess Dr. Mathis is only interested in your love."

Erika nearly broke down and cried when she saw how tenderly he looked at her. Not only was it touching, it was so nice to know he cared about her future. He obviously cared about Michael, too. Dr. Baker was hardly old enough to be her father, but she imagined Anthony would've given her a lot of the same advice he constantly gave her. An angelic smile stole across her face, settling in her eyes as she thanked him for his generosity.

Arlene was sitting at the table when Erika sauntered into her spotless kitchen. The smell of freshly perked coffee filled the air as the oven emitted its own delicious smells into the room. Heavenly croissants, Erika guessed easily, inhaling the bakery fresh aroma. Bending over to kiss Arlene's cheek, she noticed the faraway look in her aunt's eyes, which gave her cause for concern. Erika trembled, silently hoping Arlene just suffered from nothing more than a case of delayed grief about her beloved sister. Arlene didn't even look up when Erika sat down in the chair facing her. Was this going to be one of those difficult days? Arlene could be unreasonably moody when she wasn't feeling well, or when something troubled her.

Erika covered her aunt's hand with hers. "How are you feeling today, Aunt Arlene?" Erika asked anxiously.

Arlene shrugged her shoulders. "Nothing to brag on," Arlene mumbled, causing Erika to frown. "No use in complaining, anyway. There's not much that can be done about it."

It was one of those days, Erika decided sadly. "Want to talk about it? I care about how you're feeling," Erika placated, aware it probably wouldn't do any good.

Intent on watching her aunt's every reaction, Erika saw that Arlene had barely eaten the food in front of her. Her aunt was not herself at all today, and she was in one of those moods Erika had never been able to get used to. Vernice used to get like this from time to time, too, she recalled. *No one ever said life was easy,* Erika thought.

Arlene surprised Erika when she suddenly suggested they take a walk.

After removing the croissants from the oven, Erika put her jacket around Arlene's shoulders. Taking her by the hand, she led her out the back door. As they stepped outside, the wind was a little brisk, making Erika glad she'd put on a heavy sweater, since Arlene wore the jacket. She could've retrieved Arlene's own jacket, but hadn't wanted to leave her aunt's side. Their time together always seemed short and precious. Erika's work schedule was nearly as busy as the one Dr. Baker had complained about earlier.

Quietly, they walked around the spacious grounds. Green shoots sprouted everywhere, announcing that spring was definitely just around the corner. Erika watched her aunt closely as Arlene surveyed budding trees and the blue sky above. Erika would've given anything to know exactly what her aunt was thinking, but nothing in Arlene's expression gave her thoughts away.

On their way back from circling the property, Arlene sat down on a wooden bench, patting the seat next to her. At her command Erika dropped down beside her. Still, Arlene said nothing, though Erika sensed that she was somehow at peace in her lovely flower garden.

Vernice felt at peace here, too, Erika recalled. Only the good Lord knew how much Vernice had needed to feel serenity. As Erika was now aware, Vernice's life had been tumultuous, and she was grateful for any portion of peace her mother had found. Only when Vernice was at peace had Erika herself felt free enough to try to attain her own.

Arlene turned to face Erika, giving her niece a warm hug. She held her aunt's hand. "Are you really happy living out here all alone, Aunt Arlene?"

"It's not like it was when your mother was alive, but still I love it here. My sister was very good to me and she loved hanging out here with me. I miss her very much. We got along so well. I guess it's because we had so darn much in common," Arlene said, smiling slightly. "Speaking of having things in common," Arlene added, "are you still keeping that good-looking young man of yours at bay? Please tell me you two are back together."

Erika laughed. "What would you think if I said I'd like to marry him?"

A thin smile crept onto Arlene's lips. "I'd say you were a smart girl. You now know that your mother picked him out for you. But if you keep letting him run around loose, all those women out there, young and old, are going to try to steal him away."

Erika looked through her purse and came up with the tiny, velvet jewelry box. Opening it, she showed its brilliant contents to Arlene. "The good-looking doctor gave this to me the same night he asked me to marry him. What do you think of it?"

Arlene lifted the diamond ring out of the box. "It's beautiful! One question—why aren't you wearing it?"

Erika wanted to delve into her reasons, but she contained herself. "That's a good question, Auntie, one that I haven't been able to answer. Are you saying you'd approve of Michael as a nephew-in-law?"

Arlene frowned. "Approve of him? What's there not to approve? He's handsome, intelligent, sensitive, and it's my guess he's crazy in love with you. Haven't you been listening to me, girl? Just like your mother did, I knew he was the one for you the first time I saw him. I vividly remember my reaction to him the first day you brought him out here. It was a warm reaction, a good reaction."

Happiness flooded Erika's heart. "So, does that mean you'll come to my wedding?" Erika asked tearfully.

Tears leaped into Arlene's eyes. "Not only will I come to your wedding, I'm going to dance in celebration. Have you set a date yet?" Arlene could barely contain her joy.

Erika couldn't believe how well this conversation was going. She'd thought earlier that Arlene wasn't even close to being on track this day, but her aunt had proved her wrong. In this case, she didn't mind being wrong. "No, I haven't set a date. In fact, I haven't even accepted Michael's proposal yet." Her sigh was filled with discontent.

Arlene looked puzzled. "And why not? What are you waiting for?"

Erika shrugged. "I had some personal things to work out. I've had a lot on my mind, and I just couldn't give him an answer until I had everything straightened out."

Arlene shook her head. "You young people! In the sweet days of my youth a woman would've jumped at the chance to marry such a fine, handsome young man—a doctor, no less. Have you now decided to accept his proposal?"

A single tear spilled from Erika's eye. "Yes! That is, if I'm not too late. I haven't been very fair to him. Maybe he's changed his mind by now. I just don't know how he's going to react to me. I've treated him badly. I know I had to be out of my mind. Maybe he's moved on."

"Bullcraps! If he asked you to marry him, I can bet you he's still waiting for the answer. If I were you, I wouldn't keep him waiting much longer, Erika Edmonds."

Hearing the sweet sound of the surname, the name that was

truly hers, Erika almost fell off the bench. Filled with joy and excitement, she folded Arlene into her arms, kissing her gently on the mouth. "You always come through for me, don't you? Just when I think things aren't going to get any better, you reach down into that bag of miracles and sprinkle me with your magic dust. Besides age, what has made you so wise?"

A glint of deep sadness touched Arlene's eyes. "Pain, Erika. Hard, cruel pain. There have been a lot of mistakes made by this family over the years, which seem to be the causes of the pain to begin with. Happiness can't be bought or sold, Erika. Love is not a bargaining chip. Don't make the same mistakes some of us old folks have made."

Erika took a deep breath. This was an opportunity she couldn't let pass by, though she'd have to practice extreme caution in her line of questioning. "What mistakes are you talking about, Auntie? I always thought you were perfect," she teased.

Arlene sighed heavily, another sad expression invading her eyes. "It's a long story, but I'm sure I can cut down on some of the details. I need you to listen before you jump to any conclusions. Do I have your word?"

Her eyes filled with utter amazement, Erika nodded.

Arlene wrung her hands together. "Sometimes things aren't always what they seem to be, niece. Your mother carried around a tremendous burden, and I don't want that to affect your happiness. I can't allow that to happen. Infidelity is not an easy thing to live with, especially in the days of our youth. I can't let you enter into a marriage believing in fairy tales. Marriage can be difficult at best."

Arlene then launched into the story of her own difficult marriage and Vernice's troubled first marriage, which had ended with the infidelity with Anthony as the last straw. Even though Erika had already heard most of the story from Arlene, she listened intently, the negative aspects of Vernice's life hurting her greatly, as Arlene spelled them out in plain, sensible terms.

"So you see, Erika, marriage doesn't always work out the way we want it to," Arlene concluded. "I can only say that I'm sorry you weren't told all this when you were first old enough to understand it. It was a grave mistake on all of our parts. You deserved to know."

Erika hugged her aunt. "It's okay. I know now. Richard and I aren't holding any grudges. We both understand why they felt they had to do what they did. Desperation is the only answer."

Arlene looked up with a start. *"We?* Am I right in assuming you've met your brother, Erika? You've made contact with him other than by phone, haven't you?"

Erika suddenly looked frightened. She didn't want her aunt to think she had insulted her mother's memory by seeing Richard, but it was too late to take her words back. "Yes, I have met him. I hope you're not going to try and stop me from seeing him, out of loyalty to Mother. I won't be able to do that. We've accepted each other as family."

Arlene looked pained. "I would never do that, Erika. When you asked me what you should do, I could only tell you what I would do. It wouldn't have been fair to say anything else. To meet your brother, or not to, had to be your decision. I'm happy you have him in your life. You two are going to need each other. I'm sorry you were kept apart for so long. I just hope that in time you both will be able to forgive all of us who played a part in that unfair decision. Now, if you don't mind, I'd like to go inside and lie down. I have to rest up so I can be ready to dance your wedding night away with that handsome groom of yours!"

Erika wanted to ask her aunt what became of her mother's divorce papers, but she quickly decided that some things were best left alone. Arlene had already revealed more than enough.

She stood up and held out her hand. "Come on, Auntie. I'll get you settled in. But first I need a big hug," she said, pulling Arlene close to her, telling her she'd already forgiven her parents. As for her aunt, there was nothing to forgive. Aunt and niece hugged as tears of joy fell from their eyes. Erika walked Arlene inside. After she settled her back in her room and in bed, she left.

Erika's heart danced inside her chest all the way to the dorm. Before going to her apartment she looked all around for Dr. Baker, but was told he'd already left the building. Erika wanted him to be the second person to know of her decision to accept Michael's proposal. However, the most difficult part was yet to come.

Informing Michael of her long-overdue decision wasn't going to be a walk in the park. Would he still want her? she wondered, fresh tears sliding from her eyes. Would he be as forgiving of her as she'd been of her parents? Somehow she doubted it. How could she expect him to forgive her when she'd been so unforgiving toward him? She'd hurt him terribly, something she couldn't deny or ignore. Wasn't turnabout fair play?

Erika still believed in miracles. Anything short of a miracle might not be enough to undo all the damage she'd done to her relationship with Michael, all of which she was totally responsible for—regrettably so.

Listening to the song "Body and Soul" when a totally unfamiliar knock came on the door, Erika looked down at the faded black sweats she'd put on to relax in. Frowning at her attire, she hoped it was just Lorraine or one of the other dorm residents on the other side of the door. Erika gasped when she saw Lorraine and Richard, looking as happy and content as two bugs in a rug.

Erika hugged Lorraine before she hugged Richard. "Come on in, guys. This is a pleasant surprise. What brings you two out in this stormy, rainy weather?"

Erika's guests followed her into the tiny living room. Richard and Lorraine sat on the sofa. Richard stretched his arm along the back of the sofa. Erika sat in the chair, curling her legs up under her. She had seen Richard's eyes go straight to Vernice's portrait before he'd seated himself. She hadn't been able to read the expression, but some unrecognizable emotion had briefly flashed in his eyes.

Richard smiled at Erika. "Sorry we came without calling first. Speaking of us coming out in this nasty weather, Lorraine and I were going to take a drive out to the country. This unexpected rainstorm came out of nowhere, just as I turned onto University Drive. So we ate lunch in the cafeteria instead of risking Lorraine's beautiful neck out on the slippery roads. After eating, I suggested we pay you a surprise visit."

Erika looked down at her dowdy clothes again. "I would've dressed for the occasion had I known. As you can see, I wasn't expecting visitors, but I'm glad you came. I was feeling a little lonely. Can I get you two something to drink?"

Richard put his hand across his stomach. "I'm full. If Lorraine's not, she should be. Why didn't you tell your big brother this redheaded woman friend of yours has an appetite like a horse? I'm not sure I can afford to feed her on a regular basis."

As she watched the innocent verbal foreplay between Richard and her best friend, amusement glittered in her brown eyes. When Lorraine picked up a pillow and swatted him with it playfully, Erika saw all the signs of a budding romance under development. She couldn't help remembering how her romance with Michael began. A storm had hit that day, as well. Then love's storm had come—just as unexpectedly as the rainstorm Richard had mentioned.

Lorraine sucked her teeth indignantly. "Have you forgotten that I'm a doctor, the sole heiress to the Poole fortune, Attorney Glover? I don't need anybody to be able to afford to feed me. I can feed myself."

Erika felt a bit of tension tightening in her chest at Lorraine's bodacious comments. When Richard laughed and hit Lorraine back with the pillow, she relaxed, happy to know he hadn't taken Lorraine's comments personally. It also told her that Richard wasn't the least bit intimidated by Lorraine's profession, or her wealth.

"In that case, you can buy dinner tonight. And you can pay for the movie afterward," Richard teased. "I don't have a problem with equal-opportunity dating."

Erika raised an eyebrow. "So you two are dating?" Erika interjected, smiling.

Richard looked Lorraine dead in the eye, his expression serious. "Are we?"

Lorraine's mouth fell open. For several seconds she sat in stony silence. "I . . . don't . . . know," she stammered. "Well, let's see. We've been out for coffee three times since the first night we met. We've had lunch twice, including today, and we're having dinner and seeing a movie tonight. So can you tell me if we're dating or not?" she inquired, smashing the ball back into his court with a strong forehand.

Erika couldn't hide her amusement over what was transpiring between her two visitors. Amused, she sat back in her chair to await Richard's response, guessing it would be a good one. Both Richard and Lorraine had great senses of humor.

Richard hugged Lorraine to him. "Dating? First let's define that term. Since it might mean something different to you, I'm going to share with you beautiful ladies what I think it means." He rubbed his hands together. "Dating—wooing, courtship, lovemaking, being sweethearts, going steady, just to cover a few."

Smiling triumphantly, he took Lorraine's hand. "Now, considering all of those things I just mentioned, I'm going to give you the opportunity to tell me if you think what we're doing can be defined as dating. The ball is back in your court, Miss Lady."

Lorraine laughed out loud. "What is this, Richard Glover, a tennis match without a line judge? You serve and I hit the ball back, so on and so forth? I don't think so. Maybe what we're doing defies definition. But if it's going to be defined, you're the one who'll define it. The next time you call me and ask me out, you're going to have to tell me if it's a date or not. Otherwise, I'm not going to be able to honor your request. You did start this, you know."

Richard pointed a finger at Erika. "No, she started it. Erika's the one who asked the question to begin with. Erika Edmonds specifically asked if we were dating."

Laughing, Erika threw up her hands. "Okay, enough already. I'm sorry I asked. It's none of my business, anyway. But, Richard, you used the term when you talked about equal opportunity. At any rate, let me settle this. You two are simply building a friendship. Sometimes friends share coffee, lunches, dinners, and movies. So we'll define the things I just mentioned as outings. You and Richard are simply outing! Fair assessment?"

Lorraine smiled. "I'll agree to anything to get this topic of conversation over and done with. Richard, darling, you and I are outing each other. Okay?"

He grinned. "Okay. Outing!" He turned his attention to Erika. "Thank you. You've settled the little dispute between *your* best friend and me—diplomatically, I might add. Now I have to ask if you've tried to settle the dispute between you and *my* best friend?"

Erika looked disheartened. "Something tells me I've been set up by you two. Am I right? You guys came here with the specific intent of rattling my cage."

Richard shook his head in the negative. "Not at all, baby sister. I'm just curious. I haven't talked to Mikey since the night we all had dinner at my place. He never called me back that night. I've left several messages for him, to no avail. He hasn't returned any of my calls. I was hoping he was too busy getting back together with you to worry about calling me."

Erika's complexion paled. "You don't think something has happened to him, do you? Oh, God, I couldn't bear it if something bad happened to him. Maybe he's sick, and out in that huge house all alone, surrounded by nothing but forest. His closest neighbor is three to five miles away, Richard," she wailed. "It could take a long while before someone might discover something was amiss way out there."

Richard got up from his seat. Walking the few steps across the room, he knelt down in front of Erika, gathering her in his arms. "Calm down, baby girl. It's not that serious. I didn't mean to upset you like this. Michael's probably just off somewhere brooding over this whole mess. You're trembling, baby. Come on now, calm down."

Lorraine came over and sat on the arm of Erika's chair. "It's okay, sweetie," she whispered, stroking Erika's hair. "If it'll make you feel any better, Richard and I will drive out to Michael's house to make sure everything's okay with him."

"Would you like us to do that, baby?" Richard asked, brushing away Erika's tears.

Erika took a moment to pull herself together. "It's raining too hard now. Maybe you should just try to call him again. If you don't hear from him by tonight, I'll be the one to go there. It's time for Michael and me to at least talk about our problems."

Erika decided it was best not to say anything to anyone else about her wanting to marry Michael. She already regretted what she'd said to her aunt. It was wrong to talk about her decision to accept Michael's proposal of marriage without knowing if it still stood. Michael might have had a change of heart by now. Though it would kill her, she wouldn't blame him. After all, she had walked away from their relationship.

Richard hugged his sister. "I think that's a good start. Nothing will ever get solved when the lines of communication are completely shut down. You and Michael have a lot going for you. Don't let the chance of a lifetime slip through your fingers if all that's keeping you away is a bruised ego."

Lorraine tugged at Richard's sweater. "Enough said, already, Richard. Erika has to take this at her own pace. It does no good to rush headlong into anything. She'll know when she's ready. She's a big girl."

Richard embraced both women. "You're right. Now let's

play a game of Scrabble, or get some other type of intellectual stimulation. Until this weather calms down, I'm staying right here. Before we get started, I'm going to use this brand-new telephone to check on our mutual friend."

Erika laughed. "Help yourself. I'll get the Scrabble board. If you're as bad at spelling as your best friend, Lorraine and I are going to blow you away, my dear, sweet brother."

Nineteen

Spring was now in full bloom. The rains had come and gone, and the days were now warm and sunny, the colors of spring vivid and lively. Yet Michael's heart was still surrounded with the bitter cold of winter. Nothing could warm him and the vivid colors of spring did nothing to brighten his days or his somber moods.

Erika Edmonds had become his spring, all year long. Only she'd left him before their love was given every chance to blossom and mature into an eternity of spring days, warm summer nights, breezy fall evenings, and toasty warm winters—winters that would find them wrapped in each other's arms, in front of the fireplace.

For the last few weeks Michael had spent his days and his evenings listening to all the songs they'd danced to and made sizzling love by. "Body and Soul" was the musical selection he found himself playing most often. Having committed the words to memory, he'd even locked the song into the memory of the CD player.

Seated on the sofa in the room that Erika had dubbed "the greenhouse," he laughed bitterly, recalling how he'd coded the song into the CD's memory as number thirteen, an unlucky number. Perhaps he should've coded it into the system as the number seven or eleven, he thought unhappily, hating the fact that Erika wasn't there with him to solve the dilemma.

But this wasn't a crap game. A few lucky rolls of the dice

weren't going to bring Erika back to him. Just for luck, he recoded the song as number seven; just for kicks, he coded it as number eleven, too.

As he moved back to the sofa, the doorbell rang. Not expecting anyone, he had no desire to answer it, had no desire to see anyone, had no intention of answering the door, period.

It was probably someone peddling something despite the "No Soliciting" sign posted on the front door. There wasn't anything he wanted that could be provided by a salesperson. What he wanted couldn't be peddled, nor could it be purchased with any amount of money.

When the bell pealed again, he used the remote control to turn up the volume on the stereo, hoping to drown out the ringing sound. The walls were soundproof, so no one could hear the music and guess that he was at home. When the bell continued to peal annoyingly, he saw that his efforts had been of no consequence. While covering his ears, he let go with a loud expletive. Whoever it was, was certainly persistent. He jumped up from the sofa.

Feeling extremely irritated, he made his way to the door. Ready to vent his anger on the intruder, he swung the door open wide. His breath caught at the sight of her. *Gorgeous!* It was the first word that had come to his mind the day they crashed into each other.

Standing before him, dressed in a rose-pink linen dress and jacket, were all his dreams, all his hopes. All of them were bound up in the tiny woman who owned all of his love, all of his heart, all of his soul. Her eyes glistened like morning's first dew. Her hair appeared to be slightly longer as its full body swept her shoulders like a silken wrap. The wine-colored lips still pouted with passion, shimmering from the glossy lip color she wore.

As their eyes locked in a bewildered embrace, Erika indulged herself in a few delicious thoughts of her own. Unable to tear her eyes away, she found herself still so amazed by the more than six-foot hunk of pliant steel packaged in exquisite

Indian-brown flesh, which appeared to have darkened just a tad more.

Perhaps he'd been soaking up the early spring rays, she thought. His hazel eyes appeared tired, but could still effect the piercing gaze tunneling right into the very heart of her soul. The brick-house physique looked slightly thinner, yet she felt sure it was still more than capable of bringing her the same staggering pleasure it had brought her so many times before.

Bringing her hand from behind her back, she handed him a single red rose. "This is for you, Michael. I hope you like it."

Keeping her entranced with his eyes, he lifted the rose to his nose and inhaled deeply. It was then that he noticed she had worn her engagement ring. His breath caught again, yet he remained silent. He was too stunned to speak.

Erika touched his hand gently. "Are you going to invite me in?" she asked timidly, praying he wouldn't slam the door in her face, even if she did deserve it.

Michael made a sweeping gesture to approve her entry, closing the door once she was inside the foyer. "Seven come eleven," he muttered under his breath.

Looking unsure of herself Erika turned to him. "Excuse me?"

He gave her a slight smile. "I was just thinking aloud. Nothing important," he added, knowing it was so very important. He lifted the rose to his nose again. "Thank you. It's very beautiful. Would you like to sit out on the patio? It's a lovely day outside." *And I've been inside mourning the absence of the spring in my life for far too long.*

Erika smiled softly instead of reaching to kiss the mouth that made her insides feel like Jell-O shaking about in her stomach. "I would really like that, Michael," she said, hating the formality of their conversation. After all, they weren't strangers.

Without further comment, Michael led the way to the patio. He pushed back the sliding glass doors and allowed Erika to precede him. Once outside, he raised the flowered umbrella centered in the glass table and pulled out two chairs.

Michael waited until she was seated before he sat down. "It's good to see you, Erika. You look beautiful. What brings you out this way?"

He sounded so casual. But there was nothing casual about the way his heart ran a marathon inside his chest.

"Oh, I just happened to be in the neighborhood," she responded, using the same casual tone. Then her expression grew serious. "I came here hoping to right a wrong, which is something I finally realized you were trying to do the last night we shared together. I can only hope you'll be more gracious than I was. I was wrong, Michael. I love you. I never stopped. And I'm so sorry. Can you forgive me? Do you still love me? Do you still want to marry me?" she fired off breathlessly, not missing a beat.

Astounded by her veracity, Michael gazed at her through slightly hooded eyes. How long had he waited for her to come to him? How long had he hoped and prayed she'd say the very words she'd just spoken? It seemed like forever. His ego was telling him to reject her, make it hard for her, to not give in to her so easily. But his heart was busy warring with his ego, an ego he rarely allowed to surface. He had no idea which one was going to win, but he rooted for his heart.

There should be no ego involved in true love, Michael argued with his inner self. How could he reject the only woman he'd ever really loved? Hadn't those professing to love her rejected her enough? She hadn't deserved any of the pain that had been heaped on her slender shoulders. How could he even think of sending any more pain her way?

Momentarily, Michael looked down at her left hand, stunned to see that she'd removed her engagement ring. Or had he really seen it on her finger to begin with? Had it just been wishful thinking on his part?

"Erika, there are so many things we need to discuss before

I can answer the majority of your questions. But I can tell you this—I can't forgive you."

Erika was taken aback. Of all the things she'd asked of him she'd been sure he would at least forgive her. Michael saw the light go out of her eyes. The sadness in them floored him.

"There's nothing to forgive. I've not held anything against you. Believe it or not, I understood your pain. I understand because I felt it, Erika." Michael reached across the table and took her hand. "I didn't come to you because I knew you needed time. You've taken time and now you've come back. I know what this must be costing you, but I'm afraid I'm going to need to ask you for a little time."

What the hell was he saying? No amount of time would tell him any more than he already knew. He knew that all her questions could be resolved with one three-letter word—yes!

Before he allowed himself to give further voice to his thoughts, he stood up and swept her into his arms, crushing her petite body against his own. His lips pressed into her temple, moved down to her cheek, urgently claimed her pouting lips.

Winding her arms around his neck, she gave herself up to the insanity his passion stirred within her, gave herself up to the need burning deep within. Relieved to be back in his arms, she prayed that this moment would finally mean eternity for them.

Michael wanted to make her his, right then and there, but he'd been waiting to bring an unfulfilled promise to fruition. Releasing her for a moment, he held her away from him. Unable to stand her being that far away from him for another second, he brought her back into his arms, tilting her face upward until their eyes connected. "Are you in my life to stay, Erika? Forever?"

"Yes, Michael," she breathed, "yes. For as long as you want me."

Hungrily, he covered her mouth again, which helped him

regain his strength. Without uttering another word, he directed her out to the garage, where they got into the Pathfinder.

Driving like a maniac through the rural district, Michael didn't slow down until he reached his destination thirty minutes later—the barn on his parents' property.

Michael jumped out of the vehicle. Running around to the passenger side, he opened the door for Erika, who appeared to be in a trance. It was as if she'd just discovered the beauty of the countryside for the first time.

In slow motion, Erika moved out of the seat and into Michael's arms. "Oh, I get goosebumps just looking at all this splendor. Both times I visited here were at night, so I didn't receive the full benefits of this magnificent farm. I'm absolutely mesmerized."

Taking her by the hand, he led her around the property. Erika gushed and gasped during the entire minitour. Then Michael opened the door of the red barn and steered her inside. Sunlight filtered into the barn from the tiny windows above the hayloft.

As she looked around the massive barn, Erika slowly inhaled the scents of freshly pitched hay and Scotch pine. Unable to detect any animal smells in the area, she assumed no farm animals were kept in this particular barn, though she knew that they had a team of horses—the same team that had taken her on her very first winter sleigh ride.

A small bird swooped down from somewhere near the hayloft. Smiling gently, Erika watched as it flew out the entrance. When Michael closed the door, they found themselves submerged in darkness, with only the light from tiny windows to guide their path.

Following Michael's instructions, Erika climbed up into the hayloft. He came up right behind her, ready to break another of her falls if necessary. Once they reached the top, Michael used a pitchfork to make them a large, loose pallet of hay.

Dropping down on the pallet, he lowered Erika down beside him. "Do you remember us making a date to make love in the hayloft?" Blushing like a newlywed, she smiled and nodded.

Lying back in the hay, Michael drew her down against his body, positioning her head on his chest. For several minutes they lay there quietly, drinking in the serenity encircling them. As Michael slipped the linen jacket from Erika's shoulders, his lips traced feathery kisses up and down her bare arms.

Welcoming the delicious insanity Michael's fiery touch brought to her entire anatomy, Erika closed her eyes. As Michael's fingers reached for the zipper on the back of her dress, she dropped her head forward to give him easier access. Slowly, he pulled the zipper down, the sound of it echoing throughout the barn. In one delicate motion, he removed her dress.

Gathering her hair in his hands, he moved it to one side, planting moist kisses on her neck and down her back. Impatiently, he undid the clasp on her bra. As his hands melted against her aching breasts, she moaned with wantonness. She'd been missing this, but most of all she had missed Michael's presence in her life.

Laying her back down in the hay, he worried the waistband of her pink silk panties with his teeth, not releasing until he had the wisp of material drawn down over her hips and over her feet. Looking at her nude body made him ache with desire. First, he wanted them to have a slow, delicious ride to ecstasy, wanted the passion between them to last forever.

Guiding Erika's hand to the buttons on his shirt, he hotly instructed her with his eyes as to what he wanted her to do. Obeying their heated commands, Erika unhurriedly undid the buttons, pausing after each one to kiss the flesh she'd just exposed. Michael moaned as her lips and tongue connected with each of his taut nipples.

Growing even more impatient, he directed her shaking hands to the waistband of his sweatpants, but Erika pulled her hand away. She had other plans for her lover.

As she stood up, she reached her hand out to Michael, helping him to his feet. Moving into a dark corner of the hayloft, where the bales of hay had been stacked into tall piles, Erika backed Michael against one of the bundles. Starting at the top of his head, she passionately kissed her way down to the top of the sweatpants. Methodically, she inched the material down his body, until the pants rested around his ankles. Lifting one of his feet, she slid one leg off, then the other, and tossed the pants out of the way.

Falling to her knees on the soft hay, she started at his feet and worked her euphonious purple-passion style of magic over the length and breadth of his entire body. Erika's mouth and hands inflammably roved and tenderly caressed every inch of every muscle Michael possessed. Getting to her feet, she pressed his back into the hay, molding her nudity against his explosive heat. Michael gritted his teeth, praying for mercy against the fire in Erika's touch.

In one fluid motion Michael turned her around so that her back faced the hay. Lifting her leg, he drew it up around his waist, his flaming fingers reaching down to delicately taunt the opening of her luscious flower. Erika squirmed against his touch. Squeezing his buttocks tightly, she drew his male structure of marble snugly against her. As his rigidity pressed against her belly, a cavalcade of moisture and heat spread through her entire being. As if she didn't feel on fire already, hot tears of relief rolled down her cheeks.

The foreplay was arresting, yet Michael took a minute to protect them. Frantically, they awaited what was yet to come. Both sensing the urgent callings of each other's bodies, Michael finally filled her with his granite tenderness and immediately began to receive all the endowments Erika so wantonly offered.

Their legs became unstable and began to tremble. Still inside of her, Michael carried her back to the pallet of hay. Laying her down there gently, he came down on top of her.

Writhing and tenderly meshing, until neither of them could maintain control, they completed each other with the fulfilling love only they were capable of providing each other—what no other person in the world could give them.

As their climax burst forth, the atmosphere darkened considerably. Lightning struck, thunder rolled loudly, then the sounds of torrential rains slammed against the metal rooftop. The *ping, ping* of the raindrops had a tranquilizing effect.

Michael laughed against Erika's parted lips. "It appears we've whipped up a powerful storm inside and out," he whispered softly. "For a minute I thought it was all in my blown mind. You do blow my mind, you know, gorgeous."

A bright smile stole across Erika's features. "Just as you blow mine, Dr. Mathis. We've been creating mighty storms from the moment we torpedoed into each other. I'm happy to be back in your arms, Michael. I've missed you so," she cried. In response, Michael kissed her thoroughly. He got up and pulled a green military-style blanket from a top shelf. Lying back down, he covered their nude bodies with the clean blanket.

Erika melted against him as she laid her head in the well of his arm. "A few things have occurred to me since we parted, Michael, but nothing compared to the miracle of your love."

He kissed her forehead. "Speaking of a miracle, I know of a couple myself. Your coming back to me is definitely one of them. After I share some good news with you, you can tell me about yours, Erika." Erika's eyes widened in anticipation of his news.

He looked down at her. "We received full board approval for your pernicious anemia screening project and the preventive health plans. The board has also agreed to hear you out on all your other community-service ideas," he sang out. "How's that for a miracle?"

Erika squealed in delight. "Oh, I can't believe all these wonderful things are happening for us. We do make a great team. It appears that all my prayers are being answered. I'm so happy now, Michael."

Erika began telling Michael about her budding relationship

with her brother. She then spoke of the chemistry she'd witnessed between Lorraine and Richard as she informed him that they were now "outing." Covering every minute detail, she told him about her most recent visit with her aunt. Lastly, she discussed with him all she'd learned about her parents' past.

Michael squeezed her gently. "I'm proud of how you've handled it. But if you and Aunt Arlene discussed all these things some time ago, why has it taken you so long to come to me?"

Erika lifted her head and propped her elbow on Michael's chest. "You're a doctor so I'm sure you can guess. Besides being busy at the hospital, I had a few more personal things to work out. But, Michael, I'm here now. I'm here to stay. Does that work for you as much as it works for me?" She saw the answer there in his eyes, yet she wanted to hear him say the words.

"Erika, without you in my life, nothing works for me. Yes, it works for me." He studied her intently for a few moments. "Did I just imagine that you were wearing your engagement ring when I first saw you?"

Laughing sweetly, she reached for the discarded linen jacket. Pulling the ring from the pocket, she held it up. "No, you didn't imagine it. I was wearing it, but I thought it was pretty presumptuous of me. When it looked as if you might not let me in, I slid it off my finger and put it in my pocket. Are you . . . ready to put it . . . back where . . . it belongs?" Erika asked hesitantly, looking into his eyes with uncertainty in hers.

Michael got on his knees and took the ring from her hand. With tears in his eyes, he gazed tenderly into her bewildered ones. "Will you marry me, Erika Edmonds? Will you share the rest of your life with me? Will you be my best friend, and the mother of my children?" he asked in an emotionally charged voice.

"Yes, Michael," she breathed, tears swimming in her eyes. "Yes, yes, yes!"

Kissing her as though he'd never kissed her before, Michael slid the ring onto her left hand. "I can't wait to share our news with all those who've been rooting for us."

Erika smiled sheepishly. "A couple of those people already know. Of course, as we've discussed, I told my aunt first. Then I told Dr. Baker. I discussed it with him over the phone last night. But we still have to tell your parents and Richard and Lorraine. I kind of thought it would be nice for us to tell them together."

He smiled broadly. "I think we should throw an amazing engagement party. Together, we can tell everyone that we're close to. I'm sure my brother would like to be present for such a celestial celebration. Patrick Mathis is a romantic at heart, just like his older brother."

His expression grew sober. "Erika, several people told me to bombard you with an arsenal of romantic notions, but I just couldn't do that. It wouldn't have been right. I couldn't discount your badly injured feelings. I knew you needed time to sort out everything you'd been put through."

He softly kissed her eyelids. "I vowed to give you your space even though Lorraine warned me not to, but I don't think I counted on you taking such an extensive liberty. As each day passed, I promised myself I'd call you the next morning. My courage waned with the dawn. I wanted you to come to me, and not because of my ego. I knew that if you did, you'd come of your own free will. The decision to share a lifetime is not something we can rush. I'm happy you decided to choose a lifetime spent with me.

"That's all over with now, and I desperately need you to fill all my empty space. If it's okay with you, I'd like to go all out for our engagement. I want to throw a party that even the Clintons would have cause to envy."

Her tears spilled onto his bare chest. "Darling, thank you for being so patient with me," she sobbed. "I'm glad I wasn't too late. I don't know how I would've managed the rest of my life without you to keep me grounded. And I think the engagement party is a great idea, Michael. I know where to find the perfect dress for such a special occasion."

Erika flicked at his lips with her tongue, drawing his mouth down over hers. Pushing her fingers through his hair, she looked into his eyes. "I have redefined the meaning of our lovemaking. I'd never thought of it as an exhilarating contact sport, but I do now. Since our plans for the future have been settled, care to indulge me in another game, Dr. Mathis?"

"Yes, gorgeous. For the rest of our lives I'm going to love teaching you all its finer points!"

"Michael Mathis, I'm going to love having you as my very own private tutor!"

Twenty

Wearing the white sequined dress she'd seen featured as part of the spring fashions in *Essence* magazine, Erika danced before the bathroom mirror. The dress had been an expensive purchase, but was worth every cent she'd paid for it. She'd even purchased matching shoes.

Erika smiled at her reflection. "A girl should look her best on the evening of her official engagement party," she said excitedly, making one final inspection of her stunning attire and newly acquired windswept hairstyle. Walking across the room, she picked up her small evening clutch bag and went into the living room.

As she waited for Michael to arrive, she thought of how easily she could've messed up the rest of her life. Had she not come to terms with her parents' mistakes, Michael would've slipped through her fingers and she would've been left with nothing but her raging anger.

The anger was all gone now and she really understood what her parents had gone through. Having an illicit affair in those days had to have been tough on them. She would learn from their mistakes instead of holding them against her mother and father. No one had the right to sit in judgment of Anthony and Vernice, not even their own children.

Erika wanted to meet Michael's every need, but she wasn't going to forget to meet her own. She would always try to let Michael know exactly what she needed from him. By meeting each other's needs, they wouldn't have the urge to have them fulfilled elsewhere. Therefore, their marriage should be strong, healthy and free of desperate deceptions. Their children would be loved and cherished and have all their needs met, as well. Erika and Michael wanted children, but intended to fulfill their personal and professional goals before starting a family.

The Edmonds-Mathis wedding was planned for the late fall. The ceremony would be a small, intimate affair. Just family and a few very special friends would be invited, which would include many of the same people who would attend their engagement party, to be held at the posh home of Dr. and Mrs. Jules Baker.

Erika and Michael had wanted to rent a reception hall for the party, but Dr. Baker and his wife, Jada, wouldn't hear of it. They'd insisted on having it at their home. Michael, in turn, had insisted on paying for the entire bash. Erika had purchased a lovely party dress for Arlene, as well. Arlene had plenty of beautiful clothes, but Erika had wanted to do something special for her aunt since she could now afford to do so.

The insurance check was now deposited in her savings account. She'd tried to pay Richard back, in full, for the debts he'd paid off for her, but he'd refused to accept the money. The Marlboro Realty Agency had agreed to handle the contract on her childhood home. The house had been leased to a family with three delightful children.

Erika had met the Burns family, a delightful crew. The nine-year-old twin boys and their eight-year-old sister had taken to Erika right off. The parents, Judyann and John, had extended an open invitation for Erika and Michael to come by any time. Because the family was new in town, they were thrilled to learn that Michael was a pediatrician. While Erika had found loving tenants for the family home, Michael had gained three new patients.

Michael's familiar knock sounded on the door and Erika responded excitedly to the summons. He'd been given his own key to her apartment, but with Aunt Arlene in tow he thought it best not to use it. Even though he knew Arlene was a very wise woman, for him, respect was the name of the game.

As usual, Michael's formal attire was a perfect representation of exquisiteness. His strong, masculine image was something to be reckoned with. Erika couldn't take her eyes off her handsome African prince.

Speechless. Michael couldn't take his eyes off her, either. Erika looked like a beautiful wildflower dipped in the sweetness of honey, and she smelled as though she'd been immersed in a bouquet of jasmine blossoms. She never ceased to send his senses reeling and every time he laid eyes on her gorgeous face his heart rate went absolutely crazy.

Bending his head, he kissed her softly on the mouth. "If this is an example of what I have to look forward to for the rest of my life, I can see I'm going to be a very happy man. You are dazzling, gorgeous," he said excitedly, kissing her again and again.

Arlene had a wondrous twinkle in her eyes, quietly observing how much Erika and Michael were in love. She didn't need a crystal ball to know Erika's future was secure in the hands of Michael Mathis. Knowing her niece was happy and that she had a good man who brought her sweet contentment, she thought Vernice and Anthony would've been proud of their lovely daughter and handsome son-in-law-to-be. The love Erika and Michael shared couldn't possibly be missed. They fit together perfectly, like a hand in a glove.

Dressed in an ice-blue, satin suit with rhinestone buttons, Arlene was all class and elegance. Her slate-gray hair was neatly fashioned in a thick bun. "If you two don't hurry up and come out of that trance you're in, you're going to be late for your own party." Arlene laughed. "I've never seen two people more in love than you two. I pray that you stay that way forever and a day. Happy and in love."

All smiles, Erika and Michael hugged each other.

Slipping from Michael's embrace, Erika hugged her aunt, pecking both of her cheeks with gentle kisses. "You look just marvelous! And you're right, Aunt Arlene. We'd better be going." Erika turned to face Michael. "Ready, handsome?"

"Ready, gorgeous," he responded, smiling all over.

As Michael and his two stunning companions entered the marble foyer of Dr. Baker's English Tudor home, Jules and Jada greeted their guests warmly. Dr. Baker made the necessary introductions before he and Jada escorted their guests into the spacious living areas.

Jada Baker, a tall, slender woman, possessed the most expressive, golden-brown eyes Erika had ever seen. They were a perfect complement to her rich, mahogany complexion. A portrait of finesse, she wore a knockout Dior gown fashioned of pale-peach silk crepe. She and her handsome husband were quite an impressive-looking couple, Erika marveled.

Whoever was responsible for decorating the house had done a magnificent job. It appeared to Erika they'd had an unlimited budget to work with. The extraordinary decor smacked of British and other European influences. Mirrors were everywhere, giving even more depth to the already massive rooms. The entire house was open and airy.

The party room was decorated with fresh flowers, pastel streamers and colorful balloons. Along with fine china and silverware, a sumptuous feast of hors d'oeuvres and other delicacies was laid out on grand buffet tables. Golden champagne bubbled and flowed through clear tubes from a silver fountain. Though Michael had paid for everything, the Bakers had gone all out on the decorations. Everything was laid out beautifully.

Erika's breath caught when Lorraine appeared on the arm of Richard. Lorraine's fancy attire definitely made a fashion statement. She looked good and well-rested. Swirls of pink chiffon swished and swayed as Richard escorted Lorraine across the room to meet with her best friend. Erika couldn't help noticing the intimate way in which Richard looked at Lorraine.

As they neared, Erika looked down at the pink satin shoes

and the rest of Lorraine's attire. Then her eyes came to rest on Lorraine's new coiffure. Her auburn hair had been highlighted with subtle shades of gold. Her hair had never looked more beautiful, and Erika was delighted with the highlights and the new style.

"Lorraine," Erika exclaimed, kissing her on the forehead. "You are mesmerizing! What have you done to yourself?" Erika asked, smiling knowingly.

Smiling sweetly, Lorraine winked at her best friend. "Trade secrets, darling. I'll tell you all about it when the party is over."

Michael noticed the genuine look of love in Erika's eyes as she fussed over Lorraine. Quietly slipping forward, he held out his arm to Arlene, who took it without a moment's hesitation. "We'll be back, Erika," he said, giving his fiancée an arresting smile. "Aunt Arlene and I have to sharpen our dancing skills for the wedding reception." Looking ready to party the night away, Arlene sashayed off with Michael, holding on to his arm as they made their way across the room.

Looking very happy, Erika glanced at her wristwatch, wondering why Michael's parents hadn't arrived yet. Before Erika could inhale another breath of air, Wilimina and Lawrence smiled at her from across the room. There was another man with them. Erika hadn't met him yet, but she knew he had to be Patrick Mathis. Even though she'd seen pictures of Patrick, he looked so much like Michael that anyone could easily guess they were brothers or somehow closely related.

When the two groups met up, everyone started talking at once. They all laughed. Lawrence took control of the conversation by introducing his other son to Erika. Wilimina greeted her future daughter-in-law, hugging her tenderly. She had already come to love Erika as if she were her very own child. Her son loved Erika and that alone would've been enough for her.

Making her feel just as Wilimina and Lawrence had made her feel the first time she'd met them, Patrick kissed and hugged his future sister-in-law. "It's nice to finally meet you, Erika. Every time Michael calls me he can't get through the conversation without mentioning your name." Patrick looked all around the room. "This is turning out to be some dinner party. I thought Michael said *intimate*." Patrick laughed.

Michael walked up. "It is intimate, little brother," he interjected from behind, gathering the small group together in one spot. "Erika and I are going to be married! Is that intimate enough for you?"

Since their loud hoots and cheers drew the attention of the other guests, Michael may as well have gone on and announced it to everyone at once. Everyone in the small group kissing and hugging one another caused many of the other guests to draw their own conclusions.

Taking Erika's hand, Michael guided her over to where the Bakers stood. "I think I've blown it," Michael said, smiling sheepishly. "Do you mind if we go ahead and make our surprise announcement now?"

Dr. Baker patted Michael on the back. "Go for it. This place is already buzzing with speculation. It seems as though the hospital grapevine exists in here," Dr. Baker joked, drawing laughter from the others. "I'll gather all the guests and get them quiet."

Michael looped Erika's arm through his and they walked to the center of the room, where they waited a few minutes until everyone calmed down. He smiled brightly. "Good evening. Greetings to all our family members and special guests. We're so glad you could be with us this evening. As you may have already guessed, this is an auspicious occasion and Erika and I wanted to celebrate it with our friends and family. Some of you are aware that Erika and I have been dating, and others have certainly been speculating about it." Everyone laughed.

"Well, all the rumors can be put to rest now. Erika and I are crazy in love with each other, and we're going to be married in the fall," he announced proudly. All the guests began to clap and cheer, shouting their congratulations. "Thank you all very much. May you enjoy this special evening as much as my lovely fiancée and I."

"Let's hear something from the bride-to-be," Richard shouted above the din.

Unable to hide her joy for Erika, Lorraine looked on through tears.

Smiling, Erika looked over at Richard and shook her finger. "I don't know what else to say. Michael has said it all. We are crazy about each other and we can't wait to be married. There is someone very special to me. I'd like to ask him a question," she said, keeping her eyes focused on Richard. "I'd like to ask my brother, Richard Edmonds, to give me away on my wedding day. Can you hook a little sister up with one of those muscular arms?" Though smiling, she looked anxiously at Aunt Arlene, who eyed Richard intently.

Only those closest to Erika knew about the unusual circumstances surrounding the two siblings, which made it easier for her to address him as her brother. She was more concerned with how Arlene was really taking it, knowing how loyal the two sisters had been to each other. It was too late to worry about it now, she thought gravely.

Stepping forward, Richard kissed Erika gently on the mouth, choking back tears. "I would be delighted to give you away, Erika Edmonds. It's not every day that a brother gets to marry off his sister to his very best friend. The pleasure will be all mine!" he assured, embracing Erika and Michael warmly.

Once all the hugs and congratulations were out of the way, soft music filled the air and the festivities began. While some guests milled around the buffet tables, others chose to take to the area reserved for dancing.

Still anxious about the look she'd seen on her aunt's face, Erika immediately went to Arlene and guided her to another part of the house. Arlene wasn't too happy about being dragged away from all the lively action, and she let Erika know it in no uncertain terms.

"I understand, Aunt Arlene. We'll go back to the party in

just a few minutes. I saw you watching Richard, Auntie. Are you really okay with the relationship he and I are trying to build? Are you truly happy for us? We do need each other."

Arlene suddenly realized Erika might have misunderstood the intense looks she'd been giving Richard. "Oh, sweetheart, of course I can accept your relationship. It's just that he looks so much like Anthony—I'm stunned by how much. Erika, it's nice that you two have accepted each other. I have no reason not to accept the relationship you have with him. He seems like a real nice man. He talked to me earlier, and I like him. He also promised to dance with me later."

Erika was totally bewildered. It would be nice for everyone to come together as a family. *Anthony would be all for it,* Erika thought quietly. *This is really going to work,* she decided.

Arlene tugged at Erika's hand, dragging her out of her bewildered state. "Can we go back to the party now? I feel like dancing again, Erika. I don't get out that often, you know."

Erika began to laugh and cry at the same time, feeling the tension flow right out of her. "Yes, we can go now." Looking into her aunt's eyes, Erika placed her hands on her shoulders. "I love you, Aunt Arlene. I love my mother and father. I know they'd be happy for Michael and me. My only regret is that they're not here in the physical sense. Yet their spirits are most definitely present. Thank you for all your understanding."

Arlene pulled Erika close to her and hugged her tightly. "I love you, too, Erika," Arlene exclaimed, unshed tears stinging her eyes. "I do love you so!" Hand in hand and smiling, they returned to the party.

As Michael swept Erika into his arms, Richard steered Arlene to the dancing area. Erika and Michael watched as Richard charmed Arlene with his gentle kindness.

Erika touched Michael's face tenderly. "You, Richard, Lawrence and Patrick are a lot alike. Since I'm on a lifelong diet, I don't know that I can stand to be around all you men dripping with syrup, but I'm going to love having a great big happy family."

Michael smiled gently. "We may be syrupy, but I'm the only one who plans to overdose you with sweet, seductive treats, gorge you with gentle tenderness and saturate your entire body and soul with delicious love. I can assure you that you won't gain an ounce of weight from any of it."

Erika slanted an eyebrow. "Are you sure about that?" she asked, rubbing her hands down over her flat abdomen.

Michael got a mischievous glint in his eyes as he caught the meaning of her gesture. "Well, now that you mention it, carrying our child will cause some weight gain, but think of all the fun we'll have creating our very own family. And think of the fun we'll have when it's time to take the excess weight off. Does 'contact sport' ring a bell?"

She kissed him softly. "Loud and clear, Dr. Mathis. Loud and clear."

After several dances and many seemingly endless conversations, Erika and Michael slipped away from the party for a few quiet minutes alone. With his arm around Erika's shoulder, he guided her out onto the terrace, where it looked to be a perfect night for lovers.

The bright stars dazzled. The crescent moon hung lazily in the purple-hazed skies, illuminating the two lovers in the whiteness of its beams. Standing by the dimly but romantically lit pool, they saw their reflections in the bluish, moon-kissed waters, the reflections of love.

Wrapping Erika in his warm strength, he possessed her lips in an awesome kiss, causing her to stand on her toes. As he lifted his head, his gaze sank into the depths of her eyes. "This time next year we'll be husband and wife, Erika. We'll be as one. I love you like crazy, Erika Edmonds."

"Yes, Michael," she whispered softly, "as one. Like Lawrence and Wilimina, we'll join our wings together and fly as one. I love you like crazy, too, Michael Mathis." Michael and Erika hugged each other tenderly.

He looked deeply into her eyes. "Do you remember what

you told me about the couple you had sketched in the cafeteria the night of our first date?" She smiled broadly.

"Anything created from love is love!" they exclaimed simultaneously.

AUTHOR'S NOTE

Because pernicious anemia is often reported as a disease that's more common in individuals of northern European descent, I felt compelled to shed some light on this serious subject. After contacting Dr. Tanya Rutledge, an Atlanta based gastroenterologist, I asked her to write an article that would help us understand this disease much better. In reading her article below, you will find that, like other ethnic groups, African-Americans are indeed affected by pernicious anemia. My mother died from this disease, which could've been treated easily and effectively had it been caught in time. She was diagnosed as having Alzheimer's disease before the anemia was discovered.

Pernicious anemia is the most common cause of vitamin B12 deficiency. Vitamin B12, cobalamin, is required for normal red blood cell maturation and functioning of the central nervous system. Pernicious anemia, an autoimmune disease, leads to the destruction of parietal cells, the acid-producing cells of the stomach. Loss of parietal cells results in gastric atrophy, diminished gastric acid production and a deficiency of intrinsic factor, a protein required for B12 absorption. The destruction of the parietal cell is mediated by the immune system primarily through autoantibodies. The risk of developing pernicious anemia is increased in individuals with other autoimmune diseases, such as Graves' disease, Hashimoto's thyroiditis, and vitiligo. Relatives of individuals with pernicious anemia have a twenty-fold greater risk of developing the disease than the general population. The classic description of a patient with pernicious anemia as a middle-aged person of Northern European descent no longer holds true. Pernicious anemia affects all ethnic backgrounds, especially African-Americans.

The signs and symptoms of pernicious anemia are attributable to B12 deficiency. Affected individuals may have a variety of mild to severe symptoms or be relatively asymptomatic with only laboratory abnormalities. The primary symptoms are related to anemia. The red blood cells produced in individuals with pernicious anemia are often macrocytic (larger than normal). Additionally, the other cells produced in the bone marrow, such as white cells and platelets are also affected. Symptoms of anemia can include fatigue, angina, or palpitations. The skin may have a pale, sallow appearance. Glossitis, a beefy, red and painful tongue, and loss of appetite may occur. Episodic diarrhea may be present related to altered intestinal function. However, the most worrisome symptoms are neurologic. The earliest manifestations may be numbness and tingling in the hands and feet. Later, weakness and difficulty with ambulation can develop. The most disturbing are changes in mentation, with loss of memory and irritability to dementia or frank psychosis developing.

Pernicious anemia is usually diagnosed by assessing vitamin B12 levels in the blood. A Schilling test and antibody measurements can be performed to confirm loss of intrinsic factor as the etiology. Treatment of pernicious anemia is simple and effective. The mainstay of therapy is B12 replacement. Vitamin B12 should be administered intramuscularly on a monthly basis. Therapy is life long. Unfortunately, the neurologic manifestations may not completely resolve with treatment. Therefore, early screening and intervention for pernicious anemia is warranted for this easily correctable disorder. Lastly, individuals with pernicious anemia are at increased risk for the development of gastric cancer, thus screening for gastric cancer in older individuals is advised.

Tanya M. Rutledge, M.D.
Gastroenterologist
Atlanta, GA

Dear Readers:

I sincerely hope that you enjoyed reading DESPERATE DECEPTIONS from cover to cover. I'm interested in hearing your comments. I'd love to know how you feel about Erika and Michael's story. Without the reader, there is no me, as an author. Please enclose a self-addressed, stamped envelope with all your correspondence.

Please mail your correspondence to:

> Linda Hudson-Smith
> 2026C North Riverside Avenue
> Box 109
> Rialto, CA 92377

You can e-mail your comments to:

> *LHS4romance@yahoo.com*

Web site:

> http://www.romantictales.com/linda/index.html

ABOUT THE AUTHOR

Born in Canonsburg, Pennsylvania, and raised in the town of Washington, PA, Linda Hudson-Smith has traveled the world as an enthusiastic witness to other cultures and lifestyles. Her husband's twenty-year military career gave her the opportunity to live in Japan, Germany, and other parts of Europe, as well as many cities across the United States. Hudson-Smith's extensive travel experience helps her craft stories set in a variety of beautiful and romantic locations.

She is a member of Romance Writers of America. *Romance in Color* recently chose her as Rising Star for the month of January. ICE UNDER FIRE, her debut Arabesque novel, has received rave reviews and earned rapturous letters from fans. Voted as Best New Author, A.A.O.W.G. and Romantic Tales presented Hudson-Smith with the 2000 Gold Pen Award. SOULFUL SERENADE, released August 2000, has also received great reviews and was selected by readers as the Best Cover for that month. Though novel writing remains her first love, she is currently cultivating her screenwriting skills.

Dedicated to inspiring readers to overcome adversity against all odds, Hudson-Smith is a member and advocate of the Lupus Foundation of America, the NAACP, and is a supporter of the American Cancer Society. She also enjoys her volunteer work at a local nursing and rehabilitation center. Linda resides in California with her husband, and is the mother of two sons and has a son and daughter through her extended family.

COMING IN APRIL 2001 FROM ARABESQUE ROMANCES

__HIS 1-800 WIFE
by Shirley Hailstock   1-58314-157-X $5.99US/$7.99CAN
Fed up with her meddling family, Catherine Carson had a plan . . . make a deal with a nice guy who would agree to marry her for six months, then divorce. She knew Jarrod Greene was just the man for the job—until she sparked an unexpected desire. Now, Catherine must discover what she really wants if she's to find everything she's ever dreamed of.

__DANGEROUS PASSIONS
by Louré Bussey   1-58314-129-4 $5.99US/$7.99CAN
It's been eighteen years since Marita Sommers found herself caught up in a powerful romance—and entangled in a shocking crime that nearly destroyed her life. Marita vowed never again to let her heart rule her head. But now, drawn to a family friend, she once again enters a shadowy world of sweeping passion . . . and peril.

__A ROYAL VOW
by Tamara Sneed   1-58314-143-X $5.99US/$7.99CAN
As heir to the throne of an island nation, Davis Beriyia's life has been planned out for him, including who he will marry. Determined to have one last chance at freedom before his marriage, he disguises himself as a building handyman. But when he falls for Abbie Barnes, Davis realizes that he would trade his kingdom for the chance to win her heart.

__DREAM WEDDING
by Alice Greenhowe Wootson
                    1-58314-149-9 $5.99US/$7.99CAN
If sparks aren't flying with her fiancé, Missy Harrison doesn't care—she had her fill of passion and turmoil in high school with Jimmy Scott. Or so she thought. On the way to her hometown to finalize the last-minute wedding details, her car breaks down, and Jimmy shows up in the tow truck . . . looking better than ever.

Call toll free **1-888-345-BOOK** to order by phone or use this coupon to order by mail. ALL BOOKS AVAILABLE APRIL 1, 2001.

Name_____
Address_____
City_____ State_____ Zip_____
Please send me the books that I have checked above.
I am enclosing $_____
Plus postage and handling* $_____
Sales tax (in NY, TN, and DC) $_____
Total amount enclosed $_____
*Add $2.50 for the first book and $.50 for each additional book.
Send check or money order (no cash or CODs) to: **Arabesque Romances, Dept. C.O., 850 Third Avenue 16th Floor, New York, NY 10022**
Prices and numbers subject to change without notice. Valid only in the U.S. All orders subject to availability. **NO ADVANCE ORDERS.**
Visit our website at **www.arabesquebooks.com**.